MISS BUNCLE, MARRIED

The brilliant and unerring blend of satire and subtle wit displayed by Miss Stevenson in her immensely popular *Miss Buncle's Book* is present in full measure in this sequel. *Miss Buncle, Married* is a sparkling comedy of life in an old-fashioned English county town. Even in the peaceful atmosphere of Wandlebury, Barbara Buncle, now married, succeeds in attracting adventures—for her love of "putting her fingers into other people's pies" remains, as ever, unsubdued.

Books by D. E. Stevenson in the
Ulverscroft Large Print Series:

KATE HARDY
ANNA AND HER DAUGHTERS
AMBERWELL
SUMMERHILLS
CHARLOTTE FAIRLIE
KATHERINE WENTWORTH
KATHERINE'S MARRIAGE
CELIA'S HOUSE
WINTER AND ROUGH WEATHER
LISTENING VALLEY
BEL LAMINGTON
FLETCHERS END
SPRING MAGIC
THE ENGLISH AIR
THE HOUSE OF THE DEER
THE FOUR GRACES
STILL GLIDES THE STREAM
MUSIC IN THE HILLS
CROOKED ADAM
THE TALL STRANGER
GERALD AND ELIZABETH
THE HOUSE ON THE CLIFF
VITTORIA COTTAGE
SARAH MORRIS REMEMBERS
SARAH'S COTTAGE
FIVE WINDOWS
GREEN MONEY
MISS BUNCLE'S BOOK
MISS BUNCLE, MARRIED

D. E. STEVENSON

MISS BUNCLE, MARRIED

BEING THE FURTHER ADVENTURES OF THE CELEBRATED AUTHORESS

Complete and Unabridged

ULVERSCROFT
Leicester

First published by
Herbert Jenkins Ltd., 1936

First Large Print Edition
published November 1982
by arrangement with
Collins, London & Glasgow

British Library CIP Data

Stevenson, D.E.
  Miss Buncle married.—Large print ed.
  (Ulverscroft large print series: romance)
  I. Title
  823'.912[F]   PR6037.T458

  ISBN 0-7089-0876-4

0708   908   764   2956

Published by
F. A. Thorpe (Publishing) Ltd.
Anstey, Leicestershire
Printed and Bound in Great Britain by
T. J. Press (Padstow) Ltd., Padstow, Cornwall

1

MR. AND MRS. ABBOTT

"WE had better move," said Mr. Abbott casually. Mrs. Abbott's hand was arrested in mid-air as it went towards the handle of the coffee pot. Her grey eyes widened, her mouth opened (displaying a set of exceptionally fine teeth) and remained open, but no sound came. The pleasant dining-room was very quiet, a fire burnt briskly in the grate, the pale wintry sunshine flowed in at the window on to the red and blue Turkey carpet, the carved oak furniture and the motionless forms of Mr. and Mrs. Abbott sitting at the breakfast table. On the table the silver glittered and the china shone—as china does when it is well washed and polished by careful hands. It was a Sunday morning as could easily be deduced from the lateness of the hour and the unnatural quiet outside as well as inside the Abbotts' small, but comfortable house.

1

"I said we had better move," Mr. Abbott repeated.

"Yes—I *thought* you said that," declared Mrs. Abbott incredulously.

Mr. Abbott lowered his paper and looked at his wife over the top of his spectacles. It was a Sunday paper, of course, and Mr. Abbott had been glancing over the publishers' announcements. He was a publisher himself so the advertisements interested him enormously, but did not deceive him. The news that Messrs. Faction & Whiting were publishing the Greatest Novel of the Century, crammed with Adventure, scintillating with Brilliance, and bubbling with Humour, merely roused in Mr. Abbott's bosom a faint kind of wonder as to what they paid their advertising agent. He put down the paper without regret, and looked at his wife, and, as he looked at her, he smiled because she was nice to look at, and because he loved her, and because she amused and interested him enormously. They had been married for nine months now, and sometimes he thought he knew her through and through, and sometimes he thought he didn't know the first thing about her—theirs was a most satisfactory marriage.

"Yes," I said 'move'," he repeated (in what

Barbara Abbott secretly called "Arthur's *smiling* voice"). "Why not move, Barbara? It would solve all our difficulties in one blow. We could have a nice house, further out of town, with a nice garden—trees and things——" added Mr. Abbott, waving his hand vaguely, as if to conjure up the nice house before Barbara's eyes, and the queer thing was he succeeded. Barbara immediately beheld a nice house with a nice garden, further out of town. The whole thing rose before her eyes in a sort of vision—lawns and trees and flower beds with roses in them, and a nice house in the middle—all bathed in sunshine.

"Yes," she said breathlessly, "yes, why not? If you wouldn't mind leaving Sunnydene— there's no *reason*, I mean——"

"Exactly," nodded her husband, "you *see*. There's no reason at all, and it would solve all our difficulties."

They looked at each other and grinned a little self-consciously—their difficulties were so absurd. Had any two, apparently sane, people ever landed themselves in such a foolish ridiculous mess?

The human mind is a marvellous organism. Whilst Mr. Abbott was still grinning a trifle self-consciously at his wife, he returned through time and saw the events of the last twenty-four hours in a flash. He helped himself to more marmalade, and thought—*queer*, if I hadn't drunk any of Mrs. Cluloe's port (and why did I when I knew it would be rubbish—you can't trust port in a woman's house—I *knew* that and yet, like a fool, I drank it). If I hadn't drunk any of Mrs. Cluloe's port, I wouldn't have had a ghastly headache all yesterday, and if I hadn't had a ghastly headache all yesterday, I wouldn't be suggesting to Barbara that we should move. It *is* queer!

"What are you thinking about, Arthur?" Mrs. Abbott enquired.

"Yesterday," replied her husband succinctly.

Yesterday morning, Mr. Abbott had risen with a dreadful headache. He rose late, bolted his breakfast, and rushed for the 8.57 train to town. It was imperative that he should catch the 8.57 because he had an important interview with Mr. Shillingsworth. If Mr. Abbott was not in the office when Mr. Shillingsworth arrived—there and waiting, all smiles and joviality—there would be trouble. It was all the more annoying because the day was

Saturday, and Mr. Abbott usually took Saturdays off, and played golf with John Hutson who lived next door and had exactly the same handicap as his own. Mr. Abbott had had to put off John Hutson the night before and rush up to town, with a bursting headache, at Mr. Shillingsworth's behest.

Mr. Shillingsworth was a well-known novelist, and Mr. Abbott was his publisher. Mr. Shillingsworth gave Messrs. Abbott & Spicer more trouble, and caused them more annoyance than all their other authors put together, but they hung on to him, and placated and soothed him because his books sold. (Personally Mr. Abbott was of the opinion that Shillingsworth's books were tripe, but they undoubtedly sold.) The new novel was frightful rubbish—they all thought so at the office—but they had decided to take it all the same, because, if they didn't take it, somebody else would, and somebody else would make a good deal of money over it, and Messrs. Abbott & Spicer would lose Shillingsworth for ever.

Mr. Abbott thought of all this going up in the train, and it annoyed him intensely—he hated publishing rubbish—and what with his hurry, and his headache, and the loss of his morning's golf and his annoyance over Shillingsworth's rubbish, he arrived at the office in a most unenviable condition.

"What on earth's up with the boss?" demanded Mr. Abbott's private secretary, bursting out of Mr. Abbott's private room like a bomb. "I never saw him 'so het up'. He threw the letters at me and told me to go back to school, because I made a slip, and spelt omitted with two Ms."

"Marriage, that's what," said the head clerk, who was a bachelor. "Marriage. You mark my words, he'll never be the same again."

Mr. Abbott was all honey to Mr. Shillingsworth (when he arrived fifty minutes late for his appointment). It was a frightful effort to be all honey, and it left Mr. Abbott with arrears of bad temper to work off on his next visitor. His head ached much worse by this time, and he was beginning to feel a little sick. So when Mr. Spicer, the junior partner of the firm, looked in for a chat, and sat on the edge of Mr. Abbott's desk, smoking his foul pipe and swinging one leg in a *dégagé* manner, Mr. Abbott did not welcome him as cordially as usual.

Mr. Spicer was quite oblivious of the thunderous atmosphere. He chatted cheerfully about various matters, and then, quite suddenly, and apropos of nothing that had been said, he poked Mr. Abbott in the ribs and enquired slyly—"What about another John Smith—eh? Is there another John Smith coming along soon?"

"No," said Mr. Abbott shortly.

"Oh, come now, that's bad. That won't do at all," Spicer complained, "you must stir up your wife. You mustn't let her slack off like this. We can do with another best seller like *Disturber of the Peace*; it went like hot cakes—you know that yourself—and *The Pen is Mightier*——is doing splendidly. I ordered the sixth edition to-day. We must have another book by John Smith—the time is ripe—you tell her to get to work on another of the same ilk."

"No," said Mr. Abbott again.

Mr. Spicer rushed upon his fate. "I'll tell you what to do," he said cheerfully, "buy her a new pen—a nice fat one—and a big sheaf of nice white paper, and see what that does. If *that* doesn't do the trick——"

"You mind your own business," snapped Mr. Abbott, "you leave my wife alone. There aren't going to be any more John Smiths. My wife isn't going to write any more—why should she?"

"But, land-sakes!" cried Spicer, in surprise and consternation, "John Smith is a best-seller, Surely you're not going to stop her writing. Think of the *waste*," cried Spicer, almost wringing his hands, "think of the waste. Here are two books, the funniest—bar none—I've ever read—*real satire*—and you say there aren't going to be any more. She *must* go on writing—she's got a public. She's a genius—and you marry her, and shut her up in your kitchen, and tell her to get on with the cooking."

This last was a joke, of course, but Mr. Abbott was in no mood for jokes. He beat on the table with his clenched fist.

"She's not cooking, you fool!" he cried, "she's enjoying herself—dinner-parties, bridge——"

"My God!" said Mr. Spicer reverently. He got down off the table and went away.

Mr. Abbott mopped his brow—this is ghastly, he thought, this is ghastly. I never felt like this before—never. What on earth's the matter with me? It's all these damned dinners, and late nights. I'm too old to stand the racket. (Too old at forty-three—it was a sad thought, a frightful thought, really. It didn't comfort Mr. Abbott at all.)

2

A STRANGE DILEMMA

MR. ABBOTT caught an early train home (he was quite unfit for any more business), and found Barbara pouring out tea in the drawing-room. She was alone for a wonder, and Mr. Abbott was thankful, he sank into an easy chair with a groan of relief.

Barbara looked up and smiled. "There you are!" she said, "I'm awfully glad you're so nice and early. We're dining with Mrs. Copthorne to-night."

"Hell!" said Mr. Abbott.

Barbara was amazed. She had never heard her Arthur swear with real fervour and emphasis before (he was a very even-tempered man as a rule, quiet, kind and reliable). Barbara was struck dumb.

"Hell," said Mr. Abbott again, louder and more emphatically, "Hell, hell, *hell!*"

"Don't you *want* to go, Arthur?" enquired Barbara, somewhat unnecessarily.

The simple question was the last straw on the camel's back, or, to take an even better metaphor, the question was the last pint of water that burst the dam. Mr. Abbott's dam burst, and a flood of eloquence poured forth over Barbara's defenceless head. Mr. Abbott got up and walked about the room, knocking against chairs and incidental tables in his blind passage, and all the time the flood of eloquence continued. He told Barbara all he had suffered and endured, he told her exactly how he felt about dinner-parties, with bridge to follow, and exactly how he felt about the friends of whose hospitality he and Barbara had partaken in the last few months. He inveighed against their rapacity at bridge, and the third-rate quality of the port and cigars they supplied. His diatribe veered from the general to the particular, and then back to the general again.

It took a long time, and a great deal of energy, and when Mr. Abbott finally ended with the distressing statement: "This life is killing me, killing me, I tell you"—he was quite breathless, and somewhat ashamed. The outburst had done him good, and he began to realise that it was not Arthur Abbott who had been speaking—not Arthur Abbott at all. It was some other Being, a suffering Being, an illogical, unreasonable, irritable Being, who had usurped Arthur Abbott's body and had ridden it all day long. This Being had behaved quite extraordinarily badly all day long; had been rude to Mr. Abbott's secretary (a most estimable and quite invaluable young woman); had quarrelled senselessly with Mr. Abbott's partner; and now, to crown everything, was bullying Mr. Abbott's wife.

"But Arthur," Barbara enquired again, when the flow of eloquence had ceased. "But Arthur, don't you *like* it—the dinners and bridge and things? I thought you liked it. Why do we do it if you don't like it?"

"Why do we do it?" echoed Mr. Abbott, stopping short in his pacing, and gazing at her in amazement.

"Yes, why do we?"

"We do it because you like it, of course," Arthur told her in calmer accents. The Being that had ridden him all day was seeping out of him now. Barbara was having a curiously soothing effect upon his tortured nerves. "It's all right," he continued, "it's quite all right, Barbara. Don't take any notice of what I said. It's just that I've had a frightful headache all day, and everything has been rather——"

"But I don't like it either," said Barbara simply.

"You—you don't like it either!"

"I hate it, really," she replied, "I'm no good at bridge, you see, and it bores me rather. I've done my best to get better at it. I've had lessons and I've read Culbertson till my head swims, but it doesn't seem to do me much good——"

"But Barbara——"

She swept on—"I was wondering how I was going to go on bearing it for ever and ever, but if *you* don't *like* going out to parties and playing bridge then we needn't."

Arthur Abbott gazed at his wife in amazement, which gradually gave place to amusement—she was a priceless person, his Barbara. Life was so simple to her, she was so matter-of-fact, so absolutely and peerlessly sane. He began to laugh, and Barbara laughed too—*her* laughter was from relief. She was tremendously relieved to discover that she need no longer look forward with dismay to thirty years of dining and bridging with her neighbours. (It might have been even more than thirty years, she reflected, because Mrs. Copthorne was sixty-five if she was a day, and

13

she still played bridge, and played quite a sound game, and held the most devastating post-mortems over every hand. At sixty-five, Barbara thought, you really ought to be beyond caring so frightfully if your partner, in a moment of absent-mindedness, trumped your trick. You ought to be knitting socks for your grandchildren or something like that.)

"Why on earth didn't you say you hated it all before?" Mr. Abbott enquired when at last he could speak. "Why didn't you tell me——"

"Why didn't *you* tell *me?*" retorted Barbara.

"I thought you were enjoying it."

"And I thought *you* were. After all they were all your friends," Barbara pointed out, "so, of course, I thought you liked them. They called on me and invited us, and, of course, we had to ask them back——"

"And then they asked us again," put in Arthur.

"So we had to ask them again," Barbara added.

"Are you sure?" Arthur enquired, smitten by a sudden horrible suspicion. "Are you quite sure you're not just saying it—I mean it isn't just because you think that I——"

"I'm sure," she replied, nodding vigorously,

14

"quite, quite sure. It was a sort of night-mare——"

It was a little while before they were able to convince themselves and each other of their sincerity, but eventually they realised that they were in complete accord. Both craved for quiet evenings by their own fireside, both were bored by dinner-parties and bridge.

"We'll never play again," said Barbara happily.

But, alas, it was not so simple as that. The Abbotts were involved with their friends in a series of gaieties; they had half a dozen engagements booked, and more rolling in daily. The Abbotts were a popular couple. Mr. Abbott played a good hand of bridge, and Barbara was pronounced to be "really very sweet." Her bridge was poor, of course, and completely lacking in character—you never knew where you were with Barbara Abbott as your partner. Sometimes she played quite reasonably for a hand or two, and then her eyes would stray round the room, and she would fall into a kind of trance and have to be told to play, and would waken up and ask what was trumps. It says a good deal for Barbara's personality and her friends' charity, that, in spite of such glaring faults

15

they liked her, but like her they did—everybody thought that Arthur Abbott had done well for himself when he married her. They had given him up for a confirmed bachelor years ago, and they were amazed when he took a holiday in the height of the publishing season, and returned to Sunnydene with a wife. *"It just showed"*—they said.

They all called, of course, and some of the more curious tried to find out where the new Mrs. Abbott had come from, and who she was before Arthur married her. But, after a few not very searching questions, they gave it up—it didn't really matter who she was. They liked her, and she was obviously a lady, and obviously had money of her own. She dressed well, with a simplicity that they knew was expensive, and she had a small car which she was learning to drive herself—what did it matter who or what she was, it was none of their business.[1]

Thus the Abbotts had been accepted, had become popular, and had been involved in a social round of engagements from which they were now trying to extricate themselves. How

[1] Mrs. Abbott's "past" may be discovered in *Miss Buncle's Book* by the same author.

was it to be done? That was the question. What excuse had they? The truth was too fantastic to be admitted openly—they would look such fools. . . .

Barbara produced her engagement book and they pored over it while they drank their tea, and Barbara consumed crumpets in vast quantities, and Arthur nibbled toast.

"I don't see how we can get out of the Smiths'," Barbara said, "or the Gorings' either, for that matter. And Sybil Beauchamp will never speak to me again if we let her down on the 9th."

"We must make a clean sweep," Arthur declared.

"But how?" objected Barbara. "What excuse can we make? To-night's easy, of course," she continued. "There's your head-ache—but I had better go and ring her up now, so that she can make up her tables."

She bolted the last crumpet and wiped her buttery fingers on her handkerchief. "You can be thinking of something while I'm away," she added hopefully.

Mrs. Copthorne was exceedingly annoyed when she heard about Mr. Abbott's head-ache, for now she was left with six—an inconvenient number for bridge—and it was too late to get anyone else—(except, perhaps, the curate, and even that only made seven).

Barbara soothed her and rang off feeling rather frightened. If everybody was going to be as difficult as Mrs. Copthorne they would never escape—never. It was a ghastly thought.

She went slowly into the back premises to find the Rasts (the married couple who cooked and buttled so impeccably for Arthur and herself), and here more difficulties materialised, difficulties requiring just as much tact and patience as the egregious Mrs. Copthorne. There was nobody in the kitchen but Dorcas (Barbara's own personal maid), and Dorcas was ironing.

"Lawks, what a turn you gave me, Miss Bar—Mrs. Abbott, I mean," Dorcas exclaimed, "creeping in so silent like that. I put out your black lace to-night (you don't want to mess up your best at old Mrs. Copthorne's) and I'm giving your velvet a press while Mrs. Rast is out. Her face is enough to turn the milk sour."

"Where are they?" Barbara enquired, looking round the kitchen vaguely as if she expected Rast and Mrs. Rast to appear from behind the dresser or out of the stove. "Where are they, Dorcas?"

"Who?—The Rasts?—Out," said Dorcas, dumping down her iron with a bang. "Both of them's out—gone to the pictures. They're on speaking terms for a wonder."

"Oh dear, what a bother!" Barbara said.

"Good riddance, I think," replied Dorcas. "But you better go and start dressing, or you'll be late, *Madame*."

Barbara smiled. When Dorcas called her "madame" or spoke of her as "Mrs. Abbott," she invariably said it in inverted commas, as if that were not Barbara's name at all, but only a sort of secret which she and Barbara shared to the exclusion of everybody else. Dorcas had been with her all her life; first as her nurse, and then as her maid and general factotum in the little house at Silverstream, so it was difficult for Dorcas to realise that Barbara was now not only grown up, but actually married.

Barbara felt the same about herself. She still felt that she had to grow up. Sometimes in the middle of a party, she would suddenly be overwhelmed by the conviction that she was not really grown up—not like other people. Surely other people of her age had

19

not got all the queer childish ideas and inhibitions that she had; were not beset by shyness at awkward moments; were not burdened by a total inability to express themselves in decent English, as Barbara was. The queer thing was that Barbara would *write* decent English, had, in fact, written two novels which had sold like hot cakes, and, like hot cakes, had given quite a number of innocent people a good deal of pain; but, when it came to talking, Barbara was lost.

No, she was not like other people. Other people took grown-up things as a matter of course—things like late dinner, and wine, driving cars and going to the theatre; things like marriage and housekeeping and ordering commodities from the shops; whereas *she* was just playing at it all the time, pretending to be grown-up, when, really and truly all the time, she was just Barbara—a plain, gawky child. She had the same body (bigger now, but indubitably the same, even to the rather intriguing brown mark, shaped like a little mouse, on her right thigh. Nobody ever saw it, of course—except herself, and even then, only in her bath—but it was still there—a visual testimony to the fact that she was still the same as she had always been, Barbara

Buncle and no other). She still had the same, rather unsatisfactory hair (though its poverty was now somewhat mitigated by a permanent wave), and she was still frightened of "bright" people, and of thunder, and big dogs, and dentists, and still had the same courage to bear her fears without a sound. Last, but not least, she still enjoyed the same things—ice cream, and sweet cakes, and crumpets with the butter oozing out of them—and she still loved being out at night when the stars were shining, and going late to bed, and having breakfast in bed. Some day, she was convinced, somebody would find out that she was an impostor in the adult world.

"You better go and get dressed, 'madame', " said Dorcas again. "You haven't too much time, and your hair's all over the place. I'll come and do you up when I've finished this——"

"But we're not going," said Barbara. "That's what I came in to see Mrs. Rast about. Mr. Abbott's got a headache——"

"There now!" exclaimed Dorcas, "there now—and the Rasts out! What a to do!—not but what I can cook something for your suppers just as nice as her——"

"Of course you can, Dorcas," agreed Barbara diplomatically.

"Yes," said Dorcas complacently, "we managed all right at Tanglewood Cottage, didn't we, Miss Barbara—Mrs. Abbott I mean—but Mrs. Rast will go clean dotty when she hears I've been poking round her larder."

"Well, you'll have to," said Barbara. "I don't see how she can be more disagreeable than she always is, and Mr. Abbott will want something to eat——"

"He'll get it, don't you worry," Dorcas promised. "I'm not afraid of that old cat. I can stand up for myself, I hope."

"I wonder what there *is!*" Barbara said, moving vaguely in the direction of the larder.

"Never you mind what there is, 'madame,'" Dorcas told her. "I'll see you get something tasty. Off you go back to the pore gentleman, and leave it to me."

She turned off the iron as she spoke, and bustled away to see what she could find, leaving Barbara to return to her suffering husband.

Thus it was that the Abbotts had a very comfortable little meal together, and spent a quiet evening by the fire. It was extraordinarily pleasant and peaceful despite the problem that vexed their minds. The problem was so absurd that they could not help laughing over it, but it was a very real problem all the same.

"I don't see what we're to *do*," said Barbara, for perhaps the twentieth time. "You can't have a headache every night, can you?"

Arthur agreed that he couldn't. "It's gone now, anyhow," he admitted.

"How angry Mrs. Copthorne would be!" Barbara exclaimed, with a little gurgle of delight.

No solution to the problem was arrived at that night, but the following morning at breakfast Arthur hit on the one and only way out of their dilemma. It came to him quite suddenly in the middle of reading Messrs. Faction & Whiting's advertising announcements, it came to him as a ray of light, a veritable inspiration straight from Heaven— they would *move*.

3

A BLOODLESS VICTORY

THERE straightway ensued a strenuous period for Barbara Abbott—it was she, of course, who was to find the perfect house (obviously Arthur could not be expected to range the Home Counties looking at houses—he had his work to do). Barbara flung herself into her task with all her energy—she really enjoyed it, for she was of an adventurous spirit—she visited house agents; she answered advertisements; she advertised in the paper and waded through the replies. She ranged the countryside daily in her small car—which she could now drive with a fair degree of competence—Kent and Surrey, Essex and Bucks became familiar country to Barbara. She visited big houses and small houses, old houses, and new houses; houses with no water at all and houses that stood ankle deep in water. She visited houses buried in trees, dark and gloomy as the tomb, and houses set upon hilltops where the four winds blew through the flimsy masonry and the doors banged all day long, but she saw nothing that pleased her, nothing that satisfied her. The truth was Barbara had a picture of the ideal house in her mind's eye. It had arisen, all unsought, that first morning when Arthur had said "A nice house, further out of town, with a nice garden—trees and things." The picture in Barbara's mind was a concrete picture, quite incapable of alteration, and nothing she saw approximated to the picture, so nothing she saw would do.

Every night when Barbara returned to Sunnydene, worn out and bedraggled with her fruitless search, Arthur would enquire, "Well, any luck to-day? Seen anything?" and Barbara would reply with invariable truthfulness "I've seen five houses (or nine or three, as occasion demanded) but none of them are any good." And she would add, hopefully, "But I'm going to Farnham to-morrow (or it might be Hatfield). The agents have told me about a house *there* which sounds as if it might do."

As week succeeded week Arthur began to despair. "Surely you've seen something that might suit us!" he would say; and Barbara would reply, somewhat wearily, but still firmly and hopefully, "not yet."

In one way their original problem was solved, for Barbara now possessed a splendid excuse for shirking the little dinners and the bridge. She was far too tired when she returned from house-hunting, far too tired out to go to parties, and Arthur was so devoted that nothing would induce him to go out and leave her alone. One or two hostesses were so misguided as to insist on the Abbotts accepting their hospitality, but they did not repeat their mistake. Barbara was genuinely tired after her long days in the open air, and her bridge was so deplorable that even her best friends were annoyed. At Mrs. Copthorne's she actually fell asleep in a corner of the sofa before the gentlemen had finished their port, and, as her husband forbade anyone to waken her, she slumbered peacefully the whole evening, while one table was obliged to play "cut throat," and everyone talked in whispers. It really was not good enough, and now that those charming Fitz-Georges had taken Oak Lodge, there were plenty of people to make up two—or even three tables—without bothering about the Abbotts.

So the Abbotts were left in peace and, gradually, they drifted out of the social whirl and were partially forgotten; and people felt (as people do, when they know that their friends are leaving the neighbourhood), that it was really not much good bothering about the Abbotts any more.

So the weeks passed and April came, and the tiny garden of Sunnydene was full of yellow daffodils, blowing gaily in the breeze; and one fine Saturday morning Mr. Abbott came down to breakfast wearing his golfing shoes, and a brand new suit of plus-fours which became him mightily.

Barbara looked up from the letter she was reading and said "Oh! You're wearing it to-day! I like it awfully, it makes you look so nice and big."

"Yes," said Mr. Abbott, well satisfied with his wife's praise. "Yes, I thought I would. I'm playing with John," and he sat down to his breakfast, feeling at peace with the world.

"Where are you going to-day, Barbara?" he enquired, for it was now an established custom in the Abbott household that Barbara should sally forth early every day and return late. Arthur would have been surprised at any deviation from this fixed routine, he would

27

have been even more surprised (by this time) if the truly Herculean efforts of his wife had produced a suitable house for his inspection, so inured to disappointment had he become.

"It's a place called Wandlebury," Barbara replied. "The agents told me about it yesterday—The Archway House, Wandlebury—I may as well look at it, I suppose."

"By all means," agreed Mr. Abbott with cheerful hopelessness.

"It seems awfully difficult to get just exactly what we want," complained Barbara, a trifle wearily.

"Yes it does, doesn't it?" he agreed again. "As a matter of fact, you know, there's no *real need* for us to leave here. It's very convenient for town, and it's really very peaceful now that we don't have to go out at night——"

"But it's only because I'm house-hunting that we don't have to," Barbara reminded him, "it would all start again if I stopped being out all day."

This was true, of course, so there was nothing more to be said.

Barbara glanced at the clock, and saw with dismay that it was nine-thirty. It was the hour at which she repaired to the kitchen to interview Mrs. Rast about the food. She rose reluctantly; not only did she actively dislike Mrs. Rast, but she always felt that nine-thirty was a bad hour at which to order food—the worst hour in the day for that arduous and uncongenial task. At nine-thirty Barbara was glutted with bacon and eggs and drugged with coffee, and invariably felt as if she never wanted another mouthful of food in her life. She knew, of course (academically), that by lunch time she would feel quite differently about the matter, and would welcome a succulent meal cooked to perfection by Mrs. Rast—nay, she would even be annoyed if it were not forthcoming—but she could not really and truly believe it.

Barbara had never done any housekeeping before she was married. In the old days at Tanglewood Cottage she had left the food question entirely to Dorcas. Dorcas had ordered what was required, and had fed Barbara on boiled neck-of-mutton or stew, and milk puddings, with an occasional pie to vary the monotony, and Barbara had eaten it meekly. Food did not interest her in the least; it was a necessity, not a pleasure (indeed it was not until she was married that Barbara realised it was possible to be interested in what you ate), but Arthur, though by no means a glutton, liked his food, and liked it to be of good quality, well cooked, and of reasonable variety. Barbara found it difficult.

It was impossible to continue to leave the food question to Dorcas—for Dorcas had now become a maid—and, as such had nothing whatever to do with food—Mrs. Rast would not have stood it, and Arthur would never have eaten such meals as Dorcas chose. This being so Barbara was forced to take an interest in food and, moreover, forced to take an interest in food at nine-thirty a.m., when she was full to the brim with a solid mass of breakfast, and in no condition to exercise her selective faculties.

Mrs. Rast was no help, she took a delight in being no help to Barbara. For years Mrs. Rast had run the house, ordered everything, and fed Mr. Abbott as a gentleman should be fed, but now that he had got married she knew her place. (Let the new wife arrange the meals— he'd soon see the difference—said Mrs. Rast darkly.) Every morning she stood and looked at Barbara with her head on one side and her arms folded across her thin chest, and said "Yes, madame," "No, madame," or "I reely couldn't say, madame. Just as *you* like, of course," while Barbara gazed at her, and tried vainly and desperately to think of something that Arthur would like to eat, and wondered whether Mrs. Rast knew how disagreeable she looked, and whether it was any pleasure to her to look like that.

It was not only to her new mistress that Mrs. Rast was disagreeable, she was disagreeable to everyone; she quarrelled with everyone; she fought with her husband week in and week out. Sometimes for days at a time this extraordinary couple were not on speaking terms with each other, and, when this happened they communicated with each other in writing. Barbara had come across the slate which they used during hostilities, and had read the curt message written upon it in Rast's niggling hand "SHE WANTS TEA AT FOUR." Arthur was aware of all this, he had had the Rasts for years and had found them excellent servants. He laughed at their peculiarities—but Barbara couldn't laugh. To Barbara there was something very horrible about it, and she felt that the bad feelings harboured by the Rasts lay like a cloud upon the house. (It was the only cloud that marred the clear sky of her married life.) She would look at Rast, as he handed her the vegetables and mark his tight lips, the streaks of ill-temper engraved from nose to chin, and the deep wrinkle between his narrowly-placed eyes, and she would think, with a little shudder: there's hatred in that man, and deceit and cruelty—all sorts of slimy things—and Mrs. Rast is worse. Sometimes she felt as if the Rasts had filled the house with a miasma of wickedness, and would be impelled to rush to the windows and throw them wide open to let in the fresh air.

The Rasts quarrelled with each other, they were cruel and disagreeable to each other, but they were as one in their hatred of Barbara. She felt their hatred like a solid thing, weighing upon her shoulders. She was their common enemy. They waited upon her, and carried out her orders with exactness and promptitude, but, for all that, she could feel the hatred seeping out of them at every pore. Several times she had tried saying to Arthur—"The Rasts hate me, you know," and Arthur, usually so understanding, had not understood at all. He had either said "Nonsense! Nobody could possibly hate you, you're not a hateable person, Barbara," or else he had said "They've got more to do, with a lady in the house, but they'll soon get used to it," and another time he had said "I don't know why you keep on saying they hate you. They do their work all right, don't they? Well then, what more do you want?" Barbara was constitutionally incapable of describing what she wanted, she struggled for a few moments, and then said "I wish they'd smile sometimes," whereupon Arthur had roared with laughing and exclaimed "Can you imagine old Rast *smiling?* It would split his face. Honestly, Barbara, you would have difficulty in replacing the Rasts—look at the bother other people have with servants."

This particular morning Mrs. Rast looked more than usually sour. She listened in silence while Barbara arranged the meals for the week-end, and at last she announced that she would like to speak to Mrs. Abbott for a moment.

Barbara was terrified, but she managed to convey her willingness to listen to Mrs. Rast.

"There 'ave bin roomours," said Mrs. Rast darkly, "I'm not one to listen to roomours, not as a general rule, but when they affects yourself they 'as to be listened to."

"Rumours!" enquired Barbara.

"Roomours," agreed Mrs. Rast. "It 'as bin said at table in Rast's 'earing that you are looking for another 'ouse."

"Yes, of course we are."

"It seems to Rast and me that we ought to 'ave bin told," said Mrs. Rast indignantly. "Me and Rast feels after the years we 'ave bin with Mr. Abbott, and given every satisfaction, not to say working our fingers to the bone, we ought to 'ave bin *told.*"

"I thought everyone knew I was looking for a house," said Barbara in surprise. "What did you think I was doing?"

"What you do isn't nothing to do with us, madame," replied the unpleasant woman frigidly.

"And anyhow I haven't found anything yet," Barbara added.

"It's unsettling," Mrs. Rast said. "Very unsettling, that's what it is. Me and Rast 'asn't felt so unsettled for years. When you think of all the years me and Rast 'as served Mr. Abbott it's very unsettling to find you aren't trusted."

Barbara felt sure there must be a good answer to this, but she couldn't find it. She felt, deep within her, that it was unfair. The Rasts had known all along that she was looking for a house—it was a ramp, that was what it was—she felt her anger rising.

"Not *trusted*," Mrs. Rast continued. "That's what's worrying Rast and me."

34

"I'll tell you when I find a house," Barbara said.

"And may I ask where the new 'ouse will be?" enquired Mrs. Rast with elaborate humility.

"I don't know, I haven't found it yet."

"It will not be in this neighbour'ood, I presoome."

"No—no, it certainly won't be here," said Barbara firmly—the whole object of the move would be annulled if they did not move far enough away—

Mrs. Rast drew back her head and tucked in her chin, it was an ugly gesture, rather like the recoil of a snake before it strikes—"I see," she said. "Well, Rast and me feels that we would rather not leave the neighbour'ood. It suits us, and we 'ave our friends 'ere—we 'ave ties in this neighbour'ood."

"You mean——" Barbara could not believe her ears—"You mean you want to leave——"

"I mean we don't want to leave," said Mrs. Rast significantly, "and what's more, if Mr. Abbott was aware that Rast and me was wedded to the neighbour'ood—so to speak—well, we 'ave bin with Mr. Abbott a long time—we knows 'is ways, you see."

Barbara did see. It was the most frightful

35

impertinence. She and Arthur were to remain at Sunnydene to suit the Rasts. *Whatever next?* she thought. She was angry, but she was also frightened—how would Arthur see it? Arthur was already a trifle lukewarm about leaving Sunnydene. She saw the doors of the cage closing and she thought—I shall be here for ever and ever, growing old, playing bridge, waited upon by the Rasts. I must be strong, she thought, I must be firm, I'm too Barbara Buncle-ish, that's what's the matter with me. And then quite suddenly her rage rose to the surface, and she wasn't frightened any more.

"Mrs. Rast," she said, getting up out of the chair, and frowning at Mrs. Rast in a majestic manner, "Mrs. Rast, I consider your remarks impertinent. I shall be glad if you and your husband will look for another situation at the end of the month."

Mrs. Rast was aghast—as anybody well might have been—at the metamorphosis she was witnessing. It was like seeing a sheep turn into a tiger before your eyes. She did not recover the use of her tongue until her mistress had left the kitchen.

Arthur had not yet gone to play golf. He was waiting in the hall for John Hutson to call for him (practising a little putting on the hall carpet) when Barbara, still simmering with rage, emerged from the kitchen premises.

"There you are, Arthur," she remarked, with forced brightness. "Hasn't Mr. Hutson called for you yet?"

"No," said Arthur, putting assiduously.

"The Rasts are leaving," added Barbara casually.

"The Rasts—leaving?" exclaimed Arthur, with alarm and consternation. "Good heavens! How frightful! What's the matter? Do they want more wages or something? Couldn't you persuade——"

"They don't want to leave Hampstead Heath," Barbara told him.

Arthur's face cleared. "Oh," he said, "Oh well—there's no real need for us to go, is there? I mean—well—there's no real need. I was just thinking this morning—besides, you haven't found a house yet. Did you explain?"

"I told her we hadn't fixed on a house," Barbara admitted, she was still boiling with rage, but the rage was well in hand (it was a servant not a master). She thought: Arthur's in a groove—he *shall* move.

"Oh well!" Arthur said, oblivious of the

hidden storm, "Oh well! That's all right then."

"Are you going to stay on here?" enquired Barbara.

"What d'you mean?" cried Arthur, suddenly aghast.

"I'm leaving here you see," Barbara explained calmly. "But, of course, *you* needn't——"

"Barbara! Barbara, of course, I didn't mean I wanted to stay here—no, of course not."

"You must mean something."

"No, nothing. Nothing at all," said Arthur earnestly. "Of course I'm as keen as ever to find a house—as keen as ever."

"If you'd rather stay——"

"No, no—certainly not. We must move——"

"You see I've half left here already," Barbara explained, waving her hand vaguely. "It's a funny sort of feeling—I've left here, but I haven't gone anywhere else. I'm sort of in the air. but I couldn't possibly come back here and settle down again—I simply couldn't."

"Barbara, don't be absurd. We're going to move, I tell you." He was thoroughly alarmed now; it was so unlike Barbara to behave like this—could she be ill, he wondered—ghastly thought! What on earth would happen if Barbara took ill?

He was moved by his guardian angel to do the right thing, the only thing in the utterly unprecedented circumstances, he seized her in his arms and kissed her thoroughly—he had had eleven months' experience in kissing Barbara, and he was rather good at the job. "There," he said, "there—it's all right, darling, isn't it?"

Much to his relief, Barbara responded adequately. "Of course, it's all right, silly," she replied, kissing him in return.

They were still locked in each other's arms, when Mr. Hutson opened the front door and walked in—he was a privileged visitor.

"Are you ready, Arthur? Oh Lord, I'm sorry!" he exclaimed trying to back out again.

They drew apart, full of confusion.

"We were just—er—saying good-bye," said Barbara blushing furiously.

"Barbara's going to Wandlebury—she's going to look at a house, you know——" added Arthur, babbling with embarrassment. "We're leaving here to-morrow—or the next day. I told you we were leaving, didn't I? I

39

mean you've heard me say we were leaving here——"

"Yes, of course. Everybody knows you're leaving," agreed John Hutson. "But surely you're not going to-morrow—it's Sunday, you know."

"Well, perhaps not exactly to-morrow, but quite soon—quite, quite soon," Arthur assured him, "quite, *quite* soon—just as soon as ever we can—as soon as Barbara finds a house for us to move into. It was my idea to leave here, you know—I've told you that, haven't I? My idea entirely—yes—I can't bear this place—can't think how I've stuck it so long."

"It's not a bad place," ventured Mr. Hutson—a trifle bewildered by his friend's vehemence.

"Oh, it *is*," Arthur told him earnestly. "It's a bad place—not a good place at all. Barbara and I are leaving immediately."

They walked down the path, Arthur still assuring his friend of the imminence of their departure. Mr. Hutson's small car was waiting at the gate. Mr. Hutson got in and started the engine, Mr. Abbott stowed his clubs into the tonneau.

"I say," he said, hesitating with his foot on

40

the step. "I say, John, I think I had better run back for a moment and say good-bye to Barbara—you don't mind waiting a moment, do you?"

"I thought you *said* good-bye to her!" exclaimed Mr. Hutson in amazement.

"Not properly," Arthur told him seriously. "I think I had better say good-bye to her properly."

He ran back to the house and disappeared from view.

"So that's marriage!" said Mr. Hutson to himself. "Most extraordinary!"

4

WANDLEBURY

ENGLISH towns and villages have as many idiosyncrasies as prima donnas. Some of them hide themselves amongst woods, or lurk behind hills, to burst into the motorist's view as the road winds round a corner; others are set upon a hill-top, their roofs and spires stretching heavenwards for all the world to see. Others, again, lie upon a plain, so that the traveller sees them before him for miles, growing gradually bigger, changing from a toy village to a real one as he approaches. Some indulge in outlying suburbs of villas and bungalows, very new and tidy; others in long rows of workmen's cottages with children playing round the doors.

Barbara approached Wandlebury from the north, she had lost her way, and had been misdirected by a congenital idiot in charge of two ancient farm-carts full of manure. She had wandered helplessly into muddy lanes, and had nearly bogged the car in trying to turn at a field gate—turning was still a troublesome and somewhat exhausting business for Barbara Abbott. She had begun to wonder whether Wandlebury had walked away in the night, leaving the countryside unblotted by its tenancy. For miles she had expected to see the place at every turn in the road; for miles she had said to herself, "I'm almost there—that next corner will disclose it to me." If the country had not been so beautiful she would have been annoyed, she might even have given up the chase and gone home in despair, but the country was beautiful— not flat, nor exactly hilly, but rolling as English country ought to be. The day was bright and breezy, cloud-shadows moved over the fields like smoke, and, like smoke, they faded and disappeared. A haze of tender green was spread upon the fields, as the seeds, which had lain dormant for so long, thrust forth their green blades to the warmth of the sun. Barbara could not be annoyed—it was not in her to be annoyed on such a day, and in such surroundings. Besides, she was distinctly above herself to-day, she had won a battle—a pitched battle against the forces of evil, and she had "managed" Arthur beautifully. *I'm coming on*, she thought.

43

At this moment, a moment of psychological importance in Barbara's development, she turned the corner of a high wall and found herself in the middle of a town—it was Wandlebury at last, and Wandlebury just when she had ceased to expect it. There was no gradual approach to the place, no hideous growths of brick and plaster to be penetrated before the core of the town was reached—one moment Barbara had been in the country, the real country of hedges and fields and trees, and the next moment she was in the town.

It was a very small town, of course—a sleepy, sunshiny place that looked as if the rush and hurry of the modern world had overlooked its existence. Barbara found herself in a big square, paved with cobbles. There was a fountain in the middle; the water from the fountain flowed away in a wide runnel, it made a pretty whispering sound. A few pigeons, the iridescent feathers gleaming in the sunshine, strutted about, pecking hopefully amongst the cobbles, or sat and preened themselves on the edge of the wide shallow basin of the fountain. One side of the square was occupied by County Buildings of Georgian character, they were four stories high with pediments over the principal windows and a heavily ornamented cornice along the edge of the flat roof. High pillars of Doric design graced the broad doorstep, supporting two small balconies with carved stone balustrades. Between the balconies an arched window lent a pleasing dignity to the design, and broke the monotony of the long line of tall windows whose large panes glittered in the morning sunshine. The whole effect of the buildings was bold, and simple, and massive.

The second side of the square consisted of a row of private houses, which had been turned into offices and banks. They matched the County Buildings in period and design, were flat faced and pillared, with little flights of wide steps leading up to porticoed doorways. On the third side was a row of shops, and, on the fourth, the Inn.

The Inn, which bore the intriguing sign of "The Apollo and Boot," was the oldest building in the square; it was pure Elizabethan, with small windows, timbered orders and a gabled roof. The archway, which admitted travellers to the inn-yard, was high and pointed, and above the archway was a row of latticed windows with diamond-shaped panes. Barbara felt, as she looked at the Inn, that the sound of the coach-wheels of a previous century had not died away. She could so easily imagine the coaches, dashing round the corner, lurching in through the tall archway, and drawing up with a clatter of hooves on the cobbled yard. She could imagine the horn blowing, the ostlers running out to change the horses, and the quaintly dressed passengers climbing down from the top of the coach with stiff and weary limbs. Mr. Pickwick, she thought, and Weller—yes, Sam Weller, that was his name—and the long lanky Mr. Winkle who fought in the duel. It's all exactly like that, she thought (trying to catch the aroma of the book, the bird's eye view which we reproduce when we try to remember something read long ago and build up from an incident or a character in the story). It's all exactly like the background of *Pickwick Papers*. How Arthur will love it, she thought, and her heart warmed towards him, for she was desperately fond of Arthur. The recollection of the little scene this morning made her smile—but her eyes were a trifle wet. As if I would have gone away and left him! She thought tenderly, what an absurd darling he is! It was all just bluff on my part (at least I suppose it was. I

46

didn't really *think* it was bluff at the time) and how I ever found the courage to do it, beats me. But, after all, it was really for his own good, he was getting into such a dull groove, and I know he'll be happy here—and so shall I. Already she was determined that the house she was going to look at was the right house—Wandlebury was the place she had been looking for—she knew it in her bones.

Through the tall arch of the Apollo and Boot she drove her car, and was half ashamed of its insignificance and modernity in that ancient yard. She parked it carefully in one corner—there was nobody about—and went into the Coffee Room for lunch.

The Coffee Room was disappointing, it was dark and rather dirty—somebody had tried to bring it up to date, and had succeeded in spoiling the atmosphere without achieving his object. But Barbara did not notice the room, she sat by the window and looked out at the square, at the fountain and the pigeons, and the pale grey buildings, and, above them, the pale blue sky; and suddenly, as she looked, the square was invaded by a flock of sheep, driven by boys, who cried shrilly to each other, and waved their sticks; and a

47

strong smell of disinfectant from the sheep's hot bodies drifted up to her as she sat at the window, and caught her by the throat.

But they didn't use disinfectant in those days, said Barbara to herself—it was a sure proof that Wandlebury was really here in the twentieth century.

5

JUBILEE PORT

AFTER Barbara had finished her lunch she set out on foot for the lawyer's office, where she was to enquire about The Archway House. The waiter had told her that it was no distance—no distance at all—and Barbara felt she could sample the unique flavour of Wandlebury better on foot than awheel. She strolled across the square, looking about her with interest and enjoyment. The square was full of ghosts—or so it seemed to Barbara—jolly little ghosts out of Arthur's set of Dickens. Little gentlemen with whiskers on their cheeks, clad in smalls, with tight-fitting blue coats and glossy boots; and ladies with poke-bonnets and curls, the silken rustle of whose skirts blended with the whisper of the running water in the wide gutter. It was all the easier to see these ghosts because, apart from them, the square was empty. There were no cars, no pedestrians, no signs whatever of the modern inhabitants of the town. But to Barbara the square was not empty, nor deserted, and this was strange, because Barbara always said that she had no imagination at all. To Barbara "an imagination" was a definite thing, it was like a leg, or an arm, or an ear, and when she said she hadn't got "an imagination" she visualised herself as a sort of mental cripple, a person who had been born without the usual supply of assets. "I have no imagination," she would say, sadly, and she would go on to explain that *that* was the reason she had had to put her neighbours into her books. It seemed unkind of them to be annoyed at finding themselves there, they really ought to have been sorry for her—it was not her fault that she had been born without "an imagination," was it? This being the case, it was very strange, very strange indeed that she should have seen poke-bonnets and whiskers in Wandlebury, and heard the rustle of silken petticoats in the deserted square.

It was quite impossible to lose your way, once you were actually in the town of Wandlebury, because all the important part of the town was centred in the square; and very soon Barbara found the names "TUPPER, TYLER, & TUPPER" on a brass plate, and went briskly up the wide flat steps (worn a bit at the edges) to a dark-green, porticoed door. The bell was the kind you pull from its socket, and it made a terrific jangling somewhere below Barbara's feet. The noise had scarcely subsided when the green door was flung open, and a dapper little man with a round, chubby, pink face, and a round, shiny bald head stood before her framed in the lintel.

"Mr. Tupper?" enquired Barbara politely.

"Tyler," he amended, bowing from the waist with old-fashioned courtesy, "Mr. Tyler—at your service—ahem. We have been—ah—expecting you all morning. Will you—ah—walk this way. My partner is—ah—unfortunately—ah—indisposed, but I have no doubt that I shall be able to—hum—hum——" and so saying Mr. Tyler led the way across the hall, rubbing his hands together busily and importantly.

Barbara followed, a trifle surprised at the warmth of her welcome. She had frequented the offices of lawyers and house agents for months, and was used to various kinds of treatment at their hands. She had met with cold indifference, verging on rudeness; she had also met with politeness and helpfulness,

51

but she had never encountered such graciousness as this.

She found herself in a large and lofty room, looking out towards the back on to lawns and trees. The walls were shelved, almost to the roof, and the shelves were filled with large black tin boxes upon which, in white letters, she could read the names of Messrs. Tupper, Tyler & Tupper's august clients. Amongst these she discerned Lady Chevis Cobbe, C.P.R. Wrench, Colonel Thane, Rev. Edwin Dance, M. Winkworth, Cobbe Estate, Sir Lucian Agnew, Chevis Estate, Wandlebury Orphanage, etc.

Mr. Tyler waved her to a chair near the window, a large and somewhat shabby leather chair; it was exceedingly comfortable. Barbara sank into its embrace with a sigh of relief. She had not realised she was tired, but she was—her morning had been a strenuous one, and her lunch at the Apollo and Boot had not refreshed her.

"You will take a glass of sherry, I hope," said Mr. Tyler graciously, "or perhaps you would prefer port wine?"

Barbara did not want either, it was one of her peculiarities that she detested the taste of wine, but Mr. Tyler was so pressing, so emphatically of the opinion that it would do her good, so absurdly distressed at her refusal, that Barbara was obliged to change her mind and partake of his hospitality.

"I haven't very much time," she told him, sipping the horrible stuff (which, incidentally, was '87 Jubilee Port, and had been most carefully—not to say lovingly—matured in Messrs. Tupper, Tyler & Tupper's vast underground cellars)—"I haven't very much time—so if you would——"

"Certainly—by all means," he agreed. "I have the document ready. If you will just glance through it—we shall require witnesses, of course. Two of the clerks——"

"Surely we don't need witnesses!" Barbara exclaimed.

"I quite understand your feelings," said Mr. Tyler earnestly. "We have been—ah—most discreet—I assure you—most discreet. My partner and I fully—ah—appreciate your desire for—ah—discretion. Our clerks are extremely—ah—discreet."

"But I don't understand——" began Barbara.

"The witnesses"—explained Mr. Tyler. "It is—ah—absolutely essential to have witnesses—but they will merely witness your signature—that is all."

"I haven't even seen it yet!" cried Barbara—did he want her to buy the house without seeing it—what an extraordinary idea!

"Of course, of course," agreed Mr. Tyler with ready apprehension. "You would like to see it first—to con it over—ah—at your leisure."

Barbara agreed. (What strange words the man used! She had "seen over" houses, she had "inspected" houses, she had even "viewed" them, but she had never been invited to "con" a house at her leisure.)

"I will send for the draft at once," said Mr. Tyler, smiling at her over the top of his tortoise-shell spectacles.

Here was another word, strange to Barbara. She supposed a draft must be some kind of conveyance—an old-fashioned kind of cab, perhaps—to take her to see the house. It's just what you would expect in a place like Wandlebury, she thought, it *must* be a kind of vehicle—don't they have "draft horses?"

"I've got my car at the Inn," Barbara told him.

"Quite so, quite so," nodded Mr. Tyler. "A car is a most useful—ah—invention. You came in your car, and you—ah—left it at the

Inn. By the way, I hope you found—ah—everything prepared to your liking?"

"You mean at the Inn?" enquired Barbara in a bewildered voice.

"Dear me, no—at the *house*," explained Mr. Tyler.

"Oh, I haven't seen the house yet," Barbara told him. "I only came to Wandlebury this morning."

"Dear me!" exclaimed Mr. Tyler again. "Dear me! We thought you were—ah—arriving yesterday."

"No, I only came this morning, and I came straight here. The agents said you had got the keys."

Mr. Tyler laughed heartily. "But the house is open," he assured her. "Everything is—ah—prepared for your comfort. We have been most careful to—ah—see that everything was—ah—prepared."

Barbara was getting more and more perplexed. How had Mr. Tyler known that she was coming—unless, of course, the house agent had written. She supposed that was what had happened. She had drunk her glass of port by this time—every drop of it, because Mr. Tyler was really so kind and she was very anxious not to seem ungrateful—and, although the taste was horrid, the wine had given her a warm comfortable feeling in her inside. She felt soothed, and a trifle sleepy, her critical faculties were a trifle blunted. Mr. Tyler was funny and old-fashioned, Wandlebury itself was funny and old-fashioned—it was all very pleasant and peaceful. The waste of time had ceased to worry her—what did *time* matter, thought Barbara vaguely—she would see the house presently, and she was sure she would like it. People always said it was no use trying to hurry these old-fashioned lawyers. She was still ruminating when the door opened and a young man came in with a legal looking document in his hand. He laid it on the table and said something to Mr. Tyler in a low voice.

"Ah yes—ahem—this is what we want," said Mr. Tyler importantly. "What did you say, Mr. Benson? The telephone? Dear me, how very—ah—inconvenient. We are all slaves to the telephone these days—all slaves. Perhaps your ladyship will be good enough to excuse me while I attend to this—hum—ha— matter. I will leave you to glance over the draft."

"But need I?" enquired Barbara, who felt it would be much pleasanter to sit and doze a little while Mr. Tyler was away. "Is it neces-

56

sary? I mean couldn't I see the house first?"

"I am afraid it will be necessary, or at least advisable, for you to glance over the draft," Mr. Tyler told her. "You will find it in order—I have no doubt of that, for we followed your—ah—instructions with the—ah—greatest care—I will explain everything when I return."

He handed her the document with a low bow, and hurried away.

Barbara took the document; it was all rather queer, but Mr. Tyler had said he would explain everything when he returned. She was glad of that, because there were quite a lot of things she wanted him to explain. The document, on the face of it, did not seem to bear any reference to The Archway House, but Mr. Tyler had told her to read it—nay, he had said it was essential that she should read it—so she supposed she had better do so—she was an amenable women.

The typewritten document appeared to be a will. Barbara had seen her father's will and had had it explained to her, so she was able to decipher the peculiar language quite easily. The will started by declaring that it was the last will of Matilda Victoria Chevis Cobbe, revoking all other wills and testaments made by that lady and bequeathing all her worldly goods (and she seemed to be extraordinarily well endowed with worldly goods) to her deceased husband's niece, Jeronina Mary Cobbe, commonly residing at Ganthorne Lodge, Ganthorne. This bequest was, strangely, to hold good only on the condition that the said Jeronina Mary Cobbe was unmarried, at the time of the testator's death. If the said Jeronina Mary Cobbe were married at the time of the testator's death, the bequest was to go to Archibald Edward Cobbe, the brother of the said Jeronina, with various provisos and conditions which did not interest Barbara in the least. There were legacies to different people, Bertrand Chevis and Sir Lucian Agnew and Dr. Charles Wrench, and smaller ones to servants and dependants, and there were bequests to charities such as Indigent Gentlewomen and Necessitous Governesses and Children's Homes and Hospitals, but, look as she would, Barbara could find nothing about The Archway House in the will, nothing at all. At the end of the will there was a blank space for the signature of the testator, and on this was scribbled in pencil M.V.C.C., and below were two more blank spaces for the signatures of the witnesses.

The whole thing was most peculiar, thought Barbara (who was now beginning to recover from Mr. Tyler's port), most peculiar. What a strange will it was with that clause disinheriting the said Jeronina Mary Cobbe if she were married at the time of the testator's death. Barbara looked again, more carefully, to see if she had made any mistake, but there was no mistake at all. It was perfectly clear. If Jeronina (and what a funny name—rather *nice*, Barbara thought), if Jeronina was unmarried she was the residuary legatee, and raked in everything; if she was married she was fobbed off with two thousand pounds and some jewellery. Quite nice, of course, Barbara reflected, quite nice if you weren't expecting more, but a mere drop in the ocean compared with what the said Jeronina would get if she remained single. How funny not to want that girl to get married, Barbara thought. Matilda Thingummibob must be mad. (Barbara, herself, was delighted with matrimony and thought it the most desirable state on earth.)

Mr. Tyler was away a long time. He returned full of the most abject apologies. Barbara was delighted to see him, not only because she had taken a fancy to the kind little man, but also because she had been floundering in the bog of bewilderment too long. She was ready for the explanation which had been promised her.

"Most aggravating!" said Mr. Tyler, bustling in like a fussy little steam-boat. "Most aggravating. A call from Bournemouth—cut off in the middle—I cannot tell you how—hum—had *distressed* I am that this should have occurred during your visit. It was most unfortunate—most unfortunate. You will understand that we are—hum—ha—short-handed at present with Mr. Tupper indisposed. We prefer to keep matters in—ha—our own hands which makes things—ha—difficult. Young Mr. Tupper is—ah—an exceedingly capable young man, but he is—ha—*young*."

Barbara assured him that she quite understood.

"Exceedingly kind, exceedingly gracious," murmured Mr. Tyler. "May I give you—ah—a little more port wine? No?"

"No, thank you," said Barbara firmly.

"Ah well," said Mr. Tyler, rubbing his hands. "Ah well. And now to business. You have—ah—glanced over the draft, so no time

60

has been wasted. I trust it meets with your—ah—approval?"

"But there's nothing in it about the house," objected Barbara.

"The house?" said Mr. Tyler. "You are, of course, referring to Chevis Place. The house is part of the—ah—estate. It goes to Miss Cobbe as residuary legatee. That was what you—ah—intended was it not?"

Barbara gazed at him in amazement. "There's some mistake," she said, in a bewildered voice. "I don't know what you're talking about at all. You must think I'm somebody else, or something."

"My dear Lady Chevis Cobbe, how could I——"

"I'm not, I'm not," Barbara cried. "I'm not her at all. I thought there was something queer about it——"

The colour faded from Mr. Tyler's rubicund countenance, he staggered to a chair.

"What?" he said. "What? You are not Lady Chevis Cobbe?"

"No, I'm not—I never even *heard* of her," Barbara assured him.

"Oh dear! Oh dear me, this is dreadful, this is really dreadful!"

"I'm Mrs. Abbott," continued Barbara,

61

"Mrs. Arthur Abbott, and I came here to look at The Archway House."

Mr. Tyler took out a handkerchief and mopped his face—"This is terrible," he said. "This is truly terrible. I shall never get over this—never."

"I'm very sorry," Barbara told him (her heart was touched at the sight of so much suffering). "I really am awfully sorry, but I'd no idea—I mean I thought you knew who I was. You seemed to be expecting me——"

"I was expecting *her*," said Mr. Tyler faintly.

"Oh, I *see*," said Barbara nodding.

"Oh dear! Oh dear me!" lamented Mr. Tyler. "And her ladyship was so insistent on discretion—I shall never get over it."

"Well, you'll be very silly, then," said Barbara firmly. "There's no harm done so far as I can see, except that I've wasted an awful lot of time reading that silly document of yours."

"You had no business to read it," said Mr. Tyler, pulling himself together a little. "Surely you must have seen that it did not concern you."

"I didn't want to read it," retorted Barbara indignantly. "You told me it was necessary.

You *said* I was to read it. You said you'd explain everything when you came back."

"Because I thought you were her ladyship," explained Mr. Tyler.

"How could you think that?"

"Because you're like her. I was expecting Lady Chevis Cobbe, and you're like her. I don't know her ladyship very well—my partner does all her business—and naturally I thought—oh dear, and she was so anxious that this will should be kept a complete secret——"

"I shan't tell anybody about it," Barbara promised. She was really very sorry for Mr. Tyler. He was quite broken. He had lost all his funny pompous manner, and had become quite human and not a little pathetic. "I shan't tell anybody," she assured him.

"You will ruin me if you do," said Mr. Tyler frankly.

"Well, I've told you that I won't," repeated Barbara again.

"Did you actually—er—*read* the will?" enquired Mr. Tyler, a trifle more hopefully. "Ladies sometimes find our legal phraseology a trifle obscure, so perhaps——"

"Well, not very carefully," Barbara replied, stretching the truth a good deal in

63

her desire to comfort him, and feeling very uncomfortable about the whole thing. "The people were all just names to me. I don't know any of them."

"That's true," agreed Mr. Tyler eagerly, "you don't know any of them. Now, if it had been any of the local people it would have been quite different—it would have been disastrous, simply disastrous—but, of course, it could not have happened, because I know them. Yes. But you don't know anybody here—that's true."

Barbara was glad to see Mr. Tyler recovering, not only because she was a humane woman, and took no pleasure in the sight of a fellow creature in distress, but also because she hoped she would soon be able to lead the conversation round to the subject of The Archway House. She had wasted far too much time already, drinking port, and reading wills. I had better hurry, she thought, or I shall have no time to see the house properly, and I must see it properly, after coming all this way. So, after a few more soothing and consolatory words, Barbara came to the point and demanded the keys of The Archway House.

Mr. Tyler was only too happy to oblige. He

decided that when Mrs. Abbott had gone he would mix himself a pretty strong dose of whisky and soda. Wine was all very well in its way, but, after a severe shock, such as he had experienced, whisky and soda was the best thing—his whole body craved for the stuff.

"I will send a clerk with you," he said, as he unlocked the safe and took out a large bunch of keys, somewhat rusty in appearance. "A clerk, yes. The gate may be a little stiff to open. Mr. Pinthorpe shall go with you and see that you have—ha—every facility. You will find The Archway House in slight disrepair, of course. It has not had a tenant for a considerable period, but the roof is sound—yes—the roof is—ah—sound."

6

THE ARCHWAY HOUSE

BARBARA was drawn to Mr. Pinthorpe from the first. She was drawn to him strongly, and for a particular reason with which all authors will sympathise. Mr. Pinthorpe was reading one of her books. It was *Disturber of the Peace* (Barbara's first-born, and secret favourite) and he was reading it with such intense interest and absorption that he did not notice the approach of the junior partner of his firm until that gentleman addressed him by name in a peremptory manner. It was fortunate for Mr. Pinthorpe that he had gained Barbara's heart with such suddenness and security, for Mr. Pinthorpe's appearance was so against him, that nobody, not (you would suppose) his own mother, could have been drawn to him by his looks. He was thin and tall, with long arms, and long thin legs, and a very small round nob of a head set on a long thin neck. His face was extremely unprepossessing owing to a sallow skin, an abnormally long and pointed nose, and very small black eyes, which were so completely socketless, that they reminded the beholder of the boot-buttons sewn on to the face of a rag doll. Mr. Pinthorpe possessed no eyebrows at all, and his hair, which he wore parted in the middle, was very thin and lank, and more than a trifle untidy.

"Mr. Pinthorpe!" exclaimed Mr. Tyler sharply.

The wretched youth leapt to his feet, and crammed his book into the pocket of his coat, which was large and baggy and had evidently been used for the purpose before.

"Have you nothing better to do——" began Mr. Tyler in a hectoring manner—but he got no further. Barbara was not the woman to stand aside and see her public bullied like this, besides how could he have found any-thing better to do than read *Disturber of the Peace*? She held out her hand and smiled at Mr. Pinthorpe as if he had been the most handsome and delightful man she had ever seen.

"How do you do, Mr. Pinthorpe," she said sweetly. "Mr. Tyler says you are going to be very kind and show me over The Archway

House. I *do* hope it won't be a frightful bother for you."

It is doubtful which of the two men was the more amazed at Barbara's advances. Mr. Tyler was struck dumb. Mr. Pinthorpe was almost too surprised to respond. But, after a moment's hesitation, and a questioning glance at the junior partner, he took her hand and shook it gravely. There was no other mode of action open to him.

"Mr. Pinthorpe," said Mr. Tyler (this time in an entirely different tone of voice). "Mr. Pinthorpe, you will take Mrs.—ah—Abbott, you will take Mrs. Abbott and show her over The Archway House. Mrs. Abbott has an idea that the house may suit her require-ments—ahem. You will give Mrs.—er— Abbott every facility—every facility and—ah—information. Here are the keys."

Mr. Pinthorpe accepted the keys like a man in a dream, and, a few moments later, the oddly assorted couple was walking across the square while Mr. Tyler watched from the top of the steps.

Mr. Tyler was still feeling shaken. He had made a ghastly mistake—simply ghastly. He hoped that Mrs. Abbott would not like The Archway House. He thought it most unlikely that she would like it. The place was in appalling condition, and most people who went to look at the place with a view to purchase, took one dismayed glance at the desolation and fled incontinently, never to return. He hoped with all his soul that *that* was what Mrs. Abbott would do, because he never wanted to see her again. It would be too terrible if she bought it, and remained in Wandlebury; every time he set eyes upon her he would be reminded of his foolishness, of the dreadful blunder he had made. Mr. Tyler hated making blunders. When he blundered he remembered it with acute discomfort. He was aware that this particular blunder would remain a thorn in his mind for years and years.

Mr. Tyler pursed up his lips and blew them out—phew! He began to hum a hymn tune in harmony with his discomfort. It went something like this:

"Through the night of doubt and sorrow
(I shall never get over it—never)
"Onward goes the Pilgrim Band
(why on earth didn't I make sure who
she was?)
"Singing songs of expectation

69

(I was expecting her, of course.)
"Marching to the Promised Land
      (and she *is* like her—no doubt of it)
"Soon shall come the great awakening
      (and what if Tupper gets to hear of it)
"Soon the rending of the tomb
      (that would be the end of everything)
"Then the scattering of the shadows
      (but perhaps she won't like the house)
"And the end of toil and gloom
      (and I shall never see her again)."

Somewhat comforted by the optimistic sentiments of the last line Mr. Tyler returned to the office and poured out his whisky and soda. If she seems keen on it, he thought, I must tell her about the rats. It has been empty so long that there are sure to be rats in it—yes—it would be only fair to warn her—only *fair.*

*   *   *

Meanwhile Barbara, walking along by the side of her escort, could not help being conscious of the bulge in his pocket. She wondered how to attack the subject uppermost in her mind. She loved discussing her

70

books, it was so interesting to hear what people thought of them, and Mr. Pinthorpe had evidently liked *Disturber of the Peace* very much indeed, or he would not have been deaf and blind to the approach of his employer. Mr. Pinthorpe made no effort at conversation, he strode along the flagged pavement with strangely uneven steps. At first Barbara thought he must be lame, but, after a few minutes, she realised that he was stepping carefully in the middle of each flag-stone, and, as the flag-stones were alternately large and small, the effort to synchronise his steps to their dimensions was giving him some trouble. It was not the sort of amusement that Barbara had expected would appeal to a man who had the sense to appreciate her writings, but Barbara was willing to forgive Mr. Pinthorpe a good deal. Lots of people were odd, she reflected, and Mr. Pinthorpe had every right to his idiosyncrasies.

"Do you like reading?" she asked him at last.

"Some things," said Mr. Pinthorpe darkly, and then he added, "He'd no call to get annoyed. I do all they give me to do, don't I? If they don't give me anything to do, have I got to sit and twiddle my thumbs all day? I'm

71

better reading than twiddling my thumbs, aren't I?"

Naturally Barbara agreed—she agreed fervently (what better occupation could anybody have than reading the works of John Smith?).

"How do you like it?" she asked him.

"What? That book? It's pretty funny. Some bits of it are a scream. Have you read it yourself?"

Barbara said she had.

"I know people just like that," said Mr. Pinthorpe, waxing quite confidential with all the encouragement he was getting. "There's a dame here the very spit of Mrs. Horsely Downs—might almost be her."

"Really!" exclaimed Barbara.

"Mhm," nodded Mr. Pinthorpe. "Funny, isn't it? And I'll tell you another funny thing," he continued. "Talking of people being like each other—you're like somebody. You'll never guess who you're like."

"Lady Chevis Cobbe," said Barbara promptly.

The young man was rather disappointed at the success of Mrs. Abbott's first guess, but he had suffered many disappointments in his short life and was inured to them. "That's right," he said, "it's Lady Chevis Cobbe.

72

You *are* like her, and I should know. I was brought up on the estate, I was. We saw her ladyship ever so often. If you were a little more high and haughty and your hair was grey you might *be* her."

"She's older than me?" Barbara enquired with her usual disregard of English grammar.

"Oh, yes," agreed Mr. Pinthorpe. "She's older—a lot older. You're more like what she *was*, if you know what I mean. She's a funny one," he continued confidentially. "A bit balmy, if you ask me—bats in the belfry—you know."

Barbara enquired with interest what kind of bats inhabited her ladyship's belfry.

"Oh well!" said the young man. "I suppose I shouldn't say, really. It's rather professional, you know; but I don't see what harm could come of telling *you*. Her bats is making wills, and it's a pretty expensive kind of bats—not that *that* matters to her ladyship. She's for ever quarrelling with her relations, and then down she comes to us, and out comes her will to be altered. Keeps us busy, I can tell you."

By this time they had left the square, and were skirting a high wall built by grey stone blocks with a flat parapet of flag-stones. Trees hung over the top of the wall—beech and oak, and horse chestnut—all in bud, and some with pale-green fronds waiting to be uncurled by the warm spring sunshine; and presently they came to a big wrought-iron gate, set in an archway, and Mr. Pinthorpe took the bunch of keys out of his pocket and fitted one of them into the lock.

"Is this it?" demanded Barbara, somewhat unnecessarily.

"Yes," replied Mr. Pinthorpe. "My! this gate wants oiling," he continued, wrestling with it fiercely. "It's just as well I'm here, or you'd never have got in. Old Mrs. Williams, who's supposed to keep the place aired—but doesn't—goes in the back way. I don't suppose this gate's been opened for years."

"Why hasn't somebody bought it?" Barbara wanted to know.

"Ghosts," replied Mr. Pinthorpe tersely. "At least, that's what I heard. Shouldn't have told you that, I don't suppose."

"I'm not afraid of ghosts," said Barbara stoutly.

The drive was muddy, and deep in last year's leaves, it was like a tunnel, curving away into the unknown, a tunnel made of the closely overhanging branches of the trees.

Brambles trailed across the paths; nettles rose like pale green sentinels from the damp yellow undergrowth; rabbits scuttled away hastily at the sound of human steps.

"It seems awfully neglected," said Barbara in dismay. She had built so much upon The Archway House. All the hindrances that she had encountered had only served to whet her curiosity. She had made up her mind that The Archway House was the end of her search. But this was dreadful, this desolation, this air of neglect that hung about the place—how *awful*, she thought, how *awful* if this place won't do either!

"It hasn't been lived in for years," agreed Mr. Pinthorpe casually, "years and years and years. Don't know when it was lived in last. We keep the place wind and watertight for the owner, but that's as much as he can do. Poor as a church mouse, he is, just crazy to sell, but *we* can't find a buyer with the place in this condition."

They went on through the tunnel. Yellow sunlight fell through the budding branches and flecked the ground with yellow light. Barbara was excited . . . she caught a glimpse of stone ahead, and hurried forward. . . .

The house burst upon her view. It was a

rectangular building after a design by Adams, not very large but beautifully proportioned. It was two storeys high. The front of the house (which Barbara was looking at) had a door in the middle, and three windows on each side (this was on the ground floor, of course,) above were seven windows, tall and ornamental. The door was so high that it looked narrow, three broad, flat steps led up to the porticoed doorstep. As Barbara emerged from the tunnel, the roof came into view; it was flat, ornamented by a plain cornice of Roman tuscan moulding, which was supported by flat pillars between the windows. Above the cornice, from the hidden roof, rose squat chimney stacks (one at each end of the house) with their rows of blackened pots.

Barbara opened her heart to the house then and there—she liked the bold, simple lines, she liked the dignity of its design; her eyes, tired of the fussy meanness of modern architecture, the red roofs, the steeply sloping gables, the jerry-built brick disguised by whitewash, rested gratefully upon the plain façade of The Archway House. Here was a solid rectangular building of solid stone, a building with no nonsense about it. The house sat firmly upon the ground, it was surrounded by green lawns and shady trees, the sunshine streamed upon it like a benediction. It was almost her vision—almost the house that Arthur's words and gesture had conjured up before her eyes—and, even as Barbara looked at The Archway House, the vision faded, and the real house took its place.

Mr. Pinthorpe fitted a key in the lock and opened the door. He hurried in and began to open the shutters and pull up the blinds. Barbara thought that the house seemed to welcome the sun, it had been empty and darkened for so long; and the sun seemed glad to be welcomed back, it streamed in through the tall windows on to the bare floors, it explored the walls from which the faded paper hung down in curling strips. The dust floated in the air, it eddied and swirled as Mr. Pinthorpe strode about, so that the whole place seemed full of golden smoke.

The hall was square, with white pillars, very slim and tall; a winding stair with a graceful wrought-iron balustrade curled upward to the bedroom floor. On Barbara's right was the drawing-room, beautifully proportioned, with a carved mantelpiece of Adams's design. On her left was the dining-room, with three tall windows looking on to the drive. Before her a green baize door led to the kitchen premises at the back.

From the very first the lofty ceilings pleased Barbara (it was "nice and airy"), and she liked the giraffe-high windows which let in quantities of light. She could see, in her mind's eye, long curtains hanging from the pelmets in gracious folds—they must be velvet, she thought, soft and warm, and richly coloured. There was little doubt in Barbara's mind now, it was the house she had been looking for—her house and Arthur's. The dirt of the place, the neglect, the desolation of torn wall-papers and rotted blinds, the red rust on the door-handles, the fireplaces and balustrade left her undaunted. These were things that could be put right, mere details, and, as such, of no account. Barbara saw the house as it would be when these trivial matters had been attended to, she saw the house as she was going to make it.

"And you'll like that, won't you?" she said to the house (Mr. Pinthorpe had disappeared upstairs to open the shutters in the bedroom). "You'll like it when I've made you all nice, and washed your face and brushed your hair for you. You've been waiting for me all this time, and now I've found you."

Barbara poked about, opening doors, and re-creating the whole house in her mind. She discovered a smaller room beyond the drawing-room, and gave it to Arthur on the spot. It should be his study—a proper "man's-room." There were dead flies on the windowsill and cobwebs in every corner, and the old-fashioned basketgrate was broken, and red with rust, but Barbara saw it cosy and comfortable with a brown carpet on the floor, and two comfortable leather chairs before a blazing log fire. We shall sit here on cold nights, she told herself delightedly, and listen to the wind howling in the trees . . .

The rooms upstairs were large and square, they were quite as disreputable as those on the ground floor and Barbara was quite as pleased with them. She opened the window in "her" bedroom and gazed out—the view was perfect. Beyond the trees was a graceful line of hills, patterned with fields and small dark copses. Barbara had never possessed a "view" before—a view of her very own. Tanglewood Cottage was buried in tall trees, and Sunnydene was set amongst rows of villas, each a replica of itself. If there ever had been any doubt at all in Barbara's mind as to the desirability of The Archway House, it was gone now. "*This is my house*" she said, and sat herself down on the broad window-seat in a possessive manner.

Mr. Pinthorpe had finished his god-like occupation of bringing light into dark places, and now he returned to the lady who had been given into his charge, and stood and stared at her. She *was* a rum one (he reflected) sitting there and looking out of the window. Most people, seeing a house for the first time, poked into every corner, and complained about the dirt, and asked all sorts of searching questions about the drains, and the water supply, and whether it was built on sandy soil. Mr. Pinthorpe had been told to give this lady every facility and all the information she desired. He had given her every facility by opening up the place, and he was now prepared to be put through a catechism regarding the hidden merits and demerits of the house. He could answer quite comfortably and truthfully about the drains and the water, for they were in Messrs. Tupper, Tyler & Tupper's charge, and the roof was sound—he knew that. And he knew that if he were asked whether the place were damp the right reply was that "it only needed firing," because it was so obviously damp that it was no use to

80

deny it. Some people asked one thing, and some people another—there was no hard and fast rule. You said the best you could of a house and made as little as possible of its glaring defects. Mr. Pinthorpe rather prided himself upon the way he could show off houses.

But Barbara didn't want to ask any questions about the house—none at all. There was no need for her to ask questions since she had definitely and irrevocably made up her mind to have it. She looked at Mr. Pinthorpe as if she were seeing him for the first time and didn't much like the look of him.

"Go away," she said quietly—almost casually.

"Go away!" echoed Mr. Pinthorpe, unable to believe his ears.

"Yes," said Barbara, waving her hand vaguely. "Go away. I want to—to think."

He looked at her doubtfully; should he obey this extraordinary request, or not? He had been sent to look after her and he was therefore responsible both for her and for the house. Supposing he went away and left her, and she *took* something, where would he be then? He looked round the room, and considered the matter—there was nothing she could take, nothing at all. There was nothing in the house except dust, and cobwebs, and dead flies.

"All right," he said, "I'll wait for you downstairs."

She scarcely seemed to hear what he said (just waved her hand for him to go) and Mr. Pinthorpe felt rather annoyed. She *was* rum. She had been so matey coming along the street, and now she seemed to have forgotten his existence—she *was* rum. He sighed, and went downstairs, and sat down on the front doorstep in the sun. Then he took his book out of his pocket and got on with the story.

7

VISITORS—SUPERNATURAL AND OTHERWISE

WHEN Mr. Abbott was brought to see the house his wife had selected he was positively aghast. He saw it as it was, and not as it might become. It happened, most unfortunately, to be a wet day, rather dark and chilly for the time of year. The rain blew against the tall bare windows in gusts, the paper hanging from the walls flapped dismally. There was a dankness in the air, and a musty smell permeated every room; there were cobwebs in every corner; the plaster was peeling off the walls and falling from the ceilings in fine grey flakes. The truth was that Barbara would have been wiser to put off Arthur's visit, and to have brought him down to see The Archway House on a dry sunny day, but this never occurred to her for a moment. She was so besotted with The Archway House herself, that she had no qualms at all about Arthur's reaction to it.

Arthur had heard such glowing accounts of the place that he was in no way prepared for what he saw, so he was immeasurably disappointed, nay he was horrified beyond words. He had visualised a comfortable, cosy sort of house, and he beheld a ruin. Barbara must be mad, he thought miserably. He was quite certain she was mad when she opened the door of a dank, dusty apartment behind the drawing-room and showed him his study.

"You can have all your books here—won't it be cosy?" she exclaimed, looking round the dismal place with a rapt expression in her eyes. "You've always wanted a room of your very own, haven't you?"

"It's rather—dark," he objected feebly.

"That's only because of the tree in front of the window," she replied. "We'll have that cut down, of course. Monkey puzzles are horrid anyhow, so it won't be any loss."

"I wonder it there are any rats," Mr. Abbott remarked, hoping it would choke her off.

"Oh, there *are*," said Barbara airily, "there *are* rats. Mr. Tyler told me about the rats when I went back and saw him at his office.

But we can easily get rid of rats—you poison them off."

To do Barbara justice she had no idea that Arthur was not delighted with the house. She was so enchanted with it herself that it never crossed her mind that there could be any two opinions about it. And Arthur was afraid to say too much; he had not forgotten the strange way that Barbara had behaved when he suggested staying on at Sunnydene. It had given him a shock, a very severe shock. At the back of his mind was the unexpressed, almost unconscious, fear, that if he did not approve of this house (which had obviously bewitched Barbara) she would buy it herself, out of the proceeds of her books, and leave him behind at Sunnydene. This being so, his protests were extremely feeble—so feeble that Barbara never noticed them.

She dragged him round the place, pointing out its amenities with eager pride, and then she haled him off to the lawyer's office to buy it. Mr. Abbott followed miserably. He saw that his wife intended to have the house at all costs. He only hoped that she would not allow this fact to become apparent in the transactions. But he need not have been anxious on this score, for Barbara was no fool. She intended to acquire The Archway House, but there was no sense in paying a fancy price for it. Barbara wanted to spend "a lot of money" on the house, and, if they got it cheap, there would be all the more to spend on doing it up.

Mr. Tupper had evidently recovered from his indisposition, it was he, and not the junior partner, who received them and conducted the business. Barbara veiled her eagerness from Mr. Tupper with admirable self-control, she pointed out that they would have to spend a lot of money on repairs before The Archway House could be made habitable. This was so obvious that Mr. Tupper was forced to agree.

It was Arthur, of course, who did most of the talking. Barbara sat in the shabby leather chair and threw in a few words now and then. She listened to all that was said with intense interest. It really was amazing, she thought, you bought a house as easily as you bought a hat—or very nearly. It was most extraordinary! She was sorry not to see Mr. Tyler again, she had liked the little man. His pompous manner had intrigued her—especially as she had seen through it and below it, to the very human, and rather pathetic core of the little man himself. Mr. Tupper was not nearly so nice—he was dry and business-like—a lawyer and nothing more. There was no royal welcome forthcoming on this occasion, and it was quite easy to refuse the glass of sherry which he offered her—Mr. Tyler would not have taken her refusal so lightly, so casually as this. Of course Mr. Tyler thought I was somebody else, Barbara reflected (as she sat by the window and watched Arthur sip his sherry with obvious enjoyment) and I suppose that was why he was so nice to me. He thought I was that Matilda woman— Lady Something-or-other Cobbe—already the memory of the incident was fading from her mind, but it was to return later.

"There are rats," she said, breaking into the discussion with dramatic suddenness. "We can't pay all that for a house with rats in it, you know."

"Rats—oh, I think not," deprecated Mr. Tupper with an indulgent smile. "I *think* not. Ladies are sometimes——"

"But there are, *really*," asserted Barbara confidently. "Mr. Tyler told me himself, the first day I was here."

The lawyer's eyebrows rose in surprise. He began to say something and then changed his mind about it. "Mr. Tyler must have been mad—mistaken I mean——" he amended frowning. But the price came down a little all the same. It was quite possible that there *were* rats in The Archway House, quite possible, and his instructions were to sell the place for what he could get. It had been empty for years and the owner needed the money badly.

The price came down gradually to a figure that even Arthur considered a bargain. It was quite a ridiculous price. He bought the house, and then, with a magnificent gesture, he gave it to his wife.

Barbara was enchanted. What a husband! What a house! It was the most marvellous present she had ever had. Her gratitude was quite embarrassing. Arthur was a little uncomfortable about it. They had decided long ago that Arthur was to buy the house, and Barbara was to "do it up." Arthur had got off very easily with his part of the bargain—he had bought a ruin for half nothing—but Barbara's part was going to cost a small fortune. It was only fair—so thought Mr. Abbott—that the house, which was going to cost Barbara more than himself, should belong to her when it was finished. He tried to explain all this to his wife as they drove home to Sunnydene together but Barbara only saw what she wanted to see—the amazing generosity of her husband, and the superlative beauty of her house.

No sooner was the house hers than Barbara filled it with plumbers, joiners, electricians and decorators. The peace of the sunlit rooms was disturbed by the noise of hammering and of men's voices, by the sound of heavy footsteps clattering on the parquet floors. The dust swirled from forgotten corners in choking blinding clouds, and settled again over everything in a thick grey film. Charwomen with buckets of dirty water cluttered the stairs, and crawled patiently over the floors waging an endless battle with the dirt. The place was like an inferno, and Barbara drove its denizens like a whirlwind. She cajoled the foremen and bullied the underlings from morning to night—sometimes, when occasion seemed to demand a change of tactics, she reversed the process. The workmen were all terrified of Mrs. Abbott, she was the most impatient lady they had ever met.

Barbara's efforts to make The Archway House a place for heroes to live in were hindered and impeded at an alarming extent by "the ghost." She had never seen this apparition herself but apparently she was unique in this. Local charwomen refused to come and work in the haunted house, and those recruited from other districts soon got to hear of it and faded away mysteriously with their work half done. None of them would remain in the house after the workmen had left, and this was trying, because it was only after the workmen had left, that the field was clear for the cleaning to be done. The ghost was a very annoying sort of ghost—a kind of *Poltergeist*—an embodiment of mischief. Its great delight seemed to consist in hindering the work. Pails and brooms and workmen's tools disappeared from their rightful places and were discovered hours later, in different parts of the house. Barbara soon got extremely sick of the ghost. But she carried on bravely with all her preparations—no ghost on earth was going to make the slightest difference to her arrangements. She worked like a slave herself and saw that everyone else worked like a slave. And through it all the ghost continued to play a villain's part. It appeared to charwomen, and sent them into hysterics, it appeared to workmen and interfered with their work. Some said it was a tall figure in white draperies, that wrung its hands and coughed dismally, others said it was headless and moved with the clanking of chains.

Weeks passed, and, gradually out of the chaos, a pattern emerged, and The Archway House began to look like a human habitation. As the time drew near for the furnishing of the rooms Barbara began to feel a little anxious. She was fully aware of the limitations of her taste, and she was desperately keen to have everything right, to choose for her house the sort of furniture that the house would like. Nothing—or very little—that had been suitable for Sunnydene, or Tanglewood Cottage was suitable for The Archway House. She and Arthur were agreed on this—and she was to have a free hand to get what she liked. It was a delightful prospect, of course, but it was also very perplexing. Barbara spent long hours thinking it over and wondering what she should do. I shan't try to have period furniture, she thought, I should only do it all wrong and it would look silly. I shall just have ordinary, plain furniture—rather large, because of the rooms being so big and high— plain, comfortable furniture and not too much of it.

This was sensible and right in theory but

the details still worried her. It was easy to say "plain comfortable furniture" but when it came to choosing the actual pieces she found it extremely difficult to decide. Which of the hundred odd suites of chesterfield sofas and easy chairs would her house *like*—that was the question—and how would the things look when they were removed from their neighbours and stood alone in the drawing-room of The Archway House. "I can't decide now," said Barbara, to the polite young man who had spent the whole afternoon showing her his stock. "I can't possibly decide now. I shall have to think about it." The polite young man could have slain Barbara then and there, but he controlled his desires and replied wearily, "Just as you like, Moddam."

Barbara spent the following day at The Archway House, harrying the electricians who had slacked off a little in her unavoidable absence. It was a warlike sort of day, but, after the electricians had gone, Peace descended, and spread her gleaming wings in the empty rooms. Barbara wandered round gloating over her treasure. She tip-toed through the silent house. How still it was without the workmen, how restful and refreshing! Barbara felt herself to be part of the silence. The house welcomed her, and the welcome made her feel happy and at home. Slowly she became aware of Unseen Presences in the empty rooms—the aura of those who had lived in the house and loved it. And these Unseen Presences were friendly towards her, they welcomed her coming—she was sure of it—they could do her no harm. There was nothing ghostly about this aura, nothing supernatural, nothing frightening, it was more a sort of warm atmosphere, comfortable to the spirit as the warmth of a good fire is comfortable to the body.

How funny it would be if I saw the ghost, Barbara thought, it's funny, really, that I haven't seen it before. And then she reflected that it was "funny" about the ghost in more ways than one, for the ghost was obviously unfriendly to her (in that it hindered her activities in every way it could). It was a malign ghost, and yet the atmosphere of the house was friendly—how could that be?

She wandered into the empty drawing-room and gazed round, trying to see it furnished with the furniture she had looked at in the store. The chesterfield here, and the chairs there, the china cabinet against the bare wall, the bureau in the corner near the window—how would it look? She paced it out, and reflected, and paced it out again. She went to the window and stood there looking out. The gardens were beginning to look better now. The grass had been cut and the paths weeded. But there was still moss on the steps leading down to the terrace, and the grey stone lions which stood on either side of the steps were cracked and discoloured with damp. I must speak to Grimes about that, Barbara thought.

She was just making up her mind to leave the place and go home when the front door-bell rang. It pealed loudly through the empty house, startling the echoes—Barbara nearly jumped out of her skin. Her first thought was that it must be the ghost, but that was ridiculous, of course; ghosts didn't ring front door-bells, they drifted in through keyholes or something (Barbara was a little vague as to how they actually got in, but she was perfectly certain that they never rang front door-bells). She listened to the bell for a few moments, thinking what a frightful noise it was making, until she suddenly realised that she had better go and see who it was.

Barbara found a small girl standing on the doorstep, a child with tangled brown hair and a small thin face covered with freckles. She was clad in a bright-blue overall, very short and shapeless, and stained with earth. Her hands and her bare legs were dirty, and scarred with scratches. Barbara was amazed when she saw the child, she had expected something much larger—the noise had been so tremendous.

"Oh!" she said feebly. "I couldn't think *who* it was."

"They're digging up the flags," said the child, without the usual preliminaries of convention. "You can't *mean* them to."

"Flags!" echoed Barbara in bewilderment.

"P'raps you call them irises," said the child impatiently. "Some people do. But you can't mean them to be dug up and thrown away. They're so lovely in the spring—all yellow and mauve with spiky grey-green leaves——"

"You had better come in, and tell me about it," Barbara said.

The child followed her into the house, and they sat down together on the stairs.

"I don't mind about the rest of the garden so much," the child explained. "After all you've bought it, so it's yours now, and I suppose you can spoil it if you want to. But the flags are down near the stream—miles away from the house. You haven't ever been down there, have you?"

"Only once," Barbara admitted. "I've been so busy, you see."

"Do you *want* them dug up and thrown away?" continued the child with some exasperation. "I mean it seems so silly, that's why I came. I simply had to come. Lanky said it wouldn't be any good, but I had to try."

Barbara was beginning to understand. "Of course I'll tell them not to," she said quickly. "I don't want to spoil anything. You see I just told the men to tidy up the garden."

"I suppose you want the garden tidy?"

"Yes," replied Barbara in some surprise.

"We think it's nicer as it is."

"Well, I'm afraid I don't," Barbara admitted. "I'm afraid I want the garden tidy, but, of course, I don't want to take away anything that's really nice. Men are so stupid," she added with conviction, "unless you can be after them all the time—and I've been so busy with the house."

"Oh, the *house*," said the child scornfully. "You can do what you like with the house. I hate houses. It's the garden that *matters*. We live next door, you see, and we like this garden much better than ours—it's ever so much nicer for playing in. Of course, if you're going to have it tidied up it will spoil it frightfully." She clasped her hands round her dirty bare knees and rocked herself backwards, lifting her chin, and shaking back her hair from her forehead. It was an elfin face, pointed and delicate in profile. The eyes were dark and very brilliant beneath the small, but definitely arched, eyebrows.

"Who are you?" enquired Barbara with interest.

"Trivona Marvell," replied the child. "Most people call me Trivvie—*you* can if you like. I don't think you're bad," she added frankly. "Lanky says you're a vandal, but I don't think you're bad at all. You'll remember about the flags, won't you?"

Barbara said she would. She decided to go down to the stream to-morrow and see what the men were doing. The last thing she wanted was to alter the place—it must remain exactly as it had always been.

"I suppose we shan't be able to play here once you've really come?" Trivvie enquired hopefully. "I mean you won't want children in your garden—p'raps you've got children of your own?"

"No," said Barbara.

"I think the garden will miss us," said Trivvie sadly. "I think it will be rather lonely without any children. I think it likes us playing in it, you know."

Barbara rose at once—it was a lure she couldn't resist—hadn't she always said, from the very beginning, that The Archway House—and incidentally The Archway House garden was to have what it wanted.

"I don't mind you playing in the garden a bit," she proclaimed rashly.

"Really!" cried Trivvie in amazement. "D'you mean it? Oh, you *are* decent! I shan't let Lanky call you a vandal again—not ever. In fact I'll sock him one, if he does. We shan't bother you, you know; in fact I don't suppose you'll ever *see* us. We don't like this part of the garden a bit—just the stream and the wood—so you see it really won't bother you, will it? As a matter of fact," she added ingenuously, "as a matter of fact we were going to play in it, anyhow. We had quite decided that—and you'd never have known—but when you were so decent about the flags I thought I'd just see what you said. Even if you'd said 'No, we couldn't,' it wouldn't have made any difference."

Barbara was struck dumb by this frank statement, she made no reply.

"Well," said Trivona, rising and holding out her hand. "I must go now—good-bye. Froggy will be looking everywhere for me, and she gets in such a wax if she can't find me. Good-bye."

"Good-bye," said Barbara, whose voice had returned to her; and then she enquired, for she was exceedingly interested in her fellow creatures, "Who is Froggy?"

"Oh, Froggy's our governess," replied Trivona, standing on one leg in the empty hall, as if poised for flight. "Her real name's Miss Foddy, you know. And Lanky's my brother—his real name's Lancreste, and he's two years older than me."

"Have you only got one brother?" asked Barbara.

"Oh no, of course not. I've got Amby as well. Amby's younger than me."

"What unusual names!"

"Mhm! Rather silly, aren't they? Trivona is a goddess you know—the Goddess of the Trent—and Lancreste and Ambrose were Archbishops or something. I really *must* go now——"

★   ★   ★

Barbara's second visitor was the vicar's wife. She arrived just as the furniture was being carried into the house. It was the most awkward moment she could have chosen, for Barbara required all her wits to direct the men as to which room each piece was to adorn. It was difficult enough to recognise the chairs and tables, the book-cases and cupboards and beds beneath their sack-cloth wrappings, without having to carry on a conversation with the vicar's wife at the same time.

"I hope you belong to Our Church, Mrs. Abbott," said Mrs. Dance, advancing upon Barbara with a somewhat toothy smile.

"Oh yes—yes, of course," Barbara replied, shaking her hand vaguely. "In the study, please," she cried, trying to direct the furniture-man. "No, not there, this room—I'll open the door for you. Mind the wall—oh, please mind the wall—yes, of course, I expect we do. What is your Church?"

"I'm chapel, mum," said the furniture-man, setting down the bookcase and wiping his hands on the seat of his trousers. "I'm chapel, I am." He was somewhat surprised at the question—most people didn't seem to mind what place of worship you attended as long as you did your work properly and were careful not to take chunks out of their walls with the edge of a cupboard. But he was a polite man, and always liked to answer people's questions when he could. "My people was chapel before me," he added, hoarsely, for the bookcase was heavy, and he was a little out of breath. "The Potts have always *been* chapel—if you see what I mean, Mum."

"I didn't really mean you," Barbara explained. "Though I'm sure it's very interesting," she added with her usual kindness and politeness." Very interesting indeed—oh wait, that doesn't go in there," she cried, rushing after another man who was bearing a bed into the dining-room. "Upstairs, please—not you, that's the dining-room table—upstairs, please, wait, and I'll show you which room—it's my bed I think—no it's the spare-room at the end of the passage, I'll show you—mind the light— that's right—look out, take care of the banisters. In the pantry," she shrieked, leaning over the stairs and signalling wildly to a third man, who was staggering into the hall with a crate of china balanced precariously upon his shoulders. "Go into the pantry."

"Why?" enquired Mrs. Dance who thought

the signals were for her, "I'd rather wait in the drawing-room."

"The drawing-room, did you say?" asked the man with the crate, lurching towards the drawing-room door.

"Where's this bed to go?" enquired the man on the landing.

"Shall I unpack this bookcase, Mum?" shouted the ever-polite Potts.

It was all very difficult. Barbara wished that Mrs. Dance would go away and leave her free to wrestle with the situation, but Mrs. Dance was determined to remain until she had received a proper answer from Mrs. Abbott, and, possibly a contribution to the Organ Fund. She lingered in the hall, dodging packing-cases and getting in everybody's way, until Barbara would willingly have given her a whole organ if she had known that was what Mrs. Dance wanted.

At last the furniture had all been carried in. The vans drove off, and Mrs. Dance and Barbara were left in the sole possession of The Archway House. They sat down on the stairs—there was nowhere else to sit—and Mrs. Dance had the opportunity she had been waiting for.

"I hope you'll like it here," she said,

dubiously. "It's very quiet, of course. You've come from London, haven't you?"

"Hampstead Heath," Barbara told her.

"That's London, isn't it?" agreed the good lady. "I'm afraid you're bound to feel quiet. There is so much going on in London."

"Yes," admitted Barbara, thinking of the dinners and bridge from which she and Arthur were escaping.

"Yes," said Mrs. Dance. "Do you like music?"

Barbara answered in the affirmative. She was not very fond of music (possibly because she knew very little about it), but she was aware that it was the correct thing to like music, and she really thought she liked it. There are very few people in the world with courage enough to admit that they do not care for music (dogs and children come into the same category) and so brand themselves for ever as Philistines in the eyes of their friends.

"Ah!" said Mrs. Dance. "Ah, that's good! You like music. You will find us very musical down here. Lady Chevis Cobbe is passionately fond of music. She has the most delightful musical evenings at Chevis Place. You will enjoy that immensely."

"I'm sure I shall," agreed Barbara politely.

"And the choir," continued the vicar's wife. "The choir at our dear little church is excellent. So different from most country choirs. The bishop always remarks upon the excellence of the choir when he comes."

Barbara said that was very nice.

"Yes, so encouraging," agreed Mrs. Dance, "but I am sorry to say that the organ is very poor. The organ is not worthy of us," said Mrs. Dance sadly. "We are making a collection for a new organ."

Barbara said what a good plan that was.

Mrs. Dance sighed. It was not the reaction she had hoped for; however, she did not despair. There was plenty of time, and, if she could not get a decent contribution out of Mrs. Abbott to-day, she would return to the charge later. She had waited patiently for some time for this little chat, and she was determined that it must not be altogether fruitless; if she could not get any money out of the woman she must try to get some information. Everybody in Wandlebury would want to know all about the new people and she had obviously got in first. Mrs. Dance knew that she would be able to lunch and tea out of the new people for days to come.

"I believe your husband is a publisher," she said, smiling toothily. "I suppose, with so many new books being published, he must make a great deal of money." Her eyes strayed round the hall as she spoke—it was amazing how nice the house looked, simply amazing when you knew what it had looked like before—all that nice white paint, and the crinkly new paper—it must have cost a small fortune.

"Oh *no*!" cried Barbara, horror-stricken by this suggestion. "Business is very bad—very bad indeed."

Private means, thought Mrs. Dance, making a note of it in her mind. Aloud she said, "I've been wondering if you are related to the Wimbornes that I know—*dear* friends of mine—the Rutlandshire branch of the family."

"No, I never heard of them," replied Barbara promptly.

"You aren't?" exclaimed Mrs. Dance in surprise. "I thought your name was Wimborne before you were married."

"Oh no—no it wasn't," Barbara said.

"How funny!" giggled Mrs. Dance. "I wonder how I can have got that idea into my head. Isn't it queer?"

Barbara agreed that it was very queer indeed. Mrs. Dance sighed again, it was extraordinarily uphill work, and she was not getting much "forrader." *Very secretive*, she thought, *and obviously ashamed of her origin*.

"Do you find the climate very trying here?" she enquired hopefully.

"Oh no," replied Barbara. "I mean we haven't really lived here yet, but I'm sure I shan't."

"Perhaps you are used to bracing air—before you were married, I mean."

"I don't notice any difference in air," admitted Barbara frankly. "All air is the same to me—even bad air. I'm so very strong, you see."

Mrs. Dane was sick of hedging. "Where did you live before you were married?" she enquired.

Unfortunately Barbara was not listening. Her eyes, wandering round the cluttered hall, had alighted upon a large crate, which, she was certain, must contain Arthur's chest of drawers, and Arthur's chest of drawers had no business to be in the hall; it ought to be in Arthur's dressing-room, of course, that small, but delightful convenient apartment leading off their conjugal bedroom.

"How trying!" Barbara murmured.

"Rye!" exclaimed Mrs. Dance. "Fancy that—most interesting, I know Rye very well, I have a cousin living there. I wonder if you know her——" She expatiated on her cousin who lived at Rye while Barbara gazed at Arthur's chest of drawers and wondered how it was to be got upstairs now that the men had gone. Perhaps the gardener—thought Barbara, not very hopefully, for even her optimistic imagination boggled at the vision of the frail form of Grimes staggering up the staircase with that enormous crate——

"No," she said absent-mindedly. "No, I don't know anybody called Skate, I'm afraid."

"I said Kate," declared Mrs. Dance—really Mrs. Abbott must be half-witted—"Kate Sparling. She has lived there for years and knows everybody."

"Where?" enquired Barbara.

"Rye," of course."

"I've never been to Rye," explained Barbara casually.

"But you said you had lived there——"

"I didn't—I couldn't possibly have said that, because I've never been there at all."

Mrs. Dance gave up the struggle. The

woman was a fool—there wasn't a doubt of it—a fool and a liar (because she had most certainly said she lived at Rye). But I mustn't go yet, thought Mrs. Dance, it isn't any good offending her at the very beginning, especially if they belong to Edwin's congregation.

"I hope the Marvells won't plague you to death," she said aloud. "They live next door in a quaint little modern bungalow. He built it himself you know, and it's supposed to be very artistic. It's certainly very inconvenient," continued Mrs. Dance giggling. "Queer shaped rooms, full of divans and things. He's a painter, of course, and the children run wild. Mrs. Marvell is very peculiar, some people say she drinks, but, of course, one must be charitable. I daresay her vague manner is not really due to drink at all. The children have the most extraordinary names. Edwin was quite worried when he had to christen them."

"Fancy!" Barbara exclaimed.

"Poor children!" continued Mrs. Dance lugubriously. "Poor children, what chance have they got to make good in the world with such a peculiar up-bringing? Really, when I look at my own child—so carefully taught and guided into the right paths—my heart positively bleeds for them."

"Dreadful!" said Barbara shaking her head sadly. She wished again that Mrs. Dance would go. The stair was very hard to sit on, and there was such a lot to do. Barbara thought of all the things she had to do while she listened with one ear to Mrs. Dance's prattle. It was quite easy to do this when you got used to it, and Barbara had had a lot of practice. In the old days, at Silverstream, Barbara had perfected herself in the art of half-listening to boring conversations. You listened just enough to know when the right time came to say—"Yes" or "No," and when to shake your head sadly, and say "Fancy!" or "Goodness!" or "How awful!" With these remarks, made at the proper time and in the proper manner, you could carry on a conversation for hours without any trouble to yourself.

Barbara was practising her most useful invention on Mrs. Dance, when, quite suddenly, she heard a name she knew, and she was all attention.

"——Lady Chevis Cobbe," Mrs. Dance was saying, "very ill indeed."

"Ill?" enquired Barbara with interest.

"I said she had *been* ill," said Mrs. Dance. "She is getting better now, and I hear she hopes to be well enough to have one of her musical evenings in November. Such a charming woman, she gave us ten pounds for the Organ Fund," added Mrs. Dance hopefully.

"Fancy her being ill!" Barbara said thoughtfully. "I wonder——"

"Perhaps you know Lady Chevis Cobbe?" suggested Mrs. Dance after waiting for a few moments—most eagerly—to know what it was that Mrs. Abbott wondered.

"No," said Barbara.

"What were you going to say?" enquired Mrs. Dance who could contain her curiosity no longer.

"Nothing," said Barbara.

"You said you wondered," urged Mrs. Dance.

"Oh, I wondered—I just wondered—what was the matter with her," said Barbara, and she blushed, because she hated having to tell lies.

"Something internal," whispered Mrs. Dance mysteriously.

She rose. She could sit no longer on the cold hard stair, not even for the sake of the

110

Organ Fund. She felt chilled to the bone, and that portion of her anatomy which had been in contact with the stone was quite numb. I only hope *I* don't get something internal, she thought, but perhaps, as it was in such a very Good Cause——

"Good-bye, Mrs. Abbott," she said. "It has been *such* a pleasure—yes, I really must go. I have promised to go and have tea with an invalid, and she would be *so* disappointed. Little things mean so much when—*Good*-bye. We shall look forward to seeing you settled here soon."

"Good-bye," Barbara said. "Good-bye, so nice of you to come——"

Mrs. Dance walked very quickly down the drive. She walked quickly, partly to warm herself up, and lessen the chance of getting a severe chill, and partly because she was going to tea with Mrs. Thane and she was late. But I shall have quite a lot to tell her, thought Mrs. Dance complacently.

8

HUSBAND AND WIFE

THE great day came at last; the Abbotts
"moved in" to their new abode. Mr.
Abbott left Sunnydene in the morning, and returned at night to The Archway
House. Everything was in order for his
arrival. Barbara and Dorcas had been there all
day getting things straight. The new servants
had arrived and settled in. Barbara was
almost as pleased with her new servants as
she was with her house. She was so thankful
to see the last of the Rasts with their endless
quarrels and sour faces. The new servants
were "nice," thought Barbara (her favourite
word), they were pleasant and agreeable, they
smiled when you spoke to them, and were
obviously delighted with the lovely, clean,
new house.

Mr. Abbott arrived about tea-time. He
motored down in his new Vauxhall with his
smart new chauffeur at the wheel. The trains
were quite good, and quite convenient—he

would use the trains occasionally, of course—but the first day he wanted to arrive in comfort, to arrive in state (as it were), so Strange had been ordered to call for him at the office at three o'clock. By this time Arthur was quite excited about the new house—almost as excited as Barbara herself—he had entirely forgotten his first dismal impressions of the place, and he would have been indignant if anybody had suggested to him that he had been coerced into buying the place by his wife.

"Most comfortable!" he said, walking round the house with his hands clasped behind his back, and his kind eyes gleaming through his spectacles. "Most comfortable!" he repeated, sinking gratefully into the larger of the two leather chairs arranged before the fire in the snug study behind the drawing-room. "Most comfortable!" he was to reiterate as he snuggled down in his beautiful new bed with the spring mattress, and the blue swansdown blankets—but that was not yet, that was a pleasure to come, there was sherry, and then dinner (a truly excellent meal achieved by the new cook), and a little stroll round the garden with Barbara to be enjoyed before the acme of comfort was experienced.

Barbara was extremely keen on the little stroll round the garden after dinner. She wanted to show Arthur the beds which had been prepared for the new roses, and, although Arthur would just as soon have remained cosily by the fire, and put off seeing the beds until the morning—when he could have seen them much better—Barbara was obviously disappointed at the suggestion, and Barbara had toiled and moiled to make the place nice (she had done so much and done it so well) that Arthur felt he owed it to her to indulge her whim.

They waited until the moon rose behind the trees, and then they went out. It was a trifle cool, not to say chilly, in the garden, for it was now the end of October, but Barbara was too hardy to mind about that.

"You see, Arthur," she said earnestly. "The roses must be *here*. Grimes has been making the crazy pavement. I think he's doing it nicely, don't you? The roses must be here so that we can look out on them from the drawing-room windows."

The rose garden was absolutely bare. There was not even a twig to be seen, not a weed marred its surface. A pile of manure filled the night air with its unrose-like odour.

"I wonder how it will look," said Arthur thoughtfully.

"Oh, Arthur, can't you *see* it?" Barbara exclaimed. "I can. I can see the roses all bursting into flower. I can *smell* them," she added, sniffing appreciatively.

"That's not roses, it's manure you smell," said Arthur in his "smiling voice." "I thought you had no imagination, Barbara. But if you can see roses in an empty bed, and smell them in manure, you must have a good deal of imagination."

Barbara had done more spectacular feats of imagination than this, but she had not realised it.

"Oh!" she said in surprise. "I believe you're right, Arthur. I believe I must have an imagination after all."

Arthur laughed. There was a tinge of heavenly foolishness in his Barbara, it was one of the surprising and delightful things about her.

They walked on, arm in arm. It was very pleasant if you kept moving; there was a freshness in the air, a tingle and a nip that Mr. Abbott found most agreeable after a day in his London office.

"I think perhaps Wandlebury has done that

to me," Barbara continued. "I'm sure I never had an imagination when I was at Hampstead Heath or Silverstream. Look at my books—it was all because of me not having an imagination that there was so much fuss about them. If I'd had an imagination I wouldn't have had to write about the Snowdons, and the Bulmers, and Mrs. Featherstone Hogg. I could have made up new people out of my head."

"They wouldn't have been so funny," said Mr. Abbott with conviction.

"Oh yes, they would," Barbara argued. "If I'd had an imagination, they would have been, because, don't you see, I could have imagined funny people. Look at Dickens, you don't suppose he ever knew anybody like Mr. Dick, or Mr. Micawber; he just made them up out of his head and everybody laughs at them." She sighed and pressed Arthur's arm. "I do wish I had an imagination," she said, "I believe it might grow if I live in Wandlebury long enough, and then I could write things out of my head. Wandlebury makes me imagine things. The first day I got here I saw people in the Square—ladies and gentlemen with whiskers and poke-bonnets——"

Arthur chuckled appreciatively. He hoped

Barbara would go on talking; he adored it when Barbara was in one of her garrulous moods. It was rubbish, he supposed, if you really analysed it, but what amusing rubbish it was! "Ladies and gentlemen with whiskers and poke-bonnets"—Barbara was delighted.

Mr. Abbott had not seen nearly enough of Barbara lately, she had been so busy, and so worried. Even when he *did* see her she was up to the neck in wall-papers or cretonnes and he had got no good of her—no good at all. But now all that was over, and Mr. Abbott would get his wife back again with all her dear funny innocent ways. He was looking forward to it immensely.

"Perhaps you imagined Mr. Tyler," he suggested, hoping to start Barbara off again. He was getting very clever at the art of making his wife talk.

"It *is* funny about Mr. Tyler," agreed Barbara elliptically, "I can't think why he's always out when we call at the office. I thought he rather liked me that first day. He was so welcoming—you know what I mean—and he made me drink port—he really wanted me to. Now Mr. Tupper doesn't mind whether I drink it or not."

"But you don't like port," Arthur objected.

"I know," said Barbara. "But even if I don't like it, I like people to *want* me to drink it. It shows they're really interested, you see. I wish you could see Mr. Tyler. I really do. I know you'd like him, Arthur. He's got a round pink face and he beams at you through his spectacles. He's not thin and dry like Mr. Tupper, and he's the sort of man who minds a lot whether you like him or not, and he likes you to think he's very clever and very important because he knows, in his inmost heart, that he's not clever or important at all. So he puts on very grown-up airs, and swanks a little in front of the clerks, because it would be so awful if the clerks found out that he's just a little boy pretending to be a grown-up lawyer."

Mr. Abbott digested all this with interest—not because he was the slightest bit interested in Mr. Tyler, a man he did not know, but because he was tremendously interested in Barbara, whom, after eighteen months of daily contact, he was just beginning to know. The strangest thing about Barbara, Arthur reflected, the strangest thing about this strange woman who was now his lawful wedded wife, was that although she understood practically nothing, she yet understood everything.

She might or might not have "an imagination" (Arthur could not be sure of that), but she certainly had an extraordinary power of getting underneath people's skins. Without being conscious of it herself she was able to sum up a person or a situation in a few minutes. People's very bones were bare to her—and she had no idea of it. She used the very simplest language to voice her thoughts— quite often her expressions were couched in doubtful grammar—but this, in some strange manner, seemed to enhance their piquant flavour. Mr. Abbott could not understand it, but the very fact that he could not understand it intrigued him all the more. It was not that Barbara was illiterate, for when she had a pen in her hand her thoughts flowed freely, and flowed in perfectly good English, and, this being so, why was it that for everyday pur- poses she employed only the most colloquial expressions, and used banalities and hack- neyed idioms? Barbara loved proverbs and worn out clichés, and this was not because she was lazy and slip-shod—as most people are who employ these phrases. (When she had insisted on calling her last book *The Pen is Mightier*——she had called it that in all sincerity, and not in a satirical spirit with her

119

tongue in her cheek as so many people had thought. No, she had called her book *The Pen is Mightier*——simply because she had discovered—somewhat to her surprise—what a mighty weapon the pen was, when wielded by her hand. She had seen the good and the evil that her first book had wrought in Silverstream, and the sheer force of her sincerity had made the trite saying her own.)

I wonder what it is, thought Mr. Abbott, as they walked round the garden in friendly contented silence, I wonder what it is that makes Barbara's books sell like they do. Has she genius—as Spicer declares—or only natural facility, natural talent? And, if it is genius, am I justified in not encouraging her to exercise it? But what is the difference, he wondered. Just where does talent merge into genius? If talent is a natural aptitude for creation with an outlook on life peculiar to oneself, then genius is to have an outlook on life, peculiar to oneself, which yet appeals to everybody. Talent is for oneself and a few others, but genius is universal. Judged by this standard, Barbara must very nearly have genius—if not quite—for her books seem to appeal to an enormous number of people in every class, and every walk of life. But I shan't worry her, he thought, I shall just leave it alone, and, if she wants to write, she can write, and if she doesn't want to, she needn't. That's what I said at the very beginning, and I shall stick to it. But I really hope, in a way, that she won't want to write (thought Mr. Abbott) because this place is delightful—simply charming—and if Barbara starts writing about our neighbours, we shall most probably have to leave Wandlebury— just as she had to leave Silverstream—in a hurry.

Mr. Abbott smiled as he thought of that midnight flitting from Silverstream. He had come down in his car as had been arranged, and had found Barbara and Dorcas ready and waiting, sitting on their suitcases—for the furniture had already gone. They were both frightened, he remembered, for they had been through a good deal already, and they knew there was worse to come. They were thankful to see him, thankful to get away from Tanglewood Cottage before the storm burst. Then, the very next day, he and Barbara had been married—a quiet affair in a dingy London church with no witnesses save the faithful Dorcas and Sam.

Mr. Abbott's thoughts stopped when they

came to Sam, and he heaved an enormous sigh, for Sam was being extraordinarily difficult and annoying at the moment.

Barbara's hand tightened on his arm. "What's the matter, Arthur?" she enquired sympathetically.

"It's Sam," replied Mr. Abbott. "I don't know what on earth I'm going to do about Sam."

Sam Abbott was the son of Mr. Abbott's eldest brother who had been killed in the war; Mr. Abbott had made himself responsible for Sam's education, and, when the right moment arrived, had taken him into the office to try him out. He meant to make a partner of Sam later on. "Abbott, Spicer & Abbott" sounded rather well—so thought the senior Abbott—but now he was beginning to feel dubious as to whether Sam would ever settle down to work and become the sort of man who would make a safe partner. The thing was, you couldn't depend on the boy. Sometimes he seemed reliable enough, sometimes he seemed positively brilliant, but sometimes he was a confounded nuisance, and Mr. Abbott would reflect gloomily that the devil must have begotten Sam and sent him to Abbott & Spicer's with the sole object of plaguing and badgering them into an early grave.

"What has Sam been doing?" Barbara enquired.

"H'm," said Mr. Abbott. It seemed rather unfair to sneak to Barbara about Sam's misdemeanours. After all the boy was only twenty-five—quite young—and his father had been killed when he was four years old, so he hadn't had much of a chance. You couldn't be very angry with him—and Elsie was weak. Elsie had spoilt the boy frightfully—not that he altogether blamed Elsie, it was difficult for a woman with a fatherless boy *not* to spoil him. But this morning, when Mr. Abbott had had to trek down to Bow Street and pay a fine for the boy, he *had* been angry, very angry indeed, and he *had* blamed Elsie. What a scene it had been! Elsie in floods of tears, and the boy ashamed and defiant in turn, and the magistrate smiling behind his hand. It wasn't anything very serious, of course (just foolishness after some sort of supper-party, and Mr. Abbott had a strong suspicion that Sam had been made a sort of scapegoat), but Mr. Abbott had never got into trouble with the police in *his* young days, why, when he was Sam's age he had been fighting in France—an officer, with men's lives dependent upon his common sense. Responsibility, thought Mr. Abbott, *that* was the thing to make a man of you. There were no wars now, thank God, and he hoped, most devoutly, that there never would be any more, but he was very glad that he had been the right age for the last war.

"What has Sam been doing?" enquired Barbara again.

"Oh, painting the town red," said Mr. Abbott, laughing a little.

"Oh!" said Barbara. She had always wondered how you painted the town red—it sounded a fine thing to do. "Don't you think we might ask him down here for a few days?" she suggested.

Mr. Abbott was in two minds about this— "Well," he said dubiously, "but Sam might not want to come."

"Why not?"

It was impossible to say why not without giving Sam away (Sam might not want to come after being severely reprimanded, not to say hauled over the coals by his uncle for his idiotic behaviour) so Mr. Abbott said vaguely:

"You don't know Sam," meaning of course

that Sam was a bit of a problem, and that you never knew where you were with him. But Barbara took his words literally (as she always took everything) and replied:

"Oh yes, I do. I saw him at the wedding—and his mother, too. Shall we have to ask *her*, Arthur?"

"She wouldn't come if you did," Arthur said, "Elsie's awfully religious, you know. One of those people who think more about their own hereafter than other people's presents. If Elsie looked after Sam properly instead of spending all her time in church—if she spent as much time and energy on Sam as she has in saving her soul—Sam wouldn't have——"

"Wouldn't have *what*?" enquired Barbara eagerly.

"Wouldn't have painted the town red," said Mr. Abbott in his "smiling voice."

By this time Mr. Abbott had almost decided to ask Sam down for a few days. Barbara was interested in Sam and obviously intended him to come. After all, thought Mr. Abbott, he couldn't do much harm *here* (he couldn't paint Wandlebury red) and, perhaps, if I heard Barbara's opinion of him, it would give me some clue to the boy. I'd like Barbara's opinion of Sam. And then he chuckled inwardly and thought—if Barbara sees through to Sam's bones, I'll eat my hat. The truth was that Mr. Abbott had thought it all over before, and it had been on the tip of his tongue, on several occasions, to suggest having Sam down to Sunnydene, but every time this had happened he had choked the words back, and left them unsaid. The reason for this strange behaviour, this swithering, this filling and backing on the part of the usually forthright and stable Mr. Abbott was rather queer. It was the recollection of Sam at the wedding, and Barbara's reaction to the vision—for vision he was. Mr. Abbott had thought himself rather smart—until he saw Sam—he had arrayed himself in his morning coat, with his neatly-striped trousers and lavender waistcoat, and he had had his topper ironed at Blockes. They had decided to have a very quiet wedding (this was necessary in the peculiar circumstances), but Mr. Abbott had felt that it was due to Barbara to wear the proper clothes to marry her in, and the proper clothes for a wedding were those enumerated above. In addition to this Mr. Abbott was aware that he looked well in morning dress (and what man does not desire to look well at his wedding?), his broad shoulders seemed even broader beneath the well fitting black cloth, his narrow hips seemed narrower beneath the chaste pin stripe of his trousers, the shining topper lent dignity to his pleasant, kindly face. These garments of Mr. Abbott's were old and valued friends, they had helped him through his first luncheon party, they had given him confidence at his first board meeting, they had accompanied him to weddings galore, and, on two occasions, had aided and upheld him in the discharge of the responsible and onerous duties of Best Man. He had worn them at Lord's, year by year when he attended the Eton and Harrow match. They had accompanied him to Ascot and had shared with him the joy of winning a good deal of money and the sorrow of losing considerably more. The morning coat and the topper (but not the other more festive accompaniments) had seen him through a good many funerals, and had helped him to conceal too much feeling—or too little.

For five years these, almost sacred, garments had been laid away, guarded by blue paper and a superfluity of moth balls, while Mr. Abbott waged war for his country, attired—very differently, but almost as becomingly—in a khaki tunic and a Sam Browne belt; and, when he returned, bearing the sheaves of victory, he had lifted the garments out of the trunk where they had reposed for so long, had shaken out the moth balls, and had thought—I wonder if I can still wear my morning coat. Of course he could still wear his morning coat, and, what was more, he would still wear the striped trousers, the lavender waistcoat, and the carefully preserved and shining topper—of course, he could wear them (and very smart he looked in them too), war was not the sort of game that put flesh on a man. They fitted him as well as ever—*and they still fitted him.*

It was rather an achievement, Mr. Abbott thought, that at forty-two you could still wear the same morning coat that you had worn at twenty, rather an achievement. Not many men of forty-two could say the same.

These things being so it was only to be expected that Mr. Abbott should decide to appear in morning dress at his wedding, and should say, off-hand to Sam, who had accepted the honour of being the Best Man, "By the way, I'm going to wear morning dress." "Oh, yes. Yes, of course, Uncle

Arthur," Sam had replied, negligently, and had turned up at St. Humbert's attired in *his*.

It was natural, Mr. Abbott supposed, if somewhat galling, to find that the clergyman had taken Sam for the bridegroom, and Mr. Abbott for his father. (The mistake was discovered and rectified in time, so no harm was done except to Mr. Abbott's vanity.) It was a natural mistake for Sam was young, and Sam, Mr. Abbott was bound to admit, was good-looking. He had upon him the radiance of youth, which the clergyman had mistaken for the radiance of a bridegroom. Mr. Abbott had realised all this and made allowances, it was Barbara's reaction to Sam that Mr. Abbott had taken to heart.

"Oh!" she had said when she saw Sam for the first time; and her eyes had strayed admiringly from the tips of Sam's patent leather Oxfords to the crown of his shining topper, dwelling on the way, with all too obvious pleasure and amazement, upon his lemon-coloured spats, his grey and white "sponge-bag" trousers, his lemon waistcoat embroidered with lemon flowers, his lemon tie with the pale silver horse-shoes, his high collar with its immaculate wings, and the lemon carnation in the buttonhole of his perfectly tailored morning coat.

"Oh!" was all she had said, but there are many kinds of "Ohs," and, besides, Mr. Abbott had seen the admiration in her eyes. It had all hurt just a little because Mr. Abbott, not unnaturally, wanted all Barbara's admiration for himself on this auspicious day. So this was the reason why, when Mr. Abbott's mind said "Invite Sam to come and stay and see what Barbara thinks of him," his heart replied, "No don't, keep Barbara, for yourself."

Mr. Abbott scarcely realised all this, of course, it was a subconscious reaction, and the little that he did realise of it he was not proud of. And now, when Barbara suggested having Sam down, he decided that it was all nonsense, and that he had got over it long ago—besides he had no excuse for not having him—none that he could produce. So, after a little hesitation, while he fought with his disinclination to have Sam and conquered it, he said to Barbara:

"All right, we'll ask Sam and see."

And with that they went in and presently retired to bed.

9

MARVELLS IN THE GARDEN

BARBARA had been at The Archway House for a week before she saw the Marvell children in her garden. It was the day of Sam's arrival, and she had been so busy preparing for his reception that she had not been out all the morning. In the afternoon she walked down to the wild strip of garden beyond the little wood, where the stream ran between banks of soft turf, and, just as she was emerging from the wood, she stopped suddenly for she heard the high-pitched sound of children's voices.

It's them, she thought, it's those Marvell children. And she walked on very quietly so as not to disturb them, and found them sailing little boats on the stream. Trivvie was squatting at the edge of the stream with her back to Barbara, but she was easily recognisable by her tangled brown hair, and the bright-blue overall which she was wearing. On the other side of the stream there was a small plump boy with fair curly hair, and a pink and white complexion; he was clad in tight brown shorts and a tight brown jersey, which made him look (thought Barbara) for all the world like a chestnut-bud before it bursts into green leaves. He was capering wildly and shouting in his thin shrill voice.

"Mine's winning, Trivvie. Cambridge is winning!"

Barbara watched them for a few minutes—they were too intent upon their game to notice her presence, but, when the race was over and Oxford had won after all—not without some sharp practice on Oxford's part, Barbara suspected—Trivvie looked up, warned by some sixth sense that they were not alone.

"Hullo, it's you!" she said, and then she added defiantly, "You said we could play here."

"I know, it's all right," Barbara replied.

"Trivvie's been bucking about you, frightfully," said the boy, gazing at Barbara with his very deep-blue eyes. "I don't think you're much to buck about."

"Shut up, silly," said Trivvie in a stage whisper. "What an owl you are! D'you want to be turned out of here."

"She better try," retorted the boy, without rancour.

Trivvie looked at him with scorn; he was silly, Ambrose was. Couldn't he see that they had better suck up to Mrs. Abbott? It was no good arguing with him now, because he could be frightfully stubborn when he liked— Trivvie knew it to her cost—but afterwards he should hear of it. Meanwhile a change of subject might be diplomatic.

"You *never* come down here, do you?" she remarked politely.

"Not often," Barbara admitted.

"Fancy having a stream of your own and not coming down to look at it, even," remarked Ambrose scornfully.

"Perhaps she's busy," Trivvie pointed out. "What d'you *do* all day?" she added, turning back to Barbara, and asking the question as if she were a visitor from the moon and had just arrived upon the earth that very day.

"How do you mean?" enquired Barbara, somewhat taken aback.

"I mean whatever do you *do*? You don't paint like Daddy, and you don't sit and be painted like Mummy, and you've got servants so you don't have to cook or make the beds,

133

and you don't have lessons and play like us, so whatever do you *do*?"

Barbara tried to give an account of her activities; she knew she had been busy all day, but it sounded very little when it was told.

Trivvie listened with growing pity to the stumbling narrative—grown-ups were odd, she thought (not for the first time) here was a perfectly strong and healthy grown-up with the whole day to do what she liked with, and nobody to say she mustn't do this or that or the other, and look at what she did—it was really pitiable. "How dull!" she said at last, sadly shaking her untidy head. "*Doesn't* it sound dull, Amby?"

Ambrose was squatting by the stream. "I wasn't listening," he said, "but I don't suppose it's any duller than what *we* have to do."

"But she doesn't *have* to," Trivvie complained. "Don't you see, Amby? She can do what she *likes*."

Barbara found it rather embarrassing to be discussed in this frank manner—just as if I wasn't here at all, she thought vaguely.

"P'raps she *can't* do what she likes," Ambrose objected, "and anyhow it can't be any sillier than what *you* do——"

"I didn't say it was silly," Trivvie pointed out. "I said it was dull—and it was dull—what are you doing, Amby?" she shrieked suddenly. "Leave my boat alone, you've swamped my boat—you beastly fat-faced baboon——" With a sudden lightning dart she was across the stream, and had seized the unsuspecting Ambrose by the collar of his jersey. The next moment they were rolling on the turf, kicking and squealing, a jumble of brown and blue, fat legs and thin legs all mixed up in inextricable confusion.

"Stop!" cried Barbara, picking her way across the stream. "Stop it at once—you'll kill each other——"

They stopped as suddenly as they started, and Trivvie sat up, shaking her hair out of her eyes with a characteristic toss.

"We won't *kill* each other," she said scornfully. "I wouldn't hurt Amby—at least not badly—it does him good to be hurt a *little*".

Ambrose sat up too, and gazed quietly round the little grove. He seemed to bear no malice for the sudden attack that he had endured—he rarely bore malice, for he was of a philosophical disposition, and took what came to him as natural manifestations of fate. In appearance as well as by nature the two young Marvells were as different as children could be—Trivvie was quicksilver, easily moved to wrath or repentance; Ambrose was stolid and stubborn as a mule. Trivvie was a brown elfin creature, thin and wiry; Ambrose was plump and chubby with rosy cheeks and fair hair.

"Trivvie's got a daimon," said Ambrose in a conversational tone. "Like Socrates, you know. Was that your daimon, Trivvie?"

"No, it wasn't," replied Trivvie promptly. "It was me. My daimon doesn't go for people—it's not that kind of daimon at all. It tells me things, it's more—more like a familiar spirit, really." She drew up her bare knees, almost to her chin, and stretched the very short skirt of her blue overalls over the knobbly bones, "There are lots of different kinds of daimons, you know," she added dreamily.

"I don't like your daimon," Ambrose said. "I think it's silly."

"My daimon doesn't mind a bit," retorted Trivvie defiantly.

Barbara thought it was time to change the subject. "You haven't told me what *you* do all day," she said, "what do you do?"

136

"Lessons, mostly," Trivvie replied, "we have to, you see."

"We don't do them all day," Ambrose put in.

"Do you go to school?" enquired Barbara.

"No, Froggy gives us lessons."

"You're lucky not to go to school."

"We *aren't* lucky," said Ambrose, contradicting her in a calm, indifferent sort of way. "We'd learn more if we went to school—Lanky says so."

"I don't think Froggy's bad——" began Trivvie.

"She's no good," said Ambrose gloomily. "She doesn't even know arithmetic properly. I asked her how many different kinds of fives there were, and she said all fives were alike."

"She said your fives were like nothing on earth."

"Shut up," said Ambrose, treating this irrelevant remark with the indifference it deserved. "Can't you see there are different kinds of fives? You can make a five with five ones, or with four and one, or with three and two—they're all different aren't they?"

"They all look the same," argued Trivvie.

"Not to me—they look quite different to me," maintained Ambrose stubbornly.

"Well, why did you ask her if you knew?"

"To see what she'd say, of course, and she didn't say what you said she said. She said my fives were extrable." He got up and tried to brush the wet mud off his shorts. "Girls don't understand," he said, frowning fiercely at nothing. "Girls don't understand—I ought to be at school—with boys."

"Oh Amby, I understand," said Trivvie anxiously. "You know I do—I do really, I was only teasing. I'm just like a boy, Amby. I can climb trees better than you."

"You're not like a boy," Ambrose told her firmly.

"I am."

"You're not."

"Why aren't I? I can climb——"

"You know why," he said. "You know as well as I do, your——"

Barbara felt it was time to interrupt the discussion—it seemed to be taking a somewhat dangerous turn—"I think that's somebody calling you," she said quickly.

They listened for a moment in silence, and Barbara heard the cries again, nearer this time—"Trivona—Ambrose." It was like a lost spirit wailing amongst the trees.

138

"It's Froggy," Trivvie exclaimed. "She's coming this way——"

With a sudden glance backwards, and a whispered injunction, "don't tell her," the two slid into the bushes and were lost to view.

Barbara was amazed at the suddenness of their departure, it left her in the air; one moment the children had been there, talking to her, and the next moment they were gone. The stream flowed by, chuckling over the stones, the branches of the bare trees rose and fell gently as the wind sighed past, the little grove was silent and deserted. Barbara stood there for a moment, bewildered, helpless, baffled; and, during that pause, Miss Foddy hove into view, her pince-nez flashing in the sun.

Miss Foddy was small and slight, with greyish brown hair, and very brown eyes behind the flashing glasses. She gave you the impression of a brown mouse—small and timorous. But, in spite of her mouse-like looks, Barbara was taken aback at her appearance on the scene; it would have been better if Barbara had vanished like the children—had gone while the going was good. Barbara was taken aback at the sight of Miss Foddy, but

Miss Foddy was positively overwhelmed at the sight of Barbara.

"Oh!" she said aghast. "Oh—I'm trespassing——"

"It's all right," Barbara assured her.

"Pray forgive me," continued Miss Foddy, positively trembling with agitation. "You are Mrs. Abbott, I presume—pray forgive me. I am not in the habit of trespassing upon your property, I assure you."

"It's really quite all right," said Barbara again.

"I am looking for the children," Miss Foddy told her, casting her eyes to left and right as she spoke. "You have not, by any chance, seen the children—my charges—the Marvell children. I am Mrs. Marvell's governess."

"How do you do," said Barbara solemnly.

"How do you do," repeated Miss Foddy, greatly pleased.

They shook hands.

The conventions having been observed, Miss Foddy enquired again about her charges, and Barbara realised that she was in a most uncomfortable predicament, and wished again, more fervently than before, that she had had the presence of mind to follow the children's example and disappear. Was she to take sides with Trivvie and Ambrose, as they had obviously expected, and deceive the wretched Miss Foddy as to their movements? Or was she to side with the Law, and indicate the route that the fugitives had taken? Barbara was practically certain that the children had not gone far, they were probably hidden in the bushes, within earshot, listening intently to every word that was being said. How could she give them away?

Barbara gazed at Miss Foddy in perplexity and distress.

"Ah, I understand, you have not seen them," Miss Foddy said, taking Barbara's embarrassment for a sign of ignorance. "No wonder you are surprised that I should have to search for the children in your grounds, Mrs. Abbott, no wonder you are surprised; but the truth is (she continued) the truth is that they have no regard for the property of others, and, what is even more lamentable, I have not been able to inculcate in them the spirit of obedience so necessary to the discipline of the young mind. I confess this with some shame, Mrs. Abbott," continued the wretched woman, whose small, greyish-brown face had gone pink to the ears. "I confess this with some shame, for I have now had the Marvell children under my care for two years, and two years should be sufficiently long to mould such young and plastic natures, but the truth is the Marvell children are a little beyond me, Mrs. Abbott. I have not been able to gain their confidence, nor even, I greatly fear, their respect. You are asking yourself," she continued, quite mistaken as to the reason for Barbara's silence. "You are asking yourself why I have not resigned my post, since I am unable to carry out my duties to my own satisfaction, but the truth is, Mrs. Abbott, that it is so extremely difficult for a woman of my age and uncertified qualifications to find a post in the present day congestion of the teaching profession, that I shrink—I positively shrink—from the consideration of such a course."

"I don't suppose anybody could manage them" said Barbara comfortingly—nor did she, when she thought of the amazing behaviour of the young Marvells.

Miss Foddy was much too pleased with this most acceptable view of the case to wonder how Mrs. Abbott could have formed such a true opinion of her charges without having seen them. She smiled at Barbara, and the smile changed her entirely; it lighted up her worn little face, and took years off her age.

"How kind you are!" she exclaimed. "How kind you are, Mrs. Abbott, and—yes—I really believe there is a great deal in what you say. Strangely enough Mrs. Marvell was good enough to make the same observation—in different words, of course—when I hinted to her, as tactfully as possible, that I found the high spirits of her children a trifle difficult to control."

"Well, you needn't worry then, need you?" said Barbara sensibly. "I mean if Mrs. Marvell herself——"

"One would imagine so," agreed Miss Foddy. "But the case is not so simple as it may seem upon the surface. Mrs. Marvell is not a very good judge of what is, or is not, the best upbringing for her children. It seems a very extraordinary allegation for me to make against the children's mother, but it is none the less true. And I cannot help feeling that the reason she is anxious to retain my services is not so much because she thinks I am the best mentor for the children, as because I am able to be of service to her in various small matters connected with the house. Mrs. Marvell is obliged to help her husband, you must understand. Her husband is somewhat exacting, and I am able to take a certain amount of routine work off her hands— routine work such as counting the washing, dusting the drawing-room, keeping the accounts, and answering any letters which are not of a strictly private nature. These duties are not, of course, the duties to which I have been accustomed, but I have never found it advisable to refuse my aid when it was asked for. So long as these duties do not encroach upon the hours devoted to the children's study (and they do not, for I rise early and perform them before breakfast) I am only too happy to be able to undertake them, and to carry them out to the best of my ability. But sometimes," said Miss Foddy (gazing at Barbara with her sad brown eyes, which reminded Barbara of the sad brown eyes of a spaniel belonging to Colonel Carter, the son of old Mrs. Carter, who had lived next door to her at Silverstream). "Sometimes, Mrs. Abbott, I cannot help feeling that it is all too much for me, and that I should have more chance of dealing firmly with the children, if my energy were not dissipated in dealing with matters of minor importance. My task is none the easier this term owing to the fact that Lancreste—Mrs. Marvell's elder son—has not returned to his preparatory school. He was unfortunate enough to contract an exceedingly virulent form of whooping-cough during the summer holidays, and the disease has left him with a small catarrhal patch at the base of the right lung. Doctor Wrench, while not anticipating any permanent injury to the organ, is still a trifle anxious, and definitely vetoes any suggestion of Lancreste returning to Rugton Hall, until the symptom has completely disappeared. I am therefore taking Lancreste for History and Mathematics, a duty which usurps a great deal of my time and energy. But this is by no means the most serious of my troubles with Lancreste, I do not grudge a moment of the time spent in helping him with his lessons—no—my most serious trouble with Lancreste is the influence he possesses over the younger children, and which he uses to incite them to behave like savages. This is all the more remarkable, because Lancreste, himself, seems quiet and well-mannered in comparison with Trivona and Ambrose, but his influence is deplorable—quite deplorable. The children are always more troublesome and difficult when Lancreste is at home."

Barbara was extremely sorry for Miss

Foddy. It seemed dreadful (Barbara thought) that a clever woman like Miss Foddy should be badgered and annoyed by the Marvell children, and worked like a slave by Mrs. Marvell until she was brought to such a pitch of desperation that she was forced to confide her troubles to the first stranger she met. Miss Foddy was obviously frightfully clever— (nobody who was not frightfully clever could talk like that. Barbara couldn't have talked like that to save her life—and we always admire in others the qualities and attributes which we lack ourselves). Barbara could no more have expressed her troubles in the flowing and erudite English employed by Miss Foddy than she could have flown to the moon.

The truth was (as Miss Foddy would have said) the truth was that things had come to a crisis for the Marvells' governess. Her position had been growing more and more difficult for weeks and she had nobody with whom she could discuss it—no confidante of any sort or kind. Poor Miss Foddy was neither fish nor flesh, she was not one of the family, and not—most certainly not—one of the servants and, to-day, with the mysterious disappearance of her charges, everything had boiled up, and she suddenly felt that she must tell somebody all about it—or burst. It was at this dangerous—not to say critical—moment that Barbara had appeared on the scene and had shown her sympathy with Miss Foddy's troubles. She had listened with interest, and had made one most penetrating and sympathetic remark. It was quite enough. Instead of bursting with a terrific explosion Miss Foddy had poured out her troubles to Barbara's willing and sympathetic ear. But, although she had been pouring them out for about ten minutes without ceasing, she had not done yet, there was more to come. And, as Mrs. Abbott's attention showed no signs of wandering, Miss Foddy was encouraged to continue.

Miss Foddy was very lonely at the Marvells'—so she told Barbara, still in that clever and cultured English which her hearer so admired—she had never been so lonely in any of her numerous posts. When she was at Mrs. Benton's she had been like one of the family, sharing in all their interests and amusements; Mrs. Winkworth's husband had been unkind to her and Miss Foddy had sympathised and upheld her in her vicissitudes; and at the Redmonds' the eldest girl was grown up—a delightful girl—and had been wont to discuss her various love-affairs with her young sister's governess. In all these houses Miss Foddy had had somebody to talk to, somebody to help, somebody who sought her out and desired her company as a human being, but at the Marvells' she had nobody— nobody at all. Mr. and Mrs. Marvell completed each other's lives—or at least they wanted no outside interference in their affairs—and the children only bore Miss Foddy's company when they were obliged to do so—they, too, were completely self-satisfied and self-contained. Miss Foddy was naturally very glad that Mr. Marvell did not ill-treat his wife, did not neglect her, or drink, or stray after younger and more attractive women like the too amiable Mr. Winkworth, but she rather wished that Mr. Marvell were not *always* at home, filling the house with his overpowering personality, because if he hadn't been, Mrs. Marvell might have talked to *her* occasionally, and discussed modern conditions, or the children's health and progress. Miss Foddy wouldn't have minded *what* it was, as long as it was something.

All this Miss Foddy poured out to Barbara—all this and more—and Barbara stood and listened to it all with careful and sympathetic attention.

"I am sure I do not know—I cannot think why I am telling you all this," said Miss Foddy at last, pulling herself up with a jerk. "You must think that I am a most garrulous person—you must think that I am insane."

"Oh no, I don't," Barbara assured her. "I think you are frightfully clever, and it's all most interesting. I'm most awfully sorry for you, Miss Foddy," and she really meant it, for Barbara—by reason of her art—was intensely interested in her fellow creatures, and could understand their feelings and sympathise with their afflictions with the sympathy of her emotions. She could have understood and sympathised even if the troubles had been communicated to her in far less vivid and exciting language than that used by the erudite Miss Froddy—but the language helped, of course, what a gift it was! Miss Foddy's troubles were now Barbara's own, and if there were a single thought in Barbara's mind of *using* Miss Foddy—of squeezing her like an orange and using the juice for her next book—it was entirely a subconscious thought, and one which Barbara would immediately and sincerely and indignantly have denied. For the truth is (as Miss Foddy would have said), the truth is that authors have no idea at all how or where they garner their harvest. The harvest is garnered by some busy imp that watches and garners daily, hourly, keeping the barns full, so that when the day of threshing comes, and the wheat is winnowed from the chaff, there shall always be enough and to spare for the making of the bread.

"It's all most interesting," Barbara told Miss Foddy. "No, really, I mean it. Of course I understand how frightfully dull it must be to have nobody to talk to. You must feel as if you were going to burst, sometimes."

"Yes," said Miss Foddy, amazed at this perspicacity. "Yes, that is exactly—*exactly* how I feel, Mrs. Abbott."

"If it would be any use," Barbara added (a trifle diffidently, for Miss Foddy really was so frightfully clever, and so very—so very *articulate*, and Barbara was neither of these most desirable things), "if it would be any use at all—if you'd *like* to, I mean—I should be awfully pleased if you'd come and have tea with me. If you have an afternoon—an afternoon to spare——" Barbara said vaguely. She

150

had been on the point of saying "*an afternoon out,*" but, somehow, that sounded more like a housemaid than a governess.

"Oh, how kind! Oh, Mrs. Abbott, that really is too kind!" cried Miss Foddy, and her face went quite pink again—but this time with pleasure and excitement. "Oh, I'm sure I could. Mrs. Marvell would spare me, I'm sure. If it would not bore you—there is nothing I would like better. Oh, how very kind to think of it——"

"Well, that's settled then," Barbara said, very much embarrassed at the wretched Miss Foddy's gratitude for such a trifling boon (you never knew what to *do* with gratitude, Barbara thought, and this gratitude was inordinate). "Don't forget, will you?" she added, somewhat unnecessarily it would seem, "I'd like to show you the house—if you're interested in houses—just let me know when you can come——" and, so saying, she fled and left Miss Foddy spilling gratitude and pleasure all over the path; and she never remembered until she was going into the house, that Trivvie and Ambrose had been hiding in the bushes all the time, and had probably heard every word of Miss Foddy's tragic lament.

And what will happen—thought Barbara, gazing at the eighteenth-century chest that graced her hall—what will happen now I'm sure I don't know. Will they be better, or will they be worse?

10

THE MUSICAL EVENING AT CHEVIS PLACE

SAM ABBOTT was in rather a chastened mood when he arrived at The Archway House for his little visit. He had wanted to refuse the invitation, but his Mother, taking a strong line (for once) with her spirited offspring, had made him accept.

"You will not bear ill-will towards Uncle Arthur," she told him, and added the somewhat hackneyed but ever valuable advice about not letting the sun go down upon your wrath.

"I can't prevent the sun going down, can I?" enquired the irrepressible youth with deplorable levity, "and, anyhow, it's Uncle Arthur's wrath, not mine. It will be simply foul, living for five days with Uncle Arthur glowering at me, and thinking all the time how different I am from what *he* was when *he* was twenty-five. It's bad enough at the office—— Oh yes, I'll go, if you want me to, but don't blame me if *anything happens.*"

Sam's spirits rose a little when he beheld The Archway House. He knew a little about architecture, and its bold simple lines pleased him. And the inside of the house was almost as pleasant as the outside; it was so right, so comfortable, and yet so dignified. Barbara saw that Sam appreciated her treasure, and showed him round, pointing out it's beauties and amenities with innocent pride.

"She's rather decent, really," said Sam to himself in surprise, as he dressed for dinner in his comfortable warm room. "Decent of her to give me a fire," he added, warming his socks before its comforting blaze. "Perhaps it won't be so absolutely foul after all. I wonder what on earth induced her to marry a crusty old beast like Uncle Arthur!"

Thus soliloquised Sam, in the privacy of his bedroom, but, even as he thus soliloquised, he was rather ashamed. He knew perfectly well in his inmost heart that Uncle Arthur was not a crusty old beast, but really quite decent in his own way; and he knew—for Sam was no fool—that most uncles, and most senior partners of reputable firms, would have been quite as crusty as Uncle Arthur if their young nephews—or

154

apprentices—had been mixed up in an affair like that filthy Bow Street business. Uncle Arthur's not bad, really (thought Sam indulgently) and if only he wouldn't buck so much about that damned war (that old people are so proud of) and keep his views about the degeneracy of the young to himself, I could get on with Uncle Arthur like a house on fire.

It was even more of a surprise to Sam, when he went downstairs, and sat down at the well-appointed dinner-table to an excellently cooked and adequately served meal, to find that the crusty old beast was a charming host, and that Uncle Arthur and his new wife were delightful together, teasing each other in a very pleasant way, and cracking jokes and enjoying themselves as if they had been quite young, like himself, instead of quite old with one foot in the grave.

What'll I be like at forty-three, he wondered, as he joined in the fun and took sides with his Aunt-by-marriage in baiting the Senior Partner of his firm—shall I be like Uncle Arthur? And this was followed by the altogether extraordinary and illuminating thought—well, I wouldn't mind if I were. For Uncle Arthur was so obviously happy, so jovial, so immeasurably delighted with the

badinage he was receiving that you couldn't
help feeling it would be very pleasant to be
like that. It's rather nice (thought Sam) it
really *is* rather nice (and rather pathetic
somehow) to see the two of them together;
because, of course, it's perfectly clear that
they're absolutely nuts on each other, and,
although it's quite an ordinary sort of thing to
see young people go right in off the deep-end,
it's pretty uncommon, I should think, to see
old people like Uncle Arthur and Barbara so
frightfully gone on each other. Gadzooks! he
thought (as he smiled at his Uncle and his
Aunt-by-marriage and joined in the general
conversation with spirit and aplomb).
Gadzooks, what a queer thing Love is! Fancy
Uncle Arthur, at *his* age, getting it so badly!
I'm jolly certain I shan't get had, anyhow—no
thank you, no marriage for this child—and he
thought of his great crony, Toby Frensham,
who had been the brightest spark you ever
saw until he had gone in, head over heels, at
the deep-end, over a girl, and how now-a-days
you couldn't get the wretched blighter to
come out and have a bit of a beano in the
evening, because he preferred to sit at home,
in his poky little flat, and gaze with adoring
eyes at the very ordinary girl he had chosen to

make his wife. It isn't even as if she were frightfully pretty or anything, Sam thought, she's just plumb ordinary, and what old Toby sees in her I can't imagine. Gadzooks, what a queer thing Love is! Now if I ever fall in love, thought Sam, if I ever fall in love—which incidentally I shan't, because I shall take jolly good care not to—it will have to be somebody really beautiful, really wonderful, a glamorous, elegant, glorious creature, quite out of the usual run of girls. But I shan't, he thought, I'm safe, really. I've knocked about town for years now, and I've never seen a skirt that could do more than send a couple of shivers up my spine.

"I think we'll celebrate," Uncle Arthur was saying. "Sam's our first guest. What do you say to a bottle of champagne, Barbara?"

"You needn't ask me," said Barbara smiling. "You know perfectly well I don't like the horrible stuff. But that's no reason why you and Sam shouldn't——"

"What!" cried Sam in amazement. "You don't like fizz! Don't you really, Barbara?"

"Is that how you address your aunt?" enquired Mr. Abbott, before Barbara could reply.

Sam laughed. "Why not?" he demanded

with youthful cheek. "I discovered her, didn't I? I was the first person to read *Disturber of the Peace.* I told you she was a genius."

"And does that give you the right to call her Barbara?" asked Mr. Abbott, with a whimsical lift of his brows.

"Well, *of course*," replied Sam promptly. "If it hadn't been for me you might never have met her, and then where would you have been? Another reader might not have appreciated the subtle humour of *The Disturber* and might have packed it up and and sent it back to John Smith with Messrs. Abbott & Spicer's compliments. You've got a lot to thank me for, I can tell you."

Mr. Abbott laughed, and so did Barbara—they were both pleased with their guest. He was an impertinent monkey, but the impertinence became him, and it was rather pleasant to be teased a little by a young and personable man. He's very amusing, Barbara thought, and very good-looking. He's rather like Arthur—a smaller and slighter edition of Arthur—and he's got Arthur's nice eyes. He's cocky, of course, but it's rather a nice kind of cockiness, quite a harmless kind. I know, now, what he reminds me of (thought

Barbara smiling to herself), he reminds me of a young cockerel standing on a wall just starting to crow. Arthur needn't be worried about him, he'll be all right. He's just trying his voice, and flapping his wings like cockerels do when they're pleased with themselves and their fine feathers, and all he needs is just something to settle him down—a nice wife would settle him down splendidly, we must look about and find a nice wife for Sam.

And, so thinking, Barbara smiled and nodded and took her part in the conversation and thoroughly enjoyed—through Arthur's and Sam's enjoyment—the excellent champagne which the former had produced from his new (but already well stocked) and capacious cellar.

*　　*　　*

It was while Sam was staying at The Archway House that the Musical Evening took place.

"It's so lucky," Barbara remarked, as they dined early. "It really is so frightfully lucky that it has just happened while Sam's here. It must be rather dull for Sam——"

"Oh no, it isn't," exclaimed Sam.

"—Staying here with two old married

people like us," continued Barbara, without heeding the interruption. "So it really is very lucky that the Musical Evening is to-night."

Sam groaned inwardly. He was not feeling at all dull at The Archway House—it was really very surprising—he found it pleasant and peaceful. He went up to town every morning with Uncle Arthur, and returned with him at night; he walked and read and conversed amusingly with his host and hostess. He liked them increasingly and was fully aware that they liked him—— No, it was not dull at all. But to-night was another matter altogether—a Musical Evening, what a frightful show it would be! It was the kind of show he detested, the kind of show that ought to be put down by law; dozens of people you didn't know—and didn't want to know— standing about and gassing to each other, and people singing (Oh, Lord! thought Sam) and light refreshments such as hock-cup, and pale coffee, and banana sandwiches.

"You have such a gay time in London," continued Barbara, smiling at him kindly. "Dances, and supper-parties, and all sorts of things. It *must* be dull for you here."

Sam didn't quite know how to reply, he glanced at Uncle Arthur and saw that he was smiling to himself—had Uncle Arthur told Barbara about that horrible show, or not? It almost looked as if he hadn't, and if he hadn't, it was decent of the Old Boy.

Barbara had received the invitation to the Musical Evening a few days ago, with a nice little note from Lady Chevis Cobbe saying that she could not pay calls at present as she was still far from strong after her illness, but she hoped so much that Mr. and Mrs. Abbott— and any guests who happened to be staying with them—would waive formality and give her the pleasure of their company at Chevis Place on the evening of the 27th November. Barbara had "accepted with pleasure". She was very pleased about it. The Musical Evening would be such a good opportunity of "getting to know people" and it would be a nice party for Sam, and, now that the night had arrived, she was really excited. It was an adventure, and she loved adventures with all her heart.

Barbara had dressed with great difficulty for this occasion; first impressions were so important, and her neighbours would see her to-night for the first time. She had driven the good Dorcas nearly frantic at the way she had changed her mind; and, when she had finished her *toilette*, discarded dresses were strewn about all over her bedroom in attitudes of despair. But the result justified everything, and even Dorcas was bound to admit that her mistress had never looked so well. She had eventually chosen a night-blue charmeuse, very simply made, with a little train; and, to go with it, the diamond pendant and diamond star which Arthur had given her as his wedding present. When she surveyed herself in the long mirror of her new bedroom-suite she was satisfied with her appearance—and justifiably satisfied. She was even more satisfied with the success of her *toilette* when Sam commented favourably upon it—a young man who painted the town red surely ought to know what was what. They were all waiting in the hall for Strange to bring round the car, and Arthur was helping Barbara to put on her evening cloak.

"You look simply topping, Barbara," said Sam. "I love the colour of your frock—what's it called?"

"Night-blue," replied Barbara, blushing with pleasure. "I'm glad you like it, Sam. I think *you* look frightfully smart," she added truthfully.

Sam preened himself (he *is* like a cockerel,

thought Barbara in amusement). "Oh well," he said deprecatingly, "but we men haven't so much scope. I like colours, you know. It would be rather fun to have a suit the colour of your frock."

"With knee-breeches, and a brocaded coat," Barbara agreed. "How splendid you would look! And Arthur," she added looking at the tall, well-set-up figure of her husband, "Arthur would look simply magnificent, wouldn't he?"

They were all in an exceedingly pleasant and amiable frame of mind when the car came round to the door, and they set forth to the Musical Evening.

The drive at Chevis Place was already cluttered with cars when the Abbotts drove up. Everybody was there, for Lady Chevis Cobbe's Musical Evening was an affair that nobody wanted to miss. It was an Annual Event, the one occasion in the year when the doors of Chevis Place were thrown open to Town as well as County, and County rubbed shoulders, very amiably, with Town as Lady Chevis Cobbe decreed that it should.

Chevis Place was a stately Elizabethan Mansion that had been altered, and added on to, and brought up to date at various periods of its career. The result, to a fanatic upon the subject of architecture, was perhaps somewhat unfortunate (the kind of man who prefers candles to lamps, and powder closets to bathrooms might have torn his hair and called the Chevis family vandals and goths) but, to the ordinary person, Chevis Place was a pleasant place, and the different styles of architecture blended well enough to produce a dignified, commodious and convenient country house. The ballroom, where the reception was being held, was a long-shaped room which had been added to Chevis Place by the present owner's grandfather. It was high-ceilinged, and bright with candelabra, which now contained cleverly concealed electric bulbs.

"Mr. and Mrs. Abbott, Mr. Sam Abbott," announced the butler in a stentorian voice, and the next moment Barbara found herself shaking hands with her hostess.

Barbara looked at Lady Chevis Cobbe with especial interest (so that's what I look like! she thought). She saw a woman of about her own height and build, with a pale face and dark-blue eyes. The lashes were dark and long, and the eyebrows finely drawn; she had rather an insignificant nose, but her mouth though a trifle wide, was well-shaped, and her teeth, when she smiled, very white and even. I suppose I *am* rather like that, Barbara thought. She's a lot older than me, of course, but I don't think I carry myself so well. I must remember not to stick out my chin—she doesn't do that.

"So glad you could come," Lady Chevis Cobbe was saying. "I was delighted when I heard somebody had bought The Archway House, it's such a pity when these nice old houses fall into disrepair. Where's Jerry?" she continued, looking round vaguely, "Oh, there you are—Jerry will introduce you to some of your new neighbours—my niece, Miss Cobbe—Mrs. Abbott," she added, and turned away to welcome her next guests.

Barbara shook hands with the niece. She was a small slight girl, rather athletic in build, with quantities of silky brown hair and straight grey eyes, set rather wide apart. Her fair skin was lightly powdered with golden freckles, which betokened a life spent in the open air.

"I've been longing to meet you," she said, with a frank friendly smile. "It's so nice when new people come to Wandlebury."

Barbara responded adequately to these

advances, she introduced Arthur and Sam to Miss Cobbe, and was in turn introduced to various people standing near. Everybody seemed interested to meet the Abbotts, and wanted to know how they liked Wandlebury. Most of the people came into Barbara's favourite category of "nice people," but there were one or two who fell somewhat short of this high standard. Two elderly ladies, dressed alike in old-fashioned brown silk dresses, seized hold of Miss Cobbe and evidently asked to be introduced to the new-comers, "Mrs. Fitch and Miss Wotton," said Jerry Cobbe, rather reluctantly. Barbara understood the reluctance in her tone, they were not very prepossessing old ladies—one was rather fat, and the other was very thin, but in spite of this they were extraordinarily alike. Sisters, I expect, Barbara thought, and the next moment they had vanished in the crowd and she had forgotten all about them. The room was filling up fast, and the air was full of the buzz of conversation. She had lost Arthur and Sam in the crush, but Jerry Cobbe stuck to her indomitably.

"I want to introduce Candia Thane," she said. "I'm sure you'll like her. Oh, here are the Marvells!"

Barbara was interested to meet the Marvells on account of their offspring—she felt convinced that the parents of Trivvie and Ambrose must be unusual, and therefore worth knowing. Mr. Marvell was certainly unusual, he was very tall and broad-shouldered, with strongly-carved features, and iron-grey hair. He wore his hair rather long, and had a wave in it that a Society Beauty might have envied. Mrs. Marvell had a queer kind of untidy elegance, her hair was brown—like Trivvie's—and cut in a straight bob, like a mediæval page, with a straight fringe across her forehead. Her eyes were brown and rather wide apart, and had a vague look, which, Barbara discovered later, was due to the fact that she was extremely short-sighted.

"How do you do," she said. "Are you the people that have come to live next door?"

Barbara answered in the affirmative, she was a little surprised that Mrs. Marvell had found it necessary to ask the question.

"The garden has been neglected for a long time," complained Mrs. Marvell.

"I know," replied Barbara. "I'm having it tidied up."

"It's rather a nuisance because of the

seeds—dandelions and things—they blow over the wall," said Mrs. Marvell, peering over Barbara's shoulder as she spoke.

"Oh, yes," said Barbara. It was difficult to know what else to say.

"Yes, it's rather a *nuisance*," said Mrs. Marvell again.

Barbara felt it was unfair to blame her for the state of The Archway House garden. It was not her fault that the place had been neglected for so long—but she found this conviction difficult to word, so she left it unuttered. I wonder (she thought) whether my garden will suffer more from her children, or hers from my dandelions—but she left this thought unuttered, too.

"Perhaps you'll come to dinner some night," said Mrs. Marvell more cheerfully. "You don't expect me to call, or anything, do you?"

"Oh no—no, of course not," murmured Barbara.

"Because I never do, you know. But come to dinner."

"We don't play bridge," said Barbara firmly.

"Bridge!" exclaimed Mrs. Marvell, as if she had never heard of the game. "Oh, *bridge.*

No, we don't play bridge. James doesn't like it."

"Neither do we."

"We play ping-pong sometimes."

"We don't play ping-pong," said Barbara.

"But we're not very good at it."

"We can't play at all."

"How funny!" said Mrs. Marvell, and then she added, "But come to dinner all the same."

"Thank you, we should like to," Barbara said politely. She thought—this is a mad conversation, quite mad. She's like the White Queen out of *Alice in Wonderland*.

At this moment all conversation suddenly ceased, and a fat woman in pink began to sing in a very loud contralto voice.

"That's the worst of these Musical Evenings," whispered Mr. Marvell who was standing on Barbara's other side.

"What is?" enquired Barbara in the same sibilant tone.

"The music of course."

Several people turned round indignantly and said, "Hush," whereupon he relapsed into gloomy silence.

When the applause was over Barbara was delighted to find her husband at her elbow.

"Well," he enquired, "how goes it? Do you know enough people yet?"

"Where *have* you been, Arthur?" she exclaimed.

"Talking to one or two fellows," he replied. "They're going to put me up for the golf club——"

"That's good," nodded Barbara. She was very much pleased at the information for she had been worrying about Arthur's golf. He enjoyed it, and it was good for him. It really was splendid news.

"Hullo!" said Arthur suddenly. "Hullo—it isn't—it can't be—it is! *Monkey*, by all that's blue!" he leant across Barbara and seized hold of a funny little man with a brown face and surprised eyebrows—"Monkey—don't you know me?"

"Badger!" cried the little man, equally thrilled at the unexpected meeting, "Badger—Good Lord it's you! Where have you come from—eh?"

"What have you been up to, you old scrounger?" cried Arthur, quite red in the face with excitement. "Look here, this is my wife. Barbara, this is Monkey Wrench—we were in France together fighting the Boches.

Monkey's a great fighter—you'd never think it to look at him, would you?"

Barbara shook hands with the little man.

"Bless my buttons, it's good to see you again!" continued Arthur. "Brings back old times—what? Remember that night at Amiens?"

"Hush, hush," said the other with feigned terror. "No lurid reminiscences here—I'm a staid respectable old medico now, and I've got my reputation to think of."

"What? A medico?" Arthur exclaimed. "Great Heavens—hadn't you killed enough people in France. Talk about blood lust——"

Barbara never knew what Dr. Wrench replied to this amazing innuendo, she was swept off to be introduced to somebody else. She had now met so many people that she was completely bewildered, it was impossible, she found, to disentangle the unfamiliar names and faces. How awful! she kept thinking (as she bowed or shook hands with another complete stranger) how awful if I meet them in the street and cut them dead! The only thing for me to do is to bow to everybody I see, because all Wandlebury must be here to-night—or very nearly—so there will be less chance of making a mistake by bowing than not bowing.

By this time Barbara had been gradually pushed up to the end of the room where the dais was situated. Silence was commanded and Sir Lucian Agnew—rather a thin weedy-looking man, with a pink and white complexion—climbed on to the dais and prepared to entertain the company.

"Our Wandlebury poet," explained Mr. Marvell, who was once more at Barbara's elbow. "Our Wandlebury poet prepared to recite an original and hitherto unpublished gem from his own immortal works."

"How clever of him!" exclaimed Barbara, looking at Sir Lucian with awe and wonder.

"It is indeed," agreed Mr. Marvell. "But perhaps we had better withhold our superlative praise, until we have heard and enjoyed Sir Lucian's effort."

Sir Lucian cleared his throat and raised his eyes to the ceiling—he evidently required no aid to memory—

"Thoughts in my Garden," said Sir Lucian slowly.

"A charm of gold-finches upon a bush
Of Michaelmas daisies or long-tailed vetch

Is busy pecking at the little seeds—
Their golden livery gleams in the sunshine.

"The weed-blanketed dung-hill boasts
A rainbow-hued murmuration
Of starlings—and, on the currant bushes,
Red and white currants hang like milky
     pearls,
Or blood-red rubies. Tits as small as mice
Hang upside down, and gorge until their
     beaks
Drip with succulence."

There was tremendous applause when Sir
Lucian finished, and then the hum of conversation burst forth once more.

"How did it strike you?" Mr. Marvell
enquired, with a satirical gleam in his fine
eyes.

"I thought it was awfully pretty," replied
Barbara, with her usual truthfulness. "But it
wasn't a poem, really, was it? I mean it didn't
rhyme."

"Sir Lucian prefers *vers libre*," explained
Mr. Marvell solemnly.

He was beginning to think that Barbara was
a most amusing woman—quite an acquisition
to Wandlebury—he took her simple sincerity
for subtilty (it was too innocent to be natural,

173

he thought), and she took his sarcasm for sincerity. But in spite of this complete misunderstanding of each other—or perhaps because of it—they got an extraordinarily well. They agreed that Sir Lucian must be frightfully clever to write poetry like that, and they agreed it was "very brave" of him to stand up and deliver his poem before such a large and critical audience, and the fact that Barbara really thought these things and Mr. Marvell didn't never became apparent.

11

THE MUSICAL EVENING—
CONTINUED

BARBARA was still discussing the poem with Mr. Marvell when Mrs. Dance spotted her, and bore down upon her with her usual toothy smile.

"There you are, Mrs. Abbott!" she exclaimed delightedly. "I've been looking for you everywhere. Isn't it a lovely party?"

Barbara had no difficulty in remembering Mrs. Dance, she had suffered too much, both mentally and physically, during that lady's call. Those large and gleaming teeth would forever be associated in Barbara's mind with the storm and stress of the furniture arriving, and an aching at the base of her spine.

"Come and sit down, Mrs. Abbott," continued Mrs. Dance, leading the way to a sofa, in the corner of the room, which happened to be unoccupied at the moment, "come and sit down, and I'll tell you who everybody is."

Mrs. Dance was unfeignedly glad when she

saw Barbara, she was feeling a trifle "out of it," and this was all the harder to bear because she knew practically everybody in the room. The truth was that Mrs. Dance was not popular in Wandlebury—and she knew it. Now, unpopular people with thick skins are usually rather happy people—they go through life quite cheerfully treading on their neighbours' toes, and bestowing their unwelcome company upon all and sundry, secure in the conviction that everybody likes them— but Mrs. Dance, unfortunately for herself was thin-skinned. She was clever enough to know that people disliked her, but not clever enough to understand the reason for their dislike. When, for instance, she saw Jeronina Cobbe, coming towards her down the street, and saw her suddenly turn and dive into the Wandlebury flower shop, Mrs. Dance was aware that Jeronina had not really wanted any flowers—how could she when her own garden was teeming with them—but had only taken this step to avoid a meeting with herself. Why didn't people like her, Mrs. Dance wondered sadly. It was not (she had made sure of this) for any of the curious reasons that one saw advertised so assiduously in the daily papers in conjunction with different brands of lozenges or powders or lotions. What could it be, then? Mrs. Dance renewed her efforts to be popular in Wandlebury; she manœuvred people into corners, and told them amusing little anecdotes about their friends; she pursued people in the street, and poured into their willing ears all sorts of little tit-bits of local gossip. The anecdotes and the tit-bits usually went down well, and Mrs. Dance would take leave of her victim thinking—*there, she really does like me now*. But the next time they met the friendship had always cooled off, and Mrs. Dance had to start all over again. What Mrs. Dance did not realise was that the person in question had been willing enough to listen to the anecdotes and tit-bits, but had afterwards reflected, consciously or unconsciously, *I wonder what Mrs. Dance says to other people about me.*

Since her old friends—or acquaintances—were so unsatisfactory, Mrs. Dance was always ready for someone new, and Mrs. Abbott was just the sort of person that Mrs. Dance liked (or at least Mrs. Dance thought she was)—a simple, and rather foolish person, but obviously well-off—so she manœuvred Barbara on to the sofa, and proceeded to put her wise as to the faults and failings of the Wandleburians.

"It's *so* lucky you came to-night," she said, bursting with friendliness. "Everybody's here. *There's* Mrs. Marvell—have you met her yet? Such queer clothes—artistic, of course. Not pretty at all (is she?) with those queer high cheek-bones and weird hair. They say it's Scotch—those cheek-bones—but I shouldn't be surprised if she had foreign blood in her. Have you met Miss Thane? That's her in green—isn't it a pity she wears green with that sallow skin? She lives with her mother at the other end of the town—not far from you. Mrs. Thane is an invalid—I don't think there's much the matter with her, myself, but she likes a lot of attention. Candia Thane will have to go back to her mother and tell her all about us, and what everybody wore, and if she doesn't remember she will have to make it up as she goes along—ha, ha!" and Mrs. Dance laughed delightedly. "Candia is such a queer name, isn't it?" she continued. "She was called Candia, because she was born there (it's in Crete, you know). She was born in Candia quite by mistake—because Mrs. Thane was on her way home, intending her to be born here—but she arrived a month

178

too soon—so like poor Candia to do the wrong thing!"

"What was Mrs. Thane doing in Crete?" enquired Barbara with interest.

"She and Colonel Thane were on their way home from Egypt or somewhere," said Mrs. Dance vaguely, "and they stopped at Crete to see some ruins or something—it was all very awkward I believe. Colonel Thane's dead now. He was out shooting and his gun went off and shot him. Some people say it wasn't an accident at all, but, of course, you can't believe all you hear." Having disposed of the Thanes to her own satisfaction Mrs. Dance turned her attention to other matters. "Have you seen anything of the Marvell kiddies yet?" she enquired. "Ambrose is a dear little boy, but Trivona is very peculiar—slightly *mental*, I'm afraid. I believe Mr. Marvell's grandmother died in an asylym so, of course, that accounts for a *lot*. Lancreste, the elder boy, is consumptive—sad, isn't it? I suppose you will be having Doctor Wrench as your doctor. I saw your husband talking to him as if he had known him before. Such an excellent doctor, but inclined to be a little unsympathetic, I always think. He doesn't really understand my little Marguerite at all—the poor child is terrified of him—she needs a great deal of care and love—so terribly highly strung, you know. Doctor Wrench doesn't understand her at all. Oh, there's Archie Cobbe! Archie's our bad boy, Mrs. Abbott. All towns have their bad boys, haven't they?"

"Does he paint the town red?" enquired Barbara looking with interest at the elegant figure in immaculate tails.

"Ha, ha!" laughed Mrs. Dance. "You *are* so amusing, Mrs. Abbott. Archie really prefers London to Wandlebury, but he can't settle down to work. A bit of a rolling-stone, I'm afraid. He's Lady Chevis Cobbe's nephew—her husband's nephew, really—he lives with his sister at Ganthorne Lodge (at least he's supposed to, but, as I said, he really prefers London to Wandlebury). Ganthorne Lodge is a sweet little house—*very* old and inconvenient: with earwigs, and no electric light, and the bath water always lukewarm, you know the kind of house I mean. Jeronina Cobbe is a charming girl—rather unwomanly perhaps; she goes about most of the time in breeches and a pullover—very modern—with no hat. Of course she has *ruined* her complexion. She runs a sort of riding-school, isn't it a queer sort of thing for a girl to do? They aren't at all well off, but, of course, they'll have plenty of money when Lady Chevis Cobbe dies—at least Archie will, everybody knows that he's the heir."

Barbara sat up and opened her eyes wide—so everybody knew that, did they? Barbara happened to know differently—and how queer, she thought, how very queer that I should know more about it than anybody else. Archie Cobbe isn't the heir at all—how angry and disappointed he will be if he thinks he is the heir and finds that he isn't! And he evidently *does* think he's the heir, Barbara reflected (as she watched the young man moving about the room talking and laughing with his Aunt's guests), he's *behaving* like an heir, there's no doubt about that. It's rather bad luck if he's banking on all that money coming to him, and I really don't think it's very fair of Lady Chevis Cobbe not to tell him about her new will.

"You see," continued Mrs. Dance (delighted with the obvious interest her information was arousing). "You see, Chevis Place and all the money belongs to Lady Chevis Cobbe in her own right. She was a Chevis, of course—very old family—and the place has belonged to the Chevis family for generations. So, when her

181

only brother was killed in France, and the property came to her, she married Sir Archibald Cobbe—one of the Cobbes of Ganthorne—and a brother of Jeronina's father—and Sir Archibald took the name of Chevis, and they called themselves Sir Archibald and Lady Chevis Cobbe. It must have been rather a blow for them to have no children to inherit, after all the bother they had taken (although Sir Archibald was only a knight so they couldn't have inherited the title), but Lady Chevis Cobbe is going to leave the place to Archie, and I suppose he will take the name of Chevis so that there will still be a Chevis at Chevis Place. It's all rather complicated, of course," added Mrs. Dance, smiling in her toothy way.

"Yes, it is," agreed Barbara—it was a good deal more complicated than Mrs. Dance suspected. Lady Chevis Cobbe was *not* going to leave the place to Archie Cobbe, she was going to leave it to his sister. Barbara had forgotten all about the will (which she had read by such a curious mistake in Mr. Tyler's office), or, at least, she had not remembered a thing about it until this moment. She had been far too busy, moving into her new house, to remember the incident. But, now, it was all coming back to her. It had been stored up in a little cupboard in her brain, and she was taking it out and looking at it. There was something that had struck her as curious about that will—what was it? Oh yes, Lady Chevis Cobbe had made a curious proviso to her bequest to "the said Jeronina" and the curious proviso had run something like this— "if at my death the said Jeronina is still unmarried——"

Very odd indeed, thought Barbara vaguely, and she decided to leave it at that—the whole thing was far too queer and complicated for her to examine now, with people laughing and talking all around her, and Mrs. Dance pouring confidences into her ear.

People really *are* queer, Barbara thought, the Wandlebury people are queer, and the Silverstream people were queer too, in their different way. I don't suppose (Barbara thought), I don't suppose there are any *ordinary* people in the world, anywhere. She was rather weary of Mrs. Dance by this time—Mrs. Dance was very tiring—and presently she managed to detach herself from the good lady, and wandered off to find Sam.

It was curious that she had seen nothing of Sam the whole evening (Arthur, she had no doubt, was securely hidden in some out-of-the-way corner exchanging reminiscences with "Monkey" Wrench). Sam knew nobody here, and she had expected to see a good deal of Sam, to have him attached to her apron strings, so to speak. But the evening had worn away in talk and laughter broken by occasional songs and piano solos, and visits to the refreshment buffet in the hall, and not once had she caught a glimpse of Sam—where on earth could he be? She wandered into the hall and looked about, and suddenly she saw Mr. Tyler.

"Oh, Mr. Tyler, how nice to see you!" Barbara exclaimed, catching hold of his arm, as he was passing by.

"Oh—how do you do," said Mr. Tyler. "Very nice—ah—I'm in rather a hurry——"

He tried to edge round Barbara as he spoke, but Barbara stood her ground. She was sincerely pleased to meet Mr. Tyler again, he was the first person she had spoken to in Wandlebury—except, of course, the waiter at the Apollo and Boot, and he didn't really count—and Mr. Tyler had been so nice to her—so very nice and kind. Barbara wanted a little chat with Mr. Tyler.

"We love The Archway House," she told

him. "It's so comfortable and cosy."

"Oh, indeed," said Mr. Tyler, "most—ah—satisfactory. I really must——"

"We haven't seen any rats, not one," added Barbara.

"Rats!"

"Not one," Barbara assured him. "But I *do* think it was so kind of you to warn me about them."

"Oh yes—I'm afraid I was—ah—misinformed," said Mr. Tyler unhappily. "Yes—misinformed."

"I wonder who can have told you——" Barbara began.

"I cannot imagine," said Mr. Tyler, and, with that, he fled, almost bumping into the large form of Mr. Abbott which was emerging from the ball-room.

"There, Arthur!" cried Barbara excitedly. "That was Mr. Tyler—did you see him?"

"Well, scarcely," said Arthur smiling. "He seemed in a hurry. Where's Sam? We ought to be going, I think."

* * *

Sam had had a much more amusing evening than he had expected—though perhaps

185

amusing is scarcely the word. He had escaped from Barbara, and the chain of introductions at the first opportunity, and had attached himself to Jeronina Cobbe. Jerry was busy, helping her Aunt, and introducing the Abbotts, but Sam bided his time, and, once she was free from her duties, he headed her off very cleverly and parked her on the stairs. Sam was rather adept at that sort of thing, he usually managed to get what he wanted, and, for some unknown reason, he had wanted to talk to Jerry Cobbe.

They sat on the stairs, just beyond the bend, so that they were hidden from the people passing through the great hall to the refreshment buffet. It was a strategic position, not secluded enough to be compromising, but quite secluded enough for a nice quiet conversation. Jerry sat two steps higher up than Sam, so that Sam had to turn sideways and look up if he wanted to see her face, and he found he wanted to do this quite often. She had such sweet hair, Sam thought—and so she had. It was very brown and silky, and it swept back from her forehead in a big glossy wave. She kept it very short, so that her head was almost like the head of a boy.

"It's nice here, isn't it?" Sam said.

"Yes," agreed Jerry. "It's nice to sit down. I'm rather tired. I've been riding all day—I keep horses you know—and then I had to change, and rush over here to help Aunt Matilda."

"You *must* be tired."

"It's because I'm not used to parties," Jerry explained. "I usually go to bed early—and I get up very early, of course. What a noise they make, talking!"

"Don't they? Rather like a Zoo."

"What do you do?" Jerry asked.

"I'm in a publishing office."

"Oh, that must be rather interesting. Tell me about it. What do you have to do? Read books and things?"

Sam told her.

They discussed modern literature.

She's not really pretty, Sam thought (looking up at the small eager face, with the broad brow and the widely set grey eyes, so frank and clear). She's not really pretty, but there's something about her. I rather like those funny little freckles on her nose and her cheeks, I suppose it's being out riding all day. She looks awfully healthy and strong, somehow.

They talked for a long time. People passed

187

and repassed in the hall, but nobody came up-stairs. Sam congratulated himself upon his astuteness in the choice of a retreat. If he had been sitting there with any other girl he would have felt bound to kiss her—a kiss would have been indicated, so to speak (she would have expected it and he would have enjoyed it in much the same way as he would have enjoyed a glass of good wine), but this girl was different from other girls of Sam's acquaintance, and Sam was intuitive enough to recognise the fact. It was rather a pity, in a way, because he would have enjoyed kissing Jerry—all the more because her face was not all messed up with paint and stuff—but Jerry did not expect to be kissed, she might even be rather angry if he attempted such a thing. She's a funny girl, he thought, quite odd, really. It's almost like talking to a man. And yet it wasn't the least like talking to a man, either—there was something about her——

Sam was quite annoyed when it was time to go home. The Musical Evening had not been such a complete washout after all.

12

THE CURE THAT FAILED

IT was the next afternoon. The sad level light of the winter's sun lay on the empty fields, and defined the peaked roofs of cottages and barns with yellow light and grey shadow. It seeped in between the bare black branches of the trees, and glittered mildly in the puddles and the water-logged ruts of the country lanes. Sam Abbott strode along twirling a heavy stick, and striking at the withered stalks of cow parsley and nettles that grew along the edges of the path. He was on his way to see Jeronina Cobbe and, as an excuse for his visit, he had a note—wangled with amazing diplomacy from Barbara—in his pocket.

It was essential that he should see Jeronina Cobbe, because the thought of her had been worrying him, and Sam was quite certain that if he saw her again he would be able to put her out of his head. It would cure him completely. He would see her in the cold light of reason and the queer effect she had made upon him would be dissipated—Sam was sure of that. He was so sure of it that he kept telling himself about it all the way. No girl was going to upset him, and disturb his night's rest—*no girl on earth*. I wonder if she'll see through the excuse, he thought (as he decapitated a withered thistle with one blow). Well, I don't care if she does. How could she, anyhow? It would be quite natural for Barbara to ask me to walk over and deliver a note.

He stopped for a moment where the lane forked—the signpost said "Ganthorne" and "Gostown"—Ganthorne was obviously right. He strode on. There were moors about him now, brown moors with boggy green patches, all very desolate on this November afternoon. I suppose she rides here, Sam thought, it must be rather fun. Quite soon he came to the place he was looking for—a small grey house, dove-coloured, with twisted chimneys. Trees grew round about it, enclosing it in a dark casket. In front of the house was the garden, damp and dreary now, and colourless save for a row of slightly-frosted chrysanthemums. To the right was a long low building—the stables where Jeronina kept her horses.

190

Sam paused at the gate and looked at the house—it was an Elizabethan gem. His eyes dwelt on it with pleasure, he noted the timbered orders; the gables, steep and darkly jutting; the mullioned windows with their diamond-shaped panes. Then he marched up to the door and rang the bell. It was an old-fashioned bell of wrought-iron, and was almost hidden amongst the bright red leaves of the Virginia creeper.

The door was opened by a fresh-faced country girl, who seemed somewhat surprised at his appearance, and informed him, reluctantly, that Miss Cobbe was over at the stables. The obvious thing to do was to hand over the note and return home, but Sam had come for a definite purpose, and he intended to see Miss Cobbe.

"I'll go and find her," he said, and suited the action to the word.

Jerry was easily found, she was standing in the stable-yard talking to a groom. She was clad in jodhpurs, brown, like an autumn beech leaf, and a brown jersey, high-necked and close-fitting. Her brown head was bare, and the wind had ruffled her silky hair, and had whipped her cheeks into a rosy glow.

"Hullo!" she said, when she saw Sam,

"have you come to see the horses?"

"I've got a letter for you," replied Sam, delivering it as he spoke.

He had the opportunity of looking at her as she opened Barbara's note and read it. Now was his chance to take a good look at her, and discover what it was about this girl that had disturbed him. He made the most of the opportunity. He studied her carefully: she was different, that was what it was. She was entirely and absolutely different from any girl he had met. There was nothing artificial about this girl, her small determined face was innocent of powder. Sam looked at the freckles on her nose, he marked the broad brow, the sensitive mouth (how pale the mouth looked without the usual smear of red!). It was rather a sad face when it was in repose, it had a sort of sad, wise look as if its owner had too many responsibilities, too many burdens for her years. Sam felt suddenly that he would like to take care of her.

Jerry lifted her eyes and smiled, and the sadness vanished. "I suppose you know— Mrs. Abbott has asked me to tea to-morrow," she said. "It's nice of her, isn't it? Will it be all right if I give you a verbal message, or had I better write?"

"It will be quite all right," Sam assured her. "You can come, I hope?"

"I'd like to come," said Jerry. "You're sure I oughtn't to write? She won't mind, I mean. Some people are rather particular about——"

"Oh, Barbara's frightfully sensible."

"You call her Barbara?" enquired Jerry in surprise. "Isn't she your step-mother?"

"No, she's my aunt by marriage," Sam explained. "Besides I always call people by their Christian names—it's so much easier——" he looked at her as he spoke, hoping that she would take the hint. It would be nice to call her Jerry. He would come to it in time, of course, but the sooner the better.

"I see," said Jerry. "Everyone here thinks you are Mr. Abbott's son—you know how people talk in country places. They haven't got anything better to do, poor dears."

They laughed together over the foolishness of "poor dears," and the atmosphere became more friendly. It was extraordinarily pleasant in the stable-yard, sheltered from the wind. The light was fading fast; from the stalls and loose-boxes came the stamp of a hoof, and champ of teeth, and the rattle of a chain, and the rather pleasant stable smell, slightly ammoniac in the nostrils. Sam felt that he and Jerry were alone in the world, he felt very near to her to-day. Last night he had talked to her about himself, but to-day he wanted to know more about *her*—what did she do, all day? What were her thoughts?

"You're fond of horses?" he said, tentatively.

"I love them," said Jerry. She was silent for a moment or two and then, when Sam did not speak, she continued. "I couldn't do without horses you know—at least, of course, that's rubbish, because I could do without them, I suppose, if I had to—but all the *goodness* would go out of my life if I had to do without horses. You see Father loved horses, and I was brought up with them."

"Yes," said Sam, nodding sympathetically.

"And then, when Father died, and we were not so well off, everyone said the horses must be sold, and, of course, I saw that too—I mean it would have been absurd to keep three horses just for me. Archie doesn't care about riding, he rides sometimes, when he's here, but he doesn't love it like I do. Well, I didn't want to sell the horses a bit, and I put it off from week to week; and then, somehow or other, I began to find people who wanted to keep horses down here for hunting, and a

194

man asked me if I would take an old favourite who was past work, and keep her for him; then some people turned up who wanted a few lessons, and they told their friends about me; and there were some children staying with Mrs. Thane for the holidays—her son's children—and they wanted to ride (it all happened so queerly, somehow), and gradually I began to see that I could keep the horses, and actually make them pay. So now," said Jerry, smiling at him in a friendly way, "So now you see before you a livery stable proprietor—a sort of riding-master—a sort of glorified groom——"

"It was splendid," said Sam earnestly. "I know there was a lot more to it than that. I mean you must have worked awfully hard, and had bad moments when you thought it wasn't going to be any good—and—and all that."

"Yes, I did," said Jerry, not a little surprised that this young man had seen what apparently nobody else had seen.

There was silence after that for a few moments—a friendly sympathetic silence—and then a groom appeared and touched his cap.

"Well, Crichton, what is it?" enquired Jerry. Crichton gave his message—Colonel White had rung up to know whether Silver Maid would be fit to ride to-morrow, and, if so, could she be sent over to the Cross Roads to-morrow by nine-thirty. Jerry gave the necessary orders clearly and concisely and the man ran off.

Gadzooks, she's capable! thought Sam—no wonder she's managed to pull through. What a girl! What guts!

"I wish I could get a groom with a little sense," said Jerry rather wearily. "They've got no initiative, these people. Well, never mind. What about tea? Would you like some, Mr. Abbott? I've been out all afternoon, and I'm starving. Perhaps you've had tea."

"No," lied Sam. "I'd love some tea, if it wouldn't be a bother——"

They walked up to the house together, talking in a desultory fashion. Jerry left Sam in the drawing-room while she went and washed, and Sam strolled about the pretty room, looking at the cushioned window seat, the pictures, and the beautiful old furniture (which was so exactly right for the room) and the gate-legged table, bearing an ample tea, which was set before the fire. Jerry was not very long, she came down with smooth hair and clean hands, and settled herself on the wide fender-stool to dispense the tea. Her legs, moulded in her close fitting jodhpurs, were cocked, one over the other, her figure was outlined faintly beneath the clinging wool of her jersey. She was strongly made—not thin and elegant, but rounded and sturdy—the muscles of her body had been developed by her active life. The firelight flickered on her fair skin (turning it ruddy) and awoke red lights in her gleaming brown hair. There was a golden circle of light from the lamp on the table—without, it was dark, and the windows were like deep-blue panels in the walls of the room.

"It's a cosy house, really," Jerry said. "Some people would think it dreadfully uncomfortable, but I'm used to it."

"It's beautiful I think," said Sam quietly.

"Yes, isn't it?" she agreed. "I'm glad you think that."

"Anybody would," said Sam.

Jerry took a large slice of wheaten bread, spread with golden butter, and bit into it with her small white teeth. It was a natural gesture—she was very hungry indeed—but to Sam, there was something symbolic about it. Jerry was like bread, he thought. She was like good wholesome wheaten bread, spread thickly with honest farm butter; and the thought crossed his mind, that a man might eat bread for ever and ever, and not tire of it, and that it would never clog his palate like sweet cakes or pastries or chololate *éclairs*.

I do care for her, Sam thought. I do care for her—it's different. It's not so much that I'm in love with her as that I love her. I'll always care for her if she'll let me. I'll work like mad at the office so that Uncle Arthur will give me a rise—it will be rather good working for her. Oh, Glory! he said to himself, what a dear she is! What a lamb! I love every bit of her.

"You must come over another day and see the horses," Jerry was saying. "It's no use now—too dark. I hate the dark winter evenings, don't you?"

"Yes," agreed Sam.

"D'you live with your Uncle and Aunt?"

"Lord no, I'm only here for a visit, but I shall be down here a good deal, I expect," said Sam hopefully. "They're awfully decent, you know," he added (quite forgetting that, less than a week ago, he had anathematised his Uncle Arthur for being a crusty old beast). "Really awfully decent—and they don't seem a bit *old*, if you know what I mean."

"They aren't old, are they?" said Jerry. "I

saw Mrs. Abbott last night. She's very nice-looking, isn't she? I thought she looked as if she'd be 'nice to know.'"

"Oh, she is—she's a dear," agreed Sam fervently—what a splendid thing it would be if Jerry and Barbara became friends. "I'm sure you'll like her awfully. You may think she's—well—rather simple, at first, but really and truly she's clever in some ways—extraordinarily clever——" (He thought, I wish I could tell her about the books, but, of course, I can't.)

"Is she?" enquired Jerry with interest.

"And they're frightfully devoted to each other," continued Sam eagerly. "It's rather nice, that, isn't it?"

Jerry nodded. "It is, rather," she agreed. "It makes a nice sort of atmosphere, doesn't it? I don't mean soppiness, of course—that sort of thing always gives me the creeps—but real friendly love."

There was silence on that. "Real, friendly love," Sam thought, that's exactly what I feel for *her*. How odd! And then he thought—I shall never forget this, never, not if I live to be a hundred, not even if I never see her again.

It would always be his—that was what he

meant—this little picture: the quiet mellow room, the glow of the lamp, the dark shadows behind the chairs, and Jerry in the firelight, all ruddy with its glow. Already the little picture was enshrined in his memory like a picture seen in the focusing lens of a camera, like a single coloured photograph taken from the roll of a cinematograph film—one stationary incident culled from the swiftly passing film of his life.

They talked a little longer of different matters, and then Sam got up to go. Jerry walked with him to the gate, and stood there, leaning on it. There was a mist rising from the ground, but it was clear overhead, quite dark and starry. Sam could not see her face—it was only a blur—but he could see it in his mind, and, somehow or other, he knew that it wore that sad, wise look which he found so pathetic.

"Mr. Abbott," she said, and it seemed strange to hear her voice so clearly in the darkness. "Mr. Abbott, do you like the town or the country best?"

"The country," replied Sam promptly—and he said it quite honestly with never a thought for the delights of London which had seemed so good to him a short while ago.

Jerry sighed. "I wish Archie liked the country," she said. "He finds it dull here. He wants to live in town, but I simply couldn't. Besides I'm making money now—just a little—and he isn't. We ought to live together—but why should I bother you."

"You aren't bothering me," said Sam. "Why ought you to live together?"

"Because it's cheaper," said Jerry simply.

"I see," nodded Sam.

"Have you ever read a book called *Great Expectations*?" Jerry enquired, somewhat naïvely. "I think Archie is very like that boy. You see he knows that some day he'll be rich, and so it doesn't seem to him worth while to settle down to anything. He gets a job, and then he gives it up because he doesn't like it, or else the job gives up Archie because he won't work hard enough, and then he's idle for a time until he finds something else. I wish," said Jerry, sighing again, "I wish Archie had no expectations."

"It's worrying you," Sam said sympathetically.

"Yes. You don't mind me telling you about it, do you? I can tell *you* about it because you're young too, and you understand how difficult the world is now. Older people don't understand the difficulties."

Sam agreed eagerly, it was exactly what he had found. "Things were so different when they were young——"

"Or else they've forgotten."

They were silent. An owl hooted in the darkness, and there was a gentle rustle in the hedge as if some small timid animal was stirring. Sam felt very near this girl. He wanted to stretch out his hand and touch hers. He could see her hand, dimly white, on the bar of the gate, but something forbade him—it was too soon. He made up his mind that he must get to know her better, must see her *often*, and then——

"Look here!" said Sam suddenly, "I wonder—I wonder if I could ride sometimes when I'm down here. I shall be down quite a lot, I expect, and it's so difficult to get enough exercise. Do you—I mean could I hire a horse—or anything?"

Jerry laughed, it was a chuckling sort of laugh, very pleasant to hear, and very infectious. "Of course you can hire a horse," she said. "Haven't I just told you I keep a livery stable? Six bob an hour is what I charge."

"But I should want lessons," Sam told her.

"You see I'm an awful duffer at riding—haven't ridden since I was ten."

"Schooling is extra, of course," Jerry said. "Ten bob a lesson inclusive."

"That would be the thing," said Sam cheerfully—if Jerry had said five guineas a lesson his reaction would have been the same. It really didn't matter what he paid as long as it gave him the opportunity of seeing her often.

"How many lessons would you want?" enquired Jerry. "It's cheaper if you have a dozen——"

"I shall want a dozen," said Sam promptly. "The only difficulty is I don't quite know when I shall be here."

"Yes, I see. Well, it wouldn't matter—you can just have them when you come. We should have to fit them in as we could. I'm busy sometimes—I suppose before breakfast would be too early for you."

"Why, it's the best time!" cried Sam— something in Jerry's voice had informed him that this was her opinion, had informed him that Jerry was up and about at daybreak, and had a wholesome scorn for those who preferred to doze sleepily in their warm beds. Her next words proved him correct in his surmise——

"That's what I think," she said in a friendly tone. "Of course, it's rather dark now, so you couldn't ride *very* early, but it would be all right about half-past eight. Lots of people hate getting up early, especially London people like you."

"I only live in London because I have to," Sam told her earnestly.

He walked back to The Archway House on air. Everything was arranged. The following day was a Saturday, and he was to have a lesson at half-past eight, which would give him time to return to The Archway House for breakfast at half-past nine. In the afternoon Jerry was coming to tea. She had promised to give him another lesson on Sunday; on Monday he was to return to town. Sam did not like the thought of returning to town, but it was no good worrying too much. Perhaps he would be able to wangle another visit out of Uncle Arthur in the near future—it ought not to be very difficult, they liked him, he knew, and he was good at wangling things.

The Sam that strode home was a totally changed being from the Sam of twenty-four hours ago. A totally changed being, with totally different tastes, and an entirely new outlook upon life. *Then* he had preferred the town to the country, *now* he preferred the country to the town. *Then* he had preferred dark girls, rather pale and languorous (elegant, decadent, decorative creatures with long silken legs), *now* he preferred—Jerry. It did not strike Sam as strange that his tastes had altered, for he was not in the habit of analysing himself. He merely thought. Gadzooks! This time yesterday I hadn't even *seen* her, I was fed up to the back teeth at the prospect of the Musical Evening. . . .

The elder Abbotts were a little surprised to hear about the riding, but not inordinately so. Sam was good at dissembling his feelings (he had had lots of practice in the art at home), he remarked casually at dinner that he wanted a bit of exercise, and had arranged to hire a nag from Miss Cobbe.

"Good name for a girl who keeps horses!" was Mr. Abbott's reaction.

Sam smiled and agreed.

"I didn't know you were keen on riding," added Mr. Abbott.

"I don't get much chance of it," Sam pointed out.

"I think it will be nice for you, Sam," said Barbara kindly.

So that's that, thought Sam complacently—it was very easy.

Sam's first riding lesson was not all bliss. He was very rusty, to say the least of it, and Jerry did not let him off lightly. She had a high sense of her responsibilities, and took care that her pupils got their money's worth. Sam was very tired, and very sore, and very humble when Jerry was done with him.

"I told you I was a duffer," he said ruefully.

"You'll soon learn," replied Jerry, with her kind smile. "Go straight home and take a boiling-hot bath with mustard in it"—she was a very practical girl.

Sam climbed stiffly into Barbara's little car—which he had borrowed for the occasion—and drove home to do her bidding.

13

TEA AND CRUMPETS AT THE ARCHWAY HOUSE

SAM was not in the drawing-room when Jerry arrived at The Archway House for tea. She asked after him with some anxiety, for she was aware that she had been a trifle hard on him.

"He's gone out for a walk with Arthur—they'll be back soon," Barbara said. "Sit near the fire, won't you? It's frightfully cold and windy, isn't it?"

"Yes, but I like it," replied Jerry.

"So do I," Barbara agreed, and then she added, "Sam enjoyed his ride this morning."

"That's good," said Jerry, smiling a little as she visualised Sam's agonised face as he trotted round and round her field, bumping about like a sack of coals. She was not going to give him away—oh dear, no! It was rather sporting of him to tell them he had enjoyed it—not quite veracious, of course, but you couldn't have everything.

"Yes," said Barbara. "We're so glad he enjoyed it. Arthur's been rather worried about Sam. He's young, you know, and he likes a gay life—quite natural at his age, of course. Arthur thinks the riding will be so good for him."

"What sort of gay life?" enquired Jerry.

"Oh, night-clubs and things," replied Barbara vaguely.

Jerry's heart sank. Somehow or other she hadn't thought Sam Abbott was "like that." There was no harm in night-clubs, of course, but the people who frequented them were not her kind, and she had rather thought that Sam Abbott *was* her kind. It was a little disappointing.

Barbara must have read her thoughts in part, for she continued, "There's absolutely no harm in night-clubs, but Arthur thinks that Sam does rather too much of it. I think Arthur worries quite unnecessarily—Sam's young and good-looking, why shouldn't he have a gay time? You're only young once."

"Yes," said Jerry.

"I was afraid he would find it dull here——"

"He likes staying with you," Jerry told her.

"He's been a dear," said Barbara. "But ten days is really long enough. I'm sure he's dying to get back to all his gaiety," and she smiled at Jerry, knowingly.

It was rather difficult to smile back, but Jerry achieved it. You fool! (she told herself). What on earth does it matter to you what he's like? You're his riding-master, that's all. For goodness' sake be your age, Jeronina Cobbe!

At this moment Sam came in, followed by Arthur Abbott and Doctor Wrench. They all had the healthy hearty appearance of people who had been blown about by a cold November gale. Sam was delighted to find Jerry sitting by the fire. It seemed ages since this morning. He sat down beside her, and began to eat buttered crumpets with obvious enjoyment.

"Barbara's crumpets are Food for Gods," he said, smiling across at the aunt-by-marriage.

"I love crumpets," Barbara agreed. "They never give me indigestion."

"Nothing ever gives you indigestion," said Arthur proudly; it was one of the things that had drawn him to Barbara Buncle—her amazing digestion—he admired her for it all the more because his own digestion was poor.

"And Barbara's tea is Drink for Gods," continued Sam, handing in his cup for more. "It's funny how seldom you can get a really good cup of tea. Good Indian tea, properly made, with some *body* about it."

Doctor Wrench agreed. "It's fine stuff when it's right," he said. "But how rarely you get it right! Peope either make it so weak that it tastes like straw, or so strong that it tastes like ink, or they buy horrible cheap stuff made of coarse leaves, full of tannin——"

"The water must be boiling," Barbara put in.

"And the tea-pot warmed," added Arthur.

They all laughed when the itinerary was finished, and agreed that they were very particular people.

Jerry had made no contribution to the conversation, and Sam felt intuitively that she was "a bit under the weather." He determined to cheer her up, and began to talk and laugh in an amusing manner, and to tease his uncle and Barbara with that slight flavour of impudence which he knew they enjoyed. They both played up to the best of their ability, and the atmosphere became more and more friendly and hilarious. Doctor Wrench, laughed until he was quite sore, and even Jerry was forced to join in the fun. The tea-party was a great success.

Presently Jerry said she must go, and Sam elected to see her safely home. They went off together in the darkness, and the two old warriors, Arthur Abbott and "Monkey" Wrench, repaired to the former's study for a good talk. Barbara was left sitting by the fire in solitary state.

"Comfortable den!" remarked Doctor Wrench, looking round the cosy room with some envy.

"Yes, isn't it," agreed its owner, complacently. "Very comfortable and cosy. We sit here in the evenings when we're alone."

"The Badger's den," said Doctor Wrench, and he looked at his old friend and laughed. "Rather different—eh?"

Arthur laughed too. He knew what Monkey was thinking of. A little picture sprang into his mind—that dug-out in France—he saw it as clearly as if he had been there yesterday—the sand-bags at the entrance—the crumbling steps—the trodden earthen floor. Gosh, what an awful hole it was! And yet it had been "home" to him for weeks—to him and Monkey.

"D'you remember that staff captain?" he asked.

"Rather," said Monkey. "Came sailing

211

along in his polished boots, and poked his nose in at the doorway—'Good Heavens,' he said—'this place stinks like a badger's den'."

"Yes," agreed Arthur, "and I daresay it did really, but we didn't care. It was warm, anyhow, wasn't it, Monkey?"

"Jolly cosy," said Monkey dreamily. "I remember how fed up you were when everybody began to call you Badger."

"Was I?" exclaimed Arthur in surprise.

"Of course you were, you ass!" said Monkey affectionately.

"You were 'Monkey' long before that," Arthur pointed out.

"I was 'Monkey' at my prep school," said Monkey chuckling. "What else could you expect with a name and a phizz like mine? . . . That's a nice young nephew of yours," continued the doctor as he sank into a leather chair and stretched out his thin legs to the fire, "most amusing beggar—full of beans, isn't he?"

"H'm," said Arthur. "He's all right, really. Very young, of course, and a bit unreliable like all these youngsters nowadays. Barbara thinks he'll outgrow it. Barbara's rather good at summing people up."

"Yes. She's watchful, isn't she? Not always

chattering nonsense like some women. I'm
sure she's right about young Sam—you
mustn't be too hard on him, Badger."

"I like that! Most people would be a damn
sight harder on him than I am. D'you know I
had to go and get him out of Bow Street the
other day."

Monkey Wrench laughed. "The young
devil! What had he been up to?"

"Oh, painting the place red."

"And you gave him a good dressing down,
I'll be bound. Told him when you were his
age you were leading a forlorn hope in
France."

"Something like that," admitted Arthur,
smiling. "But how the devil did you know,
Monkey?"

"Well, it's part of my job to read people,"
said Monkey more seriously, "and you get
into the way of doing it in season and out.
People are odd, you know——" he added
thoughtfully.

"I was wondering," Arthur said, taking his
pipe off the mantelpiece and filling the bowl,
"you haven't much scope here, have you?
Wouldn't you have been better in town?"

"I've plenty of scope," returned Monkey,
"it's the kind of doctoring that appeals to me.

I'll tell you what I feel about doctoring—if it won't bore you—you see everyone wants to specialise now, or nearly everybody who has the brains for it. They sit in their consulting rooms like so many spiders; they diagnose, and, if necessary, they operate, and then they say good-bye and send in their bill. Well, it's necessary to have people like that, I suppose, but that's not my idea of doctoring—I mean it doesn't appeal to me, personally. My idea of doctoring is to get to know your patients, to help their minds as well as their bodies——"

"A sort of medical father confessor?"

"Yes, you can't do that in town."

"I see," said Arthur slowly, "yes, I see your idea, but it still seems to me that Wandlebury can't give you much scope."

"I may not have very many patients, but I've got some very interesting ones," said Doctor Wrench. "I don't gas about my cases to other people, but I know you're safe. There's Mrs. Thane, for instance, a splendid woman. Full of courage and cheerfulness—Mrs. Thane is worth a dozen ordinary patients. And then, on the other hand, there's Agnew——"

"That poet fellow?" enquired Arthur, with interest. "There can't be much the matter with *him*. What nerve to stand up and recite like that!"

"Yes, what nerve!" agreed Monkey smiling. "But you'll be surprised to hear that that man is always in bed for days after his ordeal—absolutely laid out."

"What on earth does he do it for?"

"You may well ask. He does it every year. Sometimes I think he does it just to show he's not going to be beaten by his nerves. And sometimes I think it's because Lady Chevis Cobbe asks him to. He's her only friend, of course—her only real friend."

"What is her ladyship like?" enquired Arthur, with interest.

"She's a very strange woman. I'm frightfully worried about her at the moment—frightfully worried. I want a specialist, but she won't hear of it."

"What's wrong with *her*," Arthur asked. "She looked all right at the party the other night."

"That damned party didn't do her any good. It's her heart. I don't suppose you would understand if I told you what's wrong. It's rather an obscure thing, but definitely interesting. If she would only go slow she might live for years, but she won't go slow.

She's a queer woman, Badger, she isn't normal."

"In what way?"

"Auto apotheosis."

"Come off it, Monkey," said Arthur smiling.

"Well, if I must pander to your ignorance, she's in a mental condition in which she recognises no authority but her own—everything she does is right because *she* does it. She imagines that, owing to her having been born a Chevis, she is justified in behaving exactly as she pleases at whatever cost to other people—is that clear?"

"There are a good many people suffering from that disease," Arthur opined.

"That's not the only thing, though," continued Monkey. "Of course I oughtn't to tell you, but it's a relief to gas to somebody even if they are as abysmally ignorant as you. I won't confound you with medical terms this time——"

"Decent of you!" commented Arthur.

"I shall talk down to you, and call her condition an anti-marriage-complex," said Monkey Wrench.

"But she married, didn't she?"

"She never would have married if it hadn't

been for the Chevis name. She wanted a Chevis at Chevis Place. Cobbe was quite the wrong sort of man to deal with anything not normal. The marriage was a fiasco, and, of course, there's no heir after all."

"Bad luck!"

"Yes. A child would have made all the difference, but there you are—that's life," said Monkey, lighting his pipe and puffing hard to get it going well. "That's life, Badger—and then other people have too many."

"Yes," agreed Arthur.

"So she's a lonely woman, you see. The people who want to be friends with her she suspects of being after her money. Sir Lucian Agnew is her only real friend, and he's a queer sort of creature, too. Rather a tame cat, if you know what I mean, but I believe if she had married *him* they might have made a success of it. All these things combined have made Lady Chevis Cobbe an extraordinarily difficult person to deal with. She really is a little mad—not certifiable, of course, but definitely abnormal. She hates marriage and everything connected with it, won't have a married butler in the house—sacked a chauffeur she had had for years because he got engaged—won't even have a married lodge-keeper at the gates——"

"I suppose that's why she likes you," said Arthur, smiling. "No encumbrances, eh?"

"Yes, of course it is," replied Monkey. "It's no joke, Badger—you needn't grin. I tell you that woman causes me more trouble than all my other patients put together."

"I can well believe it," Arthur told me. "There are some people who seem born to give other people trouble. It's the same in my business——"

"Temperamental authors," suggested Monkey smiling.

"Temperamental authors," Arthur agreed.

There was a little silence after that—a friendly, sympathetic silence—the two pipes puffed away in harmony.

"I'm glad you're here, Monkey," said Arthur Abbott at last. "I'm getting old, I suppose—anyhow I've come to the time of life when one old friend seems better than all the new friends in the world."

"Same here," said Monkey, gruffly.

The pipes puffed on.

218

14

NEW FRIENDS

BARBARA and Arthur settled down very comfortably in their new abode. Barbara's days were full of small happenings. There was still a good deal to do in the house and garden; people called, and their calls had to be returned. The neighbours were nice, Barbara thought, she liked them all—some of them more than others, of course. Every morning Barbara "shopped" in Wandlebury, and there she met her neighbours engaged in the same mysterious occupation. She met them and chatted with them in the butcher's or the grocer's, or in the ice-bound fastness of the fishmonger's. In the afternoon she walked or paid calls, or hob-nobbed with Jerry who had quickly become her friend, and once or twice she had Miss Foddy to tea. Sometimes Arthur came down early from town, and, if it were fine, they took the small car and explored the country, discovering new beauties in the bare trees and fields and rolling pastures.

These were small pleasures, perhaps, but Barbara was very content, and some of the small incidents of everyday life gave her a great deal of amusement and satisfaction. There was the morning when she met Mr. Marvell in the town, for instance. Barbara happened to be in the tiny slit of a shop which was the Wandlebury Library. She was busy choosing a book, and had looked through several without finding anything adventurous enough to please her taste, when suddenly the doorway was darkened by a massive figure (with a flapping black cloak, flung carelessly round its shoulders) and a tragic voice proclaimed: "Oh dark, dark, dark, amid the blaze of noon!"

"Oh, Mr. Marvell, what a fright you gave me!" exclaimed Barbara. "It's only dark in here because of you in the doorway," she added, with her usual commonsense. But she said it kindly because she liked big men, and never made any secret of her predilection.

"Mrs. Abbott!" he returned, sweeping off his soft black hat in a low bow, "I presume you are there! I hear your voice, but you are invisible: 'Blind with the sun, his eagle eyes are dim. The darkness shields her loveliness from him'."

"It's because the pupils don't expand quickly enough," Barbara said, in a friendly tone, "or is it *contract*—I never remember. But I thought eagles' did," she added, a trifle incoherently. "Eagles' and lions'."

"Eagles and lions—The Kings of the Air and the Kings of the Beasts," said Mr. Marvell. "They can look at the sun unblinded by its glare. Have you anything I would like, Miss Carruthers?" he continued, turning to the bird-like librarian and precipitating a pyramid of cheap editions on to the floor with the edge of his cloak.

"Never mind it, Mr. Marvell," said Miss Carruthers, referring, of course, to the accident. "Never mind about it. What kind of book would you like, do you think?"

"A good bedside book—you know my taste."

"A bedside book," agreed Miss Carruthers, licking her fingers and turning over the leaves of her catalogue with rapid flicks. "Let me see now—*Bedfordshire Streams*, no, *Bedlington Terriers*, *Bedding out Plants*, no, no, *Bedlam Memories*, no——"

"Yes," said Mr. Marvell.

"It'll give you nightmare, Mr. Marvell!"

"Never mind, it might be worth it," said Mr. Marvell. "I'll take it—yes—*Bedlam Memories*—Hah!"

He took the book from Miss Carruthers, and he and Barbara left the shop, and walked down the street together.

"And how are you liking our little town?" he enquired.

Barbara assured him that she liked it immensely.

"Good," said Mr. Marvell. "Good. You and your husband must dine with us. I will get Feodore to arrange a day—neighbours, you know—neighbours," said Mr. Marvell in a jovial voice.

"Yes," said Barbara. "Yes, thank you, we should like to come."

"Good," said Mr. Marvell. He was in splendid fettle that morning; various things had conspired together to please him. His agent had written suggesting a private show, and he had just finished a picture, and was convinced that it was the best thing he had done. Mr. Marvell was in the mood for dalliance with a personable woman, and Barbara intrigued him. Before he left her he had discharged several enigmatical quotations at her head, and had complimented her on the elasticity of her walk. The quotations were too literary to be comprehensible, but the compliment to her gait was easily understood—Barbara walked home that morning with tremendous elasticity and told Arthur all about it.

Another day she encountered Mrs. Fitch and Miss Wotton—this was quite a different sort of meeting, of course, but, somehow or other, Barbara "got a kick out of it," as Sam would have said. She saw them coming towards her down the road: the short, stodgy, pudding-like figure of Mrs. Fitch and the trim, angular, anaemic Miss Wotton with her red-rimmed eyes and her blue nose. It was, of course, not their fault that their exteriors were unlovable. God had, presumably, made them what they were. The thought was incredible to Barbara—it was almost blasphemy. Could God have made them? Could He really have intended them to look like that? And, even more incredible, could He have intended them to *be* like that, for their natures were almost as revolting as their appearance (as everybody in Wandlebury could testify). It wasn't their fault, Barbara reminded herself in her usual charitable way. It really wasn't their fault that they were like that. Probably, if they had been asked, Mrs. Fitch and Miss Wotton would have chosen to be young and handsome rather than old and hideous and hairy; to be helpful and capable, rather than a nuisance and a burden to their relations and friends. They were the sort of elderly ladies who were always dropping their bags, mislaying their handkerchiefs, losing their umbrellas, and complaining bitterly to all who would hearken to them of the frightful incompetence of their servants. Miss Wotton was stone deaf, and Mrs. Fitch had a beard—that was not their fault, either, thought Barbara magnanimously, they had not *chosen* deafness, or a beard—but on the other hand, there were such things as ear-trumpets and depilatories. . . .

It's an infliction, Barbara thought, to look like that. Poor old things! People ought to be specially kind to them to make up. So she greeted them with her best smile and pointed out the beauty of the morning; and the very bleakness and drabness and misery of Mrs. Fitch and Miss Wotton made Barbara more aware of her own happiness and content.

All this time Barbara was seeing a good deal

of the Marvell children. They had made a very liberal interpretation of her permission to play in The Archway House garden. They played in it constantly; whenever they could escape from Miss Foddy they made a bee-line for the tree which leaned over the wall and was their means of ingress and egress. Barbara didn't mind. She felt that what Trivvie had said was true; the garden liked them to play in it, and Barbara wanted now (as she had wanted from the beginning) that The Archway House, and incidentally, The Archway House garden, should have exactly what it wanted and deserved. She felt, vaguely, that the garden really belonged to the young Marvells rather than to Arthur and herself. *They* had bought the place, it was true, but what was money, after all (it still seemed strange to Barbara that money had been able to buy The Archway House and all its amenities). Trivvie and Ambrose *knew* the place—they knew every tree, every bush, every bend in the stream, every stone—it was theirs by right of conquest. They knew the place as *she* would never know it if she lived there until she was a hundred years old, for—alas—she had come to it too late. It is only the very young who can make a place their own by an intimate knowledge of its geography.

They can play in the garden, Barbara thought, and I shall get to know them and understand their natures. It will be nice, Barbara thought, soliloquising in her usual colloquial manner, it will be nice for me to get to know some children. I've never known any children at all (there were none at Silverstream, except, of course, Sarah's twins, and they were only babies). Barbara was conscious that it was a Big Want in her that she knew, and had known, no children, since every newspaper and magazine, and almost every book that she opened impressed upon her the importance, and the beauty of the very young, and waxed lyrical over the sincerity, the innocence and the freshness of the opening mind, and pointed out in no uncertain language how much one could learn from the unspoilt simplicity of its Outlook upon Life.

Naturally Barbara was interested—she was an adventurous person and she wanted to experience Life to the full—naturally she looked forward to her friendship with the Marvell children with eager anticipation. Barbara had read and heard so much about this strange subject race of human beings, that she imagined she knew "quite a lot about children," but she soon discovered that nothing she had hitherto heard, or read, or thought about the very young was applicable to her next door neighbours.

The Marvell children were not children, they were savages. The only "childlike" things about them were their greed, their covetousness, their love of freedom. They had none of the virtues that Barbara had been led to expect, not one. But they were most certainly an Experience and an Adventure— Barbara granted them that—sometimes they amused her, and sometimes they annoyed her, and, if she had not had a very keen sense of humour in good working condition, the annoyance would very soon have swamped the amusement she got out of them, and she might have been led to the extreme step of banishing them from their Paradise.

The Marvell children were savages, they were red in tooth and claw. They had an Elizabethan sense of humour, and a truly Elizabethan freedom and ribaldry of speech, Barbara tried hard to get "on terms" with the children, but she never knew where she was with them. Sometimes they flitted from one subject to another like butterflies amongst flowers, so that Barbara was literally breathless in her efforts to follow their thoughts; sometimes they stuck to one subject for days, and could think and talk of nothing else, so that Barbara was bored to death. Sometimes they would converse with Barbara in a reasonable manner, so that she began to feel she was really getting to know them at last, and then, in the middle of the conversation, and for no reason at all, Trivvie would suddenly shake with soundless laughter; she would fling herself on the ground, and roll about convulsed with mysterious mirth, while Ambrose watched her in stolid silence, or remarked, with his usual bland indifference, that she would get hiccups in a minute, or wet her knickers.

On Sundays when Barbara saw them in church, sitting, one on either side of Miss Foddy, washed and brushed, and dressed in their best clothes, and heard them singing in their shrill sweet childish treble:

"We are but little children weak
Nor born in any high estate"

—she could only shake like an aspen leaf with helpless laughter; Trivvie weak, and meek!

she was as meek, and almost as helpless as a full-grown Bengal tiger.

But all this was later, of course, when Barbara had had dealings with the Marvell children, when she had tried to get to know them and failed; when she had invited them to tea, and they had eaten everything provided for them, and asked for more; when they had prepared an elephant pit on the path through the wood, and Barbara had fallen into it and grazed her knees; when they had dammed the stream to make a harbour for their boats, and the stream (naturally annoyed at the restriction) had overflowed its banks and flooded the lower part of the garden; when she had listened, with horror and sympathy, to a circumstantial account of their meeting with a wolf escaped from Bertram Bostock's menagerie (which was in Gostown at the time) and had afterwards discovered, quite by accident, that the whole story was a baseless fabrication.

After the last-mentioned incident Barbara took all they told her with an ample helping of salt, and she found to her horror that more than half they told her required this seasoning. Even when they *seemed* to be telling the truth, the truth was coloured by them, and distorted out of all recognition, and, whether it was so coloured and distorted by vanity—as in the case of the wolf—or by fear—as when they had disclaimed all knowledge of the damming of the stream—or even by a misplaced kindness and consideration for others—as when they had assured Miss Foddy that her petticoat was *not* hanging down below her skirt—the truth was never (when the Marvells had had a hand in it) anything like the clear unvarnished truth as seen by others, so that Barbara began to wonder whether the Marvells *knew* when they were telling the truth and when they were not.

Like sand they ran through Barbara's fingers—ribald, independent, unreliable. They had no sense of responsibility to God nor man. Had they a sense of responsibility to each other, Barbara wondered. It would seem that they had. Even in their most severe quarrels it only required the appearance of one of their common enemies—a "grown-up" connected with their own household—for all their differences to be forgotten, and for them to be banded together in an impregnable alliance. That, thought Barbara, is one of the few things you can really be sure of about them—their loyalty to each other—and, after all, it is a good deal. Another thing that mitigated the barbarity of the Marvell children in Barbara's eyes was their love of beauty. In Ambrose the love of beauty was a placid sort of admiration, but in Trivvie it was a fierce passion. She loved beauty and she hated ugliness with all the intensity of her young and vital nature. She loved the dog-roses in the hedge at the bottom of the garden, and the little swamp which bordered the stream with its brave show of flags; she loved the horse-chestnuts that she and Ambrose garnered so assiduously—they were so smooth and brown and shining when you took them out of their close-fitting shells. ("They're like little jewel-cases," Trivvie explained, and, for that delightful simile, Barbara forgave her a good deal.) Her hatreds were equally acute. She hated ugliness in people—Mrs. Fitch and Miss Wotton, for instance, were anathema to Trivvie—and she hated ugly things—old, worn-down bedroom-slippers, and hair-brushes that had lost their bristles, and the stain in the bottom of the bath where the paint had peeled off—it was bluish red, like a bruise—these things made her shudder with horror.

231

Barbara gradually learned these things about the Marvells. She learned, too, that the Marvells, like all savages, had superstitions and taboos. Trivvie would rather have died than walk under a ladder, she was miserable for days if a mirror were broken, or a black cat crossed her path, or if she saw a solitary magpie in the wood. There were certain words that must never be said, and certain trees which Trivvie never passed without touching lightly with her hand. Barbara never learnt more than a tenth of all these strange rites, and never knew the meaning nor the origin of those she saw—she doubted whether the Marvells themselves knew the meaning or the origin of them.

The Marvells continued to play in the garden and Barbara continued to find excuses for their misdemeanours; she excused them to herself, and to Miss Foddy, and also to Arthur, who was legitimately annoyed at the damming of the stream (Arthur would have been even more annoyed if he had heard about the elephant pit, but Barbara kept that piece of wickedness to herself) but sometimes it was difficult to find excuses, and, sometimes, quite impossible, and at last Barbara decided that she must just take the Marvells as she found them and make the best of it.

Meanwhile Sam came down to The Archway House for several long week-ends. It was essential that he should get the full benefit of his riding lessons, and Arthur and Barbara liked having him, and it required very little hinting on Sam's part to wangle an invitation out of Uncle Arthur. He was rather a subdued Sam, Barbara thought, subdued and slightly vague at times, and he had lost a good deal of his youthful cheek which had amused them so much during his first visit. She spoke to Arthur about it.

"I wonder what's the matter with Sam," she said.

"Sam!" echoed Arthur. "There's nothing the matter with Sam. He's settling down now and really working. You were quite right about him, Barbara."

"Perhaps he's working too hard," said Barbara anxiously.

Arthur roared with laughing.

The truth was that Sam was worrying about Jerry. He was not getting "any forrader" with Jerry, and he couldn't understand it. He came down and rode; he met her at tea with Barbara; he walked home with her several times through the winter's nights;

but, although Jerry was polite and friendly, she held him at arm's length, and no wiles, no stratagems could break down the invisible barrier she had erected. Sam couldn't understand it at all, he was not used to this kind of treatment, he could usually do what he liked with the female species of his acquaintance. Girls went down like ninepins before him—in vulgar parlance they threw themselves at his head—but the one girl that he wanted was absolutely unapproachable. If Jerry had wanted to complete her conquest of Sam and bind him to her with fetters of steel, she could not have taken a surer or more certain way of achieving her object, but Jerry didn't want Sam, she had made up her mind of that. She was far too frank and straightforward to act one thing and mean another, and her unapproachable manner was intended to show Sam that she had no use for him—to warn him off.

Jerry had no use for Sam, but she had plenty of use for Barbara (if the expression can be allowed), she and Barbara became friends. There was ten years difference in their ages, but that did not seem to matter. Jerry was old and wise for her years, and Barbara was young for hers. Sometimes

Barbara felt that Jerry was older than herself. It was natural in a way, for Barbara had led a very sheltered life, and Jerry had shouldered responsibilities, and there is nothing more ageing to the young than responsibilities bravely shouldered, and troubles courageously borne. Jerry had her meed of both, and she came and poured them out to Barbara and felt all the better for it. She told Barbara some of her troubles—but not all—she told her all about the horses, their spavins and their overreaches, and Dough-Boy's cough, and the blue roan who had turned out to be a cribbiter, and she told her about the owners of the horses, and how exacting and unreasonable they were; and she told her about the frightful worries she was having with her maids; but she didn't tell Barbara much about Archie, because, for one thing, she felt it wasn't very fair to Archie to discuss him, and, for another, Archie's delinquencies were not very suitable to be retailed *in toto* to an innocent like her new friend. So, when Barbara enquired after her brother, Jerry replied vaguely that he was "living in town" or "still looking for a job—it's so difficult to find a job nowadays," and Barbara had no idea that Archie's vagaries were causing his sister wakeful nights.

Mr. Tupper (of Messrs. Tupper, Tyler, & Tupper) was also concerned about Archie Cobbe's behaviour, though not to the extent of allowing it to interfere with his slumbers. He visited Jerry one afternoon—much to her amazement—and besought her to make her brother find suitable employment.

"He's looking for a job, he can't find one," said Jerry firmly, for, whatever her own opinion of Archie might be, she was loyal to the backbone and nobody but herself had any right to criticize him.

"He is spending money very freely," Mr. Tupper said. "I happen to know that he is deeply in debt and is making no attempt to curtail his expenses. It is *deplorable*."

Jerry knew this, too, and deplored it even more deeply than Mr. Tupper, but she was not going to say so. "It's because he knows that money is coming to him," she said frankly. "It's so very unsettling for a young man."

Mr. Tupper was shocked at this bald statement, he was also extremely perturbed and uncomfortable, for he was aware that money was not coming to the young gentleman in question. It was an extremely delicate subject.

"It is better not to rely too much upon—ahem—expectations," he allowed himself to say.

"That's what I think," Jerry agreed. "And I've told Archie dozens of times. But Archie's very young, and you know what boys are."

"Archie is now twenty-five," said Mr. Tupper. "Two years older than you are, I believe."

"Yes, but then I'm not a boy," Jerry told him seriously.

He smiled, for he liked Jerry. And then he thought of Archie again, and frowned. "Something must be done," he said weightily. "As you know, I am one of your trustees, and I cannot allow things to continue in this unsatisfactory way. I shall go up to town and see Archie myself. If he cannot find congenial employment in London he must return to Ganthorne."

"Yes," said Jerry without enthusiasm.

"Would it be possible for you to employ Archie here, in your—ahem—business?" enquired Mr. Tupper.

"Oh yes, of course I could," Jerry said. "I'd love to have him, of course, but you see

237

he doesn't like it—and it's difficult. I mean it's difficult to have a person living with you and being bored."

"Then he must find employment in London and stick to it," said Mr. Tupper, rising as he spoke. "I shall tell him so to-morrow, and I shall tell him plainly."

No wonder Jerry was disturbed. It was all frightfully worrying. Of course, Mr. Tupper made no impression on Archie, he went on as before, and the only thing that Mr. Tupper had accomplished by his interference was to salve his own conscience and to alarm Jerry and make her worry more. Jerry found Barbara very soothing and comforting during this difficult time. It was not necessary to confide in Barbara to gain her sympathy—you just talked to Barbara about odds and ends of things, and you came away feeling a different creature. Jerry rode over to The Archway House as often as she could, they talked about everything under the sun (except erring brothers) and consumed gallons of tea and quantities of crumpets—for Jerry's digestion was quite as good as Barbara's, and she was always hungry at tea-time.

It was a very satisfactory friendship, for

Barbara profited by it too. Jerry enlarged Barbara enormously. In a new friend we start life anew, for we create a new edition of ourselves and so become, for the time being, a new creature. Barbara had never done this interesting thing before. She had lived all her life in Silverstream and her neighbours were people who had known her from childhood, and therefore had a preconceived idea of her, so engrained, that they never *saw* her at all, any more than they saw the sponge which accompanied them daily into their baths. In creating a new Barbara for Jerry Cobbe, Barbara created a new facet of herself and was enlarged by it. She had no idea she was doing anything of the sort, of course, she merely felt that life had become very interesting, and that she, herself, was more adequate to its demands.

15

MORE NEW FRIENDS

JERRY COBBE was not the only friend that Barbara made that winter; she was the first and most important, and Mrs. Thane was the second. Barbara went to return the Thanes' call in some trepidation. She expected—on the information received from Mrs. Dance—to find a querulous invalid and a down-trodden daughter, but the Thanes were "not a bit like that." Mrs. Thane was a woman who had seen a great deal of trouble; she was disciplined to suffering; she was calm and patient; she bore her semi-invalid life and occasional pain with cheerfulness and fortitude. It was not the life she would have chosen (for she had an active mind and was intensely interested in People and Things), but she made the best of it and created a little world of her own. She could not go out into the world, but she created an atmosphere round about her, and the world came to her. Candia Thane was a large young woman, rather awkward in limb and tactless in speech. She was full of undisciplined vitality; impulsive and—to some people of lesser stamina—overpowering. Barbara liked them both (she had lots of stamina, of course). Mrs. Thane commanded her respect and Candia her affection. Candia's rather like *me*, Barbara thought, only more so.

When Barbara arrived there were two other ladies in the Thanes' drawing-room. She arrived in the middle of a discussion upon international politics. "Look at India," one of the ladies was saying. "Yes, but look at Japan," urged the other with intense vehemence. Barbara was introduced to the ladies, of course, but she never heard their names. They were already labelled, much more legibly in her retentive memory, as Mrs. Japan and Mrs. India. She was rather crushed at the far-sightedness of the two ladies—what did they see when they looked at Japan and India like that? Did their bird's-eye glance take in the whole of these Asiatic countries at a glance? Were India and Japan open before their eyes like a child's picture book? Barbara tried hard to "look at India," but all she could see was a pink excrescence like a plump baby carrot, sticking out into a

241

pale-blue sea at the southern extremity of Asia. But I haven't got an imagination, she reminded herself sadly.

After the two ladies had gone—and they went very soon—Barbara had a nice little chat with the Thanes. In age Barbara was half-way between the elderly mother and the young daughter, and she felt in sympathy with them both. She was of the transition generation, and therefore adaptable.

"Mrs. Gadgeby is very intense," said Mrs. Thane, "an interesting woman, of course, but slightly tiring."

"Is that Mrs. India or Mrs. Japan?" Barbara enquired.

Mrs. Thane was naturally a trifle surprised at the question, but when Barbara had explained matters she understood and was amused. It appeared that Mrs. Gadgeby was Mrs. India.

"I shall call her Mrs. Gandhi," said Candia, giggling.

"But not to her face, I hope," remonstrated Candia's mother.

"She'd never notice if I did," replied Candia promptly.

This little incident broke the ice, and the conversation flowed on very comfortably.

Mrs. Thane enquired whether Barbara had seen much of her next-door neighbours—the Marvell children. She was pleased to call them "the blue-eyed banditti," for she was of the generation that delights in Longfellow. Barbara replied that she had seen a good deal of them, and amused her new friends with an account of Trivvie and Ambrose, and their doings. Mrs. Thane was somewhat scandalized but not inordinately so, for she had moved with the times and was wise enough to take things as they were. She had been born in the days when children were taught to venerate the aged, but she had lived long enough to learn that she could count upon no respect from the young.

"In my young days," said Mrs. Thane smiling whimsically, "in my young days the liver wing of the chicken was given to the grown-ups and now they keep it for the children."

Candia exclaimed at that—"What rot!" she cried. "You always have the liver wing, Mother."

"Unless my grandchildren are here," Mrs. Thane agreed, laughingly. "But I'm lucky, you see. As a matter of fact," she continued more seriously, "my little remark was in-

243

tended symbolically. In my youth it was the middle-aged who ruled and the young were 'young and foolish,' and did not openly protest. But now, it is the other way about; the young think their elders foolish and make it very clear. I've sometimes wondered whether my generation was *really* foolish. A foolish generation sandwiched between two strong-minded clever generations, squashed between two mill-stones; over-ridden in youth, by age; stamped upon in age by youth. And the next generation (the children of the people who are now young) what will they be like? Will they be over-ridden by the strong-minded young, grown to middle-age? Will they be stamped upon first by their elders and then by their children? Is it a case of once a door-mat, always a door-mat?" enquired Mrs. Thane smiling.

"There isn't much door-mat about *you*," Candia said with conviction.

"I'm the exception that proves the rule," said her mother promptly. "But I've talked quite enough, it's Mrs. Abbott's turn now."

"I can't talk," Barbara told them seriously. "At least I can sometimes, but when I start I can't stop, and it's always frightfully muddled. I never know how people manage to say things that they feel. I feel things, of course, but they won't come out. I think there's a kind of block somewhere."

Barbara came away from the Thanes' feeling pleased with herself and pleased with them—a very agreeable state of mind. They're nice and friendly, she thought. Mrs. Thane's very interesting, and Candia's a dear. She didn't know, of course, that the Thanes were equally pleased with her—but it was so.

"I like her immensely," Mrs. Thane said, with surprise, when Candia returned to the drawing-room after showing Barbara out.

"Oh, you never can go by what Elva Dance says," replied Candia elliptically.

"Poor Elva!" said Mrs. Thane laughing. "I wonder what she told Mrs. Abbott about us."

*   *   *

When Barbara got home after her visit to the Thanes' she found Jerry Cobbe in her drawing-room.

"They said you wouldn't be long so I waited," Jerry told her.

"I'm so glad you did," Barbara exclaimed,

pushing a chair up to the fire for her unexpected, but ever-welcome guest.

"I wanted to see you 'specially'," continued Jerry, "not that I don't always want to see you—but things have happened——"

"What things?" enquired Barbara, with her usual keen interest in the affairs of others.

"Hyacinth and Poppy have GONE," said Jerry dramatically.

Barbara was aware that these flowery names were the names of Jerry's maids, and she was suitably sympathetic with her friend in the domestic crisis that the departure of her staff had occasioned.

"Goodness!" she exclaimed. "Both at once?"

"Both at once," nodded Jerry. "But I'm not really sorry, you know. They were a frightful trial to me. Rose and Ivy were bad enough, but Hyacinth and Poppy were absolutely the limit. What names, too!" continued Jerry wearily, tearing off her beret and throwing it on to the floor. "What names!"

"Yes," agreed Barbara, nodding sympathetically, *"What names!"*

"I think Mother would have had a fit if she had had to engage a cook called Hyacinth. Cooks, in Mother's day, were always called

Jane, or Ellen, or sometimes Mary—and they could cook, too, which was another advantage."

Barbara agreed again.

"I know it's dull for them," said Jerry, trying to be strictly impartial, "and the lamps are a nuisance, of course, but I can't help that. I can't move my house nearer to a cinema to suit my maids, and I can't afford to put electric light into it—I wish to goodness I could——"

"I know," said Barbara, in her most sympathetic voice. "What *are* you going to do?"

"I'm going to have Markie to live with me."

"Markie?" enquired Barbara.

"Yes. I rang up Markie yesterday, when Hyacinth and Poppy had gone, and fixed the whole thing. Markie and I can run the house together quite easily, and I can get one of the grooms to come in and do the heavy work. I think it ought to work out all right. I really do——"

"But who——" began Barbara.

"You see Markie is out of a job," continued Jerry smiling cheerfully, "and when I suggested it she seemed quite pleased at the idea of coming to live with me. It isn't really her line, of course, but—well—she likes me, you see. And, of course, it will be awfully nice for me to have dear old Markie to talk to in the evening. It's a bit dull with nobody there. Archie is still——"

"But who *is* Markie?" demanded Barbara.

"Markie!" exclaimed Jerry, raising her eyebrows in surprise. "Oh, of course, I forgot you don't know Markie. I'm always forgetting you've just come to Wandlebury. I feel as if I'd known you for years, and years, and years."

Barbara smiled. She was very glad Jerry felt *that* because she felt the same about Jerry, but she was still no nearer knowing who "Markie" was—this mysterious being who was to solve Jerry's domestic problem so satisfactorily.

"Who is Markie?" she asked, for the third time (for Barbara, when her interest was aroused, was a most pertinacious creature). "Who *is* Markie, Jerry?"

"Markie is really Miss Marks, my old governess," explained Jerry. "I never went to school, you know. Father wouldn't let me, and, of course, I had a splendid time at home with all the horses and hunting, and all that—so I never wanted to go. Sometimes I think it would have been better if I *had* gone to school, I wouldn't have felt so different from other girls—but that's neither here nor there," she added, "the point is I didn't go to school. I stayed at home and had Markie instead. I had her for ages, and she did all she could to educate me, and it really wasn't her fault that she didn't manage it better. It was partly my fault—I hated lessons—and partly Father's fault. If Father was going to ride he just came and dragged me away from Markie, and, of course, I was delighted—and off we went. What fun it was!" said Jerry, with a sigh for the good old days.

"Yes, it must have been," agreed her friend.

"Markie's frightfully clever, you know," Jerry continued stretching out her legs in their brown jodhpurs. "She's the sort of person who can turn her hand to anything. She can conjugate Latin verbs, or turn out a perfectly scrumptious omelet, or make beds, or keep accounts, and all the time she doesn't think she's being clever at all, she's so nice and kind and sort of *modest* about it. So you see," Jerry added, looking across at Barbara with her clear, frank, grey eyes, "you see I'm frightfully lucky to have got her."

Barbara saw that she was. She was indeed frightfully lucky, for she had really had a desperate time with maids.

Ganthorne Lodge was tucked away amongst the moors, there were no modern conveniences, and the nearest bus route was two miles from the house. Servants hated the place—as well they might—and found nothing to relieve the tedium of their existence except flirting with the grooms or quarrelling with each other. Jerry's problem had been getting more and more acute, and Barbara was thankful that it was now solved in such a satisfactory manner.

"I'm glad," she said sincerely. "I really *am* glad about it, Jerry. When is Markie coming?"

"To-morrow," said Jerry promptly. "You see the poor darling's out of a job. She's a little deaf now, and people don't realise how frightfully marvellous she is. So she simply leapt at the idea of coming back to me as a sort of glorified cook-general—it's rather pathetic, somehow."

16

CONVERSATION AT THE MARVELLS'

IT was the night of the Marvells' dinner party. Arthur and Barbara decided to walk, for the house was next door and the night was fine. There were bright stars in the sky, and the moon would rise—so Arthur said—at eight forty-five. It would light them home. Barbara hoped there would be no ping-pong, she was sure Arthur would not take to it kindly, and all her evening frocks had "tails". She was carrying her "tail" now, and her other hand was held securely in the crook of Arthur's arm. Barbara enjoyed the little walk, she loved a starry night, and she loved the feeling of being taken care of by her nice big husband.

"We needn't stay late if you're bored," she assured him, as they turned in at the Marvells' gate and walked up the little drive.

"My dear lamb," said Arthur, in his "smiling voice." "I don't go out to dinner expecting to be bored, do I?"

"I thought you were, a little," Barbara explained, and then she added with her usual desire to be strictly truthful. "In fact I know you were."

Arthur laughed.

Mrs. Marvell was alone in the drawing-room when the Abbotts were announced. She had intended to invite people to meet the Abbotts, but she had put it off from day to day, and had finally decided it was too late. She explained this to Barbara. Barbara found it difficult to think of the right reply. Should she say "What a pity!" or should she say "How nice to be just ourselves!" or should she merely say that it didn't matter? Eventually the moment for saying anything passed, and she had said nothing—which, perhaps, was best of all.

Mr. Marvell came in with a tray of glasses which he handed round, remarking that it was his own invention—a cocktail with a real kick. He was extremely upset by Barbara's refusal to try it, but she was adamant. Mr. Marvell looked bigger than ever in his own house (for his house was extremely small), he was massive, bigger than Arthur, both in height and girth.

"What a night!" he exclaimed, in his loud

booming voice, "what a glorious night!" They all agreed that it was.

Unfortunately there was not much to say about the night, except that it was glorious, and marvellous for the time of year, and that the stars were extraordinarily bright, and the air as clear as crystal, and when all this had been said, the conversation flagged a little. The Abbotts and the Marvells had not very much in common. Mrs. Marvell never bothered to talk for talking's sake, and Barbara was an observer rather than a conversationalist. She liked to be with people who talked a lot, so that she could listen, or not, as she felt inclined. Mr. Abbott knew nothing about Art. Mr. Marvell knew nothing about Business. It was all rather difficult.

The food was not very nice, it was pretentious and inadequate; but Mr. Marvell produced some excellent claret, which was a help, and, when he had had a few glasses of it, he began to warm up. Mr. Abbott also began to feel better, and decided that it was up to him, as a man of the world, to get in touch with his host. He can't talk about business, so I must talk about painting, thought Mr. Abbott, with three glasses of Château Lafîte 1917 warming the cockles of his heart.

"What is your opinion of this New Art?" he enquired.

"There is nothing new in Art," replied Mr. Marvell didactically. "It has all been done before, but I suppose you are alluding to cubism?"

Mr. Abbott said he *was*—he really had very little idea as to what he had been alluding to, but this answer seemed fairly safe. Mr. Marvell evidently expected a reply in the affirmative and Mr. Abbott felt he deserved it—the claret was excellent.

"All Art," said Mr. Marvell in his resonant voice. "All Art is a mystic experience of its creator. I cannot allow that cubism is Art, for here we find the technical devices, instead of being aids to the transmission of experience, becoming the aim and the end of their users."

"Yes," said Mr. Abbott, "yes. I've always thought there was something lacking in it."

"Lacking!" boomed Mr. Marvell, "of course there's something lacking. It lacks soul. Technical proficiency is not enough. If a man has the virility to break away from the main stream of tradition he can be forgiven for his boldness if he has something important to say—but not otherwise—not otherwise."

"Exactly," agreed Mr. Abbott. He was

really doing splendidly. He caught Barbara's eye, and saw that she was tremendously impressed by his cleverness.

"Let us go back," suggested Mr. Marvell. "Let us return and find a parallel in the history of Art, or, if we cannot find a parallel, let us at least try to find something of the same nature."

"That would be difficult," suggested Mr. Abbott boldly.

"Difficult but not impossible," said Mr. Marvell. "Not impossible, I think."

Mr. Abbott tried to look as if he were considering the history of Art with a view to finding something approaching the modern situation.

"Take the vertiginous figures of El Greco," offered Mr. Marvell generously. "What do we find there?"

Mr. Abbott had no idea what they found there, so, very wisely, he said nothing.

"We find," continued Mr. Marvell, "we find a lack of humanity which we now account for by the conclusion that El Greco was an anaphrodite."

"Really!" said Mr. Abbott. He looked at Mrs. Marvell and his wife, sitting there listening—but perhaps they had not understood.

"Yes," said Mr. Marvell with relish, "an anaphrodite. It is impossible to paint a human body without experiencing it humanly, hence the inhumanity of El Greco's Art. His Art, I say, because he was a true artist in that he expressed his own experience in his chosen medium."

"Very interesting," murmured Mr. Abbott, politely.

"Thus we get El Greco treating the human body as a decoration—to him it was a decoration and no more—he became more and more indifferent to fact, and the figures lost what little humanity they possessed. It was blasphemy," added Mr. Marvell. *"It was blasphemy."*

"Blasphemy!" exclaimed Mr. Abbott in surprise.

"He thought he knew what was beautiful better than God," explained Mr. Marvell simply.

Mr. Abbott was really interested now, he saw the point. He looked at his host with new eyes. The man was not a charlatan after all, he was sincere, and he knew what he was talking about. Mr. Abbott felt as if Mr.

Marvell had taken him by the hand and was leading him into a new country, a country of which he had never suspected the existence. It would be rather interesting to explore the country, to climb its hills and view the land under the guidance of Mr. Marvell. He was about to penetrate further into the new country when Barbara took a hand in the conversation.

"Have you painted your children's portraits, Mr. Marvell?" she enquired.

Mr. Marvell groaned. "My children are unpaintable," he lamented. "Absolutely unpaintable. If ever a miserable painter was cursed with unpaintable children——"

'But Ambrose is so pretty!" Barbara exclaimed.

Mr. Marvell nearly tore his hair, but not quite, for he was very proud of its thickness and luxuriance. "Ambrose!" he cried. "Paint Ambrose! For the lid of a chocolate box, I presume. Trivona is paintable, I admit (her bones are good, and the texture of her skin takes the light well). Trivona, I say, is paintable, but what use is that when she cannot pose for two consecutive minutes without fidgeting? Ambrose could pose for an hour but has the face of a Botticelli angel—My

257

God!" said Mr. Marvell, violently, "I could paint Ambrose with my eyes shut. An Artschool would leap at Ambrose. Here am I, stuck in the depths of the country with no models to be had for love or money, and God afflicts me with Trivona and Ambrose."

Barbara was dumbfounded, she was even a little frightened by Mr. Marvell's genuine distress. She was wondering what topic she could introduce to change the subject, when Arthur came to the rescue.

"You have another son, haven't you?" he enquired, "we haven't seen him yet."

"Lancreste has been away from home off and on," replied Mr. Marvell, wiping his forehead with a large bandana handkerchief. "Yes, he has been staying with some of our relations near the sea—Bournemouth in fact. Lancreste is not strong—he takes after his mother's side in that."

"I like their names," Barbara said. "So very unusual, aren't they?"

"Very unusual and somewhat foolish," replied their father. "Tell me the name of a child, and I will tell you the age of its parents. Your parents burden their offspring with fantastic sobriquets—Lancreste, Trivona, Ambrose, these are the choice of a callow mind. If I had a child, now, I should christen it William or Mary, Henry or Jane—or Ellen——"

"Not Ellen," said Mrs. Marvell, suddenly, in her deep, rather husky voice. "Not Ellen, dear."

"Yes, Ellen," said Mr. Marvell firmly. "Why not Ellen? It is a beautiful name, simple as an Ionic column."

"But so housemaidy," objected his wife. "And, anyway, if you like it so much, why didn't you say so when Trivona was born? You were not so very much younger then."

"Ten years," Mr. Marvell reminded her.

It was another *cul de sac*. An embarrassed silence fell on the ill-assorted party. Mrs. Marvell rose from the table suddenly and made for the door, and Barbara, realising that the meal was over, followed. Despite the fact that she was still hungry, she was quite glad to leave the table.

"Would you like to see the children?" Mrs. Marvell enquired.

Barbara said she would—what else could she say—and they went upstairs and looked at Trivona and Ambrose asleep in their beds. Ambrose looked much the same, asleep or awake, peaceful, and adorably pretty, with

259

his fair hair and rounded pink cheeks. Barbara, looking at him, could understand *even less* why his father would not paint him. He would make such a lovely picture, she thought. As she turned from him and looked at Trivona, she was assailed by a vague feeling of discomfort, for there was something very pathetic in the sleeping Trivvie. By day she was a rebel, full of the lust of life, battling for power, and yet more power, for freedom and yet more freedom; but, asleep, she was innocent, helpless. vulnerable. Barbara felt it was wrong to see Trivvie thus; it was like a treachery. Trivvie would hate to be seen without her armour on.

"Sweet, aren't they?" Mrs. Marvell whispered.

"Sweet," agreed Barbara, thinking of the elephant pit.

She looked round the nursery for Miss Foddy, but Miss Foddy was not to be seen. She had not appeared at dinner, and was still invisible. Barbara wondered where she was. The house was very small, and, although Miss Foddy was not very big, there did not seem sufficient cover to conceal her. Her bed was in the children's room; a small chaste bed, discreetly decked in a white-linen coverlet; and Miss Foddy's nightwear was discreetly hidden in a white-linen case with her initials worked in the corner. On the table beside her bed lay Miss Foddy's Bible, and a candle in a candlestick of white china, and a small tuppenny packet of bicarbonate of soda which Miss Foddy resorted to when visited by indigestion—it was all rather pathetic, Barbara thought.

"What would you like to do?" enquired Mrs. Marvell, vaguely, as they came down the steep stairs in single file. Barbara had suspected all the evening that Mrs. Marvell was not a very good hostess—she was now sure of it. If I don't say something, it will be ping-pong, Barbara thought, and anyhow she's *asked* me.

"I'd like to see Mr. Marvell's studio," she said, boldly.

"Would you?" enquired Mrs. Marvell. "Well, ask him, then."

"Will he mind?"

"He may, or he may not. It depends upon whether he's taken a fancy to you," replied Mrs. Marvell with devastating frankness.

Apparently Mr. Marvell *had* taken a fancy to Barbara (however unlikely it might have appeared in view of the way he had squashed her at dinner). He agreed at once to show her his studio. They left Mr. Abbott and Mrs. Marvell in the drawing-room, and went along a little passage and down three steps into the garden. It was bitterly cold. The moon had risen—as Arthur had so cleverly predicted—and shone down upon the Marvells' garden with a round, smooth, kindly face.

"How white a woman is, under the moon!" exclaimed Mr. Marvell in his loud sonorous voice as they went down the little path together towards a large barn-like building, which loomed up amongst the leafless trees. Barbara was a trifle startled at his words, but she comforted herself with the reflection that Mr. Marvell was probably quoting poetry—she hoped it was that.

Mr. Marvell unlocked the door of his studio, switched on the light, and motioned Barbara to enter.

The studio was a large rectangular room, full of the usual impedimenta. There was a dais, several easels, canvases in various stages of completion, lay figures with coloured draperies, chairs, stools, a divan, and a large solid table covered with paints and bottles and dirty rags and knives and brushes and palettes of different shapes and sizes. There were one or two good rugs, and an electric stove with a long flex. Mr. Marvell turned on the stove, remarking that it was cold.

Barbara was too interested in what she saw to notice the cold. She said so, adding, with her usual naïvety that she had never known "a real artist" before. The admission pleased Mr. Marvell, who read into the phrase rather more than was intended. Barbara had meant that she had never known a professional artist before. Mr. Marvell thought she meant that she had never known a true artist.

"We are rare," admitted Mr. Marvell with a self-satisfied purr.

"Oh you *are*," Barbara agreed.

Mr. Marvell proceeded to show his guest some of his work. He kept up a running commentary during the process, pointing out the various effects, and talking glibly about the grouping and the angle of the light. He thought he was talking down to the level of Barbara's obvious ignorance, but, even so, his listener only understood about a quarter of what she was hearing. What she did understand was rather embarrassing. One particular study of his wife seemed to Mr. Marvell particularly interesting. Barbara was invited to admire the richness of the impasto, the subtle flesh tones, and the balance of light and shade. She tried to admire all these truly admirable effects, but the subject of the picture was too breath-taking to allow her to bring her critical faculties into play. It was a back view of Mrs. Marvell with nothing on at all; she was lying on the divan, and was, presumably, asleep. The picture was extraordinarily life-like, but this only added to Barbara's discomfort. Mr. Marvell proceeded to tear the picture to pieces (metaphorically, of course). He pointed out its merits and defects with sincerity; he pointed out how the light fell upon the different portions of the model's anatomy, referring to these portions with a total lack of euphemism.

Goodness! thought Barbara, I'm glad Arthur's not here. She was aware that Arthur would not have liked it at all, and, the mere fact of Arthur not liking it, would have made it all seem a thousand times worse. I'm broadminded, of course, thought Barbara. It was a comforting thought. The mere fact of thinking that she was "broadminded" made her so. She mastered her alarm and confusion and made up her mind not to be shocked. This was all the easier because Mr. Marvell was so matter of fact about the whole thing—the picture might have been a still life of a jar of roses, or of a cabbage rather than the naked figure of his wife. After all, he's her husband, thought Barbara vaguely, and that seemed to help.

17

MORE CONVERSATION

ONCE Barbara had decided not to be
shocked at Mr. Marvell's pictures she
began to find them rather interesting
and, once she began to find them interesting,
she began to ask questions. Mr. Marvell
answered the questions conscientiously—they
were puerile questions, of course (Trivona was
infinitely more knowledgeable), but Barbara
interested and amused him. He was no less
pleased with her as a woman for her abysmal
ignorance on the subject of painting. Mr.
Marvell held the view, advanced satirically
by Jane Austen, that "imbecility in females is
a great enhancement of their personal
charms." He didn't quite know why he was
interested in Barbara. She was not particularly good-looking; she was not clever or fascinating; she was extraordinarily devoid of
that mysterious modern attribute, "sex
appeal"; in fact she had nothing unique
except her essential innocence—if innocence

it was. Mr. Marvell found her baffling. He had suspected for a while that her innocence was really subtlety—no woman could really be as innocent as Barbara seemed, so absolutely natural and simple-minded—but now he wasn't so sure. She was an enigma.

"Tell me," said Barbara, "why don't you like painting a pretty child like Ambrose? I can't help thinking he would make a beautiful picture."

"My dear lady!" he said, "my dear lady, there are different kinds of beauty, you'll grant me that, I hope."

Barbara granted it to him willingly.

"Beauty," said Mr. Marvell, "beauty is a dangerous word to use—what is beauty? Tell me that."

Barbara remained dumb. She knew what beauty was, but she was now aware that Mr. Marvell thought it was something quite different, and she was a little frightened of him again.

"Beauty," continued Mr. Marvell in his resonant voice, "is the greatest force in the world. Take a woman with beauty. She has in her hands an extremely powerful weapon, which she can use for good or evil. If all the beautiful women in the world could combine they could change the whole world—nothing would be beyond them, literally nothing. But beauty and intelligence rarely go hand in hand (for intelligence writes upon a face), and perhaps this is fortunate. Marry intelligence to beauty and beget ambition. A King's mistress!" cried Mr. Marvell (so carried away by his theme as to become somewhat incoherent). "Was Maintenon beautiful? Was Mary of Scotland beautiful? Or Nell Gwynne? What is beauty? A mere question of bones."

"Bones?" enquired Barbara in amazement.

"Bones," said Mr. Marvell firmly. "I could paint *you*," he continued, looking at her with a strangely impersonal stare, "I could *paint* you. You have good bones; your face is well constructed; the proportions are almost right. I could paint you and make you 'beautiful'—as you call it—are you offended?"

"I think it's rather a compliment," said Barbara slowly.

Mr. Marvell laughed. "Some people would say it was 'rather an insult'," he told her.

"Well, of course, if they were beautiful it *would* be," said Barbara with strict justice, "because they wouldn't need any alteration, would they? But I still don't see how you could paint me, and make me beautiful, and it would still be *me*."

"I would add on a little to your nose, and subtract a little from your mouth," said Mr. Marvell, grinning at her, impudently. "There are one or two other small details, of course, but these are the main alterations I would make—are you offended *now*?"

"No," said Barbara, smiling at him. "I know my mouth's too big, you see."

"Then it's hopeless," Mr. Marvell told her. "Quite hopeless. You are absolutely unique amongst women."

"Did you want to offend me?" she enquired.

"I thought you deserved it," he replied. "But now I'm not so sure. In fact, I'm almost sure you didn't."

He looked at her to see if she understood, but it was obvious that she had no idea what he was getting at. Her eyes met his with childlike honesty—it was almost impossible to flirt with a woman who was so unaware. What had she wanted when she lured him out here, wondered Mr. Marvell. It almost looked as if she had wanted to see his work—and yet how could she have wanted to see his work? The woman scarcely knew one end of a paintbrush from the other. . . .

She was looking round the studio again, now, and realising, with surprise, that all these women, clothed, partially clothed, and completely unclothed, were Mrs. Marvell.

"Why is it?" she enquired, "why is it that the pictures are all different? I mean they're all Mrs. Marvell and yet, if you saw them without knowing, you'd think they were all different people. I hope you don't mind me asking," she added, a trifle diffidently.

"Most interesting!" said Mr. Marvell gazing at her, "you find them so different. The answer to your question is—I am an artist."

Barbara had known that before, she looked at him blankly.

"We then ask ourselves," continued Mr. Marvell in his booming voice, "we then ask ourselves—what is an artist? What manner of creature is this that sees his wife differently every time he looks at her? And we find the answer *here*," said Mr. Marvell, striking himself on the chest with a dull thump. "The artist is a creature of moods—what he experiences, *that* he expresses. I experience my wife as a large stately woman—I paint a Juno. I experience my wife as a languorous beauty—I paint a Récamier. I experience my wife as a sparkling courtesan—I paint a Ninon de L'Enclos. I experience the gamin in my wife—I paint a guttersnipe."

"Yes," said Barbara breathlessly.

"I have, therefore, in my wife a variety of models," said Mr. Marvell complacently, "and the fact that I live in the backwoods, where professional models are unprocurable, is less of a disadvantage to me than it would be to another. I think I may say that I have made a virtue of necessity, for I have now painted Feodore so often that I can appreciate her finer shades. The small difference, for instance, between the Feodore of to-day and the Feodore of last week—Amazing!" added Mr. Marvell, shaking his leonine head. "Amazing!"

Barbara agreed that it was.

"Art is always amazing," he continued. "All Art," he cried, throwing out his arms as if to embrace a Universe of Art. "I am not one of those moribund creatures who deny inspiration to my fellow men. My own medium satisfies *me*, but who am I that I should limit Art to one medium? Take the musician—the composer—he perceives the spirit of Art through the organ of hearing; he experiences emotion through the ear, and, through the ear, he gives himself to the

271

World. Take the author—he appeals to a different sense. With what care and judgment he builds his book. Keeping in view a sustained line from start to finish, with every part in due relation to the whole. Stone by stone he——"

"Oh no, he doesn't!" Barbara interrupted.

"I beg your pardon——"

"I said *no, he doesn't*," repeated Barbara firmly. "It isn't like that at all, it isn't like building—not a bit. In building, you see, you know beforehand what it's going to be like—at least I suppose you do. I mean it would never do to start off building a house and find you've built a bridge, or something, when it was all finished. It's more like hunting, really," said Barbara, warming up to her subject. "Yes, it's really like hunting. You start out to hunt a stag and you find the tracks of a tiger. It's an adventure, you see, that's the beauty of it. You don't know a bit what you're going to find until you come to the end, and, even then, you don't know what you've *found*—at least you know what you've found for yourself but you don't know if you've found anything for anybody else—but that doesn't matter, really, the only thing that matters is that you *must* find *something*—some

272

sort of—well—prey. Otherwise it's no good, of course. You go questing about, like a—like a hound, and sometimes you get lost, of course, and sometimes you find things you never knew were there—I can't explain properly——" said Barbara waving her hands wildly, and almost bursting in her efforts to get it out.

Mr. Marvell stood and listened to all this with his mouth open. To say he was surprised is ludicrously to understate the case—was Balaam surprised when the ass spoke?

"You write," he said at last, when he could find a voice to say it in. The description to which he had listened was extremely muddled, and somewhat incoherent, and Mr. Marvell—although he knew very little about the art of writing—was pretty certain that the method described by Mrs. Abbott was an extremely unorthodox method of producing a well-written book; but he was intelligent enough to realise that nobody, who had not gone through the adventures described, could possibly have described them in such a vivid manner. It was, therefore, not as a question but as a positive assertion, that Mr. Marvell said *you write.*

"Oh!" exclaimed Barbara, aghast at what

she had done. "Oh, well—well, sometimes—I used to, I mean. I don't, now, ever."

"Why not?" enquired Mr. Marvell with interest.

"Oh well, you see I'm married now. There's no need——"

"Did you go hunting for the pot, or for pleasure?"

Barbara giggled. "Well, if you really want to know," she said, "I started hunting for the pot, but, quite soon, it sort of *got* me. But it's all over now," added Barbara seriously, rather as if she was a reformed drunkard and had signed the pledge. "It's all over and done with now, and I don't really like people to know about it."

"A secret—eh?" enquired Mr. Marvell smiling.

"Yes——"

"I wonder why."

Barbara was not going to tell him that. Oh no, she had told him far too much already. I must have been mad to let the cat out of the bag to Mr. Marvell, she thought, and then she looked rather pensive for a little, for her outburst to Mr. Marvell had stirred her up; and she reflected that it was really rather a pity that it was all over so completely, because, really and truly, it had been rather fun.

Mr. Marvell found her abstracted; he saw that for to-night, at any rate, Mrs. Abbott had nothing to give him. He suggested that they should return to their spouses.

*　　*　　*

Mr. Abbott had had a very trying time with Mrs. Marvell. He found her a most inarticulate person, amorphous as a jelly-fish. She laid herself upon the divan in the drawing-room, settling the cushions very comfortably behind her head and into the curves of her body. Two long, beautifully-moulded legs were exposed to Mr. Abbott's view, clad in the finest of sheer silk stockings. This done, she left the rest of Mr. Abbott's entertainment to Fate. It might have been enough entertainment for some people, but Mr. Abbott did not find it enough. He was not interested in Mrs. Marvell's legs—not in the least. He was not interested in Mrs. Marvell at all. But Mrs. Marvell was his hostess and he felt bound to converse with her. He tried her on every subject he could think of, but she had no ideas to offer upon any of them. It was up-hill work. It was frightful toil. And, all through this frightful toil, Mr. Abbott was conscious of an even more frightful uneasiness at the back of his mind. Should he have allowed Barbara to be led away to Mr. Marvell's studio like that? Should he? Was it perfectly all right, or was it not? Artists, Mr. Abbott knew, were rather queer—not like other people at all—and Barbara was so extraordinarily innocent, so ignorant of the big, wicked world. . . .

"They're a long time," said Mr. Abbott at last.

"Yes," agreed Mrs. Marvell, unhelpfully.

"I wonder what they're doing," essayed Mr. Abbott, with an apologetic laugh.

Mrs. Marvell considered this for a moment or two, and then said she didn't know.

"I think I'll go and see," said Mr. Abbott, rising to his feet.

"I shouldn't do that."

"No?"

"No, James wouldn't like it."

Mr. Abbott was even more uneasy at this ominous statement—"Wouldn't like it!" he repeated anxiously.

"No."

"I think I'll go all the same."

276

"Sit down, they'll be back soon," Mrs. Marvell said. She rolled over on the divan, and settled herself more comfortably amongst the soft down cushions. (*Just as if she were in bed!* Mr. Abbott thought.)

"Sit down," said Mrs. Marvell again. "They won't be long now."

Mr. Abbott was defeated, he sat down on the edge of the chair—it was absurd that he could not go after his own wife and find her, quite absurd, but, somehow or other, he couldn't. He sat and frowned at the fire, he was not going to look at Mrs. Marvell, horrible woman, detestable woman!

"Why are you worried?" enquired Mrs. Marvell in her queer husky voice. "Can't you trust your wife?"

Mr. Abbott couldn't believe his ears—"*What* did you say?"

"Can't you trust your wife?" repeated Mrs. Marvell in a conversational tone.

"Of course I can trust my wife," said Mr. Abbott angrily. "What an extraordinary thing to say!"

"I thought you were worried," explained Mrs. Marvell casually.

"It's your husband I don't trust," added

Mr. Abbott, who was so upset that he scarcely knew what he was saying.

"I don't think you need worry," said Mrs. Marvell, quite unmoved. "She's too old for James, really. He *does* take fancies to people sometimes, but only if they're young and pretty."

Mr. Abbott was dumb with astonishment and fury—the woman must be mad! He looked at her, and saw her peering at him with her queer brown eyes. Her untidy brown head was burrowed deep into a green cushion, so deeply burrowed that she had to hold down the edge of the cushion to see Mr. Abbott at all. The rest of her body was humped in curves along the whole length of the divan. Mr. Abbott looked at her—he had never seen a lady behave like this in her drawing-room before, or in any other room for that matter—he looked at her and came to the conclusion that she was either mad or bad—possibly both. He was wrong, of course. Mrs. Marvell was a good wife, and perfectly sane and respectable, she had merely been brought up differently from Mr. Abbott's friends. Mrs. Marvell was completely natural in her body; her body was to her what an animal's body is to an animal. She sprawled upon the divan, and burrowed into the cushions, because it was comfortable and she was extremely tired. Posing for hours at a time for an exacting man like Mr. Marvell is no light work, it tires the body and dulls the mind. At least this was the effect it had upon Mrs. Marvell. If you pose for hours you must either think a great deal or not at all—she found it better not to think at all—if you pose for hours, not thinking at all, your mind becomes a complete blank—it atrophies. Mrs. Marvell's mind had atrophied to a certain extent, it was subsidiary to her body. Her body was her chief asset, and was therefore her chief care. She cultivated her body assiduously, she massaged it, exercised it, dieted it, manicured it, and anointed it with various oils and lotions. She was fully aware that, when her body was no longer beautiful, James would insist (with perfect right) upon having a model in the house—and, once that started, where were you? So Mrs. Marvell lived for her body, and tended it carefully, and neglected her mind.

Mrs. Marvell and Mr. Abbott misunderstood each other completely. Mr. Abbott thought that Mrs. Marvell was mad or bad. Mrs. Marvell thought Mr. Abbott was a

Philistine—a dull, hypocritical old donkey, as she put it to herself—and they were both wrong. It is very unfortunate when people misunderstand each other so completely, and the saddest part of this particular case of misunderstanding was that there was no possibility of their ever coming to a better understanding of each other, because they were divided by a miasma of prejudice and ignorance.

It was into this atmosphere of prejudice and ignorance that Mr. Marvell and Barbara returned. *They* were delighted with each other, not so much because they understood each other any better than the other couple, but because they misunderstood each other differently. Mr. Abbott was thankful to behold his wife, apparently safe and sound, his one idea was to go home and take her with him. He rose and said that they must go. It was really Barbara's privilege to determine the hour of their departure, but Barbara showed signs of settling down in the drawing-room, and Mr. Abbott was desperate. I shall be rude to that dreadful woman in a minute, he thought, in fact I have been rude to her already, only she doesn't seem to mind. He rose and dragged Barbara away.

The Marvells were a little surprised at their guests' departure; they begged them to stay a little longer, and offered various inducements, such as ping-pong, or the wireless, but Mr. Abbott scarcely listened. All he wanted was to get home.

18

THE CHRISTMAS DINNER-PARTY

SAM spent Christmas with his mother, it was only right that he should; he would have enjoyed it more if he had not had to attend quite so many services in church. Sam liked church in moderation, but he did not like spending his entire holiday in the sacred edifice. He escaped as soon as was decent, and came down to The Archway House feeling more chastened than usual after his ordeal. Barbara was worried about Sam, he was not like himself at all. Unrequited love and too much church had worn out and subdued the gay young man out of all recognition. Barbara insisted on giving him breakfast in bed and Sam enjoyed it. He was in the mood for a little petting and pampering—somewhat tired, and not a little miserable—Barbara was a good soul.

The Abbotts had postponed their Christmas dinner for Sam's benefit; it was to be a party. Barbara had wanted to invite the

Marvells—to return their hospitality—but Arthur wouldn't hear of it, so they had asked Jerry Cobbe and her brother (who was with her for the festive season) and Monkey Wrench.

The party took place the night following Sam's arrival. Dr. Wrench rang up about seven o'clock and left a message to say he had had an urgent call, but would come later if he could get away. The remaining five dined off turkey and plum pudding, and pulled crackers afterwards. The dinner was excellent, and the party ought to have been a success, but, somehow or other, it fell rather flat. The host and hostess were the only people who really enjoyed it, and their enjoyment was tempered, unconsciously, by the fact that their guests were not in tune. Their guests were, in fact, thoroughly out of tune, not only with each other, but also with themselves.

Jerry and Archie Cobbe had just had a frightful row. They had actually had it on the way to the party, as they were driving over in Archie's small car. The row was all the more frightful, because it was a rare thing for them to quarrel. Jerry was a sweet-tempered person, as a rule; she was very fond of Archie, in spite of his delinquencies, and was tactful and soothing and indulgent by turns. But, to-night, she had been none of these things, and each had said enough to make it plain that they were completely at variance with each other upon the Ethics of Life. Jerry's view of Life was that "you should be independent and stand on your own feet"; and Archie's view was that your relations should "take an interest in you—especially if they have Plenty of the Needful, like Aunt Matilda."

"Why *should* Aunt Matilda?" Jerry had enquired, and Archie had replied, "Why *shouldn't* she? I'm her heir, aren't I? You'd think the old brute would be glad to fork out a bit now, instead of keeping me hanging on, longing for her to pip."

"Oh Archie!" Jerry had cried, "you don't mean that, it's *beastly*!"

"I'm beastly, am I?"

"What you said was beastly."

"I said what I thought."

"Then you *are* beastly," Jerry had cried with sudden rage. "Aunt Matilda has always been decent to us. I know she's queer, but she's kind to *us*, and there's no real need for her to be kind to us, because she isn't really any relation at all. I can't think why you haven't got any *pride*, Archie. Why don't you

284

do something, instead of idling about town?"

"Idling about town!" Archie had retorted fiercely. "Is that what you think I'm doing? You'd like me to come down here and turn myself into a sort of groom, wouldn't you? Talk of pride—you can't have much pride. You're nothing but a common hack-hirer."

"I can keep myself—you can't do that," Jerry had told him angrily.

"It's just as well," Archie had replied, bursting with rage. "It's a good thing you can keep yourself—nobody else would keep you——"

It was just like fish-wives or something, Jerry thought (as she sat at the Abbotts' festive board, and tried to swallow turkey and ham before it turned to sawdust in her mouth). It was just like fish-wives *screaming* at each other. What possessed me to say things like that to Archie? What on earth possessed me? And what on earth's the matter with me, she wondered miserably. I can't sleep at night, and I'm as irritable as a bear. I feel as if I could burst into tears, at any minute, and simply *howl*—I never felt like this before *in all my life*. She glanced across the table at Archie. How cross he looks! she thought. What *will* the Abbotts think of him? Oh dear, why didn't I keep my temper with him? I haven't seen him for weeks, and I'm so fond of him, really. It's just because I *am* so fond of him (she reflected) that I'm so angry with him, so disappointed when he doesn't seem to have any guts. But I must *talk*, she thought, it's awful of us to be so gloomy when the Abbotts have been so kind in asking us to dinner like this—and, with that, she flung herself into the conversation with forced, and slightly feverish, gaiety.

The third guest's wretchedness arose from love. Sam had loved Jerry for weeks, and he could not get any nearer to her. Every time he saw her he loved her more, and, when he was in town and didn't see her at all, he loved her more. He was almost desperate by now. And she hasn't any use for me at all, he thought, she hasn't given me the smallest encouragement—it's hopeless, absolutely hopeless. But I shall have to tell her soon—I can't wait much longer. Oh darling, darling Jerry, how sweet you are! (Sam thought she looked even sweeter than usual to-night, there was a fey quality in her gaiety, she laughed, and chattered, and chaffed, and her eyes were very bright.) Oh Jerry, Jerry, he thought, I can't bear it any more.

Dinner was over by this time, and Sam got

up and went round the table to light Jerry's cigarette—he was past caring whether the others would think it queer. He watched the brown head bent forward a little as she held her cigarette to his match; he smelt the fragrance of her hair, it was a clean fresh fragrance like the scent of wild flowers; he saw the white nape of her neck (as he stood over her) and the little rings of silky hair, and he was so moved by the nearness and dearness of her, that, when she looked up and smiled to thank him for the little service, it took him all his strength not to kiss her then and there.

Afterwards, back in his own chair—he scarcely knew how he had got there—his cheeks burned at the recollection of his impulse—how near disaster he had been! The hand that lifted his glass to his lips trembled so that a few drops of wine were spilt. . . .

Barbara saw it all, and the truth burst upon her with a blinding flash—Sam was in love with Jerry. For a few moments she was delighted, for she was a born match-maker, and she was fond of them both. They'll make a nice pair, she thought happily. Of course that's why poor Sam is so subdued, but it's bound to be all right, because Sam really is a dear and Jerry is, too. It's *lovely*. And then, quite suddenly, she remembered about the will, and came to earth with a bump—but Jerry mustn't marry, she told herself aghast, *she mustn't marry or she'll lose Chevis Place.* Goodness! said Barbara to herself, whatever shall I do? She doesn't know about the will, of course, and I can't tell her, because I promised faithfully that I wouldn't tell a soul. What can I do?

She was still wondering what she could do, when she and Jerry went into the drawing-room together (leaving the three men to drink their port in the time-honoured manner).

"It's cold, isn't it?" Barbara remarked.

"Yes," said Jerry, sinking into a chair. Her gaiety had gone now, she was deadly tired, and her head ached.

Barbara knelt down before the fire, and attacked it with the poker. "Is Mr. Cobbe going to stay with you for a bit?" she enquired.

"Yes, till Monday," Jerry replied. "Don't call him 'Mr. Cobbe', Barbara. Nobody does."

"But I scarcely know him," Barbara pointed out, "and he's rather—rather un-approachable, isn't he? I mean I shouldn't dare to call him anything else, Jerry."

"He's not really unapproachable," said Jerry, smiling faintly. "He's in rather a bad mood to-night—so am I for that matter. I've been wanting to apologise for us both all the evening. The truth is—as Miss Foddy would say—the truth is we had rather a row coming over in the car."

Barbara looked up with the poker poised in mid-air. "Oh, Jerry, I *am* sorry," she said.

"Don't be sorry," said Jerry quickly. "Don't, for goodness sake, be sorry, or I shall howl. I don't know what's the matter with me—I'm a perfect fool, that's all. How lovely your hyacinths are! Did you grow them yourself?"

"Yes, aren't they? Yes, I did," Barbara replied. "I'm awfully proud of them, really, but they aren't nearly as good as Mrs. Thane's."

"Mrs. Thane is wonderful with bulbs."

"She's altogether wonderful, I think," said Barbara thoughtfully.

At this moment the door opened and Dr. Wrench appeared. He looked cold and miserable. Barbara jumped up from the hearth-rug and welcomed him cordially. She was very fond of "Monkey" and thought him "good for Arthur"—it was so nice that Arthur had found an old friend in Wandlebury.

"I was awfully sorry I couldn't come," said Monkey, sitting down near the fire and holding out his thin hands to the cheerful blaze. "Couldn't get away before."

"But have you had dinner?" enquired his hostess anxiously. "Because you can easily have it now——"

"No, no, I've had some," replied the doctor. "They gave me some at Chevis Place——"

"Is Aunt Matilda——" began Jerry, sitting up and gazing at him in alarm.

"She's better," the doctor said. "It's all right, Jerry. She had another heart attack, but it passed off. All the same I wish you or Archie could persuade her to let me have further advice. I'm worried about her, and I don't like the responsibility at all."

"I'll try to persuade her," Jerry promised. "D'you think I should go over to Chevis Place to-night—would she like me to, I mean?"

"I'd rather you didn't. She's asleep, and it might alarm her if you went over there so late. But go in the morning, and try to get her

290

to let me bring a specialist from town, will you, Jerry?"

"Yes, of course, I will," Jerry said.

They were still talking about Lady Chevis Cobbe when Mr. Abbott and Sam came in.

"Mr. Cobbe had to go," said Arthur. "He hadn't time to say good-bye. We got talking and he ran it rather fine."

Barbara looked up in surprise.

"He had to be in town to-night," explained Mr. Abbott, "a supper-party, or something. He asked me to say good-bye for him."

Sam was watching Jerry's face—it was a habit of his—and he saw that she was surprised at the news. How queer! he thought, and then—with suppressed fury—what a bounder! For Jerry's face had gone rather white, and he saw her lips quiver. The next moment she had pulled herself together, for she was full of courage.

"Oh yes," she said. "Of course—how silly of me to forget——"

"He doesn't give us much of his company, does he?" growled Monkey, who hadn't much use for Archie Cobbe. "Here to-day, and gone to-morrow. Has he found a job, yet?"

"Not yet," said Jerry bravely.

Sam was the gainer by Archie's sudden flight, for it gave him the opportunity of seeing Jerry home.

19

A DEED OF CHIVALRY

JERRY elected to walk home, saying that she had eaten too much plum pudding, and the exercise would do her good. It was a lovely night, cold and very clear, the ground was crisp with frost beneath their feet. Sam and Jerry walked along in silence for a little while.

"I think you're tired," said Sam at last. "You should have let me take you in the car."

"I like walking," she replied, quietly. "My head was aching rather, and the air's so lovely—it was good of you to come——"

"I like it," said Sam quickly. "You *know* I like it. I've been wanting to tell you——"

"You know that Archie did not mean to go to town, to-night," Jerry interrupted him, still in that quiet voice. "I saw from your face—I saw that you knew. But you mustn't blame Archie because it was my fault, you see. We had—we had a row. You knew I was surprised."

"Yes, I knew," Sam told her.

"Do you think the others knew?"

"I don't think so," said Sam, considering the matter. He was longing to tell her what he thought of Archie, but he stifled the words. He had made up his mind to ask her to-night—to ask her if there was any hope for him at all—and he felt that if they began to argue about Archie Cobbe his opportunity would be gone.

"I'm glad the others didn't know," Jerry said. "It was just because he was angry with me—you see that, don't you?"

"Yes," said Sam.

"I hope—I hope he was polite to Mr. Abbott," continued Jerry. "It was so kind of them to ask us. I hope he thanked Mr. Abbott——"

"It's all right, *really*," Sam assured her. Uncle Arthur never thought anything——"

"Barbara knew."

"Barbara always knows," said Sam. "She's rather marvellous."

They walked on in silence. They were crossing the moor now. It stretched away from them on either side, ghostly and deserted. The muddy pools gleamed like silver shields in the pale light of the moon; far on the horizon a line of bare-branched trees traced a dark lacy pattern against the starry sky.

"Jerry!" said Sam suddenly. "Oh, Jerry, I can't bear it any more—I love you so, Jerry!"

"No," she said. "No, Sam, don't."

"Please," said Sam earnestly. "Please—isn't there any hope at all? I mean I know you don't love me *now*, but couldn't you—couldn't you try?"

"No, Sam."

"Why?"

"You don't really love me," she said, and, despite herself, her voice trembled a little.

Sam was so amazed at this totally unexpected reply that it was a moment or two before he could find his voice.

"But, Jerry, I do—frightfully," he said at last. How could she not know that he loved her? He had loved her for months, desperately. How could she not know?

"No, Sam. You don't really," she was saying. "You may think you do, but it's not real. It's just—just a passing thing."

"Oh, Jerry, how can you? I want to marry you more than anything on earth—more than I've ever wanted anything on earth—and you say it's just a passing thing—what *do* you mean?"

"I'd rather we were just friends," she said unsteadily.

"Jerry!"

"We're so different, you see."

"Different? I don't know what you mean. I'll be anything you like," said Sam wildly. "How are we different?"

"You can't change yourself—not permanently."

"I can if you want me to—somebody's been telling you things about me," Sam cried. "Uncle Arthur——"

"No, no! It's just that you're a town person, and I'm a country person," Jerry explained. They had stood still for a few minutes in the heat of their discussion, but now Jerry began to walk on, and Sam had to follow. Jerry was speaking so quietly that he had to bend his head to listen to her explanations. He could see she was upset, and he wondered if this was a sign that there was some hope for him after all. "You're a town person, and I'm a country person," she explained. "You may think that doesn't matter, but it does—I know it does. You like parties and gaiety, and I don't. That doesn't mean

296

that I think them wrong. It just means I'm no good at that sort of thing and I don't like it. You wouldn't be happy buried in the country, and I could never live in town—I couldn't—I couldn't possibly. We're different you see—it's no use."

"It's not true," Sam said earnestly. "I don't know how you've got all that into your head, Jerry, but it isn't true—not now."

"Don't Sam, it's no good——"

"You must listen," he cried. "It's only fair. I've listened to you. I tell you it's all wrong. I *did* go the pace a bit, but that was before I'd seen you, and everything seemed so stale and not worth while——"

"You can't change all of a sudden—I don't want you to—I'm not blaming you a bit—there's nothing wrong in liking gaiety, in fact it's natural," said Jerry desperately.

"But I *have* changed. I've changed to *me*," cried Sam. "It wasn't me before, but it *is* me *now*. Uncle Arthur doesn't understand," he continued incoherently. "There was a war when he was young like me—oh, I know it was beastly, and they were all frightfully brave, but that isn't the point. And I don't want another war, or anything——that isn't the point either. The point is," said Sam,

297

searching wildly for words to express his meaning, "the point is he got his adventures out of it, and I had to find my own adventures. Oh, I know I was a silly ass, but it's all over now—all over and done with. It was all over the minute I saw you."

Jerry had listened carefully to all this, and it impressed her. She saw the point that Sam had tried to make clear, and she saw that what he said might easily be true.

"You see," said Sam in a calmer tone, "you see I never wanted to go into the office. I wanted the army as a career, but Mother wouldn't hear of it. She thinks that all fighting is frightfully wicked. She hates war, and hates it all the more because of Father being killed in France. And then Uncle Arthur had paid for my education, and it seemed so ungrateful not to go into the office when he wanted me to—altogether I hadn't a chance. So there I was, stuck down in the office, and it was dull, dull, dull—*you see?*"

Jerry saw—"But you're still there," she pointed out.

"I know," admitted Sam. "But the queer thing is I'm getting to like it. I've been working like a horse ever since I met you—I made up my mind I would, it was working for you in a way—and I'm beginning to like it. Uncle Arthur's frightfully decent now he sees I'm—well—reliable and all that. And really and truly I'm beginning to see the fun of it, if you know what I mean—but perhaps you don't?"

"Yes, I *do*," Jerry said. "But isn't it only temporary? Oh, Sam, I hate to seem so difficult, but I must be sure. You see I know what it's like when people have to live together, and don't like the same things. I've been through it with Archie—but it would be far, far worse if you were married to the person. And besides," said Jerry in a very low voice—so low that Sam could scarcely hear it—"besides I couldn't bear it—I couldn't bear it, Sam, I could just bear it if you went away now, and I never saw you again, but I couldn't bear it if—if we went on—and—and then you got tired of me."

"But I won't, ever," said Sam gravely. They had reached the gate of Ganthorne Lodge by this time, and they stood still, facing each other in the cold white moonlight. Two young creatures, very serious and very earnest, oblivious of everything in the world save each other, and the supreme importance of the moment. "I won't, ever," he said gravely, "I'll love you, and love you, for ever, and ever, and ever—real friendly love, Jerry darling."

And then, somehow or other, she was in his arms, and he was kissing her upturned face—the skin cool and fragrant; the lips soft and clinging beneath his own—and Jerry, half-laughing, and half-crying, was saying, "Oh, Sam! Oh you silly, Sam, of course I love you! I've loved you all the time. It was just because I loved you so frightfully that I was afraid. But if you're sure—if you're quite, quite, quite sure——"

"I'm quite, quite, quite sure," said Sam solemnly, and he kissed her again, just to teach her not to ask such silly questions.

When they had calmed down a little they began to notice the cold. It was freezing hard by now, and the wind was perishing.

"You really must go home, Sam," said Jerry sensibly, and then she added with her deep chuckle, which was so infectious, "we shall both catch frightful colds in our heads, and I look a perfect sight when I've got a cold—you wouldn't love me any more."

"I would," Sam told her, "I'd love you if you had measles. I'd love you if you had mumps," and he kissed her again, more vehemently than before. "And anyhow," he added firmly, when this was over, "and anyhow I'm not going until I've seen you safely into the house——"

"Oh, Sam!" cried Jerry, suddenly aghast. "Oh, Sam, I haven't got the key!"

"The key?"

"The key of the front door—Archie's got it in his pocket—and Markie sleeps like a rock; she's a little deaf, you know. Oh, Sam, what are we to do?"

"We'll find a window open," Sam said confidently.

"We shan't," Jerry told him. "Not on the ground floor. Markie's terrified of burglars. She locks up everything when she's alone in the house."

"We'll try, anyhow," Sam said.

They prowled round the house together, trying all the windows, but Jerry had predicted truly, Ganthorne Lodge was secure from nocturnal marauders. Every window was shut, every catch was fastened. Markie had made certain of an undisturbed night.

"You see," said Jerry, half amused, and half appalled at their predicament, "it's absolutely hopeless. What are we going to do?"

"We'll ring the bell or shout," Sam suggested, "or throw stones at her window."

"It wouldn't be any good. She's deaf," Jerry pointed out. "The only way to wake Markie is to shake her."

They both laughed.

"I must climb up, then," said Sam, looking up at the blind face of Ganthorne Lodge consideringly.

"You can't——"

"Of course I can. There's a window half open—whose is it? Not Markie's I hope."

"It's mine," Jerry told him. "Markie sleeps with her windows tight shut—she's one of the old school who thinks the night air is bad for you."

"Does she?" enquired Sam with interest. "What a funny old trout she must be!"

"Yes," chuckled Jerry. "She is. That's exactly what she *is*—a darling, dear, funny old trout. You'll love Markie."

"Of course I shall," agreed Sam. (He was prepared to love everybody that Jerry loved.) "Now then, we mustn't waste time. That's the window for me."

"No, Sam—you can't——"

"Of course I can."

302

"No, you'll fall and break your leg or some-thing."

"Nonsense," said Sam. He felt that nothing was beyond his powers to-night, he almost felt that he could spread wings and fly into the window. It was really rather decent of old Markie to have locked up so well; a ground-floor window would have been dull. He wanted to do something spectacular for Jerry; something really worth while, and here was the spectacular, worth-while thing all ready for him to do—Sam was lucky.

"Don't be silly, Sam, you'll fall," said Jerry anxiously.

"I shan't fall," he promised.

He took off his coat and gave it to Jerry to hold. "There," he said. "Hold that. I shan't be long."

Then he started to climb. It was not really very difficult, for the creepers were old and thick and very strong. Their gnarled stems gave him good foothold. He climbed on to the roof of an outhouse, and edged his way very carefully along the ledge. Jerry's window was just above his head now. He stood up, balancing precariously, and grasped the sill. This was really the most difficult part of it all, but Sam managed it; he pulled himself up, slid the window wider open and climbed in.

Jerry had been watching breathlessly.

"Hullo, here I am!" said Sam, grinning at her out of the window. "Go round to the front door, Jerry—I shan't be a minute."

It was a good deal more than the promised minute before Sam found the front door. The house was strange to him and it was exceedingly dark. He groped his way to the door and spent some time feeling about the wall for an electric light switch until he remembered that Ganthorne Lodge did not possess this modern convenience. The landing was dark too. He groped about for some time before he could find the stair. If only I had my torch! thought Sam in disgust; but he hadn't even a match in the pocket of his dinner jacket. Fortunately the hall was a trifle less black, owing to a small window near the door, so the last bit of his task was not so blind. He found the handle of the door without much trouble and threw it open.

Jerry was standing on the step—"I thought you were lost!" she exclaimed.

"I was," said Sam, grinning, "completely lost. The place is pitch dark upstairs, and I hadn't even a match."

"It *was* clever of you," Jerry told him. "I was terrified. I don't know how you managed that last bit by the window."

Sam didn't know either, but, of course, he didn't say so. He was naturally delighted that Jerry appreciated his feat, he was quite pleased with it himself—not many fellows could have done it so neatly—but he made light of it to Jerry.

"Gadzooks, it was nothing!" he assured her. "I'm sorry I was such ages. Where are the matches?"

"I'll find them," Jerry said. "They're on the mantelpiece in the drawing-room."

She found them quite easily, for she knew the house, of course, and she was used to groping about in the dark. In a few moments she had lighted the lamp and the beautiful old room was filled with its mellow glow.

"Phew, that's better!" exclaimed Sam.

"There," said Jerry. "You must go now, Sam. I'm sorry to be inhospitable, but you must."

"I know," Sam said reluctantly.

"Wait just one minute and I'll give you a drink."

Sam didn't want a drink; he felt half drunk already—drunk with happiness—in that pleasant state of elevation and bliss when nothing seems real. But he agreed to have the drink because it would give him a few minutes more of Jerry's company.

She went away, and returned with a tray which contained a decanter and a siphon and a glass.

"Here's how!" said Sam, in the jargon of his day. "Look here, you must drink to *us*."

She drank from his glass and repeated the meaningless words—"Here's how, Sam," she said, looking up at him with her clear grey eyes full of love and happiness.

"Darling Jerry!" said Sam.

"Darling Sam!" said Jerry.

"I must go, I suppose."

"Yes. You've been simply splendid," said Jerry. "Simply splendid. I'll see you to-morrow—are you coming over to ride?"

"No, you won't see me to-morrow," Sam told her. "That's the foul bit of it. I've got to go back to town early."

"Oh *Sam*! When are you coming back?"

"I don't know—as soon as ever I can, you can bet on that."

"How hateful!"

"Isn't it? But they've been awfully decent

having me such a lot—I don't like sponging on them *too* much."

"I know."

"You'll marry me *soon*, won't you, Jerry?" he continued. "I've been most awfully patient. I've waited ages, and it's been absolute hell——"

"I can't——" replied Jerry, wrinkling her brows. "I simply can't—not until Aunt Matilda's better. We can't even be engaged—not properly, I mean."

Sam's face fell. "But, good heavens, what has *she* got to do with it?" he exclaimed. "I mean you'd be here just the same—I mean," he continued, laughing a trifle diffidently, "I mean I'm proposing to come and live here with you. It seems a bit odd, but that's what you want, isn't it?"

"Yes," said Jerry nodding eagerly. "Yes, of course, Sam darling——"

"And you can go on with the horses and everything just the same—only I'd be here to take care of you——"

"Yes—it would be *lovely*."

"I could easily go up to town every day from here," Sam pointed out. "I've got my eye on a little car—a second-hand sports model, just the very thing, frightfully cheap, so it would be quite easy. And we'd have the evenings together—and Sundays, of course."

"Yes," Jerry agreed. "Yes, it's exactly what I want—Oh Sam I'm so happy—it's *exactly* what I want. I should hate to give up the horses and everything *now*, when it's just beginning to be a success."

"Of course you would," said Sam. "Of course you would. Besides, don't you see, it would be a help. I mean I'm not getting a frightfully big screw yet—and—well, it would be a *help*. It sounds funny——"

"It sounds heavenly," Jerry told him earnestly, and so it did. Jerry was an independent person. She liked "doing things"; she liked to feel that she was a useful member of society; she liked to "stand on her own feet." If she could stand thus, with Sam's hand in hers, she would ask nothing more of Life.

"You and I together," she told him. "Partners, Sam!"

"Yes," said Sam. "Real friendly love—d'you remember saying that to me in this very room—that first day—*real friendly love*. I've never forgotten it, Jerry."

Jerry hadn't forgotten it either. They reminisced very happily for several minutes in the age old manner of lovers. It seemed most extraordinary that they should both remember so much of what the other had said and done—most extraordinary.

"Well, then," said Sam at last, returning to the subject nearest his heart, "Well, then, there's no reason to delay—is there, Jerry. You will marry me *soon*, won't you?"

"I can't—because of Aunt Matilda," Jerry repeated. "You don't understand, Sam. Aunt Matilda would be most frightfully upset if she heard I was going to be married. And I can't possibly risk upsetting her *now*, when she's so ill. She might have another heart attack and die—and then I should be a murderer."

"But if she knew you were going to be here, just the same—you could go over and see her just as often——"

"It isn't *that*," Jerry cried. "It isn't because she would miss me if I went away. It's just that she's queer about marriage—it's a sort of craze, or something. She can't bear people to get married—it makes her frantic."

"She must be mad," said Sam with conviction.

It was at this moment, when Sam had voiced his considered opinion of Lady Chevis Cobbe's idiosyncrasy, that the door of the drawing-room opened, very slowly, and a head appeared round the corner. It was a most peculiar apparition—quite terrifying in fact—a white face, very flat and expressionless, with two light-blue eyes, very dazed and glassy, surmounted by grey hair, twisted up into weird-looking horns which stuck out in all directions. The shadow cast on the wall behind the head was like the shadow of some prehistoric beast.

"Markie!" cried Jerry in amazement.

"I was awake," said Miss Marks. "I was awake, and I thought I heard a noise." She came farther into the room, disclosing a long thin body clad in a grey-flannel dressing-gown with lace-edged collar and cuffs. "I thought I heard *voices* and I wondered if you and Archie—oh, it's not Archie!" she cried, trying to back out again through the closed door.

"It's Mr. Abbott," said Jerry. "He brought me home—very kindly—you see Archie had to go back to town."

"To town? To-night?" exclaimed Miss Marks, forgetting her *déshabillé* in her surprise at the news.

"Yes, he's gone," Jerry replied. "I'll tell you all about it later."

310

"Well I never!" said Miss Marks, "but I daresay we shall manage without him quite nicely," she added with a touch of sarcasm.

"Yes," agreed Jerry.

"And it was very nice of Mr. Abbott to see you home—very nice indeed—but what have you been doing?" she enquired, peering at Sam and Jerry with her faded blue eyes, "What *have* you been doing? Mr. Abbott has torn his coat—look at the sleeve——"

"Gadzooks, so I have!" exclaimed Sam.

"And you look like a pair of conspirators," added Miss Marks perspicaciously.

The conspirators smiled at each other in a sheepish manner.

"You can't deceive Markie," said Jerry laughing. "I never *could* deceive Markie. She always knew when I'd been up to something. We'll have to let Markie into the secret."

Sam was nothing loath, he wanted to Tell The World that Jerry had consented to be his wife, he was bursting with it, absolutely bursting.

"We're going to be married," he said.

"Yes, *really*. Jerry and I. Isn't it marvellous? Can you beat it? Oh, Glory, I've never been so happy in my life!"

Miss Marks received the news with adequate

enthusiasm—she was amazed, excited, delighted. Even Sam and Jerry were satisfied with her reaction to their proposed union. They made her drink their health, and they shook hands all round, and Jerry hugged her. It was a tremendous scene. Miss Marks was able to enter into the spirit of the scene because she was a romantic woman, all the more romantic because her own life had been singularly empty of romance. She adored Jerry, and wanted the best of everything for her darling child—and the best of everything, in Miss Mark's estimation, was a good-looking, and adoring lover. Sam was indubitably both. Sam had stepped straight into Markie's romantic old heart with that first speech of his. "Isn't it marvellous?" he had cried, with his eyes shining like stars. "Can you beat it? Oh, Glory, I've never been so happy in my life!" *There* was a lover. *That* was the spirit in which to approach matrimony. *Here* was the very man for darling Jerry—the very man.

Nobody on earth could have been a more sympathetic or delightful confidante for a pair of lovers than Markie. They poured out their hopes and fears, their amazing happiness and all their difficulties in an endless stream, and she drank it in. She was joyful and sad, hopeful and anxious by turns. She nodded her head, or shook it so that the queer-shaped horns rattled together like castanets. But Markie had quite forgotten about her curlers and her dressing-gown, she was much too excited to think about things so mundane as these. She was completely and absolutely happy, and completely and absolutely absorbed in the happiness of her young friends.

"So you see it's a secret," said Jerry at last. "It's a dead secret, and nobody must know— or even suspect—because of Aunt Matilda. You see that, don't you, Markie? Because, if she got to hear about it, she might die or something—you know how odd she is—and then I should have killed her, and I should never be happy again," added Jerry earnestly. "So you won't tell a soul, will you?"

"Not a soul," agreed Markie, who loved a secret only a little less than a romance. "Of course, my dear, of course—not a soul—not a soul—a secret—a dead secret, until your poor Aunt recovers or——"

She stopped there, because, of course, she did not really wish for the demise of Lady Chevis Cobbe. It would be convenient, of course, and the poor lady was really very queer—fancy anybody being so extremely queer as to dislike the idea of romance—but still, in spite of her queerness, one could not—one did not—and even if one did, thought Miss Marks vaguely, one kept one's wishes to oneself.

20

THE GOLDEN BOY

THE days sped past. They were slightly
monotonous, but it was a pleasant
monotony, for Barbara was happy.
She had decided not to have Sam to stay
again, because of Jerry. Sam was in love with
Jerry (Barbara had discovered that interesting
fact on the night of the Christmas dinner
party) and Jerry must be protected from his
advances until Lady Chevis Cobbe was safely
dead. After that, of course, it would be quite
all right. She could have Sam down *often*, and
throw them together. It all seemed quite
simple to Barbara, and, if she was slightly
callous about the prospect of Lady Chevis
Cobbe's demise, it must be remembered that
she had only seen the lady once, and
thoroughly disapproved of her attitude
towards marriage. Barbara was a simple,
straight-forward person—black was black and
white was white to Barbara—Lady Chevis
Cobb was ill, her life was no good to her—no

good at all—and her death would be convenient, and would open up the way for the course of true love to run smooth. Barbara and Miss Marks shared the same views—but they were quite unaware of each other's opinions.

Whenever Monkey Wrench came to The Archway House Barbara enquired of him, most anxiously, about the health of his august patient, and she managed to conceal from him her pleasure when the news was bad, and her disappointment when the news was better. Monkey thought that Barbara Abbott was a kind woman—it was nice of her to be so interested in her ladyship's health—very kind. He told her all he could. During January her ladyship rallied a little, and was even well enough to be taken out for drives in her Rolls-Royce, but in February she was not so well, and Barbara's hopes soared high.

Meanwhile life went on for other people in various degrees of monotony. The young Marvells played in The Archway House garden; Miss Foddy came to tea with Barbara and entertained her hostess with erudite discourse; Mr. Marvell painted his wife assiduously; Mr. Abbott made up his publishing lists; Monkey Wrench formed the habit of dropping in to The Archway House whenever he had a spare moment; Archie Cobbe racketed about town; and Sam and Jerry wrote long, and slightly incoherent letters to each other, and longed for each other's company.

One Sunday in February Arthur and Barbara set out to walk to church. It was a gorgeous day after a spell of rain. The sun shone, and the birds sang with such fervour that the Abbotts agreed that it really felt like Spring.

"It's funny," said Barbara—and, as this was her well-known opening for a deeply significant remark, Arthur was immediately all attention. "It's funny, Arthur, but I'm always glad when it feels like Spring. Not only because Spring is a nice time of year and everybody likes it, but more, because, when Winter goes on and on, I sometimes feel as if it was going on for ever. Wouldn't it be awful if the sun stayed away—down in New Zealand, or wherever it goes—and forgot to come back here at all?"

Arthur agreed that it would be awful.

"It's a silly idea, I know," admitted Barbara. "Because of course I *know* that the world moves round, and the sun stays still; I know it, but I can never quite believe it—in my bones. So you see that's why I'm even gladder than other people when I feel that Spring is really coming. Do you ever feel that, Arthur?"

Arthur said he had never felt it. For him the seasons were fixed and immovable. He had never envisaged the possibility of Spring getting lost (so to speak). He agreed, however, that it was a frightful thought—a positively nightmare thought.

"But it's all right for this year, anyhow," said Barbara more cheerfully. "Because I really can feel Spring to-day—and so can the birds. Just listen to them, Arthur!" and she smiled to herself, and thought of the bulbs and the seeds, and the roses and all the nice things she had bestowed royally upon The Archway House garden (in the hope that the sun would return from New Zealand at its appointed time and make them grow) and how they would all be preparing, in the secret fastness of the earth, to arise like giants and do her honour.

As they neared the side gate of the church-yard (which they always used because it was so much nearer), they saw the Marvell family in front of them. Barbara hastened her steps, because she liked the Marvells, and Arthur lagged behind a little because he didn't. As a matter of fact Arthur thought that the Marvell family was a blot upon the fair landscape of Wandlebury. Mrs. Marvell was a horrible woman, simply horrible; the children were ill-bred young savages, and Mr. Marvell, himself, was a bounder of the first water. Arthur had never liked Mr. Marvell since that night at dinner when he and Barbara had spent so long in the studio together. He was aware that Barbara had a penchant for Mr. Marvell; she enjoyed his company; she admired his enormous size, his resonant voice, and his amazing memory for quotations. Arthur did not like it much when Barbara admired other men—it was foolish, perhaps, but not altogether unnatural—and Mr. Marvell had a sort of grandeur, he was imposing and overpowering. He was, in fact, (so thought Arthur), just the sort of man that women always admire. Once Arthur had made up his mind to dislike Mr. Marvell he found plenty of reasons for his attitude. There was the day that Barbara had met the fellow in Wandlebury, and had come home full of the extraordinary compliments he had paid her, and there was the night of the Musical Evening when the fellow had pursued Barbara to the other end of the room, and the two of them had hob-nobbed together for ages, laughing like a pair of old friends. Arthur didn't blame Barbara at all—he knew her too well—but he did blame Mr. Marvell, and blamed him most severely. The fellow had a wife of his own, hadn't he? Well then, he should leave other people's wives alone.

It was, therefore, with disgust and annoyance that Mr. Abbott beheld the Marvell family making its way to church on that fine February morning.

The Abbotts met the Marvells at the small side gate leading into the churchyard. Mr. and Mrs. Marvell did not attend church very regularly, but, to-day, they had elected to attend. Miss Foddy was there, too, of course, and the children, looking quite unlike themselves with Sunday clothes and Sunday faces. It was the first time Barbara had beheld Lancreste Marvell. She had heard about him incessantly, both from Miss Foddy and from his younger brother and sister, but, in spite of that, she was in no way prepared for what she saw. For, no matter how often or how well a person is described, a verbal description can never convey an accurate picture of the lineaments, and the pigment, and the aura that make up the whole personality of a human being.

It's my Golden Boy, thought Barbara, *how extraordinary!*—and she gazed at Lancreste Marvell with amazement and excitement—it really is *wonderful* (she thought), it really is one of the most exciting things that has ever happened to me. It's my Golden Boy.

Barbara's Golden Boy was the one creature of her imagination, her only child—so to speak. She had written about him in *Disturber of the Peace*. All the other characters in the the book were people she knew—real people of flesh and blood—but the Golden Boy was purely imaginary, and Barbara had always been proud of him. It was this imaginary Golden Boy who had given the book its name, for he had danced gaily into the village of Silverstream, blowing an erotic tune on his pipes, and had disturbed the peace of the sleepy little place in various subtle ways. All sorts of amazing things had happened in Silverstream (or Copperfield as Barbara had called it, in a vain attempt to disguise its identity from the world), all sorts of amazing and unprecedented things had happened, and every one of them was directly attributable to the influence of the Golden Boy. And, now, here he was in Wandlebury, as large as life and twice as natural, Barbara's very own Golden Boy. He was dressed rather differently of course, for Barbara had imagined him with very little clothing—practically none in fact—and she now beheld him arrayed in Etons, very immaculate indeed, with a brand new topper resting lovingly upon his golden hair; but what were *clothes* (when all was said and done), it was Barbara's Golden Boy—she would have known him anywhere.

She was still gazing at Lancreste in wonderment and delight when the bells stopped ringing, and the little group, which had been admiring the clemency of the weather, turned with one movement towards the gate. Lancreste seized the handle to open it for the ladies (his manners were excellent, as Miss Foddy had so often admitted) but the gate refused to open.

"It's stuck," said Lancreste, shaking it.

"Let me have a try," suggested Mr. Abbott, lending his aid.

"Won't it open?" enquired Mrs. Marvell.

"Oh dear! We shall be late!" lamented Miss Foddy.

"What various hindrances we meet,
In coming to the Mercy-Seat,"

said Mr. Marvell, in his sonorous voice. He leaned on the gate, and the extra weight burst it open so that Mr. Abbott was almost precipitated on the muddy path.

Barbara thanked Mr. Marvell, and commented favourably upon his strength (quite oblivious of the fact that her simple praise was infuriating Arthur), and the whole party trooped into church and disposed themselves in their different pews as the Voluntary came to an end.

In church Barbara could not keep her eyes off the Golden Boy. There he sat between the large black hulk of his father, and the small, green figure of his mother; there he sat with his golden head bathed in reddish light from a stained glass window, and his ethereal face raised in worship (at least it looked like that) to his Creator. It was almost too wonderful to be true. His behaviour was perfect; he knelt, and sat, and stood, and never once did his eyes stray round the church. He neither fidgeted like Trivvie, nor sucked peppermint balls like the greedy young Ambrose, and his voice, when he raised it in song, was the most beautiful voice that Barbara had ever heard. It was high above the other voices, crystal clear and as effortless as a bird's. It seemed to Barbara the embodiment of sheer beauty; there was no emotion in it, no expression at all in the clear sweet notes, and yet it thrilled her to the core and brought tears to her eyes.

I must see more of him, Barbara thought. I must get to know him, somehow. He can't possibly be horrid and troublesome like Miss Foddy always says. Look at how good and well-behaved he is, and his face is like the face of an angel—and his voice—I wonder if he would come to tea, Barbara thought. I wonder if he's going to be here in Wandlebury for a little now—I *must* see more of him, somehow. And Barbara was so busy thinking about her Golden Boy, and how she was going to inveigle him into The Archway House, and sustain him with currant buns, and iced cakes, and chocolate biscuits, that poor Mr. Dance's erudite sermon passed in at her left ear and out of her right, even more quickly than it usually did.

Arthur was also inattentive to the exhortation delivered so fervently by Mr. Dance, and *his* thoughts were even less suitable to the occasion than those of his wife. He was still

324

brooding over the scene at the wicket-gate, and anathemising the hero of the occasion in a soundless soliloquy. It was just like that big bounder to barge in like that and obtain all the kudos, thought Mr. Abbott in annoyance. The gate had stuck with the wet weather, of course; I had almost got it open, and then he barges in like a great elephant, and everybody thinks he did it. He's a most dangerous man, thought Mr. Abbott, eyeing the black-cloaked bulk of Mr. Marvell with intense dislike, a most dangerous man. I wonder what Barbara really thinks of him.

★   ★   ★

The day which had opened so auspiciously for Barbara (and so inauspiciously for her husband) continued fair and warm for the time of year. Barbara, wandering round the garden, found that her bulbs were beginning to show little shoots of green. She was enchanted at this further proof that the sun was returning to the Northern Hemisphere. She wandered down to the stream, and found it deserted, save for a thrush, which was extremely busy cracking the shell of a snail against a stone and devouring its inmate. She wandered back to the house, and found it wrapped in Sunday-afternoon peace—Arthur was asleep in his study. She wandered out again and looked at the bulbs. Somehow or other Barbara felt restless to-day. She couldn't account for it, except, of course, that she had seen her Golden Boy. The Golden Boy was a symbol of disturbance—so perhaps that accounted for it. It's funny, thought Barbara, it really *is* funny, but that Golden Boy seems to have made me restless. There can't be anything in it, of course, because the whole thing was just imaginary—it was the only thing I ever imagined until I came here and saw the people in Wandlebury Square—but all the same it seems to have had a funny sort of effect upon me; I don't feel as if I could settle down to anything.

She wandered round, and, as she wandered, she thought about her Golden Boy. What fun it was writing about him, she thought. Shall I write another book? No, I won't. No. I simply mustn't, she decided. If I wrote about the people here they might recognise themselves like the Silverstream people did, and we should have to leave The Archway House. No, I simply mustn't write another book. I'll walk over to Ganthorne Lodge and see Jerry, she thought, perhaps the exercise will do me good.

21

THE PANGS OF CREATION

THE day following Barbara's meeting with her Golden Boy was just as beautiful as its predecessor. Mr. Abbott went up to town as usual, but rather more reluctantly.

"I think I shall try and get away early," he said to his wife as he went down the steps to the car.

"No, I mustn't," said Barbara, staring through him with sightless eyes.

"What?" enquired Arthur, in amazement.

"Nothing."

"What did you say?"

"I don't know—what did *you* say, Arthur?"

"I said I was coming home early."

"Good," said Barbara, without enthusiasm.

Arthur worried about the strangeness of his wife's words and manner all the morning. What had she meant? Was it something to do with that Marvell fellow? "No, I mustn't," *that* was what she had said. What was it that she must not do?

He was still worrying about it at the back of his mind when Sam looked in and asked if he was busy.

"I ought to be, but I'm not," said Mr. Abbott, pushing his papers to one side—"What is it, Sam?"

"D'you think I could get the afternoon off?" enquired Sam diffidently.

"I don't see why you shouldn't," said his uncle kindly. "Going to golf or something?"

"No—er—not exactly," replied Sam.

He had come into the room by this time, and Mr. Abbott was able to observe that his nephew was certainly not dressed for sport. His grey lounge-suit immaculately pressed, his blue tie, and socks and handkerchief, all of which matched so perfectly, and his marvellously polished shoes betokened some less strenuous pastime: a pastime, Mr. Abbott surmised, not unconnected with the fair— sometimes designated the weaker—sex.

"H'm, you're very smart," remarked Mr. Abbott in a jocund manner.

"Yes," replied Sam complacently.

"Going out with a girl, I suppose, eh?"

"Well—er—yes, I am really," admitted

Sam, laughing a trifle selfconsciously. "That is if you don't mind me popping off like this."

"Off you go," said Mr. Abbott. "Off you go. You've been working pretty hard lately——"

"Thanks awfully, sir."

Sam walked out on air—he was going to meet Jerry who had deserted her riding stables for the afternoon. He was so excited at the prospect of seeing her again that he could hardly *breathe*.

I wonder what Sam's up to, reflected Mr. Abbott—in the intervals of dictating letters to his secretary—I wonder what the young devil's up to now. He looked a bit above himself, somehow. *A girl*—thought Mr. Abbott—hope to goodness it's the right sort of girl. If Sam gets entangled with the wrong sort of girl it will be worse than Bow Street— much worse. But I shan't say a word to Barbara—not a word. It isn't fair to either of them to tell tales out of school. But, perhaps, we'd better have the young scoundrel down to Wandlebury again—I'll suggest it to Barbara—he hasn't been down for some time now, and it's a good thing to keep an eye on him. Yes, I must keep an eye on Sam—the young rascal! And Mr. Abbott laughed to himself, and then cleared his throat and said aloud:

"Are you ready, Miss Fitch? Dear Mr. Shillingsworth. We have read your latest novel with much—er—no—er—with *intense* interest full stop we shall be glad if you will allow us er—no—er (damn it, why should I?) we shall be delighted to—er—include it in our Autumn List full stop we note that you are anxious that the book should be published early in the year semi-colon but our Spring List is already—er—complete full stop as regards the proposed cheap edition of *Burnt Trails*—bother, I can't do anything about that till I've seen Spicer."

"No," said Miss Fitch sympathetically. She scratched out the last few words on her shorthand notebook, for it was obvious to her trained intelligence that Mr. Abbott had ceased dictating his letter to Mr. Shillingsworth immediately after the name of the latter's book. She waited for Mr. Abbott's next words with her pencil poised; and her whole attitude betokened eager anticipation—it was the attitude of one who hangs upon the word of a god.

"No—o," said Mr. Abbott doubtfully. *"No,"* said Mr. Abbott firmly. "It will have to wait. Spicer's gone to Birmingham—and that being so," continued Mr. Abbott more cheerfully, "that being so I've a good mind to knock off and go home."

"Yes?" said Miss Fitch, relaxing a little.

"Yes," repeated Mr. Abbott, glancing at the window which was filled with golden sunlight. "Yes, I think so. I'll sign those letters in the morning," he added, rising from his chair to show that he really meant every word he said.

Miss Fitch rose too; she collected her papers and departed without a sound—she really was invaluable.

When Mr. Abbott arrived home, expecting to find a pleased and surprised wife at his beck and call, he was met on the doorstep by Dorcas. Dorcas with a long face and wild eyes.

"Good Heavens!" cried Mr. Abbott, leaping out of the car and dashing up the steps. "Good Heavens, Dorcas, what's happened?"

"Oh, Mr. Abbott!" said Dorcas, almost wringing her hands. "I hardly like to tell you—Oh, Mr. Abbott!"

"What is it?" he enquired frantically. Visions of Barbara eloping with that ghastly Marvell fellow zig-zagged like lightning through his mind. "What is it, Dorcas? For goodness sake tell me what's happened?"

"I've been expecting it," Dorcas said. "I've been expecting this to happen ever since she came back from church yesterday with that queer dazed look in her eyes——"

"What is it?" cried Mr. Abbott, and he seized Dorcas by the arm and shook her gently.

"She's writing," Dorcas said.

"Writing!"

"Yes, writing."

"Is that all?" said Mr. Abbott, mopping his forehead which was beaded with perspiration from the agony of mind he had endured.

"You wouldn't say—*is that all*—if you knew what it's like when she starts," Dorcas told him. "She's been writing all day. She's had no lunch. I knocked on the door and told her it was pigeon-pie, and she never even answered."

"Why didn't you go in?" enquired Mr. Abbott. He was so delighted to find that his wife's preoccupation had nothing to do with Mr. Marvell that he could not take a grave view of the situation. Dorcas was an old wife, she was making a fuss about nothing. Why shouldn't Barbara write if she wanted to?

"Why didn't you go in?" he repeated. "She was too absorbed to hear you knocking on the door, that was all."

"The door's locked," Dorcas told him. "Oh dear!" she lamented. "Oh dear, oh dear—I thought she'd got over it. We were all so happy and peaceful——"

"Don't be absurd, Dorcas," said Mr. Abbott, quite sharply. It really *was* absurd—anybody would think that Barbara had taken to drink, at least, by the way Dorcas was going on.

"Oh, if you'd just go and tell her not to, sir!" Dorcas besought him. "She's locked the door, but, perhaps, she'd open it for *you*—or you could shout at her through the window. You've no idea what it's like when she gets started on that writing—it goes on and on—she's just like a lunatic, she is *really*, sir. You don't know what it's like. She goes on and on; going without meals and sleep and wearing herself—and everybody else—to shreds."

"Don't be absurd," said Mr. Abbott again. He pushed Dorcas aside and went to the door of his study where Barbara was ensconced.

Barbara opened the door at once when she heard his voice. She stood there looking at him with dazed eyes; her hair was standing on end, and she had a smear of ink across one cheek; behind her he could see the desk littered with paper; it had overflowed on to the floor in an untidy wave, and every sheet was closely covered with Barbara's ungainly scrawl.

"I'm—busy——" she said, looking at him vaguely.

Arthur was quite frightened at her appearance; she looked as if she scarcely knew who he was.

"I know you're busy," he said, with assumed cheerfulness. "You've started another book, haven't you? Splendid work! But it's tea-time, now, so you had better knock off for a bit."

"I don't want any tea," Barbara announced firmly.

"But I want some tea," Arthur pointed out. "And I can't have my tea alone. Come along, Barbara, the crumpets will be getting cold."

"I can't leave this mess," said Barbara, indicating the sea of paper, which Arthur had already observed. "They'll tidy it up, or something——"

"That's all right," said Arthur, taking her arm. "Look, Barbara, we'll lock the door and you can put the key in your pocket." He suited the action to the word, and thought (with rueful amusement) as he handed her the key: *my room*, is it? I shall get a fat lot of use out of this room for the next few weeks!

Barbara ate quite a good tea. The crumpets were especially good, and she was naturally hungry. She was rather vague and abstracted at times, but Arthur kept her mind occupied, chatting cheerfully about anything and everything that came into his head. After tea he did not allow her to return to her work, but walked her about the garden, holding on to her arm and inviting her to admire the bulbs which were coming up very quickly in the bright sunshine.

The next morning, after Arthur had departed to the city, Barbara unlocked the study door and locked it again behind her. She spent all day there, writing as if her life depended upon it, and refusing all meals until Arthur returned, and, once more, dug her out of her retreat. This strange state of affairs went on for a fortnight, and Arthur was beginning to get extremely anxious about his wife. She looked pale and worn, and there were dark shadows under her eyes.

"I told you what it would be," Dorcas said,

when he spoke to her about her mistress. "I *knew* what it would be if once she got started. It was like this before—only worse, because, before, she wrote all night sometimes. She wasn't married then, of course."

"How long d'you think it will go on?" enquired Mr. Abbott anxiously. It seemed to him, that, at this rate, Barbara's book must very soon be finished, unless it was going to be one of these new-fashioned, extremely long books like *Anthony Adverse*.

"Oh, not long now, sir," Dorcas assured him. "It never lasts so very long. She gets rid of it so quick, you see."

Dorcas was correct as usual in her prophecy. For, the very next day when Arthur returned from the office, Barbara came to him with a bundle of papers in her hands:

"I'd like you to read it," she said. "It isn't finished, of course, but I can't do any more just now. I feel dry—if you know what I mean—it's all run out of me. But if you'd just read it, and see what you think—I've no idea what it's like myself——"

"I'll read it," said Arthur courageously—the bundle looked extraordinarily unpalatable—"I'll read it, to-night, and see what I think. Is it——" He stopped. He was about to

337

say "is it fact or fiction?" but he refrained. He had been wondering all this time whether the book was "all about Wandlebury" (just as Barbara's other books had been "all about Silverstream"), and whether they would have to leave the place when it was published, but he had had the self-control not to enquire. I can wait a bit longer, he thought, I'll know for certain when I read it, and it will really be better if I come to it with an open mind.

So, after dinner, Arthur settled himself in a comfortable chair in his study (which was once more his own) and prepared to read Barbara's book; and Barbara, after looking at him doubtfully for a moment or two, said:

"Arthur, I wonder if you'd mind if I went to bed. I'm not ill, or anything, but I'm frightfully tired. And, anyhow, I simply couldn't bear to sit here and watch you reading it——"

"Yes, of course, go to bed," said Arthur, looking at her over the top of his reading spectacles (which he had donned for the task ahead of him) and smiling at her kindly. "Of course go up to bed—and go to sleep. I won't wake you when I come up—I shall probably be late, you know—I'll tell you what I think of it in the morning."

338

"Tell me honestly, won't you?" Barbara said, kissing him on the top of his head where the hair was just beginning to get a trifle thin.

"I'll tell you honestly," he promised.

So Barbara went to bed, and Arthur sat up, reading her book, until the small hours of the morning.

22

"THERE'S MANY A SLIP——"

BARBARA had called her new book *There's Many a Slip*——She adored proverbs, of course, and this particular proverb had seemed applicable to the theme of her tale. Arthur was rather pleased with the name, it was in the "John Smith" tradition, and would go very nicely with *The Pen is Mightier*——by the same author. He was even more pleased when he began to read the book—it enthralled him. It was all the more remarkable that the book should enthrall him because it really was in the most appalling muddle, and, in many places, Barbara's writing was almost, if not quite, illegible. In moments of excitement when Barbara was in the grip of her Muse, her brain had outrun her hand, and the writing had become erratic—larger and more ungainly than any writing that Arthur had hitherto had the misfortune to encounter. But, in spite of this, Arthur persevered, and he managed to grasp the trend of the story and to appreciate its rare flavour. Barbara's cunning had not deserted her, neither had marriage dulled the sparkle of her unconscious wit.

"It's better," said Arthur to himself, before he had penetrated more than half-way through the embrangled manuscript. "It's better—and funnier."

It was better and funnier than the previous books, it was more assured, more cohesive. The language was smoother and more colourful; but, in spite of these subtle differences, it was undoubtedly a "John Smith." People who had liked the other two books—and they were legion—would like this one also, and, possibly, like it better.

The humour in this new book was slightly more conscious—so Arthur thought—it was as if the author had begun to realise that she was indeed a humorous person. In the other books the humour had been completely unconscious. Barbara had not known that they were "funny"; had not meant them to be; was, even, slightly hurt by the way that everybody insisted upon the fact that she was first and foremost a humorist. Arthur had heard her assure people that her books were "not funny at all." She had said so to Mr. Spicer, and to one or two other people who were in the secret; but none of them had believed her, of course. Spicer had laughed until he was nearly purple in the face, and had remarked afterwards, to his senior partner, "My word, your wife *is* a wag, in no mistake." Arthur was aware that his wife was not a wag—not in the way that Spicer intended—she was perfectly sincere when she said that her books were not funny. She believed them to be "not funny," and how could a book be funny without its author's knowledge?

Arthur knew all this, of course, but he had not read very far into the new book before he saw that there was a difference in the wit. The wit was not so unconscious. Barbara had begun to realise that she was a wag. The difference was so slight that nobody else would have seen it—nobody who did not know Barbara could possibly have spotted the difference. The difference was only this: in her other books Barbara had been funny without knowing it, and in this book she knew when she was being funny.

The humour in *There's Many a Slip*——lost nothing by being conscious, in fact Arthur thought it had gained. That incident about the lawyer's clerk, who had amused himself

342

by walking so carefully in the middle of each flag-stone (for instance), was amazingly well done. Arthur knew that the incident was true, because he had heard about it at the time, but the written description out-shone the verbal one, as the sun out-shines the moon, and Arthur laughed aloud in the privacy of his study at the humour of it.

He saw, of course, that this new book of Barbara's was partially true. That is to say he recognised the Wandleburians under their different sobriquets. He recognised Jerry and her brother, and the lawyers, and Lady Chevis Cobbe, and he recognised the Marvells and their opprobrious progeny. He and Barbara were Mr. and Mrs. Nun and had come to settle at Church End (which was the name that Barbara had given to Wandlebury in her book).

But why Church End? thought Arthur in perplexity.

In her previous books Barbara had hit on the most delightful pseudonyms for her various characters. Dr. Walker had become "Dr. Rider" and Major Weatherhead had become "Colonel Merryweather"; Mr. Bulmer had been thinly disguised as "Mr. Gaymer" and Mr. Fortnum had naturally become "Mr. Mason." It was all quite easy—anybody could see the connection. In this book, however, the names were disguised with more subtlety (was it because Barbara thought that this precaution would prevent their owners from recognising themselves?) and Arthur could not see the connection at all. Why, for instance, had Mr. and Mrs. Marvell become Mr. and Mrs. Colin Rhodes? And why had the vicar's wife become Mrs. Sittingbourne? What had led Barbara to disguise Mr. Tyler as Mr. Reade and Lady Chevis Cobbe as Lady Savage Brette? He decided to ask Barbara about it in the morning, and returned to his perusal of the manuscript.

The little character sketches interested Arthur enormously. Barbara was exceedingly good at getting under people's skins, and she had evidently taken a good deal of trouble with the Wandleburians. She knew the neighbours better than Arthur, of course, because she saw more of them. She was in Wandlebury all day whilst he was at the office, but Arthur knew them well enough to see that their portraits were excellent—they were life size. The character sketch of Mr. Colin Rhodes (the painter) was perhaps the most interesting from Arthur's point of view. When he had read all that Barbara had to say about Mr. Rhodes he put down the manuscript and roared with laughter. The laughter was partly amusement and partly relief— there was absolutely no need to worry any more. Barbara had seen through Mr. Rhodes. "What a fool I was!" said Arthur aloud. He saw quite distinctly that Barbara liked the man, and that he amused her enormously, but he also saw that the man only interested her as a type. It is much easier to make a striking character sketch of a person with striking characteristics than to make a character live when he is more or less like other people. Barbara had never seen anybody the least like Mr. Marvell before, and his peculiarities had provided her with invaluable copy. On the whole Barbara had been kind to Mr. Marvell (or Mr. Rhodes as she had called him), she had limned him sympathetically, and with a certain admiration. She had given him full marks for all his good points—his immense size, his good humour, his resonant voice, and his amazing memory for apt quotations—but it was abundantly clear to Arthur that there was no need for him to be jealous of the man. "If

Barbara sees him as clearly as *that*——" said Arthur to himself, and then he added, "How on earth does she do it?"

How on earth did she do it—his shy, slightly gauche Barbara? How could she write of men as she did, with such true insight? She saw them naked (as it were), stripped of all their little subterfuges, their mannerisms, the coverings that they assumed to shield their inadequate souls from the world's gaze. She saw them naked and calmly limned them so; not aware, in her kind, pleasant mind, that she was giving the show away. How did she do it? A man of genius is said to include a woman and a child amongst his elements. Was Barbara a woman of genius, harbouring amongst her purely feminine—nay, spinsterish—elements, a man's soul?

Arthur had already made up his mind that *There's Many a Slip*——was partly fact and partly fiction. The people in the book were obviously the Wandleburians, but the actual tale was fiction—so Arthur decided. The story was concerned with a will which had been made by Lady Savage Brette, disinheriting her nephew, young Mr. Philip Brette (who was obviously Jerry Cobbe's rather unpleasant brother). Nobody knew about this

346

will except Mrs. Nun, who had been given it to read by mistake, when she visited the lawyer's office to enquire about a house. This was all pure fiction, of course, and Arthur was considerably impressed by the flight of fancy on the part of his hitherto unimaginative wife. It was fiction, thought Arthur, and damn funny fiction at that. The agony of the little lawyer when he discovered his mistake was finely conceived. Barbara's imagination was growing (she had said that Wandlebury might help it grow, and obviously Wandlebury had. Arthur felt quite pleased about it, because he knew how pleased Barbara must be).

The title of *There's Many a Slip*—referred, of course, to young Mr. Philip Brette's disappointment over his expectations from his Rich Aunt. He had built upon his expectations, and when the will was read and he found himself disinherited in favour of his sister, he was extremely annoyed—in fact he was furious. He dashed off to London in his small—but speedy—car and disappeared out of the picture. The terms of Lady Savage Brette's will interested Arthur a good deal. She had left everything to her niece Miss Jennifer Brette on condition that the said

Jennifer was unmarried. Arthur happened to know that this was just the sort of peculiar will that Lady Chevis Cobbe might make, but he did not see how Barbara could have known this. How had Barbara got to know of her ladyship's peculiar attitude towards marriage? Arthur had not told her, he had kept Monkey's confidences on the subject sealed in his own breast. "I suppose there's a lot of gossip about it," said Arthur to himself.

At any rate, however Barbara had come to know about it—or surmise it—she had made good use of the knowledge in her story, for the *pièces de résistances* in her book were the machinations of Mrs. Nun to prevent her young friend Jennifer from marrying a young man called Bob Groome. This Bob Groome (whom Arthur suspected was in reality none other than his own nephew Sam) was desperately in love with Jennifer. He was in love with Jennifer to a positively alarming extent. Mrs. Nun, having seen the will, was aware that if Bob and Jennifer were to get married it would be all up with Jennifer as regards the Savage Estates, for it was only if Jennifer were unmarried that she was to inherit. Mrs. Nun's dilemma was acute, because she was inhibited, by a solemn promise to Mr. Reade, from breathing a word about the will to a living soul. She was, however, a dauntless creature, and she set to work and plotted and planned like a female Richelieu. She managed by fair means and foul to keep the young people apart, until the fortunate demise of the Rich Aunt cleared the way; whereupon Jennifer got her inheritance; and she and her lover fell upon each other's necks; and the unfortunate Philip (who had built upon everything coming to him) was cast forth into utter darkness with weeping and wailing and gnashing of teeth.

It was an excellent plot, well sustained, and well worked out, and the end was extraordinarily satisfying. Arthur was rather sorry for the disinherited young man, whose cup had been (so unceremoniously) dashed from his lips, but he was aware that other people would not share his views. The young man had no business to build upon his expectations, he had deserved all he got. In John Smith's books people always got what they deserved; it was one of the reasons why they were so popular. The general public likes people to get what they deserve: wedding bells for the hero and heroine, and utter desolation for the villain of the piece. *There's*

Many a Slip—— fulfilled these conditions admirably.

In one sense the book was finished, for the end was there; it was a whole story, complete from beginning to end—but, in another sense, the book was by no means finished. (Arthur saw exactly what Barbara had meant when she had thrust it into his hands and said "It isn't finished, of course.") The book required a good deal of padding here and there, and a great deal of polishing; and, in several places, it required cutting down or building up. It resembled a rough diamond—a diamond in the raw, so to speak. This was quite easy to understand, for Barbara had written it straight off with tremendous speed; she had had no time to polish it up as she went along. It now required calm consideration. But the book was good; it was very good indeed; it was excellent.

Arthur went to bed.

23

SAILING UNDER FALSE COLOURS

ARTHUR was wakened very early in the morning. He opened his eyes and beheld his wife's face leaning over him. The face wore an expression of anxiety and anticipation. It was just beginning to get light and the birds were singing like mad outside the window.

"What's the matter?" enquired Arthur, rising slowly from the waters of oblivion. He had been dreaming that Archie Cobbe was pursuing him with a boat-hook and demanding why Mr. Abbott had cut him off with a shilling. Mr. Abbott had been vaguely aware that the only hope for him was to get hold of Monkey. Monkey must do something about it; he must bring Lady Chevis Cobbe back to life and get her to alter her will. It was an extraordinarily vivid dream—a bit muddled, of course, as all dreams are, but extraordinarily vivid.

"Did I wake you?" Barbara asked

anxiously. "I didn't mean to wake you."

"No—at least I don't really know," Arthur said. "I was dreaming."

"I've been awake for *ages*," Barbara continued. "Simply *ages*. I've been longing to wake you up. What did you think of it, Arthur?"

"What!" exclaimed Arthur, yawning and rubbing his eyes.

"What did you think of the book?" repeated Barbara anxiously.

Arthur woke up properly. Most men would have been a little irritable at being awakened at dawn—especially if they had not got to bed until the small hours of the morning—but Arthur was not the least bit cross. He was really a very kind nice husband and his liver was in excellent order.

"It's good," he said, "definitely good."

"Oh, Arthur!—really?"

"Yes, excellent."

"Oh, Arthur, I *am* glad. Tell me the bits you like."

Arthur rolled over on to his back and gazed at the ceiling. He tried to visualise the book; to recapture the aroma of it—as it were.

"I like it all," he said. "It's a well-written book—your writing has come on a lot—and it's very funny. You know you're funny now, don't you?"

"Yes," said Barbara. "Yes, I suppose I do."

"The people are awfully good," continued Arthur thoughtfully. "It is amazing how you see people—how do you, Barbara?"

"I just watch them, I suppose," said Barbara. "I don't really know I'm watching them, but I suppose I must. People are so funny, aren't they? I mean they're so interesting—and all different. They're all so busy living their own lives (if you know what I mean) and they're all so certain that they're frightfully important. And the queer thing is that the very busy serious ones are much the funniest."

"Yes," said Arthur, wondering, a little, whether he came into the very busy, serious, and, therefore, funniest category.

"Tell me more," Barbara adjured him, settling herself comfortably upon the pillows.

"The plot is excellent," continued Arthur obediently. "The plot is really very neat indeed. I was particularly struck with the way you have blended fact with fiction."

"I don't quite understand."

"I mean the whole book is cohesive,"

Arthur explained. "If I didn't happen to know that part of the book is fact and part fiction I should never have guessed it for a moment. Take a historical novel," continued Arthur, trying to make his point clear, "take a historical novel as an example of what I mean. A historical novel is very difficult to write, not only because the atmosphere is difficult to achieve, and the small details of costume and manners are so apt to trip an author into anachronisms; but, also, and principally, because he has to blend fiction with fact. In nearly all historical novels you can see exactly where fact and fiction join—like a badly-sewn seam—the book is very apt to be patchy. You can place your finger on the different patches and say: this is history, and this is imagination. Even Scott, an acknowledged master of the historical novel, is guilty of this patchiness in places."

Barbara followed this with interest. "But my book isn't a historical novel," she pointed out.

"It *is*," said Arthur. "It really is, Barbara. It's a modern historical novel (don't you see) because a lot of it is fact. And that's why I said I admired the way you have blended fact with fiction. It all dovetails beautifully.

354

Nobody could say: "*this* is fact, and *this* is fiction," unless they happened to know—as I do—where the one ends and the other begins."

Barbara saw exactly what he meant, but she still could not see how it applied to her book. Her book was all fact. She had voyaged into the future, of course, when she had described the death of Lady Savage Brette and the reading of her will, and the beautiful *finale* where Bob and Jennifer fell upon each other's necks, but that had been easy. It had needed no imagination—or very little—to envisage that ending to her tale.

"It all dovetails beautifully," said Arthur. "The true parts about the Wandlebury people, and the imaginative parts about the will—you can never say you haven't got an imagination again," he added in his "smiling voice."

Barbara was silent. She was in rather a quandary. She saw now exactly what Arthur meant. She hated to deceive Arthur, but, if she was to keep her promise to Mr. Tyler, she must let Arthur continue in his delusion. She must let him think she had made up all that about the will—about Mrs. Nun seeing it by mistake, and all that. She felt very uncomfortable about it because she was naturally extremely truthful—but, of course, I *can't* break my promise, she thought, at least not until Lady Chevis Cobbe dies and the will is read. Then, of course, everybody will know, and I can tell Arthur all about it. Meantime (thought Barbara) I must just let him think I've got an imagination. It was sailing under false colours, and Barbara disliked it, but there was absolutely no help for it as far as she could see.

Arthur noticed her silence. He rolled over in bed and gazed at her in astonishment. "You don't mean to tell me it's *true*?" he enquired incredulously. "All that part about the will—you don't mean to tell me you actually saw the will——"

"No," said Barbara firmly. "No, Arthur."

It's *not* a lie, she thought, because, of course, I didn't mean to tell him. (This Jesuitical quibble was unlike Barbara's straightforward nature, but she was in a hole, and there was no other way out.)

Barbara's denial convinced Arthur at once, for habitually truthful people are always believed when they prevaricate, just as habitually untruthful people are often disbelieved when they tell the truth. Arthur was

356

satisfied with Barbara's "No" because she had never lied to him, and also, of course, because he was prejudiced beforehand. All that about Mrs. Nun seeing the will at the lawyer's office was much more like fiction than fact. Things like that didn't happen in the ordinary everyday world which Mr. Abbott inhabited.

"No, I thought not," he agreed. "And that's what I meant—don't you see—when I said you had blended fact and fiction so well. Because, of course, I realise that a great deal of the book is fact. All the characters are real people, and the clerk showing you over the house, and the Musical Evening, and the Marvells' dinner party and all that."

"Yes, of course," said Barbara who was thankful that the conversation had taken a safer turn.

"The people really *are* good," continued Arthur, chuckling a little. "They really are splendid—so *real*, I couldn't quite make out how you had got their names. I meant to ask you about that. Why has Mr. Marvell become Mr. Colin Rhodes, for instance?"

"Well, you see it was the names that got me into trouble before," Barbara explained. "So this time I didn't alter the names. I didn't think of their real names at all when I was choosing names for them. I just thought of what they were like, or of what they happened to be doing when I saw them. Mr. Marvell was easy—he's the biggest person I've ever seen, so I thought of the Colossus of Rhodes."

Arthur chortled happily.

"And Lady Chevis Cobbe was easy, too, because of her Musical Evening. 'Music hath charms to soothe the savage breast'," explained Barbara seriously. "I just changed it a tiny bit and called her Lady Savage Brette. It sounded rather grand, I thought."

"Excellent," agreed Arthur, "go on, Barbara."

"Well then there was Mrs. Thane—she was planting bulbs one day when I went to see her, so I called her Mrs. Philpotts. And Mr. Tyler was Mr. Reade because he kept on giving me papers to read and telling me to read them."

Arthur was enjoying himself immensely. "Why did you call Wandlebury 'Church End'?" he enquired.

"It was really Search End," she told him. "Because my search ended when I found

Wandlebury, but I thought Church End looked better."

"And what about Mrs. Dance? Why did you call her Sittingbourne?"

"Oh, that really was rather funny," said Barbara, giggling a little at the recollection of the manner in which she had named the vicar's wife. "That really *was* rather funny. You see, the day she called we had to sit on the stairs—there was nowhere else to sit—and it was frightfully hard and uncomfortable—I felt exactly as if my spine was coming *through*—and, all the time, I was longing for her to go, because I had such lots of things I wanted to do—I could hardly *bear* it——"

"Sitting-borne," said Arthur, laughing heartily.

"Yes," agreed Barbara, "it just sort of *came* to me."

"It was an inspiration," said Arthur (when he could speak).

"It's the only kind of inspiration I ever get," Barbara told him. "I mean I have to have something to help me. I never get an inspiration straight out of the blue. I've got to have a kind of jumping-board before I can jump at all—if you know what I mean—otherwise my feet remain fixed to the ground.

Other authors," she continued, rather enviously, "other authors seem to be able to jump off the ground of their own accord. I mean they can imagine things without any help, but I'm not like that."

"I like the name," said Arthur, trying to change the subject and take her mind off her disability. "I like the name of the book very much indeed. It goes very well with *The Pen is Mightier*—— and is quite in the 'John Smith' tradition. You will make a lot of money out of the book, Barbara."

"But it mustn't be published!" cried Barbara, sitting bolt-upright in bed and gazing at him with horror-stricken eyes. "I never meant it to be *published*, Arthur."

"Not published!" exclaimed her publisher in amazement.

"No, no, *no*—how could you think it, Arthur?"

"But why——"

"Because we should have to leave Wandlebury—and I couldn't—I simply couldn't. You don't *want* to leave here, do you?"

"No, of course not, but——"

"We should *have* to," Barbara assured him. "We should have to leave The Archway House, and it would break my heart."

"But why did you——"

"Because I *had* to," said Barbara earnestly. "Because I couldn't help it. I had to write the book because it was all inside me, simply bursting to come out, but I never meant it to be published—not for one moment."

"Why were you so anxious for me to like it, then?" enquired Arthur, in a bewildered voice. He had never yet met an author who did not want his—or her—book to be published.

"Because I wanted it to be good," Barbara told him. "I wanted it to be good, and I wanted you to like it. I should have been frightfully disappointed if you had thought it rubbish."

"It *is* good and I like it immensely," said Arthur. "It seems a pity——"

"No, no, *no*," she cried again. "They would recognise themselves, and we should have to leave. And, even if they didn't, I should always be thinking that they were going to, and I should never have another peaceful moment. You've no idea what it was like at Silverstream—the strain nearly wore me out. It was ghastly."

"We might alter it a little," suggested Arthur, whose soul was torn in twain. He saw

361

Barbara's point of view, and he would have been extremely sorry to leave The Archway House, but all the publisher in him (and, naturally, there was a good deal of the publisher in his make-up) wanted to publish *There's Many a Slip*—— by John Smith. It was so satisfactory to publish a book that you *knew* would sell like hot cakes, and there was no doubt that this one would. The other two books had been amazingly successful, and this one was of the same ilk—only better. John Smith's name alone would sell a couple of editions straight off—no wonder poor Arthur was torn in twain. "Couldn't we alter it a little, Barbara?" he enquired anxiously.

"I should be terrified," said Barbara with a shudder.

"It seems such a pity," Arthur pointed out, "and I really think it would be quite safe if we were to alter the people a little and——"

"But how could we?" enquired the author. "I mean the people are themselves—how could we *alter* them?"

They discussed the matter carefully (argued would be too strong a word), but they could come to no decision. They could not really understand each other's point of view. This was Barbara's fault, of course, she was extremely bad at explaining what she felt, and, when she felt very deeply about anything, she became even more incoherent and inarticulate than usual. Arthur pointed out that the people in Barbara's book could be made to look quite different without interfering in the least with the main theme, and that, if this were done, the book could be published with perfect safety. It was quite a reasonable suggestion, and Arthur was rather proud of it, but, to Barbara, the suggestion was impracticable, not to say absurd. Barbara saw the matter from the author's standpoint, and, although she could not explain it in plain English, she knew that it was impossible to alter the appearance of her characters; for an author does not consciously create his characters, they come to him ready-made with all their characteristics firmly fixed, and the author can do nothing with his character but accept or reject him—he cannot change or modify the personality that has arisen without making him unreal. If Arthur had suggested that Barbara, herself, should suddenly become small and blonde with a complexion of milk and roses, the suggestion would have seemed to Barbara no more ridiculous and impossible than his suggestion that she should alter the appearance of the people in her book. She felt all this very strongly indeed, but she could not put it into words.

"But then they wouldn't be them," was all she could manage to say, and even that was a struggle.

Arthur began to get a little muddled too, for Barbara's incoherency was frightfully infectious. "You don't want them to be them," he told her earnestly.

"But, if they're not them, they're nobody—they're nothing," said Barbara in despair.

"I only meant——" began Arthur.

"And if I make Colin Rhodes small and—and weedy," continued Barbara desperately, "If I make him small, and weedy-looking—like you said—then he isn't him, at all, and there's no point in him, at all, and how is he going to say, 'How white a woman is, under the moon!'? No small, mean-looking man could say *that*," added Barbara with conviction.

* * *

It happened to be a Saturday, and Arthur took the day off. He had not arranged to play golf so they had the whole day at their disposal, and ample opportunity to discuss *There's Many a Slip*——. They discussed it off and on all day long. Arthur continued to toy with the idea of changing the appearance of the characters and publishing the book. He even went the length of producing a pencil and paper and showing Barbara how easily it could be done. Barbara listened to all he said quite patiently, but she remained unconvinced.

"I should *die* if we had to leave The Archway House," she reiterated.

"But if we changed the appearance of the characters——"

"We can't," she said. "I *know* we can't. It's difficult to explain, Arthur, but I just know it in my bones."

Arthur was aware that when Barbara knew a thing in her bones it was conclusive. There was absolutely nothing more to be said or done. He pocketed his pencil with a sigh.

"I'm sorry," Barbara continued. "I really am most awfully sorry, but it's no good—no good at all. And anyhow I couldn't do anything *now*. I'm absolutely dry. I haven't got anything more left in me, Arthur."

"We'll put it aside, then," Arthur suggested. "We'll leave it in the meantime. Perhaps later on——"

They compromised on that. Arthur locked up the manuscript in the bottom drawer of his bureau and hung the key on his chain; but he couldn't lock up his thoughts so easily. He and Barbara went out for a walk together, and still they discussed the book.

"It seems a pity that I'm the only person who can really appreciate how clever it is," Arthur said, "other people would enjoy it, of course, but they couldn't appreciate it without knowing the Wandlebury people."

"I don't mind," said Barbara, "as long as you like it that's all that matters. I wrote it for myself and you."

"Sam knows the people here," said Arthur thoughtfully.

"Sam mustn't read it!"

"No, of course not. As a matter of fact I doubt whether anybody *could* read it until it has been re-written," Arthur said, thinking of his struggle to decipher Barbara's peculiar scrawl. "No, of course not, but what about having Sam down next weekend? He hinted to me that he would like to come, but, of course, it was no good while you were working."

"No," said Barbara.

"Eh?" enquired Arthur in surprise. "Don't you want Sam?"

"Not just now."

"Why? He'll be disappointed. As a matter of fact I said I would ask you if he could come. I thought you liked Sam."

"Yes, I do like him."

"Well, why not have him?"

"Don't let's have him" said Barbara. "Don't let's have anybody," she added with feminine guile, and she pressed Arthur's arm.

Arthur fell for this at once—what loving husband wouldn't have fallen?—he laughed a trifle self-consciously.

"Just our two selves, eh?" he said.

"Yes."

"Well, that's O.K. by me—as Sam would say," replied Arthur and he returned the pressure affectionately.

"You can tell him we're going to do the Spring Cleaning," Barbara said. "I mean if you want an excuse. It's quite true, of course; we shall have to start quite soon now."

"Right—but that's not the *real* reason, is it?" enquired Arthur pressing her arm again.

"No, that's not the real reason," replied Barbara truthfully.

367

24

"THE BEST LAID PLANS"

SAM was extremely disappointed when his hints about a visit to The Archway House fell on deaf ears. He couldn't understand it at all. I'm sure they liked having me, he thought, I'm certain of it. Why on earth won't they have me any more? He wrote to Jerry, and received long letters in reply, and that was very nice, of course, but it was not enough. Jerry came up to town once or twice, and Sam gave her tea at the club, but that was not enough, either. They couldn't talk properly, and Sam felt that Jerry was not really Jerry at all in her town clothes. She was quite different, and so was he, it was frightfully unsatisfactory. Sam wanted to go to Wandlebury; he wanted to see Jerry properly; he wanted to hold her in his arms and kiss her darling mouth.

"If they don't ask me soon I shall *ask* them to have me," Sam said. "I simply can't bear not seeing you——"

368

"But you're seeing me now," Jerry pointed out, smiling at his impatience.

"Not properly," growled Sam.

"Well, I don't see why you shouldn't ask them to have you," said Jerry thoughtfully. "Ask them, Sam."

"I will," said Sam boldly. "I've hinted till I'm blue in the face, and Uncle Arthur takes no notice, but I shall ask him straight out on Monday—we'll know where we are, then."

So on Monday Sam walked into his uncle's sanctum and enquired, with a charming smile, whether he could come to The Archway House for the week-end. "I haven't been down since Christmas," he reminded Uncle Arthur, "and it seems ages. I should love to come down for a few days—hope you don't think it awful cheek of me to suggest it," he added, with a slightly forced laugh.

"No, not at all," said Mr. Abbott. "Why shouldn't you ask? As a matter of fact we can't have you at the moment. Barbara's going to start Spring Cleaning or something."

"Oh!" said Sam in dismay.

"Later on," added Mr. Abbott kindly, "you must come later on."

"Uncle Arthur," said Sam desperately, "do

369

you think I've offended Barbara or anything? I mean I know I say silly things sometimes. D'you think she's fed up with me about anything?"

"No, no, my boy," replied his uncle heartily, "Barbara's not like that a bit."

"I wouldn't do anything to hurt Barbara for *Worlds*," continued Sam wretchedly, "not for *Worlds*. She's been so frightfully decent. Perhaps you'd tell her," he continued, humbling himself to the ground, "perhaps you'd tell her that if I've done anything, or said anything——"

"No, no!" interrupted Arthur Abbott, quite aghast at the spectacle of his young and personable relative in such distress. "No, *no!* It isn't that at all. Barbara likes you very much, she said so."

"Well, what is it, then?" enquired Sam, desperately.

This placed Arthur Abbott in rather a hole. He was not going to disclose the true reason for Sam's exclusion—it was a little secret between himself and Barbara. ("Just our two selves?" he had said, and Barbara had replied "Yes.") It was a little secret, the sort of little secret that husbands and wives share with each other, but nobody else. Other people might think it rather silly—it wasn't silly, of course, but other people might think it was—so other people must not know about it. The other reason, that Barbara had told him to offer, about the Spring Cleaning had fallen rather flat. Arthur had thought it was thin, himself, and Sam had, quite obviously, seen through it. Arthur had no third reason to offer the pertinacious Sam. As a matter of fact he was sorry for Sam. He was very fond of the boy—the more so because Sam really appeared to have settled down and got over "all that nonsense." He was finding Sam very useful now, and it was nice to see Sam's fresh young face in the dusty office, and to think—*he's mine, my blood.* (Blood is thicker than water, as Barbara would have said.)

"By the way, Sam," said Arthur Abbott, trying to turn the subject into pleasanter channels, "by the way, I was speaking to Spicer, and we have decided to—er—raise your salary. You're doing well now, and you're most useful and—er—reliable."

"Oh, thank you, sir!"

"Yes, I'm extremely pleased with the—er—way you're sticking into it—extremely pleased, Sam."

"Thank you, sir. It's most awfully good of you."

"Not at all. That's all right. You're worth it, old fellow," and Arthur Abbott patted his young nephew on the shoulder in an affectionate manner.

"I'm frightfully pleased," Sam assured him.

"That's all right. Run along, now. I've got to get some work done, you know."

"And Uncle Arthur, you'll tell Barbara," said Sam eagerly. "You'll speak to her and tell her all I've said, and if I've done anything—or had I better write?" suggested Sam. "Perhaps I should *write*——"

"Look here, Sam, this is *nonsense*," said Mr. Abbott, kindly and reassuringly, "this is absolute rubbish, Sam. I've told you that there's no reason at all——"

"There must be," said Sam wildly.

"You're getting all worked up about nothing," said Mr. Abbott, he was at his wits' end (ground between the mill-stones of Barbara and Sam). He felt that he could do no more. He had said what he had been told to say and it was no use—none at all. Sam was determined to come for the week-end, or know the reason why, and, if Barbara didn't want him for the week-end, she would have to tell him herself. "Look here," he said, shifting the responsibility to his weaker half, "look here, Sam. I'll tell you what we'll do. You get your things together, and come down with me for the night. Then you can see Barbara for yourself, and you'll see that it's all right. If you won't take my word for it," said Mr. Abbott, smiling to show Sam that this was a joke, "if you won't take my word for it the only thing is to see her for yourself."

Needless to say, Sam was enchanted with the plan. He had intended to go to a Fancy Dress Ball with the Frenshams, and to spend the night—or what remained of it—at their flat; but what was a Fancy Dress Ball in comparison with the chance of seeing Jerry? It was less than nothing. Sam threw the Frenshams overboard without a qualm. If he could not see Jerry in the evening, he could be certain of seeing her in the morning. I can sprint over to Ganthorne before breakfast, he thought, darling, *darling* Jerry!

"I've got my suitcase here, sir," he said eagerly. "No evening things, of course——"

"Good Lord, that doesn't matter!" Arthur said, laughing, "as long as you've got a tooth-brush—I can lend you anything else you need. Now, off you go—here, Sam," he added, handing over a bulky-looking manuscript, "have a look through this, will you. Tell me what you think of it. I shall be ready to go about five."

Sam gathered up the manuscript and fled to telephone to Toby Frensham. His heart was singing like a bird.

Barbara was unfeignedly pleased to see Sam. She liked him immensely and it had been a great deprivation to her to exclude him from The Archway House. She laughed at his idea that he might have offended her in some way, and assured him that he was mistaken. But, to Sam's consternation, she also made it abundantly clear that the invitation to spend a long week-end at Wandlebury was not to be forthcoming.

"How could you be so silly!" she exclaimed. "Of course I'm not offended with you, Sam, and we love having you—you *know* that. I've been busy, that's all—and, of course, we're going to start Spring Cleaning—I told Arthur to explain——"

"I did explain, but he wouldn't believe me," Arthur told her laughing.

"Couldn't I help in the Spring Cleaning?" Sam enquired anxiously. "I'm awfully good at hanging pictures and all that, you know."

Barbara was rather touched at this evidence of affection on the part of her nephew by marriage, but she steeled her heart. It would be impossible to keep an eye on Sam, and prevent him from meeting Jerry—more especially if she, herself, were busy with domestic tasks. Mrs. Nun had been able to manage it all beautifully, of course, but, although Barbara Abbott was much more adequate and adroit than Barbara Buncle had ever been, she had not yet reached the pitch of adequacy and adroitness enjoyed by Elizabeth Nun. I can't risk it, Barbara thought, and she regretfully—and very kindly—refused the noble offer.

"Later on," she said, just as Arthur had said, "you must come for a long visit later on, when the Spring Cleaning is over," and she thought to herself (somewhat callously, it must be owned) *that woman can't possibly last much longer. What a nuisance she is!*

"That's right," agreed Arthur. "That's right—a long visit later on. Meanwhile we must make the most of to-night."

"Oh, to-night!" exclaimed Barbara frowning, "I'd quite forgotten—we're going out to dinner with the Thanes. Oh dear, what a pity, isn't it? Had you forgotten, too, Arthur?"

Arthur had forgotten, too. He looked anything but pleased at being reminded of it.

"Couldn't we put it off?" he enquired, not very hopefully.

"Oh, don't bother about *me*!" cried Sam—too eagerly.

"I don't see how we *could*," said Barbara slowly. "If it was anybody else it wouldn't matter so much. But it's such a small house—Mrs. Thane's, I mean—and they will have taken such a lot of trouble to have everything nice. I really don't see how we could put it off *now*."

"Of *course* you must go," cried Sam. "Of *course* you must. I only came down to *see* you, Barbara. I shall be quite happy here till you come back. It would be dreadful to disappoint Mrs. Thane at the last minute, like this. She will have got everything ready. I shouldn't wonder if it would make her quite *ill*—she's not strong, is she? Of course you must go. I shall be all right—*really*."

Yes, thought Barbara, as she went upstairs and began to dress for the dinner-party (with the aid of the faithful Dorcas). Yes, he'll be quite happy. He'll go over and see Jerry, that's what he'll do. I can see it in his face. The moment our backs are turned he'll be off to Ganthorne like a flash of lightning. Now, how on earth am I going to prevent him—because, of course, I must prevent him. I *must* keep them apart until Lady Chevis Cobbe dies. Dear me, she thought, how unfortunate it is that we've got to go out to-night! It *would* happen like that. How I wish I was clever like Elizabeth Nun! thought Barbara, *she* would have known exactly what to do. What a nuisance it is! What a frightful nuisance! But she can't go on living for ever, and once she's dead (thought Barbara) once she's safely dead, I can have Sam here as much as I like and *throw* them together, because really and truly they're just *made* for each other. What a pity it is—thought Barbara, as she rummaged in her jewel-case for her diamond star—what a frightful pity it is that Lady Chevis Cobbe is so *queer*! It must be so unhappy to be queer like that and not like to see people happily married. I suppose it's rather wicked of me to wish she was dead, but what good is she—poor creature—to herself or anybody else? I'm sure I would rather be killed quite suddenly in a motor accident or something than linger on like that.

"Dorcas!" she said, as she sat down, and allowed her faithful slave to button her shoes. "Dorcas, don't you think it's a queer thing to pray to be delivered from sudden death?"

"How you do startle me, Miss Barbara— Mrs. Abbott, I mean!" Dorcas exclaimed. "Sudden death, indeed! What's set you thinking about sudden death—and you all dressed ready to go out to a party——"

"I'd rather die suddenly than lingeringly," Barbara told her, "wouldn't you, Dorcas?"

"I'm sure I never thought of it," replied Dorcas. "There's no sense in thinking such morbid things that I can see. I'll die when my time comes, I suppose. There," she added practically, "there's your shoes buttoned. I'll just run down and give your evening boots a wipe over. Don't you be long now, for I heard Mr. Abbott go down a minute or two ago, and he hates being kept waiting."

Dorcas bustled off, full of importance, and Barbara caught up her evening cloak and prepared to follow. She peeped into Sam's room on the way down—to say good-bye and to tell him not to wait up for them if they were late—but Sam was not there. She listened, and heard him splashing in the bathroom. Sam's clothes were hung over a chair in his room: his grey trousers, with the dangling braces attached to them, his jacket and waist-coat, his neat blue shirt, and other more intimate garments. For a moment or two Barbara stood there and looked at them—an idea was coming to her, a tremendous inspiration; she waited for it breathlessly—it came.

Barbara seized the trousers and ran back to her room; she turned back the mattress of her bed; she spread the trousers tenderly upon the frame—taking care that the creases were exactly right, for Sam's trousers were sacred garments, and worthy of the greatest consideration—she turned down the mattress again, and smoothed the counterpane. Did it look exactly as it had looked before? It did. Nobody would know that Sam's trousers were now reposing peacefully beneath her mattress, nobody could possibly guess. Barbara caught up her bag, and tripped gaily down the stairs; she donned her evening boots, and preceded her somewhat impatient husband into the waiting car.

Sam, still luxuriating in his bath, heard them drive off. He lifted his voice in song. It was all *too* right, too utterly marvellous. He would bolt the "little dinner," arranged for him by his kind hostess, and sprint over to Ganthorne Lodge. How pleased, how surprised darling Jerry would be! He dried himself with energy and returned to his bedroom. How lucky that he had crammed a clean white collar into his bag at the last moment! Here it was! Arrayed in vest and pants, Sam did one or two simple exercises—stretching and bending—just for the sheer joy of it, to feel his fit young body moving in harmony with his will. . . .

Better hurry, he thought—as he drew on his shirt and fixed his collar and tie with deft fingers—better hurry, all the more time with Jerry if I'm quick—gadzooks, where are my trousers?

Where were they, indeed? Sam hunted high and low, he rushed into the bath-room, to see if by any chance he had taken them in there with him when he went to his bath; he looked in the cupboard to see whether some fool of a housemaid had hung them up; he looked in every drawer, behind the dressing-chest, under the bed. When he had done this his hair was standing on end, and the clean collar was slightly wilted, but he had not found the trousers.

Some fool's taken them to brush, he thought and he rang the bell.

The bell was answered by Dorcas, because everybody else had gone out except the cook—and *she* couldn't be expected to answer bells.

"Did you ring, sir?" enquired Dorcas, peeping in at the door. She was somewhat taken aback at the sight of young Mr. Abbott in his shirt, with no trousers on.

"I rang," agreed Sam. "What I want to know is—where are my trousers?"

"Your trousers, sir?"

"Yes, my trousers—where are they?"

"I don't know, sir."

"Well, find out, then," said Sam irritably. "Some fool has taken away my trousers—to brush or something, I suppose—and I haven't got any others."

"I'll find out, sir," Dorcas said.

She was away a long time—or so it seemed—and Sam, having nothing else to do, hunted furiously in all the places he had hunted in before: under the bed, behind the dressing-chest, in all the drawers.

Dorcas came back empty-handed. "Nobody's taken them," she said. "They aren't anywhere downstairs. They aren't in

Mr. Abbott's room neither—I looked there—they must be here. Have you looked, sir?"

"Looked!" cried Sam in exasperation. "*Looked!* Of course, I've looked. I've looked everywhere. You look, yourself."

Dorcas came in, and looked carefully in all the places that Sam had already looked in twice.

"They don't seem to be here, sir," she said at last.

"You're quite sure of that, I suppose," said Sam sarcastically.

"Well, they don't *seem* to be," she repeated, "are you sure you brought them with you, sir?"

"My God!" exclaimed Sam. "Am I sure? Do you think I came down from London without any trousers on?"

"You were wearing them, you mean?" enquired Dorcas.

"I was wearing them," agreed Sam, "at least I imagined I was—and I really think I must have been. Somebody might have noticed if I hadn't been wearing them——"

"Well, they must be here, then," said Dorcas.

"You have said it," Sam told her.

"Well, where are they?"

"God knows," said Sam wearily. "At least I suppose He does."

Dorcas was somewhat shocked at the irreverence, but she passed it over—after all the young gentleman had a right to be annoyed—the thing was most extraordinary, most mysterious.

"Perhaps it's the ghost," said Dorcas suddenly.

"The ghost?"

"Yes, there's a ghost in The Archway House, you know. We haven't been seeing it lately, of course, but it may have come back."

"Queer kind of ghost to go off with a pair of trousers!"

"No," said Dorcas earnestly. "It's just the sort of thing it might do. It used to hide the workmen's tools, and the charwoman's pails. I'm sure it must be the ghost—what else could it be?"

Sam wasn't listening. Up to now he had been annoyed and irritated by the loss of his trousers, but now, quite suddenly, he became desperate. How was he going to see Jerry? They were the only pair of trousers he had with him, and he couldn't possibly go over to Ganthorne and see Jerry without any trousers—the thing was unthinkable.

"Look here, Dorcas," he said. "It's serious. It really is. I've got to go out. I've got a most frightfully important appointment. How am I going without any trousers?"

"Lor!" exclaimed Dorcas. "You *can't*, sir."

"But I must," Sam told her. "I simply *must*."

Dorcas began to search feverishly again. She got down on her hands and knees and peered under the bed; she began pulling out the drawers in the dressing-chest.

Sam nearly screamed—the thing was getting on his nerves. "For Heaven's sake stop it!" he said, trying to speak quietly. "For Heaven's sake, stop it, Dorcas! I've looked there twice, and you've looked there twice—d'you think the third time's lucky, or what? You've got to *help* me, Dorcas. Try and think of something, can't you?"

Dorcas tried to think of something. She was very sorry indeed for the young gentleman. She stood quite still, and frowned desperately with the effort of concentration.

"I know, sir!" she exclaimed, delighted with the sudden inspiration. "I know the very thing. I'll get you a pair of Mr. Abbott's trousers."

384

"Good Lord!" said Sam, "Uncle Arthur's trousers on me—I *ask* you! He's about four inches taller and four inches broader than me. I should look an absolute freak. I should look like something out of Bertram Bostock's Circus——"

"We could take them in round the waist," Dorcas pointed out, "and turn them up round the ankles."

Sam shuddered.

"With safety-pins," added Dorcas, anxious that her heaven-gifted inspiration should not be wasted.

"No," said Sam firmly. "No, that is *not* a good idea, Dorcas"—he would rather not see Jerry at all than go to her looking a figure of fun.

"I can't think of anything else," said Dorcas hopelessly, "unless you was to wear a pair of Mr. Abbott's golfing stockings and your overcoat. You might do that, sir."

"I might," agreed Sam, with bitter sarcasm. "There would be no chance at all of me catching a most frightful chill, would there? I might go out in my pyjamas, mightn't I? Or wrapped in a sheet—somebody might think I was the ghost—I might even——" said Sam, and then he stopped, suddenly; for, after all, why shouldn't he? Why shouldn't he wear his fancy dress, and go over and see Jerry in it? The fancy dress was there in his suitcase, all ready and waiting (it was simply *asking* to be worn) and it became him mightily as he well knew. No need to be ashamed of himself in those marvellous togs, no indeed. Sam banished the horrible vision of himself, shambling into Jerry's drawing-room with Uncle Arthur's bags in folds round his stomach, and in wrinkles down his legs; showing, Sam felt, that Uncle Arthur was, not only a bigger man, but, also (in some ways) a finer man than himself. Sam banished the vision—the nightmare vision. No, no, he knew of a better way than that.

"Hurrah!" he shouted, frightening Dorcas nearly out of her skin. "Hurrah! Of course I will. What an owl I was not to think of it before!" and he pounced upon the suitcase, and emptied the gorgeous raiment it contained in a heap on to the floor.

Dorcas fled from the frightful spectacle of a young gentleman tearing off a neat blue shirt over his untidy head.

25

SIR WALTER RALEIGH

THUS it befell that, half an hour later, Jerry, sitting lonely and rather miserable by her drawing-room fire, was startled out of her wits by the apparition of an Elizabethan Courtier. He stood in the doorway for a moment, and she gazed at him speechlessly—at his crimson, long-waisted doublet, with the puffed shoulders, and the crisp white ruff; at his crimson trunk-hose, slashed with cream velvet, and his crimson stockings and buckled shoes; at the crimson cloak, lined with cream and trimmed with fur, which swung from one shoulder with careless grace; at the flat crimson hat (trimmed with a long feather) that sat so jauntily on his curled hair; at his long thin gold-mounted rapier, and the gold chain that he wore round his neck.

"Oh—Goodness!" said Jerry in alarm.

The gentleman swept off his feathered hat in a low bow, and then, flinging pageantry to the winds, he rushed across the room, and fell on his knees, and swept her into his arms.

"Sam!" she cried in amazement.

"Jerry, darling—darling—darling," said Sam, kissing her with extreme vehemence between each word.

"Sam, how gorgeous you are! How simply gorgeous!"

"Yes, aren't I?" Sam agreed, delighted at the success of his plan, "and aren't you frightfully lucky to have such a gorgeous person of your very own?"

Jerry laughed, Sam really was a darling. He was so full of happiness and vim; so young and boyish and altogether delightful. If Jerry had not loved him to distraction already, she would have fallen in love with him now. But I couldn't possibly love him more than I did, she thought, as she looked into his eager eyes so near her own, and yet I believe I *do* love him more.

"But, Sam," she said, when she had recovered a little from her first surprise and delight at his arrival, "but Sam, darling, how did you come? Where are you going? What's happened? Here I was," she continued, without giving him time to explain, "here I was, glooming over the fire, thinking about you, and suddenly you appear, looking like—looking like——"

"Sir Walter Raleigh," said Sam, "at least that's what I'm supposed to look like, so I hope I do. Sir Walter Raleigh at the Court of Queen Elizabeth—that's me."

"But why?" Jerry not unnaturally enquired, "why Sir Walter Raleigh?"

"I liked the kit," Sam explained. "It seemed to suit me, somehow."

"Oh, it *does*," agreed Jerry—there could be no two opinions about that. "It does suit you, darling."

"I'm glad you think so," Sam told her earnestly. "Frightfully glad. Modern dress doesn't give a man much scope, does it?"

"But Sam!" exclaimed Jerry in amazement, "you didn't just get the clothes to come down and see me——"

"Good Lord, no, of course not!" cried Sam. "Did you think I had gone balmy or something, darling? I'll tell you the whole thing if you'll hold on a minute; but, first, I want to tell you something frightfully important, something frightfully nice—you'll never guess what it is, *never*—I've got my screw raised."

"Oh, Sam, how splendid!"

"Yes, isn't it? It isn't only the dibs you know—though the dibs will be jolly useful, of course—but it makes me feel I'm getting on. Uncle Arthur was frightfully nice about it. He said I was useful and reliable. He said," continued Sam, aping his Uncle's speech and manner with deplorable impertinence. "He said 'By the way, I was speaking to Spicer, and we have decided to—er—raise your salary. You're doing well now, and you're most useful and—er—reliable,' and then when I'd thanked the old buffer, he said 'Yes, I'm extremely pleased with the—er—way you're sticking into it—extremely pleased, Sam'—so what d'you think of *that*?"

"I think it's simply splendid," said Jerry, with conviction.

"Am I your good, nice, clever boy?" enquired Sam.

"You're my good, nice, clever, *darling* boy," Jerry told him.

"And it's all because of you, darling," Sam said, rubbing his cheek against her shoulder, "all for you, every bit of it—so there. And now," added Sam, sitting back, and looking at her with very bright eyes, "and now I'll tell you everything—all the rest of it—why Sir Walter Raleigh, and all that. It's frightfully

390

long, and frightfully complicated," said Sam earnestly, "so we had better have cigarettes."

They lighted cigarettes, and the long and complicated story was further delayed, because, when he lighted Jerry's cigarette for her, it reminded Sam of the Christmas dinner-party at The Archway House, and how he had nearly disgraced himself by kissing Jerry in front of everybody. And, of course, when he had told her about it, he had to kiss her; because it was so lovely to have the right to kiss her whenever he wanted to—or very nearly. At last, however, Sam got started on his long and complicated story, and he told her the whole thing from the very beginning—all about how he had bearded Uncle Arthur in his private office, and had practically demanded an invitation to The Archway House for the week-end, and how Uncle Arthur had refused to have him, and then taken pity on him, and suggested that he should come down to Wandlebury for the night; and he explained how it was that he happened to have the Sir Walter Raleigh kit in his bag; and he told her about his arrival at The Archway House, and how nice Barbara had been, but also how mysteriously adamant about not having him to stay; and he told her how delighted he was to learn that his host and hostess were going out to dinner, and how he had sung in his bath because everything was simply too right—too absolutely marvellously right—for words; and then he told her about the disappearance of his trousers.

"It was the most extraordinary thing," he said. "I know I left them on the chair with my other things—I *know* I did—and when I came back from my bath they had gone."

"Did you look everywhere?" Jerry enquired.

"My dear lamb, *of course*, I looked everywhere; and I rang for Dorcas, and *she* looked everywhere—you would have laughed if you could have seen us," Sam continued (for, looking back on the scene, the humour of it became apparent) "you *would* have laughed, Jerry—there was I, in my shirt, dancing about with impatience, and Dorcas crawling about on the floor on her hands and knees, looking under the bed—but I didn't laugh at the time, I can tell you, because I was so desperate to see you, and I didn't know how I was going to manage it without my trousers. I was desperate, simply desperate—and Dorcas made all sort of ridiculous suggestions; and then I suddenly thought of these togs, and the moment I thought of these togs, I simply leapt into them, and came—and here I am," said Sam with a sigh of contentment.

"Yes, that's all that matters," Jerry agreed (she thought: of course, his trousers were there all the time—they *must* have been there—they were under the quilt, or something. How helpless men are!—but she was far too wise to say anything of the sort). "Yes, that's all that matters," she said. "And you *do* look simply *splendid*. And it's too lovely for words having you like this, because I was feeling a bit gloomy before you came."

"Gloomy?" enquired Sam tenderly. "Why were you feeling gloomy, darling lamb?"

"Oh, nothing much. I'm not going to bother you with my small worries."

"Bother me!" cried Sam. "But that's what I'm here for—to be bothered, I mean. Of course you've got to tell me *everything*—all about *everything*. Cough it up, Jerry!" he entreated her, in the disgusting, but extraordinarily descriptive, not to say, pictoral jargon of his day. "Cough it up, Jerry. Come on, now—it's not fair me telling you all my troubles, and you not telling me yours."

"Oh well," said Jerry, smiling adoringly at

her masterful young man. "Oh well it's various things, really. I had to sack Crichton (for one thing), he was rather rude and beastly. He's been awfully slack lately, and, when I told him off, he was impertinent, so I had to sack him, and it was horrid. I paid him what I thought was fair, but he wasn't satisfied, and he began to argue. And then Brackenbridge came up—the second groom you know—and Crichton went off mumbling and grumbling in a horrid way."

"The foul brute!" exclaimed Sam, with feeling.

"Yes," said Jerry. "It really was rather horrid. So I was just sitting here, feeling mouldy and lonely—Markie's gone to the pictures with Miss Foddy—and then you came."

"You don't mean you were all alone in the house?" enquired Sam anxiously.

"I don't mind it really," Jerry assured him, "not usually, I mean. It was just to-night, somehow—everything seemed rather foul. Aunt Matilda's very ill again, and I got a worrying sort of letter from Archie, and then the groom—things sort of mounted up, if you know what I mean."

"Of course I know what you mean. It's horrid," said Sam, "and, Oh Jerry, I don't like you being here all by yourself! I do wish I could come down and take care of you."

"Well, you can't," Jerry replied. "You know what I told you about Aunt Matilda. You mustn't come down at all, because somebody might see you here, and then it would be all over Wandlebury in a few hours. People would be sure to say we were engaged if they saw you here—you know how people talk——"

"Oh, Jerry, it has been so hateful!" Sam said miserably. "These last few weeks when I couldn't see you have been absolutely frightful—you don't know——"

"Hush!" said Jerry, raising her hand and listening.

"It's a bell," said Sam. "Markie, perhaps."

"No, not Markie," Jerry declared. "Markie has the key—besides it's not really time for Markie, Oh Sam, perhaps it's Crichton——"

"If it's Crichton," said Sam grimly, and he rose to his feet, "if it's Crichton—and I only hope it *is* Crichton—I'll—I'll Crichton him——"

The bell pealed again.

"I'll Crichton him," Sam said, making for the door and uttering this strange threat with the most frightful ferocity imaginable. "Just let me get my hands on him—I'll Crichton him."

"Oh, Sam, you can't go like that!" Jerry cried, but Sam had already gone.

Sam had quite forgotten his gorgeous apparel; his one and only idea was to get at Crichton who had been "rude and beastly" to Jerry, and to give him socks. He strode to the front door and flung it open. It was dark outside, of course, but the oil lamp which had been left burning over the porch for Markie's convenience, threw a gentle radiance upon the step, and there, sure enough was Crichton—a small, sturdy sort of man, with a foxy face under his peaked cap. Sam recognised Crichton at once, he had seen the fellow often when he came over to the stables for his riding-lessons. But if Sam recognised Crichton, Crichton most certainly did not recognise Sam. When the door opened, and Crichton raised his eyes, expecting to see the small lithe figure of Miss Jerry Cobbe, and, instead of that familiar and reassuring sight, he beheld before him, in the lintel, the gorgeous figure of an Elizabethan Courtier in full rig, Crichton did not stand upon the order of his going.

"Gor Blimey!" he exclaimed, and, with that, he turned, and most incontinently fled down the path, through the wicket-gate and up the lane as fast as ever his bow legs would take him. "It wos a b—— ghost, that's wot it wos," he told his cronies afterwards, over a pint of beer at the Ganthorne Arms, "a girt big 'eadless ghost, it wos—dressed up in old-fashioned togs, it wos, all bloody, wif its 'ead under its arm."

Sam after pursuing Crichton as far as the gate, returned to Jerry, somewhat disappointed at the ease with which he had routed his enemy. He found Jerry standing in the doorway, laughing until the tears ran down her cheeks.

"Oh goodness!" she said, between her spasms of uncontrollable mirth. "Oh goodness! What an awful fright you must have given him! Oh goodness! I never saw Crichton run so fast—never——"

"The beastly coward!" said Sam, angrily. "The beastly coward—he never gave me a chance to get at him. Why the devil didn't he give me a chance? I wanted to biff the dirty little skunk."

"Look at yourself, Sam!" gasped Jerry.

Sam looked down and saw his gorgeous clothes, and his face broke slowly into a

smile. "Lord!" he said, "I never remembered—gadzooks! I suppose the little blighter
thought I was a spook."

"Of course he did," gurgled Jerry, "he expected to see poor little me, and when the
door opened and he saw *you*——" she laughed
again.

They went back into the drawing-room and
sat down by the fire.

"You see now, Jerry," said Sam. "You see
now how horrid it is for you being here alone.
You must promise me not to let Markie go
out at night and leave you. It's bad enough
being in town and not seeing you, but if I'm
terrified all the time that something will
happen——"

"It won't," Jerry assured him. "I'll be all
right really, Sam."

"If only we could see each other, *often*,"
said Sam, heaving a big sigh, "if only we
could, Jerry. I could bear it quite easily if I
could come down to Wandlebury like I used
to do, but Barbara can't have me—or
won't—she's going to Spring clean the house
or something. At any rate she made it quite
clear that she can't have me for ages. Isn't it
frightful?"

"I can't come up to town now, either,"

Jerry pointed out, "because I shall have to get a new head groom and get him into my ways——"

"I know," said Sam miserably.

"It's all because of Aunt Matilda—you know that, don't you?" Jerry pointed out. "If only she wasn't so ill——"

"I know," said Sam again.

"But as things are, we must just be patient."

"Oh, Jerry, it's simply frightful. I've been patient for months now——"

"Well, what can we do?"

They talked for a long time. Sometimes the conversation took a cheerful turn, and they luxuriated in each other's company; sometimes they thought of the future, and relapsed into gloom. The fire died down, and was revived by Sir Walter Raleigh with coal and logs; it had almost died down again by the time Markie came home. Markie was surprised and delighted beyond measure when she beheld Sam, she was thrilled to the core at his beauty and grace. No film star—not even her beloved Harold Hansome—could hold a candle to Jerry's Sam. Markie sat down and gazed at him with admiring eyes. He was beautiful—there was no other word for him—

he was beautiful. No wonder darling Jerry was crazy about him, Markie was crazy about him herself.

It was long past midnight before Sam, still gorgeous as a bird of paradise, returned to The Archway House and crept stealthily to bed.

★ ★ ★

Mr. and Mrs. Abbott were already in bed and asleep when Sam came in. They had had a pleasant evening at the Thanes', and had enjoyed an excellent dinner and a quiet chat about their neighbours. They had returned home at a reasonable hour, and, finding all quiet in The Archway House had concluded that their guest had retired to bed. Whilst Arthur was busy washing his teeth in the bathroom, Barbara had retrieved the grey trousers from beneath her mattress, and had hung them carefully over the banisters outside Sam's door. She could not help smiling as she returned to her bedroom—it had been such an excellent plan. Sam had probably dined in his pyjamas and dressing-gown—she wouldn't enquire. It was enough that she had been able to prevent him seeing Jerry.

In the morning Sam's trousers were brought in with his hot water, and laid on the chair, ready for him to wear. Sam saw them and was glad—"there they are, thank Heavens!" he said to himself. "Of *course*, they were somewhere downstairs all the time, and that old fool, Dorcas, couldn't find them. Anyhow it didn't matter, I'm rather glad they were lost, really." He was aware that he had looked far, far better as an Elizabethan Courtier than he could possibly have looked in his ordinary everyday clothes, and he was glad—not unnaturally perhaps—that Jerry had had the privilege of seeing him in that marvellous rig-out. There were other reasons, too, why he was glad.

Sam didn't bother any more about the loss of his trousers, nor did he mention the matter to Barbara—his mind was full of more important things. He was quiet and abstracted at breakfast, but this did not surprise his hostess at all. She was especially nice to Sam, and told him again, before he left for town in his uncle's car, that he must certainly come, later on, for a long visit.

"Yes, thank you, I'd like to," Sam said. "It's frightfully good of you, Barbara—thank you awfully."

Dorcas might have told Barbara a good deal about what had happened the previous evening, but she didn't say a word either; for, curiously enough, the kitchen chimney went on fire that very morning, and, what with the fright and the awful mess, and the cook's rage and fury over the occurrence, the mysterious disappearance of young Mr. Abbott's trousers (and the other incident connected with their loss) passed completely out of Dorcas's mind.

26

SOUND AND FURY

ONE fine day Mr. Abbott came home from the office much earlier than usual and found his wife getting ready to go out.

"Oh, Arthur!" she exclaimed, in dismay, "I didn't know you were coming home early. I've got to go out to tea."

"Can't you telephone and say you can't go—or something?" enquired Arthur with the selfishness and self-assurance of a spoilt husband. He had come home on purpose to have tea with his wife, and was absurdly disappointed at the prospect of tea without his wife. Besides, it was really a glorious day—the first real day of Spring—and Arthur had decided that, after tea, he and Barbara would walk round the garden together, and examine all the nice things that were coming up, and coming out in the garden. He could have done this by himself, of course, but that wouldn't be the same at all. The garden—as a garden—did not interest Arthur very much, but the garden and Barbara combined interested him enormously. Barbara was enchanting in the garden, so eager and pleased and happy, so surprised to find the things that she had planted—or caused to be planted—in the Autumn were really coming up. Barbara was more Barbara-ish than ever when she was in her garden, and Arthur could never have enough of the blend.

"Oh, no, Arthur. I couldn't possibly put it off," Barbara replied. "It would be so frightfully rude. You had better come too—they *did* ask you, but, of course, I said you wouldn't be home in time."

"Where are you going?" enquired Arthur cautiously.

"To the Marvells'."

"Good Heavens! No thanks," said Arthur. "I'll get Monkey to come round and have tea with me—if you really *must* go."

Arthur was not jealous of Mr. Marvell any more. *There's Many a Slip*—— had shown him that there was no need for him to be jealous of the man; but he did not like the Marvells at all, and he could not for the life of him understand what Barbara saw in the family.

404

"Yes, I must go," Barbara told him.

"Why on earth d'you want to go to the Marvells?"

"I think they're rather nice," Barbara replied. "Yes, you ring up Monkey—I won't stay long——" and she kissed her husband and departed to her tea-party with that peculiarly elastic step that Mr. Marvell had admired.

It astounded Barbara that Arthur did not like their next-door neighbours—they were *queer*, of course, but Barbara liked people all the more when they were queer. She found them more interesting and instructive than ordinary people, and Barbara enjoyed instruction. Barbara had received the invitation to take tea with the Marvells in much the same spirit as she would have received an invitation to participate in the chimpanzee's tea-party at the Zoo (lots of people would have received an invitation of this nature with horror and revulsion, but Barbara was always ready for a new experience) and she had accepted the invitation with much the same feelings of half nervous, half pleasurable anticipation.

It will be rather fun to see them all together, Barbara thought, as she tripped elastically down the drive. I've never seen them all together before. It will give me a kind of peep into their lives. She was aware that they would be all together for tea, because Trivvie had told her so—all except Lancreste, of course, for Lancreste had departed once more to visit his cousins at Bournemouth.

The Marvells were having tea in the dining-room when Barbara arrived. The children welcomed her boisterously; Mrs. Marvell with her usual vagueness; and Mr. Marvell cried:

"Oh, blythe newcomer, harbinger of Spring!" and invited her to sit near him by the window.

Barbara was delighted to be called a harbinger of Spring—it sounded a pleasant kind of thing to be—she cast off her furs, and sat down beside him and asked with her usual kind interest in the affairs of others, how the painting was getting on.

"Not too well," said Mr. Marvell, relapsing into gloom. "There are periods in the life of a creative artist when everything goes stale—stale and—stringy."

Barbara said sympathetically that it sounded horrid. She accepted a muffin—there were no

406

crumpets, unfortunately—and the conversation became general.

"Did you hear about the ghost?" Mrs. Marvell enquired vaguely.

"What ghost?" asked Barbara with interest. "D'you mean *our* ghost? We haven't seen it lately."

"Mummy means the one at Ganthorne Lodge," explained Trivvie with her mouth full.

"The whole thing is nonsense," said Mr. Marvell firmly.

"But Ivy *saw* it," urged Trivvie. "Ivy was going up the lane to her home, and she saw a ghost—a man in funny old-fashioned clothes. He went in at the gate and disappeared."

Barbara smiled. She had been taken in, too often, by the Marvell children's weird tales to believe a word of the story.

"I beg," said Mr. Marvell, "I beg that you will not gossip with the servants, Trivona. I have had occasion to complain of this predilection on your part before. The habit is undignified and injurious. There is no need for you and Ambrose to mix with the lower classes for information or instruction. You have your mother, and myself, and Miss Foddy, and I venture to think that, between

407

us, we can supply the necessary sustenance for your growing intelligence."

A great part of this harangue was incomprehensible to Trivvie, but she managed to follow the general trend of her father's observations in much the same way as a person can follow the general trend of a conversation carried on in an imperfectly understood foreign language.

"But none of you saw the ghost and Ivy *did*," she pointed out. "So *you* couldn't tell us about it, you see. And it isn't gossip at all, it's true."

"Do not argue, Trivona," said Mr. Marvell. "For, not only is it an extremely ill-bred habit to argue with your parents, but it also shows the intense ignorance of your untutored mind. Gossip is occasionally true," he continued. "But not this case, I think," and he went on to point out to the assembled company that there were no such things as ghosts, and that the people who saw them—or imagined they saw them—were merely the victims of their own disordered imaginations. Barbara listened attentively to this interesting, if somewhat dogmatic lecture on the subject of hallucinations; Miss Foddy busied herself cutting slices of bread and butter and honey for the children; and Mrs. Marvell stared vaguely out of the window.

Mrs. Marvell was, as usual, very tired. She had had a difficult time lately—it was not only the artist who suffered when his work went stale and stringy—the soft blur of gold and blue, and brown and green, which was all that her short-sighted eyes could make of the Spring sky and the awakening garden, was very restful and soothing. Restful and soothing, too, was the booming sound of her husband's voice as he explained his views to Mrs. Abbott. She's a nice safe friend for James, thought Mrs. Marvell to herself. I can't think why he likes her, but he does. And she's nice and safe. By this she meant that Mrs. Abbott could not appeal to, nor satisfy, the physical side of her husband, and, as that was the only side of her husband that Mrs. Marvell appreciated, Mrs. Abbott could not take anything that was *hers*. This view of conjugal rights is not so unusual as its strangeness might appear to justify. There are quite a number of people in the world who limit their jealousy in this peculiar manner.

"It's funny," said Barbara suddenly, when the lecture on hallucinations had come to an end, "it's funny the different kinds of people

409

there are in the world—I mean there are business men, and doctors, and lawyers, and artists, and people like that; and they're all so frightfully different—if you know what I mean—do you think they start being different from the very beginning, or does something happen to them to make them different?"

It was an exceedingly interesting point, and Mr. Marvell recognised it as such in spite of the somewhat muddled language in which it was clothed.

"Most wretched men," he told her in a lugubrious voice, biting into a muffin with such hearty appetite that the butter squirted through his fingers, "Most wretched men are cradled into poetry by wrong; they learn in suffering what they teach in song."

"That's poetry," said Barbara, with acumen. "I can't think how you remember so much poetry, Mr. Marvell. It's exactly what I meant, too," she added admiringly. "Something happens to make them different."

"Just so," agreed Mr. Marvell, quite pleased with the effect he had produced upon his guest. "Just so, Mrs. Abbott. In my own case, now—take my own case," said Mr. Marvell generously, "as a small and unimportant instance," he continued in his

410

sonorous voice, "a very small and unimportant instance of the great and altogether wonderful uses of adversity—Trivona, what are you whispering about?" he cried, pouncing suddenly upon the unfortunate child with the ferocity of a bull bison. "What are you whispering about, Trivona? How often have I besought you not to whisper—*how often*, I say? If your remark is not suitable for mixed company you must withhold it until you and Ambrose are alone. You see enough of Ambrose," continued Mr. Marvell irritably. "Surely you see enough of Ambrose—you are in his company from morning to night. His face is the first thing your eyes light on when you awake, and the last thing your eyes behold before you close them in slumber. I have often felt the most intense sympathy for you on this account, Trivona, but—what did you say?"

"I just said 'all right'," announced Trivvie meekly.

"Ask them *now*," said Ambrose, nudging her.

"Do not nudge," said Mr. Marvell, pouncing upon Ambrose for a change. "How often have I implored you not to nudge? It is a most unmannerly habit of yours, Ambrose. Am I the only person who tries to instil reasonable manners into you—am I?"

"No, everybody does," Ambrose admitted.

"And another thing," continued his father, in whom the unfriendliness of his Muse had engendered an unusually carping spirit. "And another thing that I object to—why must you *ask* your sister to *ask* us for whatever it is you desire? Have you no tongue? Can you not demand your own favours?"

Ambrose regarded his father with a wide innocent stare.

"It's just that you listen to Trivvie more," he said stolidly.

"What?" enquired Mr. Marvell indignantly. "What? Do you accuse me of favouritism?"

Ambrose still stared. He had no idea what favouritism was, so he did not know whether or not he had accused his father of that particular vice. He was not in the least alarmed by his father's ferocity, for he had long ago discovered that when his father was like this—all sound and fury—it signified nothing, nothing at all. Behind his innocent stare Ambrose's thoughts were busy: Grown-ups were odd (he thought). For weeks father would take no notice of you, and you could do what you liked and behave how you liked

412

with absolute safety, and then, quite suddenly, for no reason at all, he would jump on you like this. You could never depend on grown-ups (thought Ambrose). Sometimes they were useful and convenient, of course, but, mostly, they were foolish and unjust. The only thing to do when they raved like this, was just to sit still and let them rave, and get what amusement you could out of the show. Trivvie and Ambrose enjoyed the grown-up world in much the same manner as they enjoyed a circus. They were amused, scornful, or critical according to whether the various "turns" were good or bad. There were acrobats and jugglers, dressed up monkeys riding in coaches, and bears walking on their hind legs; and, amongst these strange and exciting phenomena, their father—the clown, and therefore the *pièce de résistance*—ran about, getting in everybody's way, and impotently cracking his whip.

"Go on," said Mr. Marvell, wearily. "Pray go on, Ambrose. We are all waiting with extreme interest—not to say anxiety—for this mysterious request of yours."

"It was just we wondered if Mrs. Abbott could come up to the schoolroom after tea," said Ambrose stolidly.

"A reasonable request!" remarked his father, more amiably. "A request that shows a certain amount of discrimination."

"We want to show her something," added Ambrose.

"And may we enquire what it is that you 'want to show' Mrs. Abbott?"

"It's a secret," said Trivvie quickly, and she kicked Ambrose under the table.

("All right, you owl. I know it's a secret," said Ambrose *sotto voce*.)

"A secret," said Mr. Marvell indulgently. "Dear me, this is very mysterious, very mysterious indeed. Shall we try to guess what Mrs. Abbott is to be shown?"

"You can if you like," Ambrose told him, secure in the conviction that, if his father guessed from now until Doomsday, he would never succeed in guessing correctly.

"On second thoughts perhaps I shall refrain," said Mr. Marvell. "I feel that the matter is too deep for me to pry into. Too deep," he continued, smiling. "I may feel a little hurt, perhaps, that it is Mrs. Abbott, and not myself, who has been chosen to be a repository for your secret; but, on the other hand, I feel bound to admit that you have shown perspicacity in your choice. Mrs.

Abbott is exactly the right person to share a secret, since those who have secrets of their own to guard are indubitably the best custodians of the secrets of others."

They all gazed at Barbara, and Barbara blushed. What *would* they all think, she wondered. What would Miss Foddy think—and Mrs. Marvell? It was very unfair of Mr. Marvell to allude to the secret that she had asked him to keep—(the secret that she wrote—or had written—books). It really was very unfair of him. Barbara wouldn't have believed it of Mr. Marvell. She was so annoyed with him about it, that his subsequent conversation—though abounding with apt quotations—failed to provide her with the pleasure and amusement that Mr. Marvell's conversation usually did. In fact she was quite glad when tea was over, and she escaped to the schoolroom with Trivvie and Ambrose.

27

BLACK MAGIC

THE two young Marvells were delighted to have secured Mrs. Abbott so easily. They dragged her upstairs to the small shabby room which did duty as a schoolroom and playroom combined, and prepared to show her their secret.

"You won't tell, will you?" Trivvie cried, dancing up and down in front of her like a jack-in-the-box. "Shall we make her *swear on the book*, Amby?"

"She won't," said Ambrose, phlegmatically. "Grown-ups never will."

Trivvie was aware of this strange aversion on the part of grown-ups, she had merely forgotten about it, temporarily, in the excitement of the moment.

"Oh no, neither they will," she said, and then she added more hopefully. "But p'raps her word's as good as her bond—is it, Mrs. Abbott?"

Barbara said it was, and thereby bound herself to guard the secret with her life. She was interested, by this time, and a little flattered at the honour of being chosen as the recipient of the young Marvells' confidences.

"Show her, Amby!" cried Trivvie, who could scarcely contain her impatience. "Show her, Amby—get out the box."

A box was placed carefully upon the table, and, from it was taken a clay-figure, moulded with considerable skill into a human form.

Barbara examined it with interest. "It's very good," she said honestly. "Very good indeed. Where did you get the clay?"

"Out of the stream," said Ambrose, and he added proudly, "I made it."

"You should show it to your father," said Barbara.

"No," said Ambrose. "He'd only pick it to bits——"

"No, no," cried Trivvie, "it's a secret and you promised—d'you know who it is? It's Mrs. Dance."

"Is it?"

"Yes, of course it is—look at the teeth! And look, I've stuck a pin in right through the middle—look, Mrs. Abbott—it's a charm—it's a spell—a witches' spell—look at the pin——"

Barbara was horrified. "Oh, Trivvie!" she

exclaimed. "It isn't kind. Oh, Trivvie! I mean, of course, it's just a game, and couldn't do her any harm, but you shouldn't play that kind of game—*really*, Trivvie."

"It's just a game," said Trivvie, looking rather crestfallen. "And, anyhow, she's horrid. We hate her, don't we, Amby?"

"Why do you hate her?" enquired Barbara with interest, adding hastily (for the sake of form), "you shouldn't hate people, you know."

"We hate her because she's ugly—her teeth stick out," said Trivvie.

"And she calls us kiddies," added Ambrose with a shudder.

Barbara understood the repugnance, she had felt something the same herself. She was aware that the blemishes, discovered in Mrs. Dance by the young Marvells, were really only outward signs of much more serious faults, and it was the inward woman from whom Trivvie and Ambrose recoiled. It was not really because her teeth stuck out, and because she called them "kiddies" that Trivvie and Ambrose hated Mrs. Dance, but it was because she was the *kind of woman* who thought and spoke in a manner they detested. Barbara understood and sympathised with

Trivvie and Ambrose, but she did not admit it.

"I think Mrs. Dance means to be kind," she pointed out, somewhat feebly.

Trivvie and Ambrose were not deceived, they looked at each other and grinned.

"*She* doesn't like her either," said Trivvie.

"I told you she didn't," replied Ambrose.

Barbara was more accustomed by now to the strange way in which the Marvell children discussed her with each other as if she were not there, but it still gave her an uncomfortable sensation.

"Well," she said, rather loudly, as if to make her presence felt. "Well, is that all you have to show me?"

"What else shall we show her, Amby?" enquired Trivvie, as she wrapped the effigy of Mrs. Dance in an old duster and put it carefully into its box.

"The buttons," suggested Ambrose.

Barbara knew about the buttons, of course—the buttons were no secret—everybody in Wandlebury was aware of the young Marvells' passion for collecting buttons, and practically everybody in Wandlebury had been mulcted to provide them with specimens. Barbara, herself, had contributed several odd buttons from the bottom of her workbasket to add to the valuable collection, and she knew Dorcas had been inveigled into doing the same.

"Oh, yes!" cried Trivvie eagerly. "Yes, Mrs. Abbott hasn't seen them—we *must* show her the buttons."

The largest drawer of the schoolroom bureau was, accordingly, opened, and the buttons displayed. It was, indeed, a marvellous collection; there were big buttons and small buttons, buttons with "necks," and buttons with holes; there were coloured buttons—of every hue—there were white buttons, and black buttons, and buttons of mother-of-pearl. Some of the "special ones" were in boxes, and these were forced upon Barbara's notice with requests for admiration; others, less valuable, were in a large green bag, or loose in the drawer.

Barbara admired them all, and was told the history of each one in an excited duet; while Ambrose leaned heavily upon her shoulder, and breathed heavily down her neck, and Trivvie—who hated any close contact with her fellow creatures—squatted beside the drawer and bent her untidy brown head over it in an ecstasy of worship.

"Look at that one," said Trivvie, pointing

to a brown bone button with an unwieldy neck. "I found that at the church door, just as we were going in. Froggy was *so* cross when I stopped to pick it up, but I couldn't leave it, could I?"

"Father was just behind and nearly fell over her," added Ambrose.

"He trod on my hand—but I didn't care," said Trivvie bravely.

"Look at this one—isn't he a giant?" demanded Ambrose, pointing out an enormous green button with yellow streaks. "I *bought* that one. I *bought* it in a shop," he added in an awed voice.

"And look at this teeny tiny one, isn't it a *darling*?" Trivvie crooned. "Look at it, Mrs. Abbott!"

Barbara looked obediently.

"This is the most beautiful of all," continued Trivvie, opening a pill box, and disclosing an opalescent button, reposing in a bed of cotton wool. "Isn't it *lovely*? Miss Cobbe gave it to me. It came off a blouse that belonged to her mother."

"Mrs. Anderson gave me this yellow one," continued Ambrose. "She's Lady Chevis Cobbe's housekeeper, you know—it's pretty, isn't it, Mrs. Abbott?"

"This grey one came off Mrs. Dance," added Trivvie. "It fell off one day when she was here——"

"And they're all different—every one," Ambrose told her. "It's a job, now, to get others, you know."

"Sometimes we get a button, and then we find we've got one exactly like it already—and *isn't* it a sell!" cried Trivvie.

"But that doesn't happen often," said Ambrose.

"Because, you see, we know them so well," explained Trivvie.

"We know them *all*," Ambrose said seriously, "and we know where they all came from—or very nearly——"

"Oh, Amby!" cried Trivvie suddenly. "That reminds me, I've got a new one——"

"You haven't!"

"I have, really," she declared, fishing up the leg of her knickers, which she always used as a pocket, "here it is, Amby. I thought, for a minute, I'd lost it. Isn't it a beauty?"

They put their heads together over the new button, and looked at it with excitement and delight. It was a large red wooden button—very smooth and shiny—and it possessed a "neck" which—as Barbara was now aware—added tremendously to its value.

"We haven't got it, have we?" Trivvie enquired anxiously.

"No," said Ambrose. "No, we haven't got it. I thought at first it was the same as the one I found in the station, but it isn't."

"It's bigger, much bigger," Trivvie pointed out.

"Where did you get it?" asked Ambrose with interest.

"It came off Miss Thane," replied Trivvie solemnly. "You know that red coat she wears in church? I've been watching the buttons for ages——"

"Did it *fall* off, Trivvie?" enquired Ambrose, taking it in his hand and examining it reverently.

"Well—almost," said Trivvie unashamedly.

Barbara knew that she ought to be shocked at this disgraceful revelation, she knew that she should remonstrate with the collectors, that she ought to confiscate the button, then and there, and return it to its owner; but, somehow or other, she could do none of these things. The collection of buttons was so magnificent that she was completely won over; her sympathies were entirely with the collectors. They really *are* fascinating, Barbara thought, as she picked them up, one by one and noted how each one differed from its fellows—who could have believed (she thought) that there are so many different kinds of buttons in the world? I don't wonder, thought Barbara—and then she stopped, because, of course, if she didn't wonder that the young Marvells actually *stole* buttons off the garments of their friends to add to their collection, she certainly ought to have wondered at such reprehensible behaviour. I wonder if that button off my blue coat, she thought, it didn't *seem* loose—and then she stopped again, because if the button that she had lost off her blue coat had been acquired by the young Marvells for their collection, by fair means or foul, she most certainly had not the heart to ask for it to be returned.

"Aren't they lovely?" said Trivvie, dreamily, taking up a handful of the smaller fry and letting them trickle through her fingers.

"They're simply lovely," said Barbara with conviction. "I had no idea buttons could be so fascinating—no idea." And I shan't say a word, she thought, I shan't say a single word to anyone, because it really is a stupendous collection, and they *have* been most awfully sweet and nice to me to-day, and I do believe—in spite of all the frightfully naughty and annoying things they do—they are really beginning to like me a little.

It was high time by now for Barbara to go home to her neglected husband. She returned to the drawing-room to say good-bye to her host and hostess and to find her furs. Mr. Marvell was somewhat annoyed to hear that she was going already—he had not had the nice quiet little chat with Mrs. Abbott that he had anticipated.

"You must come again, then," he said, when he saw that he could by no means persuade her to stay. "You must come some morning. I should like to make a little sketch of your head."

Barbara thought that this would be rather amusing—another adventure—and she promised to come. If the sketch were good she might buy it and give it to Arthur for his birthday. She had no idea how you bought an artist's picture, but presumably you could buy it. I wonder how I could suggest it—she thought.

The entire Marvell family came to the front door to speed her on her way. Trivvie and Ambrose announced their intention of accompanying her home. There was still an hour before bed-time, and they could spend the hour profitably in The Archway House garden.

Trivvie rushed on ahead down the drive. Her passage from the front door to the gate was peculiarly erratic, for it was one of her "taboos" that she must touch every tree in a certain fixed order as she went: The two elms on the right, then across to the oak on the left, and back again to the third elm. She was like a king-fisher, in her bright-blue overall, flashing backwards and forwards in the golden afternoon sunlight.

"I sometimes think that child is deranged," declared Mr. Marvell, watching her from the door.

"It's just a game," Barbara assured him.

Neither of them had the slightest idea of the extent to which Trivvie's life was governed and restricted by "taboos" and strange pagan rites of her own fashioning. She made them herself, of course, but, once they were made, she could not unmake them; they were fixed for ever to be a burden to her back, and a menace to her comfort and convenience. The "taboos" were multiple, and of all kinds. Sometimes they were "lasting," like the touching of the trees, sometimes they were merely passing superstitions. She would say to Ambrose, "If that blackbird flies away before I count twenty, I shall die in the night." And, if the blackbird flew away, she would creep to bed in fear and trembling, and find herself alive in the morning with surprise and delight. Ambrose, who was of more stolid make, would pretend to be scornful of these signs and portents, but sometimes—he had to own—they came true. He was always glad when the time passed, and some dire catastrophe, predicted by his sister, had failed to eventuate.

These signs and portents were bad enough in all conscience; they cast a shadow upon the children's lives—a shadow of which their relations and friends had no conception—but there was a far worse burden than these which Trivvie had to bear. The signs and portents, she could, to a certain extent, control, but the Nightmare Curse was a menace over which she had absolutely no jurisdiction. Every night before going to sleep Trivvie had to observe a mysterious and secret rite, she had to walk round the room three times, treading with her bare feet upon every pink flower in the threadbare carpet. It sounds an easy rite to accomplish, but the burden of it was in its monotonous repetition: every night, *every single night*, even when you were dead tired, even when you were ill; and, if you forgot, and crept into bed, you had to drag yourself out of your nice warm bed and do it. And then there was always the awful fear that you might forget; that you might go off to sleep before you remembered, and, if that happened the frightful dream came.

The origin of this peculiar rite was lost in oblivion; Trivvie had forgotten the origin of it herself. She knew, however, that if she failed to carry out the rite with faithful exactitude—either because she was too tired and sleepy, or because somebody was there— she invariably dreamed a very terrifying dream. The dream was horrible, and it was always the same in every detail. Trivvie found herself in the hall at Chevis Place, she was in her cotton night-dress, with bare feet, and it was very cold. But it was not the cold that made Trivvie's teeth chatter in her head, it was the frightful anticipation of what she knew was coming. In the hall, over the enormous fireplace, hung the head and neck of an enormous stag with branching antlers and glassy eyes. Trivvie could not look away, she knew—she *knew* what was coming. The stag began to move, it turned its neck this way and that, it began to struggle wildly against the wooden collar which held it in check—the wooden collar which bore a little silver plate telling the date upon which it had been killed, and the forest in which Sir Archibald Chevis Cobbe had killed it. Trivvie watched with horror, she knew what was coming and this frightful anticipation was by far the worst part of the dream—the stag struggled, reared wildly, and broke loose from its bonds; its fore-feet came crashing through the wall, tearing the paper, and scattering the plaster in clouds of dust. It leapt from behind the mantelpiece into the middle of the hall, leaving an immense hole in the wall from whence it had come. At this moment Trivvie always woke, screaming at the top of her voice, and Miss Foddy had to get up and pacify her with drinks of water and bicarbonate of soda.

Such was the Nightmare Curse, and a very peculiar and terrifying curse it was. Trivvie did not understand it, she did not even try to understand it, she merely accepted it and bore it philosophically, as a curse under which she, alone of all mankind, had to labour.

But this afternoon Trivvie was gay, no signs or portents troubled her, and bed-time, with its Nightmare Curse, was still an hour away. She waited at the gate for Ambrose and Mrs. Abbott—who had negotiated the drive in a more conventional manner—and danced along the road with them to the gate of The Archway House. On the other side of Barbara, Ambrose walked, with sedate steps, hanging on her arm.

"We like you," Trivvie said. "Don't we, Amby? We thought it was going to be horrid when you came and began spoiling the garden. Lanky still hates you, of course, but we don't, do we, Amby?"

"But I've only seen Lancreste once, in church," said Barbara who was grieved to hear that her Golden Boy was inimical to her.

"He's seen you, *often*," giggled Trivvie.

"Why haven't I seen him?"

"Because he didn't want you to. Lanky's clever, he can track like a Redskin Brave, and he knows lots of things. It was Lanky who showed us how to make the elephant trap."

"We dug it," Ambrose put in.

"And Lanky covered it with sticks and

leaves, and strewed the gravel over it so that it wouldn't show."

"I think it was horrid of you," Barbara told them. "I might easily have broken my leg——"

"But it was such *fun*," said Trivvie callously.

"Lanky wanted to drive you away," added Ambrose.

Barbara was annoyed. "It was very silly," she said. "Very silly indeed, and Lancreste can't be clever if he thought *that* would drive us away—as if grown-up people could be driven away from their home by a silly little boy's booby trap!"

"He didn't think *that* would drive you away," said Ambrose somewhat scornfully. "The elephant trap was just an extra——"

"It was the ghost, really——" began Trivvie.

"Oh, so Lancreste was the ghost, was he?" said Barbara casually; she was furious, by now, but she was not going to let them know that she was furious. Her Golden Boy had fallen from his pedestal—he was a devil, not an angel at all——

"Weren't you frightened?" enquired Trivvie with interest.

"No, of course not."

"Well, other people were. It was frightful fun. Lanky did the ghost whenever anyone came and wanted to buy The Archway House—we *all* wanted the house to stay empty, but Lanky wanted it most."

"Because of the garden," Ambrose explained.

"It doesn't matter telling you now," added Trivvie, "because Father caught him, you see. And his sheet was all muddy——"

"Father thrashed him," added Ambrose, with relish.

Barbara was glad to hear it, and Mr. Marvell went up considerably in her estimation. She was also somewhat relieved to know that the ghost would trouble The Archway House no more. Personally she had never minded the ghost, but others had minded it, and she had sometimes wondered what would happen if the ghost returned and frightened the servants—as it had frightened the charwoman—would they all leave in a body?

"And was Lancreste the ghost at Ganthorne Lodge?" she enquired.

"Oh no," replied the children in unison, and Trivvie added, in an awed voice, "That's a *real* ghost."

★　★　★

Arthur met Barbara at the door.

"What ages you've been!" he exclaimed.

"Were you bored, darling?" enquired Barbara. "I came away as soon as I could. Didn't you get Monkey to come and have tea with you?"

"Oh yes, he came," said Arthur, a trifle irritably. "But he had an urgent call—had to dash off at a moment's notice. Thank goodness I'm not a doctor. Monkey can't call his soul his own; he's at everybody's beck and call——"

"I know," agreed Barbara sympathetically. "Was it Lady Chevis Cobbe, or what?"

"It was Mrs. Dance," said Arthur. "They think she's got appendicitis——"

Barbara stood on the step and gazed at him—incredulity, horror and dismay chased each other across her face.

"It *can't* be!" she exclaimed.

"Appendicitis," Arthur told her. "They're taking her into a nursing home in Gostown to operate—it's nothing to worry about, darling. Heaps of people have appendicitis—she'll be all right in a fortnight or so——" (He thought—Good Heavens! I'd no idea that Barbara was so fond of the woman.) "Even Dance himself, isn't unduly anxious,"

Arthur continued earnestly. "It's quite a simple case. Honestly, Barbara, you needn't be so upset."

"I am—upset," said Barbara, in a faint voice.

It was only too obvious that she was upset—dreadfully upset—Arthur took her by the arm and supported her to a chair; he went for brandy and made her drink it; he stood over her, and fussed round her anxiously, watching, with tender concern, until the colour began to return to her pallid face.

"There, you're better now, darling," he said, with relief. "I was a fool to blurt it out at you like that, but I'd no idea——"

"Yes, I'm better," she agreed. "It was most extraordinary the way everything went round and round, and the hall got sort of dark——"

"Don't think about it," Arthur advised.

"No, I won't."

She sat in silence for a minute or two, holding on to Arthur's hand and trying to recover herself. It had been a most uncomfortable experience.

"I think you should go to bed," said Arthur. "I really think you should. You've been doing too much—those Marvells have upset you——"

"I must see Trivvie," said Barbara suddenly. "Yes, that's the only thing to do. I must see Trivvie at once."

"Trivvie!"

"Yes, you must go and fetch her."

"But why——"

"You'll find them down at the stream—they're sure to be there."

"But, Barbara, you're not fit——"

"If you don't go and fetch her I shall have to go and look for her myself," said Barbara firmly.

"But, my dear——"

"Go, Arthur," she besought him. "Go quickly—I must see her now—at once—immediately."

Arthur thought she was mad, but he saw that he must humour her—it was the only thing to do—he fled to find Trivvie.

I'll make her do it, Barbara thought, as she waited in the hall for Trivvie to come, I must make her do it. Of course there's no truth in it—none at all—it's merely an amazing coincidence—it must be that, it *must* be—but, all the same, I shall *make* Trivvie go straight home and take out the pin.

28

THE VULTURES GATHER

LADY Chevis Cobbe died very early one
Spring morning. Jerry had been sum-
moned from Ganthorne Lodge the night
before. She had found Sir Lucian Agnew in
the big hall, and the two of them sat over the
fire together and talked in low voices. The
cousins arrived from London and Pangbourne during the night, and were accom-
modated with rooms in the big empty house.
The accommodating of the cousins was
Jerry's job—since there was nobody else to
undertake it—and she found it a most onerous
task, for both lots of cousins were convinced
that *they* were the heirs to Chevis Place, and,
therefore, entitled to the best room. Dr.
Wrench was there, of course, and Mr.
Tupper; and the London specialist (sum-
moned by Dr. Wrench on his own responsibility) came down in his Daimler, looked at
the patient, and departed again, saying that
there was nothing more to be done, and

leaving it to be understood that it was much too late, and that, if he had been called in before, he could have done a good deal.

It was an extraordinarily wearing night, and, when it was all over, and her ladyship had departed peacefully to a Better Land (which presumably would suit her down to the ground seeing that there is said to be no marriage nor giving in marriage there) Jerry was thoroughly exhausted, and more miserable and disgusted than she had ever been before.

Jerry felt that the real sadness of Aunt Matilda's death lay in the fact that nobody really minded—nobody was heart-broken at her passing. Even she, herself, who had always been quite fond of Aunt Matilda, could not summon any tears. The truth was that Lady Chevis Cobbe, had not been a lovable woman; she was "queer," and her queerness kept her aloof from her kind; she was proud, and her pride had erected a barrier between herself and the outside world; she was suspicious of anybody who was "nice" to her, and her suspicion poisoned the atmosphere round about her.

"I believe Dr. Wrench is the one who feels it most," said Jerry to herself, as she looked at

437

the doctor's white face and shadowed eyes, "and he only feels it because he feels he ought to have been able to do more for her than he did—which is rot"—said Jerry—"because I'm perfectly certain nobody *could*. Sir Lucian feels it too, of course, but only in an *outside* sort of way. He is seeing himself all the time, and he sees himself as a man who has lost his best friend. It's really rather disgusting. And as for the Chevis relations—well—they're just *vultures*."

When morning came, the big house, which had been half empty for so long, was filled with people—people whispering together in low voices, going softly up and down the broad staircase, gathering in the dining-room for breakfast, and dispersing again on various pretexts. . . .

Jerry had intended to return to Ganthorne Lodge when breakfast was over, but Mr. Tupper told her that she was to stay.

"It will be better for you to remain here until—ahem—in the meantime," he said firmly. "After all, you knew her ladyship very well—I should like you to be here, and take control of the—er—rather equivocal situation, until—ahem."

"But I can't take *control*," said Jerry,

aghast. "None of the Chevis relations listen to *me*."

"You must do your best," Mr. Tupper told her. "After all, it is only for two days."

It was only for two days, until (as Mr. Tupper had been too delicate to say) the funeral was over and the will was read. Once the will had been read everything would be made plain. Archie would get his inheritance, and the Chevis relations would fade away— but it was the longest two days that Jerry had ever spent.

Archie Cobbe had been motoring in Cornwall with a friend; he arrived at Chevis Place the day after his Aunt's death. He was extremely annoyed to find the house full of Chevis relations, all of whom were under the impression that it was their prerogative to take command of the situation. They beheld Archie's efforts to assume control with indifference, or scorn, or repressed rage (according to their temperaments). After all, what was Archie? He was only a Cobbe. The Chevis relations were suspicious and resentful of each other, but they united in their resentment against these upstart Cobbes.

The situation was equivocal, as Mr. Tupper had said, for the house was full of people bent on showing their authority. Denis Chevis, for instance (who lived in town, and was therefore, up-to-date), informed the butler that dinner was to be served at eight-thirty, instead of at eight o'clock as hitherto; and Bertie Chevis (who lived at Pangbourne, and prided himself upon his old-fashioned ways) desired the butler to inform the cook that he preferred to dine at seven sharp. The wretched Killigrew brought these conflicting orders to Jerry, and asked what was to be done about it.

"Goodness!" said Jerry.

"It's awkward, isn't it, Miss?"

"Very awkward," she agreed, "and I think on the whole," she added with Solomon-like judgment, "I think on the whole, Killigrew, the best thing will be just to go on having dinner at the usual time."

"Yes, Miss," said Killigrew, and he heaved a sigh of relief, for what Mrs. Sheffield would have said if he had had to go to her and ask her to change the hour of dinner in such a ridiculous manner Killigrew couldn't imagine. "Yes, Miss," said Killigrew. "Yes, I think—if you will excuse me saying so—I think that will be the best way out of the dilemma."

So dinner appeared at the usual hour, and nothing was said by either of the gentlemen who had wanted it changed. There was a good deal of manœuvring for places at the long dinner-table, but it was all quite decorous, there was nothing unseemly about it. Archie managed to secure the seat at the head of the table before Denis and Bertie had time to perceive his intention—he was younger than either of them, and considerably more agile.

"Just wait till the will's read," said Bertie Chevis to his wife in the privacy of their bedroom. "I shall put that young man in his place when the will's read."

"I suppose you're quite sure it's all right, Bertie?"

"Of course it's all right," replied Bertie confidently. "Matilda showed me her will, years ago—of course, it's all right."

Denis Chevis and the partner of his bosom were holding much the same kind of conversation in *their* bedroom, which was situated at the other end of the house.

"It's all that girl's fault," Denis was explaining, "that Jerry Cobbe—ridiculous giving the Berties the best room like that—perfectly ridiculous. Have you noticed the way she and her brother try to run the whole show? Just because they live here, and saw a lot of Matilda before she died."

"I suppose you don't think they can have *got round* Matilda in any way? " enquired the partner of his bosom in anxious tones.

"Good Lord, no," replied Denis, confidently. "Matilda wouldn't leave Chevis Place to a *Cobbe*. Besides, I saw her will. She showed it to me that time I was down here—it's perfectly all right. No need at all to worry. We shall just have to be patient until the will's read."

Archie was another who was waiting impatiently for the will to be read. He was longing to get rid of the Chevis relations, and enjoy the amenities of Chevis Place at his leisure. Unlike the others he was a trifle anxious about the will. He had been shown it, of course, and he was certain it was "all right" *really*, but it seemed almost too good to be true, that, after all these years, Chevis Place was actually within his grasp. He was certain it was "all right," but he would not feel absolutely comfortable and happy until he had heard the will. Archie tried to get hold of Mr. Tupper several times during those two days, but it was extraordinarily difficult, and, even when Archie at last managed to hem him in and pin him down, Mr. Tupper was elusive and non-committal.

"I can give you no authority," said Mr. Tupper, with legal dryness, "I can give you no authority at all."

"But I'm the heir," Archie pointed out. "I'm Aunt Matilda's heir. She showed me her will, so there's no doubt about it at all. And I don't really see why I should be obliged to have the house full of all these Chevis relations. Can't you tell them that I'm the heir?"

"I can tell them nothing," said Mr. Tupper firmly. "Dr. Wrench and I are her ladyship's executors, and we have decided that nothing is to be said or done until the will has been read."

The two days passed and Lady Chevis Cobbe was buried with suitable pomp and ceremony in the tomb of her ancestors. Several heavy showers fell during the proceedings as if to show that Nature mourned her death—if no one else did. But this pretty idea occurred to none of her relations. Denis Chevis turned up the collar of his morning coat and murmured to his wife, who was standing next to him, "April showers." She agreed, and wondered, rather miserably, whether they would "have to live here now." It was a horrid damp place, she thought, and she hated the country at any time. But she comforted herself with the reflection that they would have "lots of money" and could shut up the place for the greater part of the year, and spend their time very profitably in London—Denis doesn't like the country either, she thought, that's one mercy. . . .

After the funeral the whole party gathered in the dining-room, with barely concealed anxiety and expectation on their countenances. Archie was well to the fore, advising everybody where to sit; opening this window and shutting that one, to obviate any draughts; raising one blind and lowering another, so that the room should be light enough, but not too bright for the mournful occasion.

They were all ready and waiting for some minutes before Mr. Tupper made his appearance, followed by Dr. Wrench. The subdued hum of conversation died away as the two executors came in. Mr. Tupper looked grave and important as befitted his task, but Dr. Wrench looked scared and miserable and, in very truth, he was both. There were at least three people in the room, each of whom believed himself to be the heir to Chevis Place, and believed it erroneously. Monkey knew enough about human nature to envisualise the reactions of these people when they heard the will read. There would be a scene—there would be the devil of a scene—and Monkey hated scenes. He wished devoutly, that a message would come for him which would necessitate his immediate departure from the battlefield. I wouldn't mind *what* it was, thought Monkey wretchedly, even a breech presentation would be better than this.

"Is everybody here," said Archie promptly.

"I don't see Miss Jeronina Cobbe."

"No, she's gone upstairs. She's got a headache," Archie explained. "It doesn't matter about Jerry, I can tell her all about it afterwards."

"I think Miss Jerry should be here," said Mr. Tupper, frowning, "you had better go and fetch her."

"It's no good," Archie told him a trifle irritably—why on earth couldn't the old idiot get on with the will—"It's no good bothering about Jerry. I told her to come and she wouldn't."

Dr. Wrench leant forward and whispered something to his co-executor. "Rather

upset," he whispered, "fond of her ladyship—just as well in a way—don't you
think?"

"Very well," said Mr. Tupper aloud. "I
shall read the will to you first, and I shall go
upstairs and see Miss Cobbe later—ahem."

He began to read the will.

* * *

"THIS IS THE LAST WILL AND
TESTAMENT of me MATILDA VIC-
TORIA CHEVIS COBBE sometime known
as Chevis Cobbe of Chevis Place Wandlebury
in the county of Westshire, widow. I hereby
revoke all testamentary dispositions heretofore made by me and declare this to be my
last will."

1. I appoint Alfred Tupper of Wandlebury
   aforesaid solicitor and Charles Wrench of
   the Corner House Wandlebury aforesaid
   Batchelor of Medicine to be the executors
   and trustees of this my will.

2. I declare that in the interpretation of this
   my will the expression "my trustees" shall
   (where the context permits) mean and in-

clude the trustees or trustee for the time being hereof whether original or substituted and if there be no such trustees or trustee shall (where the context permits) include the persons or person empowered by statute to exercise or perform any power or trust hereby or by statute conferred upon the trustees hereof and willing or bound to exercise or perform the same.

3. I bequeath the following specific legacies:

    (a) To my cousin Bertrand Chevis of Mill Hall Pangbourne in the county of Berkshire, the Chevis Miniatures contained in the glass table in the drawing-room at Chevis Place aforesaid.

    (b) To my cousin Denis Adam Chevis of 20 Finckle Street in the Borough of Kensington the collection of Seventeenth Century Snuff Boxes in the glass table in the library at Chevis Place aforesaid.

    (c) To my deceased husband's nephew Archibald Edward Cobbe of Ganthorne Lodge Ganthorne in the county of Westshire the gold watch and chain the property of my deceased husband.

    (d) To my friend Lucian Agnew of Kingsmill House Wandlebury aforesaid Baronet all my miniatures other than the Chevis Miniatures aforesaid and also my Rockingham tea and coffee service which he has always admired and also the Royal Worcester china bowl in the drawing-room at Chevis Place aforesaid and also the Ebony Cabinet with the Dresden china plaques which stands in my boudoir.

4. I bequeath the following pecuniary legacies:

(a) To the said Bertrand Chevis the sum of Two Thousand pounds.

(b) To the said Denis Adam Chevis the sum of Two Thousand pounds.

(c) To each of my said trustees in the event of their accepting the office of trustee the sum of Two Thousand pounds such sums to be in addition to any other sums hereinafter appearing.

(d) To each of my nephews John Bertrand Chevis and James Bertrand Chevis and to my niece Matilda Ann Chevis all of Holly Lodge Winkham in the county of Essex the sum of Five Hundred pounds respectively.

(e) To the said Charles Wrench the sum of Five Hundred pounds in consideration of his faithful services to me during my various illnesses.

(f) To my personal maid Annette Gaule . . . (here followed a list of her ladyship's servants and dependants and the various charities in which she was interested with bequests according to their desserts).

5. I give devise and bequeath all my real estate not hereby or by any codicil hereto otherwise specifically disposed of to which I may be entitled at my death or over which I may have a general power of appointment and including the Mansion House Chevis Place aforesaid unto my deceased husband's niece Jeronina Mary Cobbe of Ganthorne Lodge aforesaid absolutely Provided always that the said Jeronina Mary Cobbe shall at the time of my death be unmarried and that she shall within one year of my death endeavour to procure the Royal Licence to take the name of Chevis prefixed and in addition to her own and in default of compliance with these conditions or any of them I direct

that this bequest shall be reduced to the sum of Two Thousand pounds and all my personal jewellery and I give devise and bequeath all my real estate as aforesaid to my deceased husband's nephew the said Archibald Edward Cobbe absolutely Provided always that he shall at the time of my death be unmarried and that he shall within one year of my death endeavour to procure the Royal Licence to take the name of Chevis prefixed and in addition to his own and shall agree to reside at Chevis Place aforesaid at least eight months in every year.

6. Subject as heretofore I give devise and bequeath all the residue of my personal estate and effects unto my trustees upon trust to sell call in and convert the same into money (with power at their discretion to postpone such sale calling-in and conversion) and after payment thereout of my debts funeral and testamentary expenses to stand possessed of the same upon trust for the benefit of such person as shall become entitled to my real estate including the Mansion House Chevis Place aforesaid under the trusts and provisions herein-

before declared and contained IN WIT-
NESS whereof I the said Matilda Victoria
Chevis Cobbe the testatrix have to this my
will set my hand this 19th day of April
One thousand nine hundred and thirty
four.

SIGNED PUBLISHED AND DECLARED
by the said Matilda Victoria Chevis Cobbe as
and for her Last Will and Testament in the
presence of us present at the same time who
in her presence at her request and in the
presence of each other have hereunto sub-
scribed our names as witnesses.
  MATILDA VICTORIA CHEVIS COBBE
    Timothy Deans
      11 Downes Road, Wandlebury
        Clerk.
    Eric Pinthorpe
      Rose Cottage
        Chevis Place, Wandlebury
        Clerk.

The will was not read without interrup-
tions. Archie Cobbe, and Bertie and Denis
Chevis were equally appalled when they
began to realise that this was quite a different
will from the one each had been shown—at

different times—by Lady Chevis Cobbe. They glared at each other; they glared at Mr. Tupper; they started to their feet and were pulled down again by those who were sitting next to them. It was only because each hoped against hope for a codicil at the end, giving him the bulk of the estate, that they allowed Mr. Tupper to finish. But, when the end was reached, and no codicil was read, they all three burst into angry speech. It was abominable, it was disgraceful, it was a put-up job. What was the meaning of it—that was what they wanted to know. Chevis Place to go to a young girl barely out of her teens—Chevis Place to go to a Cobbe! What was the meaning of this injustice—it was madness, sheer madness—what was the meaning of it?

"The meaning of it is perfectly clear," said Mr. Tupper in his most legal manner. "Miss Jeronina Mary Cobbe is the residuary legatee. Apart from the various bequests which I have just read to you the whole property goes to her. The only condition which she has to fulfil to obtain possession of the property is as follows—she must be unmarried at the time of the testator's death, and, since she indubitably fulfils this condition, there is nothing to prevent her from inheriting. She must, of course, assume the name of Chevis in addition to her own, but that is purely a matter of routine and I anticipate no difficulties——"

"But Aunt Matilda showed me her will, and it was quite different," cried Archie.

"I saw a different will, myself," added Bertie Chevis.

"So did I," exclaimed Denis. "What has been done with the other wills?"

"It is quite possible that you may have seen other wills," admitted Mr. Tupper. "You may have done so. The fact is the testatrix was somewhat dubious as to the disposal of her—ahem—not inconsiderable property. She made a number of wills at—er—various times. Each of these wills was duly signed and deposited with us, and each will—as you will readily understand—cancelled the others. This document," continued Mr. Tupper, taking up the will and holding it to his bosom, as if he feared—as well he might—that the legatees would tear it in pieces, "this document is the last will made by Lady Chevis Cobbe and it is undoubtedly legal."

"She was mad when she made it," exclaimed Denis Chevis angrily, "I shall take advice—you will hear from my solicitor."

"And from mine," added Bertie, almost stuttering in excitement. "And from mine. The whole thing is—is outrageous—positively outrageous! My uncle would turn in his grave at the idea of Chevis Place going to a Cobbe. It has been in our family for generations."

"Her ladyship had the right to leave her property as she chose," Mr. Tupper pointed out. "The property was not entailed."

"It ought to have been entailed," cried Denis.

"That is scarcely the point," replied Mr. Tupper drily. "I am afraid I cannot offer any opinion as to what ought to have been done. Nor do I wish to go into the matter any further. If you desire to consult me about—er—anything connected with the various bequests and legacies you will find me at my office. Meanwhile I propose to—er—leave you." (And if Mr. Tupper did not actually say "leave you to fight it out" his manner implied it). "To—er—leave you," he said.

He placed the precious document very carefully in his black bag, and made for the door; and, such was the dignity of his deportment, that the disappointed and furious relations made way for him and let him go unscathed.

Monkey Wrench seized his hat and fled for his life.

29

THE RESIDUARY LEGATEE

JERRY was busy upstairs in her aunt's boudoir; it was the smallest room in the great house, and this was one of the reasons why Jerry liked it. She preferred small rooms, they were more comfortable and homelike, they did not call for such dignified and stately behaviour. Another reason why Jerry liked the boudoir was because she knew it best. It was here that Aunt Matilda always sat, and Jerry had sat here with her hundreds of times. She therefore felt more at home here—less lost—Jerry was rather like a dog in her hatred of strange places.

I shall be able to go home now, she thought to herself. Mr. Tupper can't keep me here any longer—I won't stay—I shall go home to-night, or to-morrow morning at the very latest—and then *Sam*.

Jerry had no headache—none at all—she was one of those fortunate people who never suffer from headaches—or very rarely. She had made the usual feminine excuse because she did not want to attend the reading of Aunt Matilda's will. It would be the most frightful scene—she knew that—and, like the doctor, Jerry abominated scenes. She liked to see her fellow creatures at their best, not at their worst, and she was aware that none of the legatees would be at their best when Aunt Matilda's will was read to them. Vultures, she thought, just vultures—that's what they are. They never bothered about Aunt Matilda when she was alive, but, now that she's dead, here they are—a pack of vultures, squabbling over her remains—disgusting brutes! thought Jerry, and she sat down to write some letters at Aunt Matilda's desk.

She was interrupted by the arrival of Mr. Tupper, looking very solemn and portentous, in his old-fashioned morning coat and black trousers, which he had donned for the occasion. Jerry told him to come in and laid down her pen—she supposed she would have to listen to him.

"I have read the will to the—er—relations," said Mr. Tupper solemnly, "and now I propose to read it to you," and with these words he opened the black bag, and took out the document which had already caused so much trouble.

"Oh no!" cried Jerry in dismay. "I mean don't bother. It wouldn't be any good, because, you see, I shouldn't understand a word—all those 'aforesaids' and 'hereinafter mentioneds' and things—honestly, I shouldn't understand a *word.* Just tell me if there's anything I ought to know."

Jerry looked very childish as she sat there, half turned from the writing-table. Her curls were ruffled, they glinted in the sun which poured through the open window; there was a smudge of ink on her nose, and two of her fingers were inky—for Jerry was no pen-woman. Mr. Tupper thought that she looked like a school-girl—she was very young, very young indeed—and his heart misgave him a little. It would have been wiser if the money had been properly tied up (he thought) and trustees appointed. It would have been much wiser. He had tried to persuade her ladyship to do this at the time, but her ladyship had not listened. Her ladyship did not care for advice, she went her own way and it was never the slightest use trying to guide or control her.

"Well," said Mr. Tupper, relaxing his

legal manner, and smiling for the first time that afternoon. "Well, I think there is something you should know, Miss Jerry. You are Lady Chevis Cobbe's residuary legatee."

Jerry gazed at him in amazement. "Me?" she enquired. "Do you mean Chevis Place and all that?"

"Yes," said Mr. Tupper, smiling more broadly than before. " 'Chevis place and all that,' describes the bequest admirably. It is far more concise than our clumsy legal phrases and equally embracing."

"My hat!" exclaimed Jerry, aghast. She looked round the room where she was sitting, and tried to believe it was hers—her very own to do what she liked with—it was incredible, quite incredible.

"But what about Archie?" she enquired at last. "Wasn't he furious? And what about Denis and Bertie Chevis? Oh dear, it's simply frightful! Why on earth did Aunt Matilda do it?"

"Her ladyship gave us no reasons for the changes she made in the disposal of her property," said Mr. Tupper, resuming his legal manner. "It did not concern us professionally. Our part was merely to draw up a legal will in conformity with her wishes. She

was not a lady who brooked interference—
you are aware of that, Miss Jerry."

"Oh, I know," said Jerry. "I'm not blaming you—*you* couldn't help it, of course."

Mr. Tupper blinked, he thought that
"blaming" was a curious word to use in the
connection. He certainly had not expected to
be "blamed" by Jerry for drawing up a will
making her a wealthy woman. From the other
legatees he had expected blame (and had got
it in full measure), not because it was in any
way his fault that the will was different from
what they had hoped, but because he was
aware that lawyers are constantly blamed for
unsatisfactory wills. It is in human nature to
blame somebody when things go wrong, and,
as testators are always safely out of the way
before their wills are made public, the
lawyers who have carried out their instructions come in for all the abuse.

"I did not anticipate blame from you," Mr.
Tupper pointed out.

"No, of course not," agreed Jerry. "I know
how frightfully stubborn Aunt Matilda was.
You couldn't help it—I know that. Didn't
Archie get anything?" she enquired anxiously.

"Two thousand pounds."

"Well, that's a good deal, isn't it?"

"I'm afraid it did not satisfy Archie."

"No," said Jerry. "No, I don't suppose it would. How *awful*, isn't it?"

"Scarcely 'awful,'" said Mr. Tupper. "Your Aunt wished you to have Chevis Place and it was for her to decide."

"Yes," said Jerry, thoughtfully.

"You did more for her than the others," he continued, "and, to my mind, the fact that she decided to make you her residuary legatee was natural in view of what you did for her."

"But I didn't do *anything*," cried Jerry. "I didn't do anything at all!"

"You came and saw her when she was ill," said Mr. Tupper.

"Anybody would have," Jerry told him. "I used to be sorry for her, you see. I used to think it must be frightfully lonely for her all alone in this huge place—I wish I'd come oftener," she added, rather sadly.

"You evidently came often enough," Mr. Tupper pointed out with dry humour.

"They'll *kill* me," exclaimed Jerry, with sudden conviction. "They'll *kill* me, I know they will."

"Surely not," objected Mr. Tupper. "Surely not. My experience leads me to believe that the fact that you are now—er—a

461

woman of considerable means will have quite the reverse effect upon her ladyship's relatives——"

"You mean they'll lick my boots?" enquired Jerry in dismay. "How ghastly!"

Mr. Tupper was still to find a reply to this extraordinary remark, when the butler appeared and announced that Mrs. Abbott had called and was waiting in the drawing-room. Would Miss Cobbe care to see her for a few moments?

"Oh, how nice of her!" exclaimed Jerry, who was thankful for a respite from the consideration of her new status. "How nice of her to come! Show her up here, Killigrew—and Killigrew," she continued, "I shan't be coming down to dinner to-night."

"No, Miss," said Killigrew, smiling in a deferential manner. "You would like dinner sent up here, Miss?"

"Yes," said Jerry. "You see, Killigrew, they might eat *me*, instead of Mrs. Sheffield's nice lamb cutlets."

"Yes, Miss," agreed Killigrew. "May I—would it be considered presuming if I was to offer my congratulations, Miss—and those of the rest of the staff?"

"Oh, thank you—no, of course it wouldn't

be, at all. I mean I'm still *me,* Killigrew, and I intend to remain me," she added with a lift of her small determined chin.

"Yes, Miss," agreed the butler.

"And I shan't forget how kind you were to me when I was little," continued Jerry. "And all the talks we had in the pantry, with you cleaning the silver, and me eating jam out of the silver jam-pot——" (and she thought to herself—Goodness, that jam-pot belongs to me now, how frightfully queer!)

"Nor me, either," replied Killigrew with spirit. "I shan't forget—nor Mrs. Anderson, nor Mrs. Sheffield, nor any of us. None of us won't forget how you used to come over here when you were a little girl. I may say, that the opinion in the Housekeeper's Room—for what it's worth—is that 'er ladyship did the right thing when she made the new will."

"Well, Killigrew, I don't know," said Jerry thoughtfully. "I really haven't had time to get used to the idea."

Mr. Tupper had been listening to this unconventional and somewhat indiscreet conversation with growing concern. He now felt that he simply *must* put an end to it.

"I think," he said, in the loudish impersonal voice which he reserved entirely for superior menials, "I think that Mrs. Abbott is still waiting downstairs, Killigrew."

Killigrew withdrew hastily.

"Dear Jerry," said Mr. Tupper kindly. "It would perhaps be better if you could adopt a little more dignified manner towards the servants. Otherwise you may have trouble with them. I am speaking as a friend, my dear—a very old friend—and entirely for your own good. I have known you since you were a small child. You are now—I would remind you—a young woman of considerable—ah—fortune, and are therefore of considerable—ah—importance in the world."

"But that's just it!" Jerry exclaimed. "I mean I can't. Really and truly I'm not a bit suited for that sort of thing. I'm not—not proud enough, or something, and it's no use trying to be something that you're *not*. I can't change myself——"

"We don't want you changed," Mr. Tupper assured her.

"Yes you do—you want me to be dignified—and I can't be." Jerry told him earnestly. "Of course you're quite right—I mean the owner of Chevis Place *ought* to be a dignified sort of person."

At this moment Barbara was announced,

464

and Jerry flew into her arms and hugged her.

"Darling," she cried. "How gorgeous to see you again! What a lamb you are to come."

Mr. Tupper went away and left them. He was disturbed and distressed. He saw breakers ahead; Jerry was right when she said she was not suited for her new position. She would either change (and change, Mr. Tupper feared, for the worse) or else she would remain as she was, innocent and guileless as a new born infant, and become a prey for fortune-hunters and spongers.

"She's too young," he said to himself, as he went downstairs. "Too young and too—too impulsive."

Archie was in the hall, putting on his coat.

"Are you going away?" enquired Mr. Tupper in surprise.

"Yes," said Archie shortly.

"Surely you are going to see your sister before you go!" exclaimed the lawyer, following the young man out of the front door.

"No, I'm not," said Archie furiously. "I don't want to see anybody, and especially not Jerry. The whole thing was a put-up job. I've said it before and I say it again. Jerry got round Aunt Matilda behind my back—when I was away in London—she came crawling round here. I know she did. But I'm not beaten yet, you needn't think it. I'm going straight to my solicitor in London—I've been duped and deceived," cried Archie incoherently. "You're all in it, every one of you— undue influence—mad, crazy, absolutely stark mad."

He sprang into his small car, which was waiting in the drive, and departed at full speed—spurts of gravel were flung from beneath his wheels——

"Trouble and more trouble," Mr. Tupper said aloud, and he walked slowly home.

30

ALARMS AND EXCURSIONS

"YOU know all about it, I suppose," said Jerry when she had hugged Barbara and bestowed her in a comfortable chair.

"All about what?" Barbara not unnaturally enquired.

"About Aunt Matilda leaving everything to me," said Jerry, "and all that. You've heard, I suppose."

"Yes," said Barbara, smiling in a pleased manner.

"Oh, Barbara, how *lovely* it is to see you again!" Jerry exclaimed, suddenly overcome by the niceness of her comfortable, soothing friend. "I feel as if I hadn't seen you for *years*—so much has happened in the last few days. It's been absolutely foul, and the Chevis relations are vultures, and I've been miserable and disgusted——"

"*Poor* Jerry!" said Barbara sympathetically.

"And now *this* on the top of everything,

467

just when I thought I was going home."

"But Jerry, it's lovely for you."

"Do you really, and truly, and honestly think so?" asked Jerry doubtfully. "I mean can you *see* me here?"

"Why, of course I can," Barbara assured her. Ever since Barbara had known Jerry she had seen her as the prospective chatelaine of Chevis Place, so, of course, she was used to the idea and found nothing alarming or unnatural in it. "Of course I can see you here, Jerry," she repeated, looking round the comfortable room with pleasure and delight writ large upon her kindly, honest countenance.

"Well, I don't know," said Jerry, still dubious. "I don't know at *all*. I can't *believe* it, somehow. And it's horrid to feel that they're all so angry with me—Archie and everybody. I suppose Aunt Matilda must have thought it would be all right—me, being here, I mean——"

"She wanted you to have it," Barbara pointed out.

"I suppose she did," Jerry agreed.

"It's lovely for you," urged Barbara.

"I suppose it is really, but I haven't got used to it yet. And, as I said before, I can't really *believe* it. Aunt Matilda wasn't a very happy sort of person, you know, in spite of all her riches, and Chevis Place, and everything—however, don't let's talk about it any more," said Jerry, in a more cheerful tone of voice. "I want to tell you about something else," said Jerry, smiling and dimpling all over. "Something *far* more interesting, and *far* more important. I wonder if you can guess—no, I'm sure you couldn't possibly guess what it is."

Barbara had only to glance at the face of her friend—flushed and eager now—and she knew at once what Jerry's secret was.

"Oh!" she exclaimed with delight, "Oh, Jerry, *you're engaged to Sam*."

Jerry threw back her head and laughed.

"That's what it is, isn't it?" enquired Barbara. "I knew it was. I was just hoping——"

"Darling!" cried Jerry. "How clever you are! How *did* you guess? Fancy you *seeing* and not saying a single *word*! But the joke is, you're not clever enough—not quite—because you see I'm not engaged to Sam at all, I'm married to him."

Barbara was struck dumb—absolutely struck dumb by the news. She gazed at Jerry in amazement and consternation.

"No wonder you're surprised," Jerry continued excitedly, "but I do hope you're not fed up with us about it. You see we *had* to do it all secretly because of poor Aunt Matilda and her funny ideas. I was afraid it would kill her if she heard about it, and then I should have been a murderer. So we didn't tell a soul except Markie—she had to be told, of course—and, as a matter of fact, she was in it from the very beginning. Markie's been an absolute lamb about it. You see we got quite desperate when we couldn't see each other— quite desperate. *You* couldn't have Sam down, and *I* couldn't go up to town and see him, because of leaving the horses. I *did* go up once or twice, for a few hours, but it wasn't much good. It was simply ghastly not being able to see each other—you can't think how desperate we were——"

"Oh, Jerry!" said Barbara, appalled at this revelation—after all the trouble she had taken to prevent Sam and Jerry from seeing each other, all she had accomplished was to drive them into each other's arms.

"We were desperate," continued Jerry earnestly. "Sam was miserable in town, and I was miserable at Ganthorne, and it seemed so silly, somehow. You see, there was nothing to

470

prevent us getting married except poor Aunt Matilda; and, as Sam said, if she wasn't told about it she wouldn't know. At first I thought we ought to wait until she was better, but Sam really was so awfully wretched, and so was I, really. So Sam said the best thing to do was just to get married and tell Aunt Matilda when she got better—you see the idea, don't you? We've been married for ten days now," continued Jerry, "and I'm certain nobody knows a thing about it. Sam comes down every night and it's simply lovely having him—simply lovely. He wears his Elizabethan dress," said Jerry chuckling, "with long red stockings and puffy sleeves, and a cloak. He really got it for a Fancy Dress Ball and then he never went to the ball after all. I'll tell you all about *that* some other time—all about the first time he wore the dress and came over to see me in it. I was so miserable that night, and then Sam appeared like a sort of fairy godmother, or something—it was *that* night that sort of settled the whole thing. We talked and talked, and Sam persuaded me to marry him—he looked so splendid, and he was so dear, and funny, and pleased with himself that I couldn't resist him—I didn't really need very much *persuading*," said Jerry honestly. "Not very much. But the whole point of the Elizabethan dress (apart from darling Sam rather fancying himself in it) is, that if anybody sees him about the place, they think he's a spook."

"But Jerry——" began Barbara who had listened to all this with increasing horror and alarm.

"I'll tell you," said Jerry, the words pouring out of her in an excited stream. "I really must tell you about that first night. He wore his fancy dress because, somehow, or other, he lost his trousers—aren't men funny, helpless *lambs*, Barbara? So he wore the Elizabethan dress, and came dashing over to Ganthorne in it, and, as I told you, I simply couldn't resist him. It wasn't the dress, exactly, but it was Sam *in* the dress—if you know what I mean—and then he scared Crichton away—quite by mistake—and that gave us the idea of him wearing it—so as to scare other people, you see."

Barbara could follow this in part (she knew about the trousers, of course), she could follow enough of it to see that it was entirely her fault that this dreadful thing had happened. Not only had she driven them into each other's arms by refusing to have Sam at

The Archway House, but she had further destroyed them by compelling Sam to visit his beloved in a dress that showed off his charms, and made him absolutely irresistible.

"Oh, Jerry!" she said, in horror-stricken tones.

"You're not angry with us, darling," Jerry coaxed, seating herself on a stool at Barbara's feet, and stroking her hand. "Don't be angry, Barbara. We're *so* happy—so frightfully happy. *You* know what it is to be happy like that, don't you? So you see, you mustn't be angry with Sam and me. And, now that poor Aunt Matilda has gone, we can tell everybody; but I wanted to tell you first—the very first of all," said Jerry, smiling up into Barbara's face.

"Oh dear!" Barbara said, thinking aloud in her perturbation of mind. "I did all I could to prevent it—I did everything I could think of, and it was the worst thing I could do—the very worst thing. It just shows you shouldn't *meddle*," she continued incoherently, "unless, of course, you're Elizabeth Nun—and I'm not, and never will be. It just shows you shouldn't meddle with things. If I had only told you about it—how I wish I had! What on earth did my promise to Mr. Tyler matter compared to this? He was horrid, any-how—afterwards, I mean—and, anyhow, he never did anything for me, except tell me the house was full of rats—which it wasn't. I see, now, I should have done one thing or the other," said Barbara wretchedly. "I should either have left it alone, altogether, and not tried to meddle, or I should have broken that idiotic promise, and told you the whole thing—oh dear, what a *fool* I am!"

"What on earth are you talking about?" demanded Jerry, with a chill feeling in her heart. "What on earth are you talking about, Barbara? Who is Elizabeth Nun? And what has Mr. Tyler got to do with me—or Sam?"

"I should have told you long ago," Barbara said. "When I saw that Sam was in love with you—that night at dinner—I should have told you the whole thing. Instead of which I just meddled and muddled, and hid Sam's trousers, and did far more harm than good—what a fool I am! What an idiot!"

"Barbara," said Jerry firmly. "If you don't leave off talking nonsense, and tell me what it's all about, I shall—I shall *shake* you."

"I don't know how to tell you—I don't know where to begin," Barbara said help-

474

lessly. "It's all so complicated—and I'm so frightfully upset——"

"You're frightening me. Tell me this," Jerry implored. "There's no reason—no real reason—why Sam and I—why we shouldn't have married each other—is there?"

"Yes, of course there is. That's what I've been trying to tell you all along."

It seemed to Jerry that her heart almost ceased to beat. It was a horrible sensation. If she were to lose Sam now—and yet how could she lose him? They were married. She could feel the ring inside her blouse, where it hung on a little gold chain from her neck—she *couldn't* lose Sam now.

"It was in the will," continued Barbara, trying to explain everything in the fewest possible words. "I saw the will myself, when I was at Mr. Tyler's office—the very first day I came to Wandlebury. Of course I didn't know you then—or anybody," said Barbara earnestly. "So, of course, I wasn't very interested."

"He showed you Aunt Matilda's will!" Jerry exclaimed in very natural amazement.

"He thought I was Lady Chevis Cobbe—it was all a mistake. The whole thing was awfully queer. He gave me port and that made it all the queerer," explained Barbara. "But the point is you don't get all this," she continued looking round the room vaguely, "you don't get Chevis Place, or anything, if you're married."

"Is that all?" cried Jerry. "My dear, how you terrified me! I thought—well, never mind; I don't really know *what* I thought— but I don't want Chevis Place, I don't really."

"You don't want Chevis Place?"

"No, and I might have known it was something like that," cried Jerry, quite wild with relief. "I might have known if I had thought for a moment—if I hadn't been too terrified to think at all."

"You mean you don't *mind*?" enquired Barbara incredulously.

"I'm thankful," said Jerry earnestly. "I've been trying to pretend that I was doubtful about it, but, all the time, I *hated* the thought of leaving Ganthorne Lodge."

"But Jerry——"

"I felt I ought to be pleased—everybody seemed to think I ought to be—and it seemed ungrateful to Aunt Matilda not to be pleased when she had been so kind, but, all the time, I hated the whole thing—inside me."

"I can't believe it," Barbara said.

"Listen, Barbara," said Jerry earnestly. "I'm just beginning to see it all plainly now. Just think what it would have meant if I had got Chevis Place, and all that money. I couldn't have done all the things I like doing any more. I couldn't have gone about in breeches; I couldn't have worked with the horses; it wouldn't have mattered about my business—whether it was a success or whether it wasn't. I should have had to be grandly dressed," said Jerry naïvely, "and I should have had to have people to stay, and entertain, and go to parties—I should have had to be thinking all the time: *Am I living up to Chevis Place?* And I couldn't ever," said Jerry. "I couldn't do it, because I'm not that kind of person at all. And Sam—Oh, Barbara, think how bad it would have been for Sam— Sam wouldn't have had to work any more. It wouldn't have been worth while, and, even if he had gone on working, all the real interest would have gone, for what would his salary have been in comparison with all Aunt Matilda's money? Sam needs work," said Jerry with her wise look. "Yes, it's good for

477

Sam to work. He would get slack and careless if he didn't have to work. You don't know how sweet Sam is about his salary," she continued, smiling up at Barbara. "He likes to give me money every week—and I like to take it from him. Housekeeping money, he calls it, and he's *so* serious and important about it. If I had all that money myself, I couldn't take it from Sam—Oh, I can't explain, but it would *all* be different, and it would all be *wrong*.

"Think of Archie," Jerry continued gravely. "Look at what this money of Aunt Matilda's has done to Archie. He knew it was coming to him (or thought he did) and it simply ruined his whole life. It made the small salaries he was able to earn seem worthless; it gave him a wrong idea of life. He depended upon the horrible money, instead of depending upon himself. And Aunt Matilda—look at Aunt Matilda," cried Jerry. "Did her money make her happy? It made her miserable, that's what it did. It cut her off from everybody—you couldn't get *near* Aunt Matilda, because she thought all the time that you wanted something out of her. Oh, Barbara, what an escape we've had!"

Jerry was quite breathless after all this. She stopped talking, and ran her fingers through

478

her curls. It had been a tremendous speech, and the making of it had cleared her own mind, and removed any doubt that might have lingered in it as to the desirability of the legacy which she had missed through her marriage. She felt much better now, clear, and sane, and practical.

"Well," she said, smiling up at Barbara. "What do you think of all that?"

"It's quite true," said Barbara slowly, ridding herself with some difficulty of the illusion that riches and happiness go hand in hand.

"Of course it's true," said Jerry confidently. "I see that now—even more clearly than I did before—so, now, the only thing to do is to get hold of Mr. Tupper and tell him that I'm married."

"Yes, I suppose we had better," agreed Barbara, still a little reluctant at the thought of all that Jerry was losing.

"I suppose you're quite sure it *was* in the will—about me only getting Chevis Place if I wasn't married," enquired Jerry anxiously.

"Quite sure," said Barbara. "It struck me as so *odd* that I read that bit twice—to make sure. But, of course, it might have been changed afterwards. Didn't Mr. Tupper say anything about it?"

"No—but, of course, he never thought for a minute that I was married," Jerry reminded her. "How could he? I mean I don't suppose it ever crossed his mind for a minute. I don't *look* married yet, do I?"

Barbara looked at her friend seriously. "No, you don't," she agreed. "You look far too young, and the ink on your nose makes you look even younger, somehow."

Jerry laughed. "I don't know why it is I always get inky when I write letters—I always do." She got up and went to a little gilt mirror which hung on the wall, and began to scrub her face with her handkerchief. "I'm not really worrying," she continued. "I'm sure the will wasn't changed. It's just exactly the sort of thing that Aunt Matilda *would* put in her will. I'm not really worrying at all."

Jerry got her hat, and they went down to Mr. Tupper's office in Barbara's car. They had thought, at first, of telephoning him; but, as Jerry pointed out, somebody might overhear the conversation, and they were not ready to impart their secret to the world. It would be better to have everything perfectly clear before saying anything to anybody.

They caught Mr. Tupper leaving his office, and explained that they wished to speak to him in private. Mr. Tupper was very gracious and friendly; he led them into his office, and gave them chairs. Barbara had not been in the room since the day that she and Arthur had bought The Archway House—it seemed a very long time ago.

"Well, young lady," said Mr. Tupper, smiling at Jerry in a kindly manner. "What can I do for you?"

Jerry explained. She told him everything except the way in which Barbara had become possessed of the information about the will. (They had decided that it was not necessary to disclose Mr. Tyler's mistake.) She told her story well, in her forceful colloquial way. Mr. Tupper listened without saying a word, but his face showed a good deal of what he was feeling; he was amazed, incredulous, and grieved in turn. In spite of Jerry's assurances that she was glad she had escaped the legacy, he did not believe it.

When Jerry had finished Mr. Tupper started. He pointed out the folly of secret marriages, and inveighed against the impatience of youth.

"If you had only *waited*," said Mr. Tupper,

almost wringing his hands at the folly and madness of it all, "if only you had waited a little. Ten days—just ten days."

"But we didn't know it would only be ten days," said Jerry, "and, besides, I'm glad we didn't, because I don't want Chevis Place."

"Well, I must compliment you upon the way you are taking your disappointment," said Mr. Tupper, searching for a gleam of comfort in the darkness of the sky. "It shows great strength of character, and——"

"No it doesn't," Jerry told him earnestly. "I'm not disappointed—not a bit. I've told you what I feel about it, and I mean every word."

She might have spared her breath. Mr. Tupper had been a lawyer for nearly forty years, and, all that time, he had been assimilating the idea that money is above all things the most desirable. Every client that darkened his doors, darkened them in the hopes that Mr. Tupper would be able to obtain more money for him, or the equivalent of more money. Subconsciously, Mr. Tupper envisaged the world—the whole civilised world—digging and burrowing, toiling and moiling, plotting and scheming to acquire this eminently desirable possession. It was not likely that a chit of a girl could upset forty years of thought in as many minutes.

"If you had allowed me to read you the will," Mr. Tupper pointed out, "this mistake—this deplorable mistake—could not have occurred, and you would have been spared a great deal of suffering. It just shows that the legal manner of procedure should never—under any circumstances—be abrogated. I blame myself very much—very much indeed. I should have insisted upon reading you the will—I should have *insisted* upon it."

Jerry was silent. She had told him her views and he did not believe her. She saw that it was useless to reiterate them.

"The estate now goes to Archie," said Mr. Tupper, with a sigh, "and I, for one, am grieved (it is extremely unprofessional of me to make such a statement, but I have done so many unprofessional things to-day, that one, more or less, scarcely matters). Archie has not behaved in a proper manner, either before the death of her ladyship, or after. I am of the opinion that Archie is quite unfit to administer the estate in the way it should be administered."

"Well, neither could I," Jerry reminded him.

483

"We could have got somebody," said Mr. Tupper. "In fact I had already thought of the very man to help us. A Major Macfarlane—an excellent fellow. He lost his arm in the War. He understands the details of running a big estate and could have taken the whole thing over—I intended to speak to you about it at the first opportunity because the estate needs a good deal of attention. Her ladyship kept everything in her own hands, and, since her illness, it has been extremely difficult—but, of course, it's no good now," said Mr. Tupper sadly. "Heaven alone knows what Archie will make of it."

"Archie will be all right," said Jerry, trying to make her voice sound confident and assured.

"Well, it can't be helped," said Mr. Tupper. "But I must say I feel that if her ladyship had known that there was any chance of Archie inheriting, she would have made different arrangements. She was not at all pleased with the way Archie was behaving—far from it—far from it."

"I don't agree with you at all," Jerry exclaimed. "I think Archie *ought* to get it. He may have behaved badly, but Aunt Matilda let him think that he was her heir, and that

484

wasn't fair—it wasn't a bit fair. And it was *because* he knew that all that money was coming to him that he was so extravagant. I know it was. And I'm quite sure," she continued, searching for words to express her complicated feelings, "I'm quite sure that if Aunt Matilda had known I was married—or even engaged—she wouldn't have wanted *me* to have Chevis Place. And it would have been horrid to have it and to feel at the same time that it wasn't what Aunt Matilda wanted. So, you see, I'm very glad that it's all turned out as it has."

"You are taking the disappointment—the grievous disappointment—extremely well," said Mr. Tupper solemnly.

31

THE JUBILEE BONFIRE

THE sixth of May was an important anniversary for Mr. and Mrs. Abbott—they had been married for two years. That it was also an important anniversary for more important people did not detract from its value in their eyes; on the contrary they were delighted to share their anniversary with their King and Queen.

"It gives you a kind of Special Feeling for them, doesn't it?" Barbara remarked, as she and Arthur faced each other across the breakfast table; and Arthur—who was in the midst of his matutinal bacon and eggs—agreed that it did.

"It makes you feel that they're Real People—just like you and me," Barbara continued dreamily. "Perhaps, even now, they're having breakfast together—just like us, only grander, of course—and feeling happy and pleased, just like us."

Arthur agreed again. It was quite possible,

486

he reflected, that Their Majesties were breakfasting together—quite possible. The fact that he could not believe they ever did anything so mundane was probably due to his lack of imagination. He could not—by any manner of means—visualise the scene; but, no doubt, that was his misfortune since Barbara obviously could.

"Do you think His Majesty has his bacon and eggs in a gold dish?" enquired Barbara, with a faraway look in her eyes.

"No," said Arthur promptly.

"Why not?"

"Because it wouldn't be *nice*. Bacon in a gold dish would be simply disgusting," said Arthur with conviction, "and I'm sure His Majesty is far too sensible to have it."

The Abbotts were breakfasting at a late hour, and in a leisurely manner, because they had decided not to go up to town and see the procession, but to reserve their energies for the bonfire and the fireworks which were due to take place in Chevis Park after dusk. Arthur was quite glad that they were not going to London to see the procession—quite glad but somewhat surprised. He had been sure that Barbara would want to see it; so sure, that he had taken tickets for seats in a stand in St. James's Street—Barbara always wanted to go everywhere and see everything—but Barbara had elected not to go. She had pointed out that it would be frightfully hot and tiring, and that they would be so exhausted when they returned that they would not enjoy the bonfire. It was quite true, of course, but, somehow or other, it did not *ring* true in Arthur's ears, and he could not help feeling, at the back of his mind, that there was another reason for Barbara's decision; a much more cogent reason; a reason that she had not explained. Arthur had no idea what the reason was—none at all—it was just a feeling he had.

The tickets were not wasted, of course, for Arthur presented them to Sam and Jerry—who were now known to be man and wife by everybody in Wandlebury, and who were living together at Ganthorne Lodge in a state of bliss—and Sam and Jerry had accepted the tickets with delight, and had promised to come and have dinner at The Archway House, and tell Uncle Arthur and Barbara "all about it." Monkey had also been invited to dine, and, after dinner, the whole party would walk over to Chevis Place for the bonfire and the other celebrations.

Arthur and Barbara spent a quiet morning in the garden—it was beautiful. The weather was perfect—real Jubilee weather—and the garden was gay with Spring flowers, and joyous with the song of birds. Arthur and Barbara sat in deck chairs, in the shadow of a huge beech tree, and talked and read in a desultory manner. The afternoon, though equally fine, was not so quiet, for all Wandlebury had been to town and seen the procession in the morning, and all Wandlebury decided to visit the Abbotts in the afternoon and tell them all that they had missed. By dinner-time the Abbotts had heard so much about the procession that they felt exactly as if they had seen it—and almost as tired. They knew exactly who was in every carriage and what they had worn; how gracious and regal Their Majesties had appeared, and how sweet and pretty the Duchesses of York and Kent. They knew all about the immense crowds—so thick that you could have walked on their shoulders over half London—they knew all about the blocked roads, and the gaily decorated streets. Even the ceremony in the Abbey was no closed book to them, for Sir Lucian Agnew had been there, and came in to tea at The

Archway House on purpose to tell the Abbotts about it. He had already composed a poem on the subject, and it needed very little persuasion on Barbara's part to induce him to recite it to them over the teacups.

Monkey Wrench and the young Abbotts came to dinner as had been arranged. Sam and Jerry were full of all they had seen and done, but they had not much opportunity of telling the others of their experiences. For one thing Arthur and Barbara were well versed in the day's events, and were even slightly bored with the subject; and, for another, Monkey Wrench had so much to say that it was difficult for anyone else to get a word in edgeways. Monkey dominated the dinner-table—Barbara had never heard him talk so much—and his conversation was entirely concerned with the Wandlebury Bonfire.

The Wandlebury Bonfire was Monkey's obsession. Archie Cobbe had given the making of it into Monkey's hands, and had allowed him to construct it on a small eminence in Chevis Park known locally as the Beacon Hill. Monkey had taken his responsibility as the designer of the Wandlebury Bonfire in no frivolous spirit; he had determined that it should be as good as, if not better than, any bonfire in the British Isles. He had gone to work in a scientific manner, had ransacked the old library at Chevis Place for information as to how a bonfire should be built, and had amassed a considerable number of interesting and relevant facts about bonfires and beacons during his researches.

Barbara was delighted that Monkey had the bonfire to occupy his mind. It had been an excellent idea of Archie's to entrust him with it. After the death of Lady Chevis Cobbe, Monkey had been wretched and miserable, for he hated losing a patient at any time, and her ladyship had been so ill (and so exacting) for so long, that, when she departed this life and had no more need of his services, he felt that there was nothing left for him to do. If there had been an epidemic of influenza—or even of chicken-pox—in Wandlebury the doctor would not have missed his august patient to anything like the same extent (for he would have had no time to grieve, and mope, and review the case for any possible mistake or omission he might have made in dealing with it), but the Wandleburians were a healthy community, and the weather had been so glorious that even chronic invalids, and dyed-in-the-wool hypochondriacs had pulled up their socks—so to speak—and had been so busy decorating their houses with bunting, and making arrangements to see the procession, that they had no time to ring up Dr. Wrench and tell him about their pains.

It was for these reasons that the bonfire was such a godsend to Monkey; and Monkey had thrown himself into its preparation with such vim and vigour that he had almost forgotten that he was a doctor, and had become, for the time being, a sort of modern Guy Fawkes.

"In the old days," said Monkey seriously, "everybody knew the right way to construct a bonfire—or a beacon—it was necessary that they should, for it was the means of communication in times of danger (take for instance the bonfires which were lighted to warn England of the approach of the Armada, and those prepared as signals of alarm in the time of Napoleon Buonaparte); bonfires in those days were not only lighted on occasions of national rejoicings. But, now, nobody knows much about them—the oldest man in the world is too young—isn't that queer? I'm sure that a great many of the bonfires which have been erected for to-night's celebrations will either flare up and burn themselves to ashes in an hour, or else they'll smoulder and go out. Now my bonfire," said Monkey earnestly, "is a rightly constructed bonfire. It will burn from the top, of course, and will burn for hours—flames and smoke," said Monkey, "tar barrels and hempen rope." He stacked his knives and forks to demonstrate the correct and the incorrect manner of laying the wood, and used Arthur's silver table-napkin ring to demonstrate the correct position of the essential barrel of tar; he commended the Boy Scouts who had aided him in his task, and Archie Cobbe for the public-spirited way in which he had given wood and tar, and had lent carts for the conveyance of the same. "The site is ideal, of course," he continued. "Simply couldn't be better. It has obviously been used for beacons and bonfires in the past—hence its name, the Beacon Hill. Personally I shouldn't be surprised if the hill was used for fires of alarm in the Druids' time," said Monkey. "In the time of the Roman occupation . . ." continued Monkey. "All down the centuries. . . ."

From the particular he diverged to the general; he gave them a history of bonfires, and the occasions upon which they had been used. He explained that the name was derived from "bone-fire" and that it had originally been a fire of bones. Other authorities—so Monkey said—had declared that the name was derived from "boon-fire," the suggestion being that all the landowners in the neighbourhood contributed material for the fire, as a gift to propitiate some deity, or in obedience to some superstition.

Barbara loved bonfires, but even she had had enough of the subject by the time that dinner was finished. She was quite glad when Monkey rose and said that he really must go.

"Just in case of anything," said Monkey anxiously. "It would be so awful if anything went wrong *now*. I'll see you later," he added. "Don't be late, will you?"

"No, of course not," Barbara assured him.

"It will be worth seeing," said Monkey. "I can promise you that. There may be *bigger* bonfires in the country to-night, but there will be no *better* bonfire than mine," he added with supreme confidence.

*   *   *

It was a glorious evening, still and warm. The sun sank slowly as if it were reluctant to depart; as if it were reluctant to look its last upon the day of rejoicing, reluctant to look its last upon the flags, the streamers, the gay decorations, and the happy throng of holiday-makers, upon whom it had smiled for so many crowded hours.

The Abbotts walked over to Chevis Place, for there was no need to hurry, the bonfire would not be lighted until dusk. The younger couple walked in front, and the older couple some yards behind.

"How happy they are!" Barbara remarked.

"No happier than we," declared Arthur, squeezing the hand that was tucked inside his arm.

Barbara returned the pressure. "It's turned out all right after all," she said contentedly. "Things usually do, somehow. You worry and fuss and try to make things go the way you think they should—and then you find that the other way was best. I'm going to try not to worry about things any more."

Arthur thought this was an excellent plan, but he was doubtful whether Barbara would be able to carry it out. Her disposition was so benevolent that she could not bear to see things going awry. She loved putting her fingers into other people's pies, and improving them (a good many people had reason to thank Barbara for the way she had improved their pies). The pies—as Barbara had indicated—rarely turned out quite as she had hoped or expected, but they were usually satisfactory. Barbara had had her fingers in a great many pies in Silverstream, and had improved them all—though not always in the way she had intended—and the Wandlebury pie was a success, too—so Arthur reflected—for Sam and Jerry were undoubtedly happier and more useful at Ganthorne Lodge than they would have been at Chevis Place, and Archie Cobbe had got what he had been wanting for years.

As they neared Chevis Place they found streams of cars and pedestrians converging from all directions; everybody for miles round Wandlebury had heard about the wonderful bonfire, and had decided to be there and see it alight.

The site chosen for the bonfire was—as Monkey had said—an ideal site. It was a flat-topped hill, covered with heather and boulders, about a quarter of a mile from the house. From here a fine view of the surrounding country could be obtained, and, incidentally, the surrounding country could obtain a fine view of the bonfire. The Abbotts were early on the scene, and were able to secure a good position on a pile of boulders. Arthur spread a rug over the boulders and they all sat down. Before them towered the dark mass of the bonfire, with trickles of black tar seeping out between the carefully packed wood. Monkey was hurrying about, full of last-minute instructions to his assistants. A donkey appeared with a huge crate of fireworks on its back, and the crate was unloaded by the Boy Scouts and secreted behind a rock. People were arriving fast by this time; groups formed and reformed. There was talk and laughter, as friends met, and recounted their experiences of the morning.

"There's Mrs. Sittingbourne!" exclaimed Arthur suddenly—he had almost forgotten what her real name was, for Barbara's choice seemed to suit her so much better.

"Where?" demanded Barbara eagerly. "Oh yes, I see her now. Oh dear, I *am* so glad she's better."

"Monkey says it wasn't appendicitis after all."

"I never thought it was."

"Would you like to go and talk to her," Arthur suggested.

"No," replied Barbara firmly. "No, let's just stay where we are—I'm enjoying it all frightfully."

Arthur was surprised. Barbara had been so odd, so mysterious, over Mrs. Dance's sudden indisposition that he had been quite worried over it. He had never succeeded in getting to the bottom of the queer faint turn that had assailed Barbara when she heard Mrs. Dance (or Mrs. Sittingbourne) was ill. It was so unlike Barbara to be mysterious. Arthur turned the whole thing over in his mind (his eyes fixed upon the good lady's toothy smile and predatory expression, as she pursued various people that she knew and engaged them in conversation). I can't believe that Barbara is really so very fond of her, he thought, she isn't Barbara's style at all. If Barbara likes her so much why doesn't she see the good lady more often? And if Barbara doesn't like her much, why was she so upset to hear she was ill?

Arthur's reflections on the subject were interrupted by the arrival of Archie Cobbe—or Archie Chevis Cobbe, as he was now to be called—he was accompanied by a tall, nice-looking man with one sleeve pinned to his breast. Archie moved about amongst the crowd, talking and laughing in a friendly manner, and inviting all and sundry to come down to Chevis Place "after the show" and partake of light refreshments. Gradually he made his way over to the pile of boulders where the Abbotts were sitting and greeted them cordially.

"This is Major Macfarlane," he said, introducing his one-armed companion. "He's going to try and teach me how to run the estate. I'm awfully lucky to have him——"

"Nonsense," said the Major. "I'm lucky to have the job—and you haven't much to learn as far as I can see."

"You're *all* to come to Chevis Place afterwards," Archie continued. "You will, won't you? It's to be a sort of house-warming. We've laid in provisions enough for a regiment—haven't we, Macfarlane? And beer, and tea, and coffee enough to float the Queen Mary—and I want *you*, especially, Jerry, to do hostess for me."

"I'll do my best," Jerry promised. "But you know I'm not much used to that sort of thing."

They chatted for a few minutes, and then Archie moved on, in his squire-like manner, to greet Mrs. Thane and Candia who had just

499

arrived on the scene. Barbara voiced all their thoughts when she exclaimed in a surprised voice:

"Isn't it queer—Archie seems to have grown."

Archie really did seem to have grown. He seemed taller and broader, his personality had expanded in the warm sun of his changed fortunes.

"Prosperity suits some people," said Monkey Wrench, who had come up to speak to them and had overheard the remark.

"Yes," agreed Jerry. "You can't think how kind and considerate he is now, and he's so anxious to do the right thing for Chevis Place—Mr. Tupper was quite wrong," she added thoughtfully.

"All he needs, now, is the right wife," said Arthur, who had succeeded in obtaining the most desirable possession for himself.

"We shall have to find him one," Barbara agreed, quite forgetting that she had decided never to meddle in the affairs of her neighbours again.

It was now almost dark, and Monkey—who had been hopping with excitement for the last half hour—decided to light his bonfire.

"It isn't *quite* time," he admitted, looking

500

at his watch, and putting it to his ear to see if by any chance it could have stopped. "It isn't *quite* time yet, but it may take a minute or two to get going, so I think I shall light up."

A ladder was brought and reared against the bonfire, and Monkey mounted with a flaming torch in his hand. Everybody had stopped talking, and watched breathlessly— he laid the torch on the top of the bonfire and climbed down. For a few moments it looked as if the torch would go out, and the bonfire remain unlighted, but only for a few moments. Gradually the top of the erection caught fire; flames ran round the edge, licking the wood; then they shot upwards in a pyramid of fire; volumes of smoke ascended into the darkening sky, and the whole bonfire leapt into life with a sound of crackling and hissing.

The glare of the flames shone, with a lurid light, upon the upturned faces of the spectators, and murmurs of approval and delight were heard on every side. Monkey's bonfire was a tremendous success.

"It's wonderful," said Barbara in admiration.

"Oh wonderful, wonderful," exclaimed a deep sonorous voice just behind her. "And

501

most wonderful, wonderful! And yet again wonderful, and, after that, out of all whooping."

Barbara had no need to look behind her to see who is was that had thus extolled Monkey's bonfire, but look behind her she did. There stood Mr. Marvell, large and majestic as ever, wrapped like a Roman Emperor in his voluminous black cloak. His head was bare, and his luxuriant wavy hair gleamed in the ruddy glow of the flames. Around him were grouped, like satellites, his family and dependants: Mrs. Marvell, Lancreste, Trivona and Ambrose, Miss Foddy and the two maids—it was an elevating sight.

"Look at them, Arthur," Barbara whispered, nudging Arthur and chuckling a little with pure delight. "Aren't they marvellous? And isn't he exactly like the Colossus of Rhodes?"

Arthur was forced to agree. There was something really noble about the little group, outlined against the darkness of the sky, and nobody could behold it without perceiving that the dominant figure in it was, indeed, more than life-size.

The night wore on. Bonfires could be seen all round, on nearly every hill. Some were large and flaming and some were small and smouldering, but none of them (everybody agreed) was nearly as good as the Wandlebury bonfire. When the interest in the bonfire began to wane the crate of fireworks was opened, and Archie let off rockets and roman candles and fairy lights. It was a splendid entertainment. Barbara liked the rockets best; away they went into the sky; they burst with a bang, and the green and red and yellow stars hung for a moment among their quiet silver brethren and then fell, light as thistledown, through the still air.

When all the fireworks were over the crowd melted away; some of them went home, but most of them straggled down to Chevis Place and were entertained there, in a royal manner, by the new squire. Jerry and Sam went with them, but Arthur and Barbara stayed behind.

It was too beautiful to leave, Barbara thought. All around them the sky was bright with stars, and before them glowed and flamed the bonfire, lighting up the dark hill-top, and making the surroundings seem darker than they really were. There was something very mysterious and lovely about the fire, and Barbara realised this to the full.

It seemed a link with the past, for fires had flamed upon this hill from pre-historic times; and it seemed a promise for the future, too, for it had drawn so many people together in friendliness and hopefulness.

They stayed on, Barbara and Arthur together, in the quiet night, watching the bonfire, and talking in low voices of many things.

"I'm not going to finish my book," she told him at last, after a long thoughtful silence.

"You must do as you like about it," he replied. "That's all I want—always—for you to do as you like. But, quite honestly, the book is better than the others—deeper and truer—it's a clever book."

"I'm going to do something much cleverer," said Barbara, smiling in rather a mysterious way.

"What are you going to do?" enquired Arthur with interest.

"I'm going to do something *much* cleverer," she repeated. "Anybody could write a book—I'm going to have a baby."

"Oh, Barbara!" exclaimed Arthur, thoroughly amazed by this totally unexpected, and absolutely stupendous revelation. "Oh, Barbara—how marvellous—how simply splendid!"

"Wonderful out of all whooping, isn't it?" said Barbara, looking at him with an expression of grave innocence such as children sometimes wear. "So you see I shall be much too busy to be bother with *There's Many a Slip*——. I shan't have any time for that sort of thing."

Arthur agreed fervently that her new adventure—her biggest yet—was a whole-time job (he relinquished *There's Many a Slip*—— without a sigh). His Barbara was an amazing woman, the most amazing woman under the sun—there was nothing beyond her powers, nothing. Arthur was convinced that he was the most fortunate man alive.

"That was why I didn't want to see the procession," Barbara continued. "I know you thought it funny, but Monkey says I've got to take care of myself, you see."

Arthur saw. That's why she nearly fainted in the hall, he thought; it wasn't anything to do with the Sittingbourne woman, but I won't remind her of that. I must take great care of her (thought Arthur), it would be frightful—simply frightful—if anything happened to Barbara. . . .

They talked for a little about the nurseries in The Archway House, and how they would have them done up; and Arthur decided that he must buy a rocking-horse, which he had seen in the window of a toy-shop not far from the office. He had looked at it as he passed, and had decided that it was the biggest, and the most splendid rocking-horse he had ever seen. I shall buy it to-morrow, he thought, just in case somebody else might like the look of it. . . .

"Isn't it funny?" said Barbara, when the subject was temporarily exhausted. "Isn't it funny, Arthur. We've only been here for about six months, but I feel we belong to Wandlebury now. We seem to have settled into the *people* as well as into the *place*—if you know what I mean. They know us, and we know them in a way you never get to know people nearer Town."

"What you do in the suburbs is your own business," Arthur pointed out. "But what you do in a little town like Wandlebury is everybody's business."

"Yes," agreed Barbara, "and I like it. I like it awfully. It's nice to feel that people are interested in you. I feel as if we had lived here for years," she continued, pursuing her previous thought in a dreamy manner. "I feel as if we had been married for years, and years, and years. Do you feel like that, Arthur?"

"In a way, I do, of course," admitted her husband. "But in another way I don't. You haven't changed a bit, you see. You're still exactly the same Barbara Buncle that you were when we first met."

"Oh, but I've changed a lot!" Barbara exclaimed. "I have, really, Arthur."

"How have you changed?" he enquired.

Barbara did not reply for a little while. It was very complicated, and she was never good at explaining what she felt. She looked back and saw the faults and failings in that ignorant, gauche spinster, Barbara Buncle, and felt her superiority in seeing them so clearly. She looked back, smugly and patronisingly upon her virgin self. She was now one with the vast regiment of Married Women, no longer barred from the councils by the stigma of virginity; they discussed marriage with her, sometimes they made her cheeks hot by the freedom with which they discussed it (Barbara could never contribute to these discussions, she had entered the married state too late in life, her nature was too set in spinsterhood), but, all the same, she was glad when they discussed marriage in her presence, for it helped to make her aware of her new status. When she had assured Arthur that she had "changed a lot" she saw just how and why she had changed. The world had broadened and deepened, and she was its citizen, full grown, and all the privileges and responsibilities of citizenship were hers. She had a man—all her own—with his life to make or mar; a house—the house of her dreams— where her lightest word was law; and, now, coming to her in the near and easily visualised future, was another dear and beautiful responsibility, a small young creature which would be utterly and absolutely dependent upon her, a new human-being to cherish and control. She had new friends, who valued her for what she was, and accepted her as she was; and she had new interests which increased and multiplied daily. Barbara saw all this quite clearly—the difference in status, and the difference in herself which made her adequate to its demands; but it was impossible—as ever—for her to put her feelings and convictions into words.

"Well, you see, I know things now," said Barbara lamely.